Eli...

GREEKS

April 2014

May 2014

Eligible
GREEKS
Tycoon's Revenge

Chantelle
SHAW

Catherine
GEORGE

Catherine
SPENCER

MILLS
BOON

Published in Great Britain 2014
by Mills & Boon, an imprint of Harlequin (UK) Limited,
Eton House, 18-24 Paradise Road, Richmond, Surrey, TW9 1SR

ELIGIBLE GREEKS: TYCOON'S REVENGE
© 2014 Harlequin Books S.A.

Proud Greek, Ruthless Revenge © 2009 Chantelle Shaw
The Power of the Legendary Greek © 2010 Catherine George
The Greek Millionaire's Mistress © 2007 Spencer Books Limited

ISBN: 978 0 263 24591 2

012-0414

Printed and bound in Spain
by Blackprint CPI, Barcelona

PROUD GREEK, RUTHLESS REVENGE

CHANTELLE SHAW

Chantelle Shaw lives on the Kent coast, five minutes from the sea, and does much of her thinking about the characters in her books while walking on the beach. She's been an avid reader from an early age. Her school friends used to hide their books when she visited—but Chantelle would retreat into her own world and still writes stories in her head all the time. Chantelle has been blissfully married to her own tall, dark and very patient hero for over twenty years, and has six children. She began to read Mills & Boon® novels as a teenager and, throughout the years of being a stay-at-home mum to her brood, found romantic fiction helped her to stay sane! She enjoys reading and writing about strong-willed, feisty women and even stronger-willed sexy heroes. Chantelle is at her happiest when writing. She is particularly inspired while cooking dinner, which unfortunately results in a lot of culinary disasters! She also loves gardening, walking and eating chocolate (followed by more walking!). Catch up with Chantelle's latest news on her website: www. chantelleshaw.com.

In memory of my darling dad, Bob Gibbs,
who encouraged me to write and
was so proud of me

CHAPTER ONE

'TAHLIA, you look divine.' Crispin Blythe, owner of the contemporary art gallery Blythe of Bayswater, greeted Tahlia Reynolds effusively. 'Those baubles you're wearing must be worth a small fortune.'

'A large fortune, actually,' Tahlia replied dryly, moving her hand to the ornate sapphire and diamond necklace at her throat. 'These "baubles" are top-grade Kashmiri sapphires.'

'Let me guess. A present from Daddy? Reynolds Gems' profits must be booming.' Crispin's smile faded slightly. 'It's good to know that some businesses are unaffected by this wretched recession.'

Tahlia frowned at the faintly bitter note in Crispin's voice. She had heard rumours that the gallery was suffering from the downturn in the economy, and for a moment she was tempted to reveal that things were far from rosy with her father's jewellery company, but she kept quiet. Reynolds Gems' financial problems would be public knowledge if the company went into liquidation, but they were not at that point yet. Perhaps she was being unrealistic, but she refused to give up hope that the company her father had built up over the past thirty years could be saved. It would not be for want of trying, she thought grimly. Her parents had used all their savings trying to keep

Reynolds afloat, while she had worked for no salary for the past three months, and had traded in the sports car her father had given her three years ago, for her twenty-first birthday, for a battered old Mini.

In desperation she had even sold her few items of jewellery, as well as many of the designer clothes that she had once been able to afford. The dress she was wearing tonight was on loan from a friend who owned a boutique, and the sapphire and diamond necklace was not her own—though it was one of Reynolds Gems' most valued pieces, stunningly beautiful and instantly eye-catching. Her father had asked her to wear it tonight in the hope of drumming up new business for Reynolds, but she was terrified of losing it, and knew she was going to spend the evening constantly checking that it was still around her neck.

She followed Crispin into the gallery, accepted a glass of champagne from a waiter, and glanced around at her fellow guests who were congregated in groups, admiring the paintings by the artist Rufus Hartman. Tahlia nodded to one or two acquaintances and allowed her eyes to drift. They came to an abrupt halt on the man who was standing on the other side of the room.

'Who is that?' she murmured curiously, feeling her heart jolt violently beneath her ribs. In a room packed with good-looking, successful men, the simmering virility of this particular man set him apart from the crowd.

'I assume you're referring to the Greek hunk in the Armani?' Crispin said archly, following the direction of her gaze. 'Thanos Savakis, billionaire head of Savakis Enterprises. He bought out the Blue-Sky holiday chain a couple of years ago, and owns several five-star hotels around the world. Careful, darling, you're drooling,' Crispin murmured wickedly as Tahlia continued to stare. 'A word of

warning: Savakis has a reputation as a womaniser. His affairs are discreet, but numerous—and short-lived. Commitment is not a word associated with Thanos Savakis—unless it's his commitment to making even more money to add to his enviable fortune,' Crispin finished with a theatrical sigh.

'Workaholic womanisers are definitely not my type,' Tahlia murmured faintly, dragging her gaze from the man and taking a sip of champagne. But her eyes were drawn inexorably towards him, and she was glad that he was looking down at the dainty blonde who was hanging onto his arm because it gave her a chance to study him.

Tall and lean, with broad shoulders sheathed in an expertly tailored jacket, he was mesmerising, and Tahlia quickly realised that she was not the only woman in the room to be fascinated by him. With his classically sculpted features, bronzed skin and gleaming black hair, which was cropped short to emphasise the proud tilt of his head, he was stunningly handsome. But teamed with his blatant sex appeal Thanos Savakis possessed some indefinable quality—a magnetism and self-assurance that set him apart from other men. He would command any situation, Tahlia decided. She sensed his innate arrogance, and although he appeared to be giving his full attention to the pretty blonde at his side, she detected the giveaway signs that he was growing impatient of his companion's chatter.

The woman was a little too eager, Tahlia mused. Instinct told her that a man as self-possessed as Thanos Savakis would be irritated by any hint of neediness, and as she watched he carefully but firmly extricated himself from the blonde's grip and strolled into the adjoining gallery.

Gorgeous, but definitely out of her league, Tahlia decided, giving herself a mental shake as she slowly became aware once more of the babble of voices around her, and the clink

of champagne flutes on a silver tray as a waiter walked past. She was shocked by the effect the sexy Greek had had on her—especially as the width of the room had separated them and he hadn't even glanced in her direction. She could not remember ever being so aware of a man. Not even James.

Her mouth tightened. Six months ago her relationship with James Hamilton had come to a shocking and explosive end, and since then she had struggled to piece her shattered heart back together. But the bitterness she felt towards him still burned as corrosively as on the night she had discovered his treachery.

'Tahlia, darling, that's vintage Krug you're gulping down, not fizzy water.' Crispin's laconic drawl dragged Tahlia back to the present. 'Can I get you another?'

She grimaced as she glanced down and saw that she had drained her glass without realising it. 'No, thanks. I'd better not.'

Crispin gave her an impatient look. 'Oh, live daringly for once. A few glasses of bubbly will help you relax.'

'Correction, a few glasses will have me giggling inanely,' Tahlia said dismally. 'And, after the recent press stories about me, I really could do without being snapped by the paparazzi clearly the worse for drink.'

Crispin gave her an amused glance. 'Yes, the tabloids do seem to have excelled themselves,' he agreed. 'The headline "Gems girl Tahlia Reynolds blamed for marriage break-up of TV soapstar Damian Casson" was particularly attention-grabbing.'

Tahlia flushed. 'It isn't true,' she said tensely. 'I was set up. I've only ever met Damian once, when we were guests at a book launch party held at a hotel. He was knocking back champagne all night and kept pestering me. I told him to get lost. The next morning he came over to my table at breakfast to apologise. We got chatting, and he told me he'd got drunk the previous night after he'd rowed with his wife and she had refused to go to the party with him. When I left, he offered to

carry my bag to the car—hence the picture of the two of us emerging from the hotel together. Neither of us had expected the media to be hanging around at nine o'clock on a Sunday morning—or at least,' she said slowly, 'I hadn't expected them to be there.'

Anger formed a tight knot in Tahlia's chest at the realisation that Damian had undoubtedly been aware of the presence of the media.

'I was shocked when a journalist asked about our relationship, but Damian told me to leave it to him and he would explain that we were simply friends.'

Instead, the handsome young actor had told the press a pack of lies about their 'amazing night of sizzling sex', Tahlia thought bitterly. If Damian's intention had been to make his wife jealous, it had obviously worked. Beverly Casson had been quoted saying she was 'distraught' that 'party girl' Tahlia had stolen her man. The story had been a scoop for the journalists—the sort of thing that would boost sales of the tabloid, and no one seemed to care that it was untrue, or that Tahlia's reputation was now in tatters.

'This sort of adverse publicity is one of the drawbacks of allowing myself to be in the public eye,' she said dully. 'For months the press have made me out to be a vacuous bimbo who turns up to every event—even the opening of an envelope. It's the price I've had to pay for promoting Reynolds Gems.'

Tahlia bit her lip. When she had graduated from university three years ago her father had made her a partner of his company and given her the role of PR executive. But the global recession had hit Reynolds hard, and in an attempt to raise the company's profile she had reluctantly agreed to feature in an advertising campaign. She had then appeared in glossy magazines, attended numerous social events, modelling fabulous diamonds and precious gems from the Reynolds Gems collection.

Before she had left for the gallery tonight she had learned that all her hard work had been for nothing.

Peter Reynolds had looked grave as he'd explained that, despite the campaign, profits at all three of Reynolds Gems' jewellery shops were down. 'To be frank, Tahlia, Reynolds is facing bankruptcy,' he'd told her. 'I've approached every major bank and financial institution for help, but they've all refused to lend us any more money.' Tahlia's heart had ached when her father had dropped his head into his hands in a gesture of utter despair. 'I'm at rock bottom,' he'd admitted hoarsely. 'I've no more money left to stave off our creditors. The only glimmer of hope on the horizon is an equity firm, Vantage Investments, who have expressed an interest in buying out the company. I've arranged to meet their CEO next week.'

Tahlia could not forget the lines of strain of her father's face, but she forced her mind back to the present and glanced around the gallery, aware that fretting about Reynolds' financial situation was not going to help. She had dreaded the prospect of attending the exhibition tonight, when her supposed love-life was headline news, but Rufus Hartman was a close friend from her university days and she could not have missed his first major exhibition.

As she strolled around the gallery with Crispin she was conscious of the curious stares from some of the other guests. 'I wonder how many people here tonight think I'm a heartless marriage-breaker,' she muttered bitterly.

'No one believes a word that's written in the gutter press,' Crispin assured her breezily.

Tahlia wished she shared his confidence, but for a moment she was tempted to slink into a quiet corner and remain there for the rest of the night. But that was ridiculous; she had done nothing to be ashamed of. Her hand strayed to her necklace.

She had come to the art gallery tonight not simply to support Rufus. She had a job to do, she reminded herself.

Crispin had mentioned that a wealthy Arab prince would be attending the exhibition. Apparently Sheikh Mussada enjoyed buying gifts for his new wife, and Tahlia hoped that if she could catch his attention he might be impressed by the sapphire necklace and request to see more Reynolds Gems jewellery. If Reynolds could earn the patronage of an Arab prince they might not need to sell to Vantage Investments after all, she mused, so lost in her thoughts that she did not realise that Crispin had led her into the second gallery until he addressed a man who was studying one of the paintings.

'Thanos—I hope you're enjoying the exhibition. May I introduce you to a fellow art-lover?' Crispin drew Tahlia forward. 'This is Tahlia Reynolds. Her company, Reynolds Gems, have sponsored Rufus throughout his career, and she has an expert knowledge of his work.'

Shock ripped through Thanos as he stared at the woman at Crispin Blythe's side. She had dominated his thoughts for so long that for a few seconds his brain struggled to comprehend that she was standing in front of him, and it took all his formidable will-power to school his expression into one of polite interest rather than murderous rage.

He had arrived in London three days ago, and at a dinner party with friends had been introduced to Crispin, who had invited him to this exhibition at his art gallery. Thanos had no particular interest in art, but these events were always useful for social networking. You never knew who you might meet, he thought derisively, as his eyes raked over Tahlia Reynolds's slender form.

He recognised her instantly. Hardly surprising when her face was plastered over the front of all the red-top tabloids,

he thought sardonically. But the photos of her in the newspapers, even the artfully posed pictures in the glossy magazines, showing her in couture gowns and stunning jewellery, did not do justice to her luminescent beauty. His eyes swept over her close-fitting blue silk cocktail dress, which matched the sapphires at her throat and was cut low to reveal a tantalising glimpse of the upper curve of her breasts.

She was exquisite, he acknowledged grimly. He welcomed the wave of black hatred that surged through him, but to his disgust another, unbidden emotion stirred within him. Nothing had prepared him for the impact of seeing Tahlia in the flesh, and to his fury he felt an unmistakable tug of sexual interest.

An awkward silence hovered in the air after Crispin's introduction, and as the gallery-owner cleared his throat Thanos acknowledged that he could not give in to his inclination to fasten his hands around Tahlia's slender neck and squeeze the life from her body.

'Miss Reynolds,' he murmured smoothly, extending his hand to her. He noted that she hesitated before she responded, and her hand shook very slightly when she placed it in his. Her fingers were slim, and as pale as milk. It would take a fraction of his strength to crush them in his grasp. He tightened his grip rather more than was necessary, and when her eyes flew to his face he stared at her impassively.

The brief pressure on her fragile bones could not compare with the pain his sister endured every day, he thought savagely. Melina had been in hospital for six long months, and would have to undergo many more weeks of physiotherapy before she would walk unaided again. Thanos did not blame the driver of the car which had ploughed into Melina. The police had assured him that the man behind the wheel had stood no chance of avoiding the young woman who had run into the road without looking.

No, he held two other people responsible for the accident which had almost ended Melina's life—and those same two people had callously broken her heart. Tahlia Reynolds was a predatory bitch who had been having an affair with Melina's husband, James Hamilton. Melina had been distraught when she had discovered them together in a hotel bedroom, and she had fled outside onto an unlit country road, straight into the path of an oncoming car.

Thanos released Tahlia's hand but continued to scrutinise her intently. According to the recent press reports she had been up to her old tricks with another married actor. Did this woman have *any* scruples? he wondered savagely. How dared she stand there staring at him with her startling bright blue eyes, her mouth curved into a hesitant smile?

Soon she would have little to smile about, he brooded. He had already dealt with his ex-brother-in-law. Immediately after Melina's accident James had fled to L.A., but the actor had quickly discovered that no Hollywood director would work with him after Thanos had threatened to withdraw his financial backing of various film projects if James Hamilton was given so much as a walk-on part. James's acting career was dead and buried, and Thanos was determined that it would never be resurrected. Now he wanted revenge on James's mistress.

Tahlia's hand was still tingling as if she had received an electric shock. Some indescribable force had certainly shot from her fingertips all the way up her arm when she had shaken Thanos Savakis's hand, and now she felt strangely light-headed. The champagne must have gone to her head, she thought ruefully. The peculiar feeling that had swept over her when Thanos's skin had briefly come into contact with hers was *not* an intense reaction to the sexiest man she had ever

laid eyes on, she told herself firmly. And yet she could not deny that he unsettled her.

'It's a pleasure to meet you, Mr Savakis,' she said politely. 'Are you here in London on business, or…?' She tailed away uncertainly, entranced by the sudden smile that lifted his features from handsome to breathtakingly gorgeous, and revealed a flash of white teeth which for some inexplicable reason made her think of the story of Red Riding Hood and the cunning wolf.

'Business…and pleasure,' Thanos drawled, relieved that he was once more in control of his hormones. He trailed his eyes over Tahlia. She was exquisitely packaged: designer dress, shoes and handbag, not to mention an eye-watering collection of sapphires and diamonds that sparkled enticingly against her creamy skin. Her outfit must have cost a fortune, he thought cynically. Tahlia was clearly used to the finer things in life, and he was going to take enormous pleasure in putting an end to her pampered, self-indulgent lifestyle.

He had expected her to show some sort of reaction when he introduced himself, but there had been no flicker of response in Tahlia's eyes at the name Savakis. Presumably she had been unaware of James Hamilton's wife's maiden name—no doubt she and James had not spared a thought for Melina during their secret assignations. Molten fury seared his insides. He wanted to vent his anger and denounce her as the heartless whore who had wrecked his sister's life—let the members of London's high society who were gathered in the gallery hear what a cheap little tart she was. But with a huge effort of will he resisted the urge. There would be time enough to tell her what he thought of her after he had brought her to her knees.

'I see that Earl Fullerton has just arrived,' Crispin Blythe murmured. 'I'll leave you two to have fun. I suggest you ask Tahlia to give you a tour of the gallery, Thanos. She has a

special relationship with the artist, and is the best person—apart from Rufus himself, of course—to talk about his work.'

'Oh, but…' Tahlia stared after Crispin, unbearably embarrassed by the obvious way he had manoeuvred her and the sexy Greek together. Thanos's mouth was still curved into a smile, but the faintly derisive gleam in his eyes unnerved her, and she could not shake off the idea that for some reason he had taken an instant dislike to her. 'I mustn't monopolise your company, Mr Savakis,' she murmured, glancing rather desperately around the gallery, in the hope that she would spot someone she knew.

'What exactly is the nature of your "special relationship" with Rufus Hartman?' Thanos queried coolly. 'Is he one of your lovers?'

For a moment Tahlia was too taken aback to reply. With a sinking feeling she realised that Thanos had probably seen the newspaper reports of her supposed affair with Damian Casson. Her temper flared. So much for Crispin's assertion that no one believed the rubbish that was written in the downmarket tabloids. 'I really don't see that it's any of your business,' she said coldly, 'but as a matter of fact Rufus isn't attracted to women,' she added. She was not sure why she had lowered her voice, because Rufus was quite open about the fact that he was gay. 'He is a good friend with an incredible talent.'

Thanos's dark eyes roamed lazily over her, as if he were mentally undressing her, and Tahlia felt horribly exposed in her low-cut gown. Her eyes seemed to be drawn to his face of their own volition, and she could not help but focus on the sensual curve of his mouth. His kiss would not be gentle. The thought crashed into her head and her face burned as she imagined him lowering his head and covering her lips with his. Heat coursed through her veins, and when she tore her

eyes from him and glanced down she was mortified to see the outline of her nipples clearly visible beneath her dress.

Tahlia had turned her head again, and seemed to be scanning the room for someone. 'Are you searching for anyone in particular?' Thanos queried, his eyes narrowing when she shrugged her slim shoulders. Her skin was so pale it was almost translucent. He noticed a dusting of gold freckles along her collarbone and the slopes of her breasts and felt a tightening sensation in his groin. His fierce awareness of her was both unexpected and infuriating, but it was satisfying to see the evidence that she was equally aware of him.

If she had been any other woman he would have wasted no time in seducing her. With her track record he doubted she would need much persuading into his bed. Disgust swept through him and he ruthlessly banished the image of peeling the straps of her blue silk gown down her shoulders and exposing her slender naked body. She was his brother-in-law's whore, he reminded himself grimly, and it was inconceivable that he could desire her when he had sworn revenge on her for the pain she had caused his sister.

Thanos's accented voice was deep and sensual, and it sent a little shiver of awareness down Tahlia's spine, but she was determined to ignore the effect he had on her. 'I'm looking for an Arab prince—Sheikh Mussada,' she said coolly. 'Do you know him?'

'I know of him—as, I imagine, does everyone else here tonight, seeing that he has recently taken over a major high street bank.'

'Yes, I believe he is the fifth richest man in the world,' Tahlia muttered distractedly, supremely conscious of the exotic scent of Thanos's aftershave. She wondered if it would appear impolite if she walked away from him, and then—recalling his dig about Rufus being 'one of her lovers'—

wondered why she should give a damn what he thought of her. The Prince must have arrived by now, she thought, as she craned her neck to peer into the larger gallery.

Thanos frowned, wondering what had caused the hectic flush on Tahlia's cheeks. 'Didn't Sheikh Mussada marry recently?' he queried tersely, a sudden suspicion forming in his brain.

'Yes, but apparently his wife hates flying, and never travels abroad with him.'

Tahlia thought of the business cards in her purse. As she had driven to the gallery she'd indulged in a daydream in which Sheikh Mussada admired her sapphire necklace and asked her where he could buy something similar. That would be Tahlia's cue to invite him to visit one of the Reynolds Gems shops—she would arrange to open the store out of hours if the Sheikh preferred, and expert assistants would be on hand to help him purchase a gift for his wife. In the daydream, Sheikh Mussada was so impressed by Reynolds' stock of jewellery that he requested their catalogue to take back to Dubai. Soon afterwards they would be flooded with orders from the Prince and his numerous wealthy relatives.

'Oh, that must be him.' Tahlia felt a spurt of excitement as the throng of guests parted and she glimpsed a man wearing traditional Arab robes. This was her chance to save her family's business. The sapphire collection she was wearing tonight was truly spectacular, and Sheikh Mussada was reputed to be an enthusiastic collector of top-quality jewellery. All she had to do was somehow gain his attention.

'Hey, don't run away.'

Warm breath feathered Tahlia's neck, whispering across the stray tendrils of hair at her nape, and she jerked her head around, startled to discover that Thanos had moved and was now standing much too close for comfort.

'Sorry?' For a few seconds she had been so caught up in her daydream about the Sheikh that she had almost forgotten about Thanos. Almost, but not entirely, she conceded ruefully. He was not an easy man to forget, and as she stared at his beautifully sculpted face and glimpsed the flare of sensual heat in his eyes her breath snagged in her throat.

'Our host has assured me you are an expert on Rufus Hartman's work, and I wholeheartedly approve of his suggestion that you should give me a guided tour of the exhibition,' he murmured.

'I assure you I'm no expert,' she replied quickly, feeling as though she were drowning in Thanos's dark eyes. His lashes were ridiculously long for a man, she mused, and his skin gleamed like polished bronze, stretched taut over his magnificent cheekbones. He swamped her senses, and her heart slammed painfully beneath her ribs when he reached out and trailed one finger very lightly down her face.

'Your skin is as soft as satin,' he said, his gravelly accent sending a frisson of awareness down her spine. 'I have to admit that I am captivated by your beauty, Tahlia.'

He had to be kidding, Tahlia decided as she struggled to drag oxygen into her lungs. Surely the sexual hunger blazing in his eyes could not be real, when a few moments ago he had been sending out distinct vibes of barely leashed hostility? She was puzzled by his sudden change of attitude, and even more confused that he was staring at her as if she were his every fantasy rolled into one.

'I…' She seemed to have lost the ability to think. She moistened her parched lips with the tip of her tongue, saw him focus intently on the betraying gesture, and felt liquid heat surge through her veins.

'Why don't we start with the landscape in the corner?' Thanos suggested briskly, and he slid his hand beneath her

elbow and steered her firmly across the room—out of Sheikh Mussada's view.

Did she get a kick out of seducing other women's husbands? he wondered furiously. He had noted the determined gleam in her eyes when she'd spotted the Sheikh—the way she had stroked her fingers over the sapphire necklace, drawing attention to her slender throat and the provocative swell of her breasts. Beneath her beautiful shell Tahlia Reynolds possessed a cold and calculating heart. James Hamilton was not blameless, but Thanos was convinced that Tahlia had deliberately seduced his sister's husband—and now she was planning to turn her sorcery on the happily married Sheikh Mussada.

Not if he could help it, he vowed grimly. He was not going to let Tahlia out of his sight for the rest of the evening—even if it meant having to pretend that he had fallen under her spell.

CHAPTER TWO

TAHLIA glanced surreptitiously at the clock on the gallery wall and was shocked to see that almost an hour had passed since Thanos had asked her to act as his guide around the exhibition. She could hardly believe she had spent so long in the exclusive company of the sexiest man in the room, and she could not help but find his attention flattering. His hand was resting lightly in the small of her back, and she was agonisingly aware of his lean, hard body, so close to her that she could feel the warmth that emanated from him and smell the subtle scent of his cologne. He seemed in no hurry for them to part company—but she was supposed to be networking, offering business cards to anyone who admired her necklace. So far she hadn't done a very good job of drumming up new business.

'I'm sure Rufus will be able to discuss his work in far more depth than I can,' she murmured, as Thanos halted in front of a painting that looked as though the artist had flung splodges of vivid colour onto the canvas, and which to Tahlia's eyes did not resemble anything vaguely recognisable.

Thanos followed her gaze across the room to where the long-haired and bearded Rufus Hartman was chatting with a group of guests.

'But he is not nearly such an attractive guide,' he

drawled, a gleam of undisguised sexual interest in his eyes
as he turned back to Tahlia, stealing her breath. Thanos
Savakis was an outrageous flirt, and her common sense
told her she should walk away from him and keep on
walking. But her usual caution seemed to have deserted her;
she was blown away by his charismatic charm, and when
his mouth curved into that devastatingly sexy smile her
heart began to race.

Thanos glanced back at the picture. 'Mr Hartman's abstract
paintings are the sort of thing I'd like to have in my new
hotel. They're contemporary and eye-catching and would suit
the modern design of the building.'

'I understand you own a chain of hotels? Crispin mentioned
it,' Tahlia admitted, flushing at Thanos's quizzical expression.

What else had Crispin told her? he wondered sardonically.
That he was a billionaire with a penchant for blondes? Had
Tahlia asked the gallery-owner to introduce them, confident
that he would find her red-gold hair and milky-pale skin in-
triguingly different from the dozens of bleached blonde,
sunbed-tanned women who were milling around the gallery,
eyeing him rather than the artwork on display?

'I own hotels in many parts of the world, including the
Caribbean and the Maldives, and I'm currently in negotiations
to buy the Ambassador Hotel, where I am staying on this trip
to London.'

Tahlia's eyes widened. The Ambassador was one of the
most exclusive hotels in the capital. She had taken little notice
when Crispin had said that Thanos was a billionaire, but now
it struck her that he could probably buy Reynolds Gems out
of his petty cash.

'My latest development is in one of the Greek Islands,'
Thanos continued. 'The Artemis is a five-star hotel, offering
the ultimate pampering experience—superbly equipped

gyms, spas and beauty parlours, together with shops selling designer clothes and jewellery.'

'It sounds wonderful,' Tahlia murmured, her mind focusing on Thanos's mention of jewellery shops within his hotel. Unconsciously her hand strayed to the row of sapphires and diamonds around her neck. The ornate necklace was not the sort of thing she usually wore, but it was undoubtedly impressive, and tonight she needed to impress.

Thanos's gaze followed the movement of her hand. 'Your necklace is almost as exquisite as the woman wearing it,' he remarked.

She blushed. 'It's just one of a wide range of pieces made by the expert goldsmiths and designers at Reynolds Gems. Our gemologists source the finest precious stones and diamonds to ensure that every piece of jewellery is of top quality.' Tahlia hesitated. Was it fair to subject Thanos to the hard sell when they were at a party, not in a boardroom? Their business needed all the help it could get, she reminded herself, and she had to seize every available opportunity to promote the company.

'Perhaps you might like to consider selling a selection of Reynolds Gems jewellery at the Artemis?' she said carefully. She opened her purse and extracted a business card. 'I believe it could be a mutually beneficial arrangement. Reynolds has an excellent reputation for superb craftsmanship, which would be in keeping with the high quality of your hotel. And we are an expanding company,' she added, as Thanos studied the card she had handed him.

'Really…?' He gave her a razor-sharp glance, and Tahlia felt the colour rise in her cheeks.

'Oh, yes. We have a dynamic management team which is always on the look out for exciting new ventures.' That, at least, wasn't a downright lie. She knew her father would jump at the chance to improve Reynolds' profits.

Thanos's slow smile once more sent heat surging through Tahlia's veins, yet at the same time she was again reminded of a wolf stalking its prey.

'That's certainly a very interesting proposition, Tahlia. I'll give your suggestion serious consideration,' he murmured.

'You will?' She forgot that she was supposed to be a hard-headed businesswoman and grinned at him. She felt as though Christmas had come early—and maybe it had, she thought excitedly. Thanos owned up-market hotels around the world, and if he allowed Reynolds Gems to promote their jewellery to his wealthy clientele it could completely turn around the company's fortunes.

Thanos's eyes narrowed on Tahlia's face. Gone was the exquisite and rather haughty-looking socialite. In her place was a young woman with an impish smile and sparkling blue eyes which were more beautiful than the most priceless of sapphires. How could she lie so blatantly and yet look so innocent? And how could he hate her and want her with equal intensity? He despised her, but at this moment he despised himself more—because he could not deny his longing to pull her into his arms and claim her soft, smiling mouth with his lips.

Suddenly he was tired of the game he had been foolish enough to start. He should have revealed from the beginning that he was her lover James Hamilton's ex-brother-in-law. He was tempted to tell Tahlia there was not a chance in hell he would enter into any 'mutually beneficial arrangement' with her or her company, but he swallowed the words. He had laid his plans carefully, and now he was poised to destroy Reynolds Gems. His moment of revenge would be sweet, and he wanted to savour the expression on her beautiful face when she realised that she had lost everything.

There was no reason to remain with her any longer. Sheikh Mussada had left the gallery some fifteen minutes ago, he

reminded himself, infuriated by the knowledge that he had prolonged his time with her because he had found her intelligent and witty conversation utterly captivating. He glanced around the gallery and saw that the blonde who had attached herself to him like a limpet when he had first arrived was giving him baleful looks. To his annoyance he could not help but compare Lisette's fluffy platinum blonde curls and her sequined dress with its plunging neckline and thigh high skirt to Tahlia's graceful elegance.

His jaw tightened and he gave Tahlia a cool smile. 'I must ask you to excuse me, Tahlia. I'm expecting a business call and need to return to my hotel.'

'Oh, but…' Tahlia stared at Thanos's retreating form, startled by his abrupt departure. He was striding away across the gallery. She felt embarrassed at the thought of calling him back, but she might never have this opportunity again. 'Can I look forward to hearing from you when you've had time to consider my idea about selling Reynolds Gems jewellery in your new hotel?' she called desperately.

Thanos paused and glanced back at her, his expression unfathomable. 'Oh, you'll certainly be hearing from me, Tahlia,' he promised softly. But for some reason his words sent a frisson of unease down her spine.

Tahlia woke early on Monday morning, with a heavy sense of dread in the pit of her stomach. Today her mother was due to see a specialist, to hear whether a mastectomy followed by a course of chemotherapy had destroyed her breast cancer. In the past few weeks Vivienne had regained some of her strength, and her hair had grown back enough that she no longer needed to wear the brightly coloured silk scarves mother and daughter had chosen together before the start of her treatment.

Her mother had been so brave, Tahlia thought, swallowing the lump in her throat. The past two years since Vivienne had been diagnosed had been a nightmare for both her parents, and she hoped with all her heart that today they would be given the news that she was completely cured.

The future of Reynolds Gems was another worry, she acknowledged grimly as she stepped into the shower. She was not hopeful that Thanos Savakis would agree to promote their jewellery at his new hotel, and if Vantage Investments decided against a buy-out, she did not know what would happen to the company her father had devoted his life to.

She would try and find out more about the situation today, she decided as she applied minimal make-up and swept her hair into a loose knot on top of her head.

The May sunshine streaming through the window was warm enough for her to choose a lightweight outfit. Her pale grey pencil skirt and matching jacket were years old, but the precarious state of her finances meant that new clothes were out of the question. She was grateful that her mother had taught her to choose classics rather than high fashion items, because the suit still looked good, and she teamed it with a lilac blouse, slipped her feet into kitten heels and checked her handbag for lipstick, keys and various other essentials, before hurrying out of her flat, praying that her ancient Mini would start this morning.

Tahlia was puzzled to see her father's car in the car park when she arrived at the Reynolds Gems shop just off Bond Street, and she raced upstairs to the office. 'I wasn't expecting to see you,' she greeted him, her smile fading when she saw the tense expression on Peter Reynolds's face. 'What's wrong?' She paled. 'You can't have heard from the hospital this early?'

'No.' Her father sought to reassure her. 'Your mother's ap-

pointment is still scheduled for eleven-thirty. I'm here because I received a call from Vantage Investments at eight o'clock this morning, informing me that they've changed the date of our meeting from Wednesday to midday today.'

'But today is impossible. Ask if we can reschedule for tomorrow.'

'I tried,' her father said wearily. 'But they say we can meet today or not at all.'

'You have to go to the hospital with Mum,' Tahlia said urgently. 'Nothing is more important than her appointment with Mr Rivers. What about asking the hospital if they can rearrange your meeting with him?'

'I've tried that too, but he's flying off to a conference later today.' Peter sighed heavily. 'I hate to put this on you, Tahlia, but I've told Steven Holt from Vantage that we'll go ahead with the meeting, although only one of the directors will be present. This will just be a preliminary meeting, but it sounds as though they are seriously interested in making a deal. Obviously if it all goes to plan I'll be involved in the negotiations, but today it's all down to you. Do you think you can handle it?'

'Of course I can,' Tahlia assured him firmly, her heart contracting when she noted the deep lines furrowing his brow. Her father looked as though he had aged ten years since her mother's illness had been diagnosed, and she was willing to do anything to alleviate his stress. 'Leave the figures for me to read through, and I'll do my best to convince Vantage to buy Reynolds Gems. You need to go home and keep Mum calm before her appointment.' She bit her lip and added huskily, 'Ring me as soon as you have any news, won't you?'

'I will,' her father assured her gravely. 'All the paperwork is on my desk,' he added distractedly, and Tahlia knew that the only thing on his mind right now was her mother.

'Go,' she said gently, giving him a little push towards the door. And with a ghost of a smile he walked out of the office.

Two hours later, Tahlia put down the documents which outlined the company's financial situation and picked up her cup, grimacing when she took a sip of cold coffee. Only a miracle could save them, she acknowledged dully. It was clear that Reynolds Gems' profit margins had been low for the past couple of years, but despite that her father had gone ahead with a costly refit of all three shops, and had had to borrow a huge amount from the bank to do so.

Now, because of the global recession that had affected so many businesses, the bank was demanding that the loan be repaid—and, as was obvious from the figures, Reynolds did not have enough money to clear its debts. Tahlia could see from various letters that her father had pleaded with other banks for help, but in the present financial climate no one was interested in rescuing a failing company.

If she failed to persuade Vantage to buy Reynolds Gems the company would go bankrupt—it was as simple as that, she acknowledged sickly. The responsibility was terrifying, and as she gathered up her briefcase and handbag she felt a churning sensation in her stomach that grew worse as she walked briskly out of the office.

Vantage Investment's offices were in the heart of the city. Tahlia knew that parking would be a nightmare, so instead of driving she took the tube to Cannon Street, arrived much too early for her meeting and had twenty agonising minutes to kill before she finally pushed open the glass doors and walked through the plush reception area, her heels echoing loudly on the marble floor. The receptionist directed her to the lift, and on the journey up to the seventh floor she peered at her reflection in the stainless steel walls. She quickly

applied another coat of lipgloss, dismayed to see that her hand was shaking.

'Miss Reynolds? I'm Steven Holt,' a sandy haired man greeted her when she emerged from the lift.

'It's a pleasure to meet you, Mr Holt,' Tahlia returned the greeting with a nervous smile, hiding her surprise that the CEO had met her, rather than his secretary or a junior manager.

He made no further conversation as she followed him along the corridor, and her confusion increased when he ushered her into a room and quietly closed the door after her. She stared blankly at the solid wood. Was she supposed to sit here and wait for him to return? Tension knotted her stomach as she turned into the room, and her heart almost leapt from her chest when she caught sight of the man sitting behind the desk, his broad shoulders and the proud tilt of his head silhouetted against the bright sunshine pouring through the window.

'Mr Savakis?' She halted abruptly and stared at him, her pulse-rate accelerating as her eyes swept over his thick black hair and hard-boned handsome face, then lowered to his impeccably tailored jacket, blinding white shirt and navy silk tie. He was even more gorgeous than the man who had tormented her dreams: a suave, sophisticated billionaire businessman—but what business did he have here at Vantage Investments, with her?

Thanos was watching her impassively, his dark eyes cold and—the word filtered into Tahlia's mind—pitiless. He made no response to her uncertain smile, simply dipped his head to indicate that she should sit down.

His silence unnerved her, and her voice was unnaturally high-pitched when she burst out, 'I don't understand. I'm here for private discussions with Mr Holt.'

'Steven Holt is the chief executive of Vantage Investments, and in ordinary circumstances your discussions would have been with him,' he told her coolly. 'But these are not ordinary

circumstances, Tahlia.' For a split second emotion flared in his eyes, and Tahlia caught her breath at the look of simmering fury he directed at her before his lashes fell, masking his expression. 'Vantage is a subsidiary company of Savakis Enterprises.'

'I see,' Tahlia said carefully, shaken by the look he had given her, and utterly bemused by it. 'Then…you must know why I'm here?'

'Oh, yes, Tahlia. I know exactly why you're here,' Thanos leaned back in his seat and brought the tips of his fingers together. He was a remote and forbidding figure, and he made no attempt to disguise the contempt in his eyes as he raked them over Tahlia's designer suit. No wonder Reynolds Gems was in trouble if Tahlia paid herself a salary well above average to finance the luxurious lifestyle she obviously took for granted, he mused cynically.

'You are hoping to persuade me to buy out your company and save it from bankruptcy. The same company that you assured me is an expanding operation with a dynamic management team,' he said mockingly.

Tahlia felt her cheeks burn as she recalled her suggestion that he might consider allowing Reynolds Gems to sell their jewellery at his new hotel. Clearly he had never had any intention of taking the idea seriously. For some reason he had just been playing her along, and the knowledge sparked her temper.

'Why didn't you tell me of your connection with Vantage Investments, instead of letting me believe there might be a way to save Reynolds?' she demanded angrily. 'Did you enjoy making a fool of me?'

'I admit I found the situation mildly amusing.'

The expression in his eyes chilled her to the bone. 'But why?' she choked. 'What have I ever done to—?' She broke off

and stared at the photograph of a young woman that he had pushed across the desk—for a second her heart stopped beating.

'I believe you have met my sister?' Thanos asked, in a dangerously soft tone.

'I…' Tahlia groped for words, her brain in freefall.

'I imagine it was not a long meeting. And there would have been a certain awkwardness to the situation, seeing that you were in bed with Melina's husband at the time. Of course my sister no longer looks as she does in that photo,' Thanos went on, in the same chilling tone of barely suppressed aggression. 'And it is unlikely she will ever dance again—which is a pity because, as you can see from the picture, she loved to dance.'

Tahlia could not formulate a reply as she stared at the photograph of the beautiful young woman whose face was so shockingly familiar. In the picture her dark hair was swept up into a chignon, rather than falling in a mass of curls around her shoulders as it had been on the night Tahlia had seen her, but there was no mistaking that this was James's wife.

'Melina was distraught after she caught you and Hamilton together. She fled from the hotel, and as she dashed across the road she was hit by a car,' Thanos said harshly. 'Eyewitnesses said she was thrown at least twenty feet into the air before she hit the ground. She was in a coma for three weeks, both her legs were broken, and she suffered spinal damage.' He ignored Tahlia's horrified gasp and went on remorselessly, 'For a while the doctors believed she would be in a wheelchair for the rest of her life. Thankfully her last round of surgery was successful, and she is having intensive physiotherapy to help her to walk, but she will never dance again,' he finished grimly, a nerve flickering in his cheek as he picked up the photo of his sister and stared at it.

The silence in the room screamed with tension, until at last Tahlia forced herself to speak. 'I…I didn't know,' she whispered.

Thanos gave a savage laugh. 'You mean you didn't hear the ambulance sirens? Or you did hear them but you were not sufficiently interested to go and find out who had been injured? Presumably you and Hamilton continued with your sexual gymnastics after Melina left?' he snarled contemptuously. 'Neither of you had the decency to follow her, even though it must have been obvious—even to a heartless bitch like you—that she was devastated at finding the man she loved in bed with his whore.'

Tahlia bowed her head while Thanos's savage fury crashed over her. His anger was no less than she deserved, she acknowledged sickly, and her mind relived that terrible night six months ago, which had started off so wonderfully.

She had felt excited and a little nervous when James had checked them in to the hotel he had booked for a romantic weekend.

'Just one key?' she'd queried tremulously, her heart thumping.

'One key, one room—one bed,' he'd replied, with that disarming grin that melted her heart. 'You know I love you, Tahlia,' he had murmured when they'd reached their suite, and he had pulled her into his arms and kissed her. 'And you love me—don't you, baby? Making love is the next step in showing our love for each other.'

She had been unable to resist him: good-looking, easygoing James, who had swept her off her feet. She had been ready for them to become lovers, and when James had started to undress her she had not hidden her eagerness. But as they had tumbled onto the bed the door had burst open, and a woman had stumbled into the room.

She would never forget the look of shock on the woman's face, the tears streaming down her cheeks and her voice crying brokenly, 'How could you, James? How could you? I am your *wife*...'

'I didn't know about your sister's accident,' she insisted shakily, dragging her mind back to the present. 'I left James almost immediately.' After his sulky confirmation that, yes, he *was* married—'but that's no reason to get hysterical, Tahlia.' 'I ran down to my car, parked at the rear of the hotel. Melina must have run out of the front of the hotel, and I drove home along a different road. I don't remember hearing sirens or anything—but I was in shock,' Tahlia said falteringly, re-membering how she had driven away, desperately trying to hold back her tears until she reached her parents' home. 'I had no idea that James was married.'

'Liar.'

The solitary word cracked through the air like a whip, and Tahlia jumped. 'I swear I didn't know—' she began, but Thanos silenced her with a savage glare.

'Of course you knew. Just as you knew that the actor you've been having an affair with recently was married. Far from attempting to hide your relationship with him, you brazenly flaunted it, allowing yourself to be snapped by the press leaving a hotel with him.' Thanos's lip curled. 'Tell me, do you enjoy a feeling of power when you have sex with other women's husbands? Women like you disgust me.'

Women like his father's mistress, Thanos brooded grimly. Wendy Jones had known that his father had a wife and children, but that had not stopped her flirting with Kosta Savakis and pursuing him with single-minded determination, uncaring of the pain and destruction their affair caused. Wendy and Tahlia were two of a kind—predatory, heartless bitches who lacked any moral decency. His hatred of the woman who had become his stepmother had burned inside him for years, and as he stared across his desk at Tahlia's pale face his fury threatened to choke him.

The icy anger in Thanos's eyes sent a shiver down Tahlia's

spine, and she said frantically, 'I promise you I did *not* know
James was married. If I had I would never have dated him, let
alone agreed to spend a weekend with him.' She jumped to
her feet and gripped the edge of the desk, breathing hard so
that her breasts rose and fell jerkily. 'When your sister burst
into the hotel room and announced that she was James's wife
I felt *terrible*. I felt as though I were the lowest life form on
the planet.'

'An apt description,' Thanos snapped, his jaw hardening.
'And I have no doubt that you felt terrible—you'd just been
caught out, and you knew James was likely to end his affair
with you so that he could try and persuade his wealthy wife
to forgive him. I don't understand what you saw in my
brother-in-law,' he added scathingly. 'James Hamilton is a
penniless, talentless waste of space. But, according to the
press reports, you seem to get a kick out of sleeping with other
women's husbands.'

The colour leached from Tahlia's face, and for a second she
was tempted to flee from the room, but she forced herself to
meet Thanos's cold stare. 'The reports in the tabloids about my
supposed affair with Damian Casson are a complete fabrica-
tion,' she said stiltedly. 'And I have instructed my solicitor to
proceed with legal action against the papers involved.' Her eyes
dropped to the photograph of Thanos's sister and she swal-
lowed. 'I am so sorry,' she whispered. 'I wish I could apologise
to Melina, and explain to her that James deceived both of us.'

'Do you think I would allow you anywhere near my sister?'
Thanos demanded harshly. 'Melina has suffered enough,
without having to hear your lies.'

He had also risen to his feet, and was surveying her with
visible contempt. She could understand why he was angry,
Tahlia conceded, but his refusal to listen to her and his deter-
mination to believe the worst of her sparked her temper.

'I am not lying,' she told him with quiet dignity. 'And I am not the woman portrayed by the tabloids. I had no idea that James had a wife.' Tears stung her eyes, and she lowered her head so that Thanos would not see them. She had felt a fool that night in the hotel, when James's treachery had been revealed, but her emotions were of little significance compared to the pain—both mental and physical—that Thanos's sister must be suffering.

'I'm so sorry,' she repeated shakily. She had been an innocent pawn in James's game, but she still felt responsible for his wife's terrible accident.

'It's too damned late to be sorry,' Thanos grated. 'It's a pity you did not feel this touching remorse *before* you slept with my sister's husband.'

'I never slept with him,' Tahlia said quickly. 'Although I realise that will be small comfort to Melina. I admit that I had intended to become James's lover. The night that Melina found us at the hotel would have been our first night together.' She swallowed, but forced herself to go on, aware that Thanos and his sister deserved her honesty. 'I had fallen in love with James—although I realise now that I never really knew him at all,' she added bitterly.

She was good, Thanos conceded grimly. She almost had him convinced that she was as innocent as she protested—and the shimmer of tears in those beautiful blue eyes was a nice touch. If it wasn't for the story in the tabloids about her affair with another married actor he might have been tempted to believe her.

But perhaps he *wanted* to believe that Tahlia had been hoodwinked by James Hamilton because of his own inconvenient physical attraction to her? he brooded irritably. Today she was the epitome of understated elegance: her slim-fitting skirt skimmed the gentle flare of her hips, and the cut of her

jacket emphasised her tiny waist, while her soft lilac-coloured blouse complemented her creamy complexion. The scattering of freckles across her nose and cheeks matched her red-gold hair, while the long lashes fringing those startlingly blue eyes were a slightly darker shade of gold.

She might be lovely on the outside, but inside she was rotten to the core, and all the evidence proved that she had known just what she was doing when she began her affair with James, Thanos reminded himself. He was not going to be duped by her lies simply because his hormones were raging out of control. His mouth tightened and he forced himself to move away from her, strolling across the room to stare out of the window at the view of the city.

Tahlia watched him, her eyes roaming over his broad shoulders and the arrogant tilt of his head. Despair settled like a lead weight in her stomach.

'You never had any intention of buying out Reynolds Gems, did you?' she said dully.

'None whatsoever,' he replied coolly. 'It seemed entirely fair that you should suffer a fraction of the misery my sister has suffered, and so I decided to destroy your company. But, to be honest, bringing about Reynolds Gems' downfall has not been difficult. Some of the decisions taken by the company during the last two years have been downright reckless, and they are directly responsible for Reynolds' current financial situation. I simply tricked you into thinking that Vantage Investments would offer a rescue package, and you were gullible enough— or more likely greedy enough—to be fooled into believing you could hang on to your self-indulgent lifestyle.'

It was no coincidence that Reynolds Gems' problems had begun at the same time as her mother's illness had been diagnosed, Tahlia acknowledged. During that terrible time business had come a long way down her father's list of pri-

orities, and she felt guilty that she had not become more involved with running the company.

'Reynolds Gems is my father's company, not mine,' she said quietly. 'If you destroy it you will be hurting him.'

'You became a partner three years ago. My investigations were very thorough,' Thanos said coldly, turning away from the window to give her a sardonic look. 'It's too bad your father will lose the company he built from scratch, but he shouldn't have brought his daughter up to be an immoral slut.'

Anger, swift and white-hot, churned inside Tahlia. Her eyes flew to the clock above the desk and she felt a pang of dread. Had her mother been told that her battle with breast cancer had been successful? Or, as the specialist had warned might happen, had the cancer spread? Even if the news was bad, her father would hide his fears and support Vivienne, just as he had done every day for the past two years. Only Tahlia knew that sometimes he sat alone in his study and wept. Peter Reynolds, of all people, did not deserve Thanos's disdain.

Shaking with fury, she marched across the office and stood directly in front of Thanos. 'Think what you like about me, but don't you *dare* say a word against my father. He is a better man than you will ever be.'

'Not in business,' Thanos drawled sarcastically.

Tahlia flushed. 'I accept he had made some unwise decisions, but there were reasons…' She glanced at Thanos's mocking expression and halted abruptly. She refused to discuss her mother's health problems with him when she was sure he would accuse her of lying to gain his sympathy. Her anger dissipated as quickly as it had arrived, leaving her feeling drained and despairing as the realisation hit her that there was no hope of saving Reynolds Gems from the administrators.

'I wish more than anything that I'd never met James

Hamilton,' she said huskily. 'And I hope with all my heart that your sister makes a full recovery.'

She swung away from him, choking back the tears she was determined would not fall until she was outside his office. Her knee collided painfully with the coffee table.

'Damn it!' She stumbled, dropped her briefcase, and bit back an oath as it burst open and spilled its contents over the floor.

No doubt Thanos was enjoying seeing her on her knees, she thought furiously, as she knelt and began to scoop up the pages of figures that spelled the demise of Reynolds Gems. She dashed her hand over her eyes and froze when she realised that he had crouched beside her and was helping to gather up her paperwork.

'Thank you.' She took the papers he handed her and slowly lifted her head, startled to find him so close. The tang of his cologne drifted around her, teasing her senses, and she could feel the dry heat emanating from his body. How could she be so agonisingly aware of him when he had made it clear that he despised her? she wondered despairingly.

It was suddenly imperative that she stood up and moved away from him, before he realised the effect he had on her, but her muscles had seized up. Her eyes were drawn to his— and shock ricocheted through her when she glimpsed the unmistakable feral desire blazing in their depths.

CHAPTER THREE

How could he feel this overwhelming sexual attraction to Tahlia when he loathed her? Thanos wondered furiously. His brain acknowledged that she was an immoral slut, but his body was responding with humiliating eagerness to the delicate fragrance of her perfume. He could not tear his eyes from the soft curve of her mouth, and the tantalising fullness of her lips was proving an irresistible temptation. His desire for her was an unexpected complication that filled him with self-disgust, but no amount of reminding himself of Melina's injuries could banish the fierce urge to crush Tahlia's lips beneath his.

Thanos was going to kiss her. Tahlia saw the smouldering intent in his eyes seconds before he lowered his head, and she was stunned by the realisation that she wanted him to. He believed she had slept with his sister's husband, and he had made his opinion of her quite clear, but for reasons she could not understand she made no attempt to deny him and simply waited, heart thumping, for his mouth to claim hers.

The first brush of his mouth sent a quiver of reaction through her. His lips were firm, sliding demandingly over hers, but Tahlia's pride belatedly came to her aid and she clamped her mouth shut, fighting the overwhelming tempta-

tion to respond to him. He hated her, she reminded herself. And he thought he had good reason to destroy Reynolds Gems in a bid to hurt her. He adamantly refused to believe that she had not set out to deliberately steal his sister's husband, and if she gave in to the urgent clamouring of her body and kissed him back it would surely confirm his belief that she was the immoral slut he had accused her of being.

But she had recognised the sizzling sexual chemistry between them at the art gallery, and now it was raging out of control, consuming them both. When he caught hold of her hand and drew her to her feet she went unresistingly—now they were standing so close, yet not quite touching, and her senses were inflamed by the subtle scent of male pheromones, the intoxicating heat emanating from his hard body that made her long to close the gap between them and have him crush her against his muscular chest.

His lips hardened, became more urgent, and her will-power crumbled beneath the onslaught. With a little gasp she opened her mouth, and he immediately thrust his tongue deep into its moist warmth, exploring her with shocking eroticism as he snaked his arm around her waist and jerked her close, hip to hip, her soft breasts pressed against his rock-solid body.

His hungry passion was like nothing she had ever experienced before, and it drove every thought from her head other than her frantic need for him to continue kissing her. She forgot that they were standing in his office, forgot that he owned Vantage Investments and had refused to save Reynolds Gems from collapse. She was only aware of him, of the demanding pressure of his lips and the faint abrasion of his jaw against the softer skin of her cheek as he angled her head and deepened the kiss to another level that was flagrantly erotic.

She was aware of the melting warmth between her thighs, and the rigid proof of his arousal pressing into her belly. With

a low moan of capitulation she moved her hands to his shoulders. She would have wound her arms around his neck, but he abruptly snatched his mouth from hers and jerked his head back, his eyes glittering with contempt as he stared down at her.

'What's the matter Tahlia—has Damian Casson come to his senses and dumped you in favour of his wife? Surely you won't find *me* a good substitute to relieve your sexual frustrations when you're only attracted to married men?' he taunted, his voice dripping with sarcasm that made her skin crawl.

Tahlia gasped, and acting purely on impulse she raised her arm and cracked her hand across his cheek. 'You arrogant bastard,' she choked, shaking with anger and humiliation. '*You* kissed *me*. What were you trying to do—prove how irresistible you are?'

'I certainly proved something,' Thanos drawled as he strolled back across the room and leaned his hip against his desk, folding his arms across his chest in an indolent stance that disguised the fact that his heart was slamming beneath his ribs. 'The sexual alchemy between us is as potent as it is inexplicable, and I admit I kissed you because I was curious to see how you would react.' His eyes narrowed on her white face. 'Hit me again and I promise you will regret it.'

Tahlia stared at the livid red mark on his cheek and felt sick. She had never struck another human being in her life, and she was shocked and ashamed by her violent display of temper. It was no good reminding herself that Thanos had deserved it. He had kissed her, but she had wanted him to, she owned miserably. Despite knowing his low opinion of her, she had been unable to resist him. What did that say about her morals? she wondered despairingly.

Thanos kept his expression deliberately blank, giving no clue to the internal battle raging inside him as he sought to bring his hormones back under control. Kissing her had been

a mistake, he acknowledged grimly. He was furious with himself for succumbing to the temptation of her lush mouth, and his temper was not improved by the knowledge that he wanted to kiss her again, to slide his lips down her throat to the pulse beating frenetically at its base, then tug the pins from her hair and run his fingers through the pale red silk.

He studied her dispassionately, wondering if the tears clinging like tiny sparkling diamonds to her lashes were meant to make him feel remorse or pity. He felt neither. She deserved to lose her company, and she would still not suffer a fraction of the trauma his sister had suffered.

He had planned Tahlia's downfall during the endless days and nights he had sat at Melina's bedside, waiting for her to regain consciousness. He had felt so helpless and so afraid, he remembered grimly. He who had never feared anything, who had fought his way out of poverty to the pinnacle of success, had been scared that he was going to lose the one person in the world he truly loved. Now Melina was out of danger, and slowly recovering from her injuries, but he would never forget the accident that had so nearly claimed her life— and he would never forgive the two people he deemed responsible for it.

In the current financial climate Tahlia would never find another buyer for Reynolds Gems. Everything was going just as he had planned. But that was not entirely true, he acknowledged irritably. He could not remember the last time he had wanted a woman as badly as he wanted Tahlia and his hunger for her angered him. He had first-hand proof that she was a woman like his father's mistress, yet still he was consumed with this damnable longing to possess her.

Maybe he should seize what he wanted and be damned, he mused grimly. He had planned to take revenge for his sister by fooling Tahlia into believing that his company would buy

Reynolds Gems and then withdrawing his offer of financial support at the last minute. He had no interest in saving Reynolds' three failing jewellery shops, but those shops *were* in prime London locations. The current recession meant that the property market had all but collapsed; he knew Peter Reynolds had tried and failed to sell the shops, and that now his creditors had run out of patience, but eventually the financial climate would improve and the shops would be lucrative investments.

Thanos's business brain told him he would be a fool to turn down the opportunity to increase his property portfolio—and wouldn't his revenge be all the sweeter if he made it personal? Buying out Reynolds Gems would save Tahlia from financial ruin, but he would demand repayment in full—in his bed!

The tense silence stretched Tahlia's nerves, and her skin prickled beneath Thanos's intent gaze. He appeared relaxed, but he reminded her of a panther: sleek, dark and dangerous as it eyed its prey. She had to get out of his office, she thought wildly. Gather what little dignity she had left and leave.

She retrieved her briefcase from the floor, where she had dropped it, and turned towards the door.

'There might be a way I could be persuaded to buy Reynolds Gems…'

His soft drawl stopped her in her tracks, and she swung back to face him, her heart thumping. It was probably a trick, she told herself, or a joke at her expense, but she was desperate for a lifeline—however tenuous.

'How?' she demanded baldly.

'The time-honoured tradition of bartering—each of us has something the other wants,' he elucidated, when she stared at him blankly. 'It's possible we could negotiate a deal.'

Tahlia frowned. 'What do I have that you want? I have nothing.'

Dark eyes burned into her, and she felt a fierce tugging sensation deep in her pelvis. 'Don't be naïve, Tahlia,' he said, in a faintly bored tone. 'You know perfectly well what I want.' He crossed the room in two strides and slid his hand beneath her chin, holding her prisoner and forcing her to meet his gaze. '*You,*' he said bluntly. 'I want to take you to bed and enjoy the delectable body that you share so willingly with your numerous lovers.' He ignored her gasp of outrage and continued coolly. 'In return for your sexual favours I am prepared to buy Reynolds Gems for the full asking price.'

A bubble of hysteria rose in Tahlia's throat. She had been right; it *was* a cruel joke. But there had been no hint of amusement in Thanos's voice, and the feral heat in his eyes scorched her skin. 'But…you don't like me,' she faltered, picking from the random threads of thought that whirled in her head.

That did seem to amuse him, and he laughed derisively. 'It is not necessary for me to *like* you. I want to have sex with you; I'm not suggesting that we become best friends.'

Tahlia flushed at his mockery. 'I have always thought that lovers should also be friends.' Thanos could not have made it clearer that he was only interested in using her body for his sexual satisfaction. 'I am not a piece of meat,' she told him scathingly, 'and I am not for sale.'

Thanos's eyes narrowed. How dared Tahlia speak to him in that contemptuous tone when, according to the press reports, she dropped her knickers for any Z-list celebrity who gave her the time of day?

'Everything and everyone is for sale for the right price,' he told her mockingly. 'You should be grateful of my offer. Who else do you think will be prepared to shell out a six-figure sum for a failing company? That's a damn good rate for even the most inventive hooker. And besides,' he drawled, tightening his grip on her chin when she tried to jerk out of his grasp,

'we both know you would not find it such an ordeal to share my bed. You might want to deny the sexual chemistry that burns between us, but your body is more honest.'

At that moment Tahlia would have given her life to deny his sardonic taunt, but from the moment he had moved close to her the exotic tang of his aftershave, mixed with another subtle masculine scent, had pervaded her senses and lit a flame inside her. Her breasts felt heavy, and she caught her breath when he trailed his free hand down her front and discovered the hard peaks of her nipples jutting beneath her silk blouse.

Anger was her only weapon against the insidious warmth that licked through her veins. He thought she was no better than a prostitute. She would not, *could* not give in to the voice in her head which urged her to agree to his outrageous proposal. It would be devastating to lose Reynolds Gems, but far worse to sacrifice her pride and her self-respect.

'Hell will freeze over before I agree to your disgusting suggestion,' she snapped.

He shrugged. 'Are you prepared to stand by and allow your father to lose the company he has devoted his life to for the past thirty years?'

Tahlia swallowed the lump that had formed in her throat. 'Emotional blackmail is despicable. My father would never expect me to sell my body, even if it means losing everything he owns. You seem to think that your wealth gives you special privileges. Obviously you were born with a silver spoon in your mouth,' she flung at him, remembering that Crispin Blythe had said that Thanos was a billionaire. 'You believe your money can buy you anything. But it can't buy me.'

'In that case I may as well take what you give away freely to so many other men,' he bit out savagely, seizing her shoulders and slamming her against his chest. He lowered his head and captured her mouth with bruising force. Tahlia gave a

shocked cry, and he took advantage of her parted lips to thrust his tongue between them, exploring her with a bold eroticism that made her tremble. Anger came to her rescue and she pushed against his chest, but he merely tightened his arms around her until she felt as though she were trapped in a vice. She was determined not to respond to him, but he seemed to sense her resolve and eased the pressure of his mouth a fraction, changing the kiss from one of domination to a sensual tasting that she found utterly irresistible.

She felt as though her bones were dissolving. Her legs no longer seemed capable of bearing her weight, and she sagged against him, relaxing her balled fists and splaying her hands over his chest, feeling the heat of his body through his shirt. She felt his fingers slide up her nape and with a deft movement he released the pins from her chignon so that her hair uncoiled and fell in a scented silky curtain around her shoulders. He made a muffled noise in his throat and buried his hands in her hair, angling her head while he deepened the kiss. She responded helplessly, closing her eyes as she sank deeper into the velvet softness of his caress.

Lost in a world of sensory pleasure, she was unprepared when he suddenly lifted his head and stared down at her. The cold contempt in his dark eyes doused her in a wave of humiliation as she realised that she was clinging to him.

'My offer still stands,' he said coolly.

She jerked away from him, tears of shame burning her eyes. There was no evidence in his mocking expression that he had been stirred by the kiss, while *she* was a seething mass of emotions and could not disguise the effect he had on her.

'My answer is still the same,' she said curtly. 'I am not for sale.'

She was sure he would taunt her with the fact that she had offered no resistance when he had kissed her again, but he

shrugged uninterestedly and flicked back his cuff to glance
at his watch.

'In that case I believe we have covered everything,' he said
coolly. 'Perhaps you'll have better luck securing a rescue plan
for Reynolds Gems elsewhere?'

He must know that her father had approached a number of
banks for help and had been refused. But pleading with him
would be utterly pointless, and would decimate what little
dignity she had left. Somehow she forced her limbs to move,
snatched up her briefcase, and even managed to bid him a cool
goodbye before she swept out of his office with her head held
high, determined to deny him the pleasure of witnessing her
utter devastation.

Tahlia caught the tube back to Bond Street on auto-pilot, stunned
by the events that had taken place in Thanos's office. She could
not believe he had made the foul suggestion that she should sleep
with him in return for him buying Reynolds Gems. When she
had first met him at the art gallery her instincts had warned her
that he was ruthless, but now she knew just what kind of a man
he was: a man who would pay for sex with a woman who he
had admitted he despised. Unquestionably she had made the
right decision when she had turned him down. There was no way
on earth she would ever agree to be Thanos Savakis's whore.
She was furious with herself for allowing him to kiss her—and
worse by far was the fact that while she had been in his arms
she had forgotten everything—even her mother.

Her phone rang as she walked into her office, and her heart
lurched when she saw that the caller was her father. 'Is it good
news?' she asked him tensely, hardly daring to breathe as she
waited for his reply.

'The best,' he assured her gently. 'The consultant gave
your mother the all-clear.'

Tahlia could hear the relief in Peter Reynolds's voice, and tears stung her eyes. 'Thank God,' she whispered shakily. 'Mum must be overjoyed.'

'We both are,' Peter said in a choked voice. 'We're going out to dinner tonight to celebrate—my credit card can just about take it. Will you come?' He hesitated, and then added, 'There's something I need to discuss with you.'

'Of course I'll come,' Tahlia agreed, puzzled by her father's tone. Her mother had beaten cancer and the world was suddenly a wonderful place, so why did he sound so tense? 'Dad, what's the matter?'

There was another long pause before Peter spoke. 'I've had a letter from the bank, threatening to repossess Carlton House.'

'What?' Tahlia's legs gave way and she dropped onto a chair. 'What do you mean? I don't understand. How can the bank repossess Carlton when you and Mum jointly own it?'

'I had to remortgage the house as well as take the loan when we refurbished the shops,' Peter explained flatly. 'Your mother agreed to it because I assured her it was just a temporary solution to a cashflow problem with the company, and she thinks I've already repaid it. I was hoping the bank would give me some leeway, but I'm behind with the repayments and they are demanding I pay the arrears immediately. 'There's no money left, Tahlia. I've used every penny of my personal savings trying to keep Reynolds afloat. I hope to God Vantage Investments are serious about buying Reynolds Gems,' he said thickly, 'because if not I will be solely responsible for losing Carlton and breaking your mother's heart. How did the meeting go?' he asked; a note of desperation audible in his voice. 'Steven Holt sounded pretty keen when I spoke to him a few days ago.'

Tahlia's brain seemed to have stopped functioning. Her parents could not lose Carlton House. It was inconceivable.

In her mind she pictured the graceful old manor house that had been built during the reign of Elizabeth I and which had been passed down through her mother's family for generations. The house was a listed building and had been a serious drain on her parents' finances for years, but they had swiftly dismissed any idea that they might be better to sell Carlton and move to a smaller house which required less upkeep.

Her mother would be utterly heartbroken if she was forced to move from the home she loved now, and after the past two gruelling years of fear and chemotherapy she did not deserve to suffer further misery.

'Yes.' She uttered the word instinctively, because she could not bring herself to say no—to reveal that the meeting had not gone as she or her father had expected, and that the CEO of Vantage Investments had been instructed to sound enthusiastic about buying out Reynolds by Thanos Savakis, head of Vantage's parent company Savakis Enterprises, a man whose only agenda was revenge.

'As you said, it was only a preliminary meeting. There are still a few points to discuss before a buy-out is absolutely certain. Leave things with me while you concentrate on Mum,' she added hurriedly. 'Why don't you take her to Cornwall and stay with Aunt Jess for a few days? You could both do with a break, and Jess would love to see you both.'

She gripped the phone, willing herself to remain calm. 'Dad…you're not serious about the possibility of losing Carlton, are you? I mean, there has to be a way…'

'The only way I can settle the debt on the house is by selling the company,' Peter said flatly. 'A while back there were a couple of other firms who were interested in buying Reynolds, but I turned them down because Vantage Investments offered the best deal. If Vantage should change their mind I'm sunk. The bank is putting pressure on me, and

there's no time to find a new buyer. You say that a few things need to be ironed out? I think I should call Steven Holt.'

'*No.*' Tahlia fought to keep the panic from her voice. If her father phoned Vantage he would learn from Thanos that there was no deal and never had been, that the offer to buy Reynolds had just been part of a cruel trick designed to punish *her*. This was her fault, she thought despairingly. If Vantage had not approached her father he would have sold Reynolds to one of the other firms who had been interested, and Carlton House would be safe.

'*Are you prepared to stand by and allow your father to lose the company…?*' Thanos's voice mocked her. The thought had torn her apart, but she had rejected his solution, vowing to find another way to save Reynolds. The defeated note in her father's voice now made it clear there was no other way. It was not simply the company that was in danger but Carlton House, and her parents' happiness and peace of mind.

'*Each of us has something the other wants.*' Thanos was a billionaire who had the means to buy Reynolds, and in return he wanted…

A tremor ran through her. He wanted to have sex with her. She couldn't do it, she thought wildly. But hard on the heels of that thought came the acknowledgement that she had no choice. Her father had admitted he was at rock bottom, and she was at the limit on her own overdraft and credit cards. She could not raise enough money to cover one mortgage repayment on Carlton, let alone clear the arrears.

'There are just a couple of minor points that need clarification before Vantage agrees to the deal,' she told her father, forcing herself to sound calm. 'I'll get back to them and sort it out. Can I speak to Mum?' she asked quickly, before her father could argue.

'Oh, yes—of course…' There was a moment's silence, and then Vivienne's voice sounded down the line.

'Tahlia! Isn't it wonderful?' she said tremulously. 'I feel as though I've been given a second chance at life.'

The raw emotion in her mother's voice tore at Tahlia's heart, and she swallowed the tears that clogged her throat. 'I hope you enjoy every minute of it, Mum,' she whispered. 'You and Dad deserve to be happy.'

And she would do everything in her power to help them, she vowed fiercely as she put down the phone. Even the unthinkable.

Thanos emerged from the *en suite* bathroom and padded across the bedroom to answer the phone, his brows lowering in a frown as he listened to the message relayed by the receptionist. He hesitated for a few moments, wondering why Tahlia Reynolds was standing in the lobby of his hotel at eleven o'clock at night, and silently acknowledged that he was intrigued.

'Inform Miss Reynolds that I will see her in my suite in fifteen minutes,' he murmured, before he replaced the receiver. It wouldn't hurt Tahlia to cool her heels, and if the reason for her unexpected visit was sufficiently important she would wait until he was ready to see her. He also needed to get dressed—unless he intended to greet her wearing nothing but a towel around his hips. When he recalled his body's involuntary reaction to her at their last meeting it was clear that clothes were a necessity, he conceded, his mouth curving into a self-derisive grimace.

To his annoyance his curiosity grew over the following quarter of an hour, and after pouring himself a liberal malt Scotch he paced restlessly around his suite. What did Tahlia want? Had she, after all, decided to offer her body in return for him saving her father from financial ruin? His mouth twisted as he recalled her scathing refusal to sell herself to him

earlier in the day. Her reaction had surprised him, he acknowledged. He had first-hand evidence that she had the morals of an alley cat, and the recent story of her affair with another married actor was not the first time her love-life had been reported in the press.

He had been certain that she would agree to sleep with him in return for his agreement to buy Reynolds Gems, but instead she had looked as scandalised as if she were a vestal virgin—which was a laughable notion, he thought sardonically.

'Hell will freeze over before I agree to your disgusting suggestion,' she'd flung at him with icy scorn. So why was she here now? Undoubtedly she wanted something. In his experience women always did, he thought cynically. He stared out of the window at the night-time view of London: the myriad lights of buildings and cars glowing like bright jewels against the black velvet sky, the illuminated London Eye sparkling like an enormous static Catherine wheel. His mind flew back six months to another hotel—this time in Athens—and another woman whose visit had been unexpected.

He had been shocked when Yalena had phoned him out of the blue and suggested they meet up. Fifteen years had passed since the woman he had loved had broken off their engagement and married his best friend, and he admitted he had been curious to gauge his reaction when he met Yalena and Takis again. But Yalena had come to his hotel alone, dressed like a tart and clearly confident that Thanos would not turn down her offer to leave her husband for him. She had made a mistake all those years ago, she had told him tearfully. She realised now that she loved him, not Takis—although Thanos noted that she had only arrived at that conclusion since his name had been included on the list of the world's top one hundred richest men.

Yalena had been dismissive of the fact that her husband

adored her, and worked hard to give her a good lifestyle, and Thanos had felt a mixture of disgust and disappointment that he had been so wrong about her. For years he had put her on a pedestal—the discovery that she was an avaricious gold-digger, just like every other woman he had ever met, had filled him with contempt and the bitter realisation that he had been a fool to waste his emotions on her.

The knock on the door dragged him from his memories. Tahlia was here. He finished the whisky, savouring its warmth as it slid down his throat. What would he do if she *had* come to offer herself to him? He felt a tightening sensation in his groin, and his nostrils flared as sexual heat flooded through him. He wanted her badly, and he could afford her. Why not indulge himself? he brooded. He hadn't had sex for months. Combining visiting Melina in hospital with running a billion-pound company had meant that he'd had neither the time nor the inclination for his usual meaningless sexual liaisons with lovers who knew better than to expect commitment from him. Celibacy did not suit him, he owned as he strode across the suite. His body felt taut, hungry for satisfaction, and antici-pation licked in his veins.

The door of Thanos's suite swung open and Tahlia wondered if he could hear her heart beating frantically against her ribs.

'Tahlia,' he greeted her coolly.

His heavily accented voice caused a delicious little shiver to run down her spine, and at the same time exacerbated the tension that had shredded her nerves during the fifteen minutes she had been forced to wait downstairs in the bar. He stood back for her to enter, and for a few seconds her resolve wobbled, and she was tempted to turn tail and flee. But somehow her legs continued to propel her forward—like a lamb into the wolf's lair, the voice in her head whispered as she moved into the centre of the room. Another tremor ran

through her when she heard the click of the door closing behind her.

'You are the mistress of surprise,' Thanos drawled as he strolled towards her.

'What do you mean?' she queried sharply, colour storming into her cheeks. The word *mistress* touched a raw nerve. Thanos believed she had been James Hamilton's mistress. He assumed that she was sexually experienced. The fact that she was not made what she was about to do even harder.

'I did not expect to see you at the art gallery, and I did not anticipate you turning up here tonight.' Nor had he anticipated his reaction to her when he had opened the door—the way his heart had slammed in his chest at the sight of her, looking utterly exquisite in the same blue silk gown she had been wearing the other evening. His desire for her weakened him, and he resented the effect she had on him. 'What do you want, Tahlia?' he demanded tersely, moving away from her to avoid the subtle drift of her perfume that teased his senses.

Tahlia shot him a quick glance that encompassed his black silk shirt, open at the throat to reveal a few inches of bronzed skin covered with crisp, dark hairs, and his superbly tailored black trousers which drew her attention to his lean hips and muscular thighs. The table lamps placed strategically around the room emitted a soft apricot glow that threw his sculpted cheekbones into sharp relief and danced across his gleaming jet-black hair.

He was unfairly gorgeous, and her stomach muscles clenched as she relived those moments in his office when he had crushed her against his body and his lips had claimed hers with untamed passion. No woman would ever tame Thanos, she brooded. Beneath his veneer of urbane sophistication she sensed power and ruthless ambition, a magnetism that commanded the respect of other men and drew beautiful women

to him in droves—yet none would own him or control him, and only the most foolish would try.

The expression on his coldly handsome face was not encouraging, but she had spent the evening listening to her mother's excited chatter about her plans for the garden at Carlton House while her father had looked increasingly strained and haunted. She had finally accepted that she would do whatever it took to prevent her parents from losing their home.

Her mouth felt dry. She licked her lips nervously and prayed that when she spoke her voice would not waver. She did not want him to know how much this was costing her. 'I've come to tell you that I accept your offer,' she said baldly, lifting her head and meeting his midnight gaze steadily. 'I'll sleep with you in return for you buying Reynolds Gems, for the price my father stipulated to Vantage Investments.'

CHAPTER FOUR

FOR several long, agonising seconds Thanos said nothing, but then his brows rose and he drawled mockingly, 'I will expect you to do rather more than *sleep* in return for paying a fortune for your family's failing company.'

His body had reacted predictably to the knowledge that Tahlia was his for the taking; his arousal had been instant and uncomfortably hard. But inexplicably he'd also felt a surge of savage disappointment. When she had rejected his offer earlier that day he'd felt a grudging sense of admiration for her, but now he felt nothing but contempt. She was prepared to sell her body to protect her financial security. She was a gold-digger. He would have no compunction about taking her to bed and sating his inconvenient desire for her.

He dropped his gaze to the low-cut neckline of her dress and the provocative thrust of her breasts. *Theos,* she was beautiful. Heat surged through him and he ruthlessly ignored the faint whisper of regret that it had to be like this, that making love to her would be nothing more than a business transaction. What else could it be? he brooded. He wanted her; she wanted him to bail out her father. It was as simple and clinical as that.

Tahlia caught her breath when Thanos reached out and removed the diamanté clip that secured her chignon. Her hair

fell down around her shoulders as soft as silk against her skin, and she watched his eyes darken as he wound a few pale red-gold strands around his fingers. He stayed like that for timeless seconds, his dark eyes scorching her, and then she gasped when his strong arms suddenly closed around her and he jerked her hard against his chest, his dark head swooping and his mouth claiming hers in a kiss of pure possession.

His dominance was absolute as he forced her head back on her slender neck and kissed her fiercely, demanding her complete compliance and proving beyond doubt his mastery. Instinct warned her that Thanos would be a skilled and highly experienced lover, but he had no idea that she was a novice— a virgin who had no real idea of how to please a man.

The hard ridge of his arousal nudging insistently against her thigh was proof that he wanted her, and his low growl of satisfaction when he slid his tongue deep into her mouth filled her with a mixture of apprehension and feminine triumph that she could have such an affect on him. Her senses were swamped by the subtle scent of his aftershave, and fire licked through her veins when she placed her hands on his chest and traced the bunched muscles beneath his shirt. He was so intensely, intoxicatingly male, and he aroused feelings inside her that no other man had ever made her feel.

But the voice of caution in her head, which she had ignored during the taxi ride to his hotel, was demanding to be heard.

This had gone way too far. She should never have started it in the first place, she thought frantically when he finally broke the kiss and drew back a fraction to stare down at her, his eyes glittering with sexual hunger. She ran her tongue over her lips; swollen and sensitive from the unsparing pressure of his mouth, and felt a lightning flare of reaction at her mental image of him making love to her. Her decision to offer herself to him had been born of a desperate desire to help her father.

But to sell herself to a man who despised her, who made no
effort to disguise his contempt of her? That was beyond des-
peration—it was insane.

She opened her mouth to tell him she had made a horren-
dous mistake. But as she was about to utter the words a picture
flashed into her mind of her mother as she had been a few
months ago, painfully thin and fragile, with a silk scarf
wrapped around her head to disguise the fact that she had lost
her hair after numerous bouts of chemotherapy. Tonight,
Vivienne had still looked fragile, but her head was now
covered in baby-fine curls and her smile had been that of a
woman who had cheated death and was looking forward to
the rest of her life. Her parents had suffered enough, Tahlia
thought fiercely. She could not sit back and allow them to lose
their home.

'You don't come cheap, Tahlia,' Thanos murmured, with
a deliberate inflexion on the word *cheap* that brought a flush
of colour to her cheeks. 'Before I agree to pay such a substan-
tial sum for Reynolds Gems, I think it only fair that I should
see what I'm getting for my money.'

'I don't understand,' she faltered, snatching a sharp breath
when he hooked his finger beneath the shoulder strap of her
dress and drew it down her arm.

'I think you do,' he said softly. 'Your dress is charming, but
I want to see what is beneath the pretty packaging. Take it off,'
he ordered, when she remained rigidly unmoving.

End this now, the sensible voice in Tahlia's head urged
frantically. *Tell him you've changed your mind, and get out
of here fast.*

And then what? demanded the reckless voice inside her that
she had not known existed until tonight. Go back to her parents
and watch her father's emotional devastation as he broke the
news to her mother that they would have to leave Carlton House?

She stared wildly at the door while her mind engaged in a fierce debate. Go—or stay, and sell her soul to the devil?

'How can I be certain that you will buy Reynolds Gems?' she asked Thanos shakily. 'I need some sort of assurance.'

'My word is the only assurance I'm prepared to give.' Thanos's eyes narrowed when she opened her mouth to argue. 'Take it—or leave it,' he shrugged uninterestedly. 'We can call the deal off.'

Tahlia's brain was racing. She had no option but to take him at his word. He was calling the shots. One night in his bed would mean that her parents' retirement would be free from financial worries. They need not know what she had done to secure their future. No one would know apart from her. And faced with the choice of sacrificing her self-respect or ensuring her parents' happiness there was no contest.

Without giving herself time to reconsider, she reached behind her and slowly slid the zip of her dress down her spine. She shot him a lightning glance, and her stomach dipped when she found him watching her intently, the expression in his dark eyes unfathomable. Don't think. Just get it over with, she told herself. And, taking a deep breath, she drew the straps of her dress down, revealing inch by inch the silver-grey strapless bra she was wearing beneath. She prayed he could not see that her hands were shaking. For this one night she must play the part of seductive temptress.

Her silk dress whispered against her skin as she drew it down over her stomach and hips and allowed the material to slither down her thighs and pool around her ankles. Her French knickers matched her bra, and her stockings were gossamer fine, topped with a wide band of lace which secured them around her slender thighs. She stepped carefully over her dress, terrified that she would stumble on her four-inch stiletto heels. She could not bring herself to look at him, but he slid

his hand beneath her chin and tilted her face to his. The sultry gleam in his eyes filled her with trepidation, and at the same time a fierce jolt of shameful excitement.

She was exquisite, Thanos acknowledged, his heart kicking in his chest. He hated himself for his reaction to her, for the urgent tide of desire that swept through his body that weakened and unmanned him. He knew Tahlia possessed the morals of a whore, and he knew the pain she had caused his sister, but his awareness of her consumed him and overrode every other consideration but his need to make love to her.

He inhaled sharply, re-imposing control over his hormones, and trailed his eyes over her in a cool assessment.

'Very nice,' he drawled, watching in fascination as twin spots of colour flared on her pale cheeks. Her ability to blush at will was a useful trick in her armoury, as was her air of innocence, he reminded himself impatiently. But he could not prevent himself from reaching out and tracing the fragile line of her collarbone. Her skin felt like satin beneath his fingertips, and her long pale amber hair fell in a curtain of silk around her shoulders. He brushed it aside to reveal the slender column of her throat, then lowered his mouth to the pulse beating frenetically at its base. She smelled divine, her light floral perfume tantalising his senses and driving every thought from his head other than his burning need to possess her.

Tahlia held her breath when Thanos trailed his lips along her jaw in a feather-light caress that sent a tremor through her. Was he going to make love to her right now? Remove her bra and knickers and stroke his strong hands over her naked body before tugging her down onto the sofa? His mouth was tantalisingly close, and the gleam in his eyes filled her with apprehension—and at the same time a wild and uncontrollable excitement. There was no point in kidding herself; she wanted

him to kiss her. She snatched a frantic little breath as he slowly lowered his head.

He claimed her mouth in a kiss of determined intent, forcing her lips apart and thrusting his tongue between them to explore her with erotic thoroughness. To her shame, Tahlia was lost from the first touch; he was so big and powerful, and she knew that if she fought him she would lose. Besides, she did not *want* to fight him, she acknowledged with searing honesty. Heat was coursing through her veins, and she felt boneless and supremely conscious of the melting warmth pooling between her thighs.

He increased the pressure of his mouth and slid one hand into her hair, while the other roamed up and down her body, skimmed her hips and slender waist, then curled around one breast. The brush of his thumb pad over her nipple caused it to harden beneath her sheer lace bra.

She had not expected the firestorm of emotions that raged through her. Her whole body seemed to be burning up, and the throbbing hardness of Thanos's arousal thrusting into her pelvis turned the fire into a raging inferno. She slid her hands over his chest, feeling the heat of his body through his silk shirt, and suddenly it was not enough. She wanted to feel his bare flesh beneath her fingertips. Fingers shaking slightly, she began to unfasten his buttons, revealing olive-gold skin covered with fine dark hairs, but before she had reached halfway down his abdomen he lifted his head, and his hands closed over hers in a vice like grip.

'Your eagerness to share my bed is flattering,' he drawled, watching dispassionately as colour surged into Tahlia's cheeks. 'But we have an early start in the morning, and I prefer to wait and enjoy you at my leisure.'

He had known from the moment he had taken her in his arms that one night would not be enough to pacify the

ravenous beast that had taken charge of his body, Thanos acknowledged. His desire for her was beyond anything he had experienced with any other woman, and he would not be satisfied with a hurried sex session—a few snatched hours of pleasure before he left for an urgent business meeting tomorrow. For reasons he could not fathom Tahlia was a drug in his veins, and he intended to make her his mistress for as long as it took to slake his hunger for her.

'*We* have an early start?' Tahlia mumbled, so excruciatingly embarrassed by her ardent response to him and his cool rejection of her that she wanted to crawl away and die. 'I don't understand.' Had he changed his mind about wanting her? Sick fear surged through her. Had he ordered her to take off her dress because it had amused him to tease her before he revealed that he would not buy Reynolds Gems?

'It's quite simple,' he told her, picking up her dress and handing it to her. His harsh, 'Cover yourself,' brought another flare of scorching colour to her cheeks. 'I'm flying to the Greek island of Mykonos to visit my new hotel first thing in the morning—and you're coming with me. I shall require your services for one month,' he continued smoothly, ignoring Tahlia's gasp of shock. 'That should satisfy my more basic urges. I've no doubt I'll have grown bored of you after you've shared my bed for a few weeks.'

'I'm not going anywhere with you and—and certainly not for a month,' Tahlia stammered when she finally found her voice. She wobbled precariously on her high heels as she stepped into her dress and tugged it up over her hips, with scant regard for the fragile material. She thrust her arms through the straps, gasping when Thanos spun her round and slid the zip up the length of her spine.

He swung her back to face him and cupped her chin in his hand, forcing her to meet his sardonic gaze. 'You are excep-

tionally lovely, Tahlia, but even *you* must admit that a six-figure sum for one night of sex with you would be an extravagance—even for a billionaire.'

She blanched at the flare of contempt in his eyes, and accepted that she had taken leave of her sanity when she had agreed to sell herself to him. 'I have responsibilities here—commitments, a job...' Although she would not have one for much longer if Thanos bought out Reynolds Gems, she acknowledged dismally. The future was frighteningly uncertain. 'I can't spend a month in Greece with you,' she said dully. 'It's impossible.'

Thanos shrugged and withdrew his mobile phone from his trouser pocket. 'That's a pity, because I was just about to call Steven Holt and instruct him to proceed with buying Reynolds Gems. But if you've changed your mind I'll tell him not to go ahead.'

She was halfway across the room, heading for the door. But his words stopped her in her tracks. She turned slowly back to face him, her brain whirling. 'You can't phone him now—it's almost midnight,' she pointed out.

'I can do whatever I like,' he informed her, with a supreme arrogance that took her breath away. 'I did not make my fortune by working nine till five. My employees know that I expect them to be available whenever I need them.'

Presumably he would have the same expectation of her if she went to Greece with him? A tremor ran down Tahlia's spine at the thought. She could carry on walking out of the door and out of Thanos's life—and all her instincts were screaming at her that she *should* walk away—but he was offering her the chance to save Carlton House from repossession, the voice in her head argued. The price was high. Could she survive a month as Thanos's mistress? What was one month compared to the rest of her parents' lives?

She snatched a breath and squared her shoulders as she met his hooded gaze. 'I want written assurance that you will honour our deal. I'm afraid I don't trust your word.'

Anger surged through Thanos at her disdainful tone, but he refrained from pointing out that she was not in a position to demand anything. 'My legal team will take care of it,' he told her dismissively. 'Would you like your duties to be listed—how many times a night I will expect you to pleasure me, perhaps a description of positions...?'

'That won't be necessary,' Tahlia said sharply, conscious that her face was burning hotter than a furnace. 'I just want to be sure my father's financial worries will be over.'

'How very altruistic of you,' he murmured sardonically.

She frowned. 'What's that supposed to mean?'

He crossed to the door and held it open. 'Don't waste your breath trying to convince me that your desire to save Reynolds Gems from bankruptcy is to help your father. You have expensive tastes,' he drawled, sliding his finger over the diamanté strap of her dress and then trailing an insolent path down to her cleavage. 'Your sole interest is in ensuring your own financial security—isn't it, Tahlia?' He paused, his eyes narrowing as he glimpsed the sudden shimmer of her tears, and for a second something tugged at his insides at the knowledge that he had hurt her. He dismissed the thought ruthlessly. She deserved to be hurt—just as she had hurt Melina. 'I'll drive you home,' he said brusquely, standing aside for her to precede him out of his suite. 'You need to pack.'

There was simply no point in arguing with him, Tahlia accepted miserably as she followed him into the lift. Thanos had judged her, and he was so pig-headed that nothing she did or said would change his opinion of her. But she had glimpsed the flare of feral hunger in his eyes before his lashes swept down and hid his expression. He desired her, and he had agreed

to buy Reynolds Gems in order to have her in his bed for one month. She could only pray that she would not spend the rest of her life regretting her decision to become his mistress.

After giving Thanos stilted directions to her flat Tahlia lapsed into silence, and he seemed to be lost in his own thoughts.

'I'll pick you up at eight o'clock tomorrow morning,' he told her as he parked outside her flat. 'Don't keep me waiting. And Tahlia?' he called, when she flung open the car door and hurried up her front path. 'Remember the reason why you're accompanying me on this trip and pack accordingly, won't you? I'm already fantasising about seeing you in sexy underwear like the tantalising wisps of lace you're wearing tonight.'

Face flaming, she bit back a retort which would have singed his ears and stepped into her flat, slamming the front door behind her and sagging against it. What *had* she done? she thought despairingly, burying her face in her hands as the enormity of the deal she had struck with Thanos sunk in. She had saved her parents from the devastation of losing their home, she reminded herself grimly. And with that thought in mind she dug out a suitcase from the cupboard under the stairs, pulled open her wardrobe and began to sort through its meagre contents for outfits suitable to take to Greece.

'Are you ready?' Thanos demanded curtly, when she opened the door to him at one minute past eight the following morning.

'Almost,' she muttered, annoyed that her heart immediately began to race at the sight of him, in a lightweight stone-coloured jacket and trousers, teamed with a cream shirt which was open at the throat so that she could see a tantalising V of bronzed skin. His black hair gleamed like jet in the early morning sunshine, and his beautifully sculpted features and sensual mouth caused a peculiar dragging sensation in the pit

of Tahlia's stomach. 'Unfortunately Charlie is proving rather stubborn to persuade out of my bedroom.'

Black eyebrows winged skywards. 'Spare me the details of your tangled love-life,' he drawled, in the sardonic tone she detested.

'Charlie is my cat,' Tahlia informed him tightly. 'He's actually the laziest cat on the planet, and spends most of his time sleeping on my bed.' She noted Thanos's impatient frown and chewed on her bottom lip. 'You'll have to help me get him into the cat-carrier.'

She disappeared through a door and Thanos followed, glancing curiously around her bedroom. He had expected something more…seductive, he mused. The soft lemon walls, pale carpet and floral curtains and bedspread were fresh and pretty, but he could not imagine her entertaining a stream of lovers here.

A hissing sound like a kettle coming to the boil came from under the dresser, and he stared in surprise at the fat ginger cat whose yellow eyes were fixed menacingly on him. Tahlia was on her knees, dangling a rubber toy in front of the cat to tempt it into the carrier.

'Come on, Charlie,' she crooned. 'Come and play.' The hissing grew louder, and the cat suddenly sprang, hooking its claws in Tahlia's hand. 'Quick—grab him!' she yelled.

'You must be joking.' Instead Thanos manoeuvred the carrier over the cat, and after a brief tussle Tahlia managed to deposit the ball of orange fur inside and hastily secured the door. Blood was running down her hand and the cat was still spitting furiously. *'Theos,'* he muttered. 'What breed is it—a wild cat?'

'He's just a bit sensitive,' Tahlia told him seriously. 'I got him from the cat rescue centre, and I think he was badly treated by his previous owners. He's a sweetie, really.'

'I'll take your word for it. You'd better put some antiseptic

on that scratch.' Thanos frowned. Giving a home to a stray cat with homicidal tendencies did not fit in with his image of Tahlia, he brooded irritably. He picked up her suitcase and cast another look around her room, pausing at the photograph on the bedside table. 'Is this your brother?' he asked curiously, as he studied the picture of Tahlia and a tall man with bright red hair.

'No, I don't have any siblings.' She slipped on her jacket and flicked her hair back from her face. 'That's Michael. We met on my first day at university, when he told me that redheads should always stick together.' She smiled softly at the memory. 'Michael was studying to be a vet, but he died of meningitis a few months before he graduated.'

Thanos heard the sudden huskiness in her voice. 'Was he your boyfriend?' he queried abruptly, irritated with himself for his curiosity. Tahlia's personal life had nothing to do with him.

She shrugged. 'We'd been dating for a few months.' Over the years she had come to terms with losing Michael, but only her closest friends knew how devastated she had been by his death. She had no intention of confiding in Thanos. She picked up the cat-carrier and glanced at him. 'I'm ready to leave now.'

Tahlia's tone warned Thanos that she did not want to continue the conversation, and he was suddenly impatient to leave. He did not want to hear that she had suffered a tragedy in her past. For the past six months he had envisaged her as a cold-hearted bitch, and he refused to contemplate any possibility that he might have been wrong.

'I hope you're not planning to try and smuggle that cat through Customs?' he said tersely as they walked out to the car.

'Of course not. Hobson is going to look after him. He used to be my parents' butler, but he's semi-retired now, and lives in an annexe of Carlton House,' Tahlia explained. 'We'll have to take Charlie over to him.'

'Is the house on the way to Gatwick?'

'The opposite direction, I'm afraid. But I can't leave Charlie to fend for himself. I guess it's a case of love me, love my cat,' she quipped, as Thanos deposited the cat carrier on the back seat and opened the front passenger door for her.

'Hell will freeze over before I do either,' Thanos said violently.

He fired the ignition and pulled away from the kerb, but his scathing comment hung in the air between them, and Tahlia quickly turned her head and stared out of the window, wondering why her eyes were stinging with stupid tears. Thanos could not make it plainer that he hated her, but she was shocked at how much his contempt hurt.

She said nothing more, apart from giving him directions to Carlton House, and only glanced at him when he drove through the gates and gave a low whistle.

'I see why your parents are so keen to hang on to the house,' he said dryly, as he stared up at the ivy-covered walls and the three storeys of mullioned windows glinting in the sunlight. 'It's spectacular.'

'For many generations it was passed down to the oldest son of the family, but my mother was an only child so she inherited it,' Tahlia explained. 'It's a Grade I listed building, and to be honest the cost of its upkeep is a nightmare. My parents do their best to maintain it, even though it's a drain on their resources, and Mum is very proud of her heritage. She loves Carlton House. It would break her heart to leave it—'

She broke off, blushing at the knowledge that she had agreed to become Thanos's mistress to keep Carlton House safe. The front door of the house suddenly swung open, and an elderly, impeccably dressed man walked slowly down the front steps.

'Who is that?'

'That's Hobson.'

Thanos frowned. 'He can't still work for your parents, surely? He must be ninety.'

'We think he's in his late seventies, although he won't actually admit his true age,' Tahlia explained as she climbed out of the car and took the cat-carrier from the back seat. 'He started working here as a butler for my grandparents; my parents feel that Carlton is as much his house as it is theirs. My father has promised Hobson that he will always have a home here.' Her smile faded as the implication of her words struck her. If Carlton was repossessed, where would Hobson go? He had no family, and he would be as distraught as her parents if he had to leave the house that had been his home for fifty years.

It wasn't going to happen, she reassured herself as she walked up the drive to greet the butler. Thanos had promised to buy Reynolds Gems, Carlton would be safe, and she would take the secret that she had sold herself to him to her grave.

'I was wondering how you had booked me onto a flight at such short notice,' Tahlia murmured an hour later, as she followed Thanos across the tarmac at Gatwick airport. 'I suppose I should have guessed you own a plane.'

'I travel extensively for my business, and the Lear jet is more convenient than relying on scheduled flights,' he replied, his eyes narrowing on her faintly stunned expression as she followed him onto the plane. His lip curled into a sardonic grimace as he watched her glance around at the plush leather seats. Women were always impressed by the jet, and several of his ex-lovers had been eager to join the mile-high club. He could spend the flight to Greece enjoying Tahlia's gorgeous body in the luxurious bedroom at the far end of the plane— she was hardly likely to object, he mused cynically. She had

made it clear she would do whatever pleased him in return for him shelling out a lot of money for Reynolds Gems.

He could not deny he was tempted, he thought irritably, and he skimmed his eyes over her, from her silky red-gold hair—worn loose today, and falling in a smooth sheet down her back—to her elegant cream skirt and jacket teamed with a sapphire-coloured blouse which matched the startling blue of her eyes, finally to her shapely legs sheathed in fine hose, their slender length emphasised by her three-inch stiletto heels. She looked cool and classy, and he felt a violent urge to lower his head and kiss her until her lips were no longer coated in a pale gloss but were red and swollen, as she parted them invitingly beneath his, as she had done in his hotel suite the previous night. Beneath her haughty façade this aristocratic English rose was hot, and she had already shown her willingness to explore the sexual chemistry that simmered between them. But he wanted to enjoy her at his leisure. He would have to curb his impatience until they reached Greece.

Four hours later, Tahlia stared out of the window as the plane swooped low over a cobalt-blue sea sparkling beneath a cloudless sky, dotted with several emerald islands. 'I hadn't expected the land to be so green,' she murmured, her spirits lifting as she absorbed the spectacular view of the Cyclades Islands.

'That's Mykonos just ahead of us.' Thanos's deep voice sounded close to her ear, and she jerked her head around to find that he had closed his laptop, which he had been working on for the entire flight. 'The smaller island closest to it is Delos. It is uninhabited, but it's one of the most important archaeological sites in Greece, and is believed in Greek mythology to be the birthplace of the goddess Artemis—hence the name of my new hotel,' he added with a faint smile.

Tahlia's eyes were drawn to the sensual curve of his mouth

and her heart flipped. She had been agonisingly conscious of him during the flight, but as soon as the jet had taken off he had become absorbed in his work and not spared her a word or glance. He had not brought her to Greece for her conversational skills, she reminded herself heavily. Her sole duty for the next month was to please him in bed—but considering her lack of experience in that department she feared he was going to be disappointed.

The Artemis Hotel was situated a few kilometres from Mykonos Town, at the charming beach resort of Agios Ioannis. The vast white-walled, flat-roofed building was impressive, and the reception area no less so, with its pale marble floors and pillars teamed with beautiful leather sofas and chairs in muted shades of blue and grey.

'The whole place is stunning,' Tahlia commented when Thanos had given her a lightning tour of the four dining rooms, six bars and the spa and leisure complex.

'I'm pleased with it,' he replied as he led the way along a velvet-carpeted corridor. The walls were hung with numerous works of art, many of them contemporary pieces, and Tahlia wondered if Thanos had bought any of Rufus Hartman's paintings from the art exhibition where they had first met. She grimaced. Was it really only a few days ago? It felt like a lifetime.

'This is my private suite,' he explained as he halted at the end of the corridor and flung open a door.

Tahlia followed him into an airy sitting room, her heart suddenly beating too fast as she glanced through a door to her right and glimpsed a king-sized bed. She wondered if Thanos expected her to begin her duties as his mistress immediately, but he had walked over to the long wall of windows and opened the French doors leading to the terrace. She followed him, and caught her breath at the uninterrupted view of the crystalline sea and an aquamarine swimming pool below them.

'The suite has its own pool,' he explained, indicating the rectangular pool to one side of the terrace. 'The main pool you can see below us is actually a salt-water pool, separated from the sea by a terraced area where guests can sunbathe and enjoy the view of the bay.'

'It's beautiful,' Tahlia murmured as she stared down at the hotel's pool, which had been cleverly designed so that it appeared to spill into the sea beyond. She lifted her face to the sun, her hair rippling in the warm Aegean breeze.

Thanos resisted the urge to wind the silky strands around his hand, pull her in and capture her mouth in a hungry kiss that he knew instinctively could only end when he swept her into his arms and carried her through to the bedroom. She unsettled him more than he cared to admit, and he found his reaction to her intensely irritating. Even forcing himself to think of Melina—now staying at a rehabilitation clinic in the US, where she was slowly learning to walk again—did not diminish his awareness of the woman at his side.

Had his father struggled to control his attraction to the English tart Wendy Jones, who had become his mistress? he brooded. For the first time in his life he understood the guilt associated with wanting a woman when it was morally wrong to desire her.

He swung round abruptly and walked back across the terrace. 'You have the rest of the day to enjoy the view. I have a meeting scheduled with my management team, which I imagine will last for several hours.'

Tahlia frowned, unsure of exactly what her role in his life was to be. 'What do you expect me to do while you're gone?' she asked as she followed him back inside.

He shrugged dismissively. 'Whatever you like. You can swim, or read—all the rooms at the Artemis have a selection of current magazines. And of course you will need to prepare for tonight.'

Tahlia's mouth suddenly felt dry at the prospect of the night ahead. In what way did he expect her to prepare? Did the Artemis also leave copies of the *Kama Sutra* in the rooms, for guests to flick through? she wondered, panic churning in the pit of her stomach.

Thanos's eyes narrowed on the hectic flush staining her cheeks. 'Tonight we're dining with the mayor of Mykonos and other council dignitaries. You'll need to dress up.' He gave her a mocking smile. 'Wear something sexy, hmm…? After all, the sole reason you are here is to please me.' He gathered up his briefcase, but instead of heading for the door he walked towards her, his mouth curving into an amused smile that was not reflected in his cold eyes. 'You can start by pleasing me now,' he said coolly, and he cupped her chin in his hand and bent his head, bringing his mouth down on hers before she had a chance to pull away.

The kiss was hard, almost brutal, a statement of possession and a warning of intent that tonight he would demand so much more. Tahlia wanted to deny him, wanted to firm her lips against his probing tongue, but to her shame the moment he touched her she was lost, swept up in the fire that consumed them both. She had been acutely aware of him ever since he had picked her up from her flat that morning, and now her senses were set alight by the scent of his cologne and another, totally masculine scent that belonged to this man alone.

He caught her despairing sigh and ruthlessly took advantage of her parted lips to thrust his tongue between them, exploring the moist warmth of her mouth until she was boneless and clung to him, sliding her hands to his shoulders and running her fingers through the thick dark hair that curled at his nape.

He was breathing hard when he finally released her, and Tahlia took a tiny shard of comfort in the fact that he could

not hide the evidence that he was affected by the wild passion they shared.

'I'll see you later,' he said tersely, stepping away from her, but she had the impression that his control was balanced on a knife-edge, and that if she gave any indication that she wanted him to stay he would seize her in his arms once more and kiss her until kissing was not enough for either of them.

She remained silent, shocked and ashamed by her reaction to him, and with a curt nod he strode from the room. Only then did she release her breath. It was crazy and utterly inexplicable, she thought shakily as she held her fingers against her swollen mouth. Thanos believed he had good reason to despise her, and she was well aware that his one aim was to punish her. Yet neither of them, it seemed, could control the wildfire sexual attraction which blazed between them.

CHAPTER FIVE

THERE was no sign of Tahlia when Thanos walked into his private suite that evening, but it was late, and he assumed that she was getting changed for dinner. His meeting had overrun by several long and frustrating hours, and the discovery that preparations for the party to celebrate the official opening of the Artemis were way behind schedule had put him in a foul mood. He needed to have been in Greece these past few months, to oversee the completion of the new hotel, but thanks to Tahlia and his sleazeball ex-brother-in-law he had been at Melina's hospital bedside in the States instead of running his company.

He crossed to the bar and poured himself a large Scotch, added ice to the glass and took a long sip as he strolled onto the terrace. Dusk had fallen, painting the sky in hues of purple and indigo, and the first stars glimmered as brightly as the lights of the tavernas and hotels that delineated the coast. But the peaceful scene did nothing to lift his mood, and when a faint noise from behind him alerted him to Tahlia's presence he swung round, his brows lowering in a slashing frown as he studied her.

'What made you think that dressing like a nun would please me?' he queried, in a dangerously soft tone. He noted her mutinous expression and his mouth curled into a hard

smile. 'Or did you deliberately choose your most unattractive outfit to flout me?'

His guess was not too far from the truth, and Tahlia blushed. At the same time she felt a spurt of annoyance at his description of her as unattractive. It was true her faithful black skirt was years old and unfashionably long, and her cream silk-organza blouse with its high neck and a row of tiny pearl buttons running down the front could in no way be called sexy. But she had swept her hair up into an elegant chignon and taken care with her make-up. She didn't think she looked a complete frump. Thanos, however, clearly held a different opinion.

'I'm not taking you to dinner when you look like my maiden aunt,' he said tersely. 'Go and get changed while I shower, and be ready to leave in fifteen minutes.' His brows rose when she did not move. 'Of course I could always strip you myself—but if that happens I can guarantee we will miss dinner altogether.'

Tahlia flushed at the hungry gleam in his eyes. 'You can't tell me what to do. You don't own me,' she said angrily, frantically trying to banish the image of Thanos removing her clothes and then his, and the even more shocking idea of them showering together.

His mocking smile told her he had read her mind, and her insides squirmed in embarrassment. 'For the next month I can do exactly what I like with you,' he warned her, in a voice laced with such blatant sexual intent that a shiver ran the length of her spine. His patience suddenly evaporated, and he caught hold of her hand and marched her across the lounge to the bedroom. 'I'll find you something suitable to wear,' he growled, but his frown deepened when he flung open the wardrobe and flicked through the few outfits she had brought with her.

'Why did you bring so little with you when you knew you were coming to Greece for a month?' His eyes narrowed. 'Or

did you hope I would grow bored of you sooner?' He reached out and tugged the clip from her carefully arranged chignon, so that her hair tumbled around her shoulders. The sultry gleam in his dark gaze sent a tremor through Tahlia's body as stark awareness uncoiled in the pit of her stomach. 'If so, then I fear you will be disappointed,' he murmured, lowering his head so that his breath fanned her lips. 'The sexual chemistry between us is at combustion point, my beautiful English rose, and I am seriously beginning to doubt that one month will satisfy my desire for you.'

His mouth was so close to hers that Tahlia shut her eyes, certain that he was about to kiss her. The exotic scent of his cologne swamped her senses, and there was no thought in her head to resist him. But to her shock he suddenly moved away from her. Startled, she let her lashes fly open, and she found that she was standing with her mouth still parted in readiness for his kiss. The sound of his soft, mocking laughter filled her with mortification at the shameful sense of longing that he would snatch her into his arms and ravage her mouth with primitive passion.

Thanos closed the wardrobe with a decisive snap. 'There is nothing in there that excites me,' he said bluntly. 'You will have to stay as you are tonight, but tomorrow you will go shopping. We'll be attending many social events while we are here and you'll need several evening dresses, as well as daywear.'

Tahlia thought of her latest credit card bill, which she had no means of paying off, and shook her head. 'I can't afford to buy new clothes,' she admitted wearily, her temper flaring at Thanos's sardonic expression. He believed she led the life of a pampered princess, but nothing could be further from the truth. 'The clothes I've brought with me are all that I own. My father hasn't been able to pay my salary for the last three months. Every penny went into keeping Reynolds Gems solvent. I worked for nothing in the desperate hope

that we could save the company,' she explained when he looked disbelieving. 'I sold most of my clothes, and my jewellery, but I didn't make enough to cover my bills and living expenses. I'm struggling to cover even the minimum payment on my credit cards, and a shopping spree is out of the question. You'll just have to take me as I am,' she finished defiantly, and then blushed scarlet as she realised what she had said.

'I am very much looking forward to taking you, Tahlia,' Thanos assured her gravely, the glinting amusement in his eyes masking his shock at her assertion that her life in London had *not* been one of luxury and over-indulgence, as he had assumed.

Of course she could be lying, he mused. Experience had taught him that most women were accomplished liars—none more so than Yalena, when she had been sleeping with one of his closest friends at the same time as swearing her love for him. But his gut instinct told him that Tahlia was telling the truth about her financial situation. No wonder she had agreed to be his mistress in return for him buying her father's company, he thought cynically. He knew from the numerous photos of her in the press that she liked to dress in haute couture. No doubt she would spend her share of the proceeds of the sale of Reynolds Gems on restocking her wardrobe.

He glanced at his watch, and then strolled towards the *en suite* bathroom. 'We're running seriously late, so I'll have to wait until tonight for the pleasure of taking you to bed,' he drawled. 'As for shopping—I will be paying for your clothes. Think of it as one of the perks of being my mistress,' he said in a harder tone, when she opened her mouth to argue. 'I want to see you in sexy clothes that flatter your gorgeous body. Not in an outfit that makes you look as though you are auditioning for a role in *The Sound of Music*.'

* * *

Dinner was the ordeal Tahlia had expected. In ordinary circumstances she would have enjoyed the stunning décor and the ambience of the Artemis's gold-star restaurant, where a celebrated French chef had prepared four superb courses. But from the moment Thanos led her over to the table where his guests were already seated and introduced her as his 'companion' she felt so painfully self-conscious—everyone must have guessed she was his mistress—that she could do no more than toy with her food.

As well as the dignitaries from Mykonos, three of Thanos's top executives were also present, and although everyone spoke in English rather than Greek, her attempts at conversation with them were stilted. They clearly thought she was a bimbo, and one of the executives, a man Thanos had introduced as Antonis Lykaios, watched her avidly throughout the meal, trailing his eyes over her as if he were mentally undressing her.

Tahlia was torn between longing for the evening to be over and praying that it would last for ever—because what was to come next was certain to be a hundred times worse, she brooded. Her eyes were drawn to Thanos. He looked breathtaking tonight, in a black dinner suit and a white silk shirt, his dark hair swept back from his brow and the flickering light from the table's centrepiece of candles highlighting the sharp edges of his cheekbones. He was urbane, sophisticated, and no doubt a skilful lover, she thought, feeling a rush of shaming heat flood through her when he looked across the table and their glances locked.

The voices around her faded, and she was reminded of the first time she had seen him at the art gallery, when she had felt as though they were the only two people in the universe. She watched his eyes darken with a sensual promise that made her mouth run dry, and butterflies leapt in her stomach. It was not Thanos she was afraid of, she acknowledged

bleakly; it was herself and her pathetic inability to resist him. It was utterly ridiculous to feel so drawn to a man who openly admitted that he despised her, but when she had first seen him at Rufus Hartman's exhibition—before she had learned that he blamed her for his sister's accident—she had felt an emotional bond with him which defied logic or common sense. A voice in her head had whispered that he was the 'the one' she had been waiting all her life to meet.

'Would you like more wine, Tahlia?' Antonis Lykaios leaned towards her, proffering a bottle of Chardonnay, and Tahlia was so grateful for the excuse to drag her eyes from Thanos that she forgot how her skin had crawled when Antonis had leered at her and smiled at him.

Across the table Thanos fought the urge to rearrange his junior executive's handsome face with his fist—before continuing the caveman tactics by throwing Tahlia over his shoulder and carrying her off to his bed. How *dared* she flirt with Lykaios in front of him? he thought furiously. But what had he expected? In recent months the British tabloids had regularly reported on her energetic love-life with Z-list celebrities. Clearly she would flirt with any man under seventy.

He gave a brief nod to his chief executive, indicating that it was time to bring the evening to an end, before his gaze strayed back to Tahlia. His initial opinion that her outfit was unflattering had been wrong, he thought irritably. At first glance she looked chaste and demure in the high-necked blouse, but look closer and it was possible to see the outline of her breasts beneath the sheer material. His fingers itched to unfasten every one of those tiny buttons and slowly reveal her delectable body. With her pale red-gold hair falling in a silky curtain around her shoulders and a subtle pink gloss on her lips she looked incredibly sexy, and he was infuriated by

the knowledge that he was not the only man at the dinner table who could not keep his eyes off her.

The dinner party eventually came to an end, and Tahlia stifled a sigh of relief when the guests stood up from the table. Antonis Lykaios seemed to have taken her smile as a sign that she was interested in him; twice she had had to forcibly remove his hand from her thigh beneath the table-cloth, and she forced herself not to flinch now, when he lifted her fingers to his mouth and kissed them in a theatrical farewell gesture. She saw Thanos's brows lower in a slashing frown, and her sense of foreboding escalated when they crossed the marble vestibule to the lift and he surveyed her in a brooding silence as they travelled to the top floor.

'I realise that you automatically flirt with anyone in trousers,' he drawled as followed her into his suite, discarding his jacket and tie and flinging them carelessly over the back of a chair. 'But Antonis Lykaios is engaged, and I will not allow you to sink your predatory claws into him.'

'I pity his fiancée,' she snapped, her temper flaring at the undisguised contempt in his voice. 'Your executive was flirting with *me*, and I'd be grateful if you would tell him to keep his sweaty hands to himself in future.' She closed her eyes against the pain stabbing at her skull, aware that her headache was due as much to the two glasses of wine she had drunk although she had eaten very little dinner, as to her rising nervous tension. Thanos was heart-stoppingly sexy, with his dark hair falling onto his brow, but he also looked grim and forbidding, and the prospect of giving her virginity to him when he had made it plain that he despised her was suddenly unendurable.

She lifted a hand to massage her temples, and pleaded shakily, 'Thanos, can we talk?'

His dark brows lifted in an expression of arrogant amuse-

ment. 'Talking is the last thing I have in mind for tonight.' He
strolled towards her and drew her hand away from her face.
'We made a deal, Tahlia,' he reminded her, his voice suddenly
harsh and his eyes glittering with cold indifference. 'And now
the time has come for you to honour your side of it.'

Her heart was thudding so hard that it hurt to breathe.
'Please…' she cried urgently. 'I swear I had no idea that
James was married to your sister…'

She was prevented from saying any more when Thanos
placed his finger across her lips. 'Save your lies—and your
tears.' He surveyed her over-bright eyes dispassionately, and
brushed away the single tear that slipped down her cheek
with his thumb. 'I'm not taken in by either,' he said savagely,
and lowered his head, capturing her mouth in a punishing kiss
that sought to dominate as he forced her lips apart with a bold
flick of his tongue.

Once again he had moved with the speed of a panther,
pouncing for the kill, and once again Tahlia was unprepared
for the molten heat that swept through her the instant he
touched her. What was wrong with her? she wondered de-
spairingly. Pride dictated that she should remain stiff and un-
responsive in Thanos's arms, but he intoxicated her senses so
that she could not think logically, and she was conscious only
of the slight abrasion of his cheek against hers, the tingling
sensation in her breasts as he crushed her against his chest.

Thanos finally lifted his head and stared down at her, his
eyes gleaming when she unconsciously traced her tongue
over her swollen lips. 'This madness is not mine alone. You
feel it too,' he grated, his fury and frustration palpable—and
yet Tahlia sensed that his anger was directed as much at
himself as her, and she knew that, like her, he was startled by
the intensity of the sexual chemistry which blazed between
them. 'You are like a fever in my blood,' he said hoarsely. 'I

wanted you from the moment I saw you, and now I cannot wait any longer.'

'Thanos…no!' She gave a shocked cry when he moved his hands to the neck of her blouse and wrenched the fragile material apart, so that little pearl buttons pinged in all directions. Before she had time to react he reached around and unsnapped her bra, casting the delicate scrap of lace to the floor so that her small pale breasts were exposed to his heated gaze.

He was breathing hard, and Tahlia watched in fascination as dull colour flared along his magnificent cheekbones. The feral hunger in his eyes made her tremble with a mixture of apprehension and an unbidden shivery excitement. No man had ever looked at her the way Thanos was doing now, and she instinctively tried to cover her breasts with her hands.

He caught her wrists and tugged them down to her sides. 'Don't hide yourself from me,' he said harshly. 'I want to feast my eyes on every inch of your delectable body.'

His words made Tahlia tremble—not with fear, she acknowledged, but with a feverish excitement she could not deny. Her heart slammed in her chest when he pushed her hair over her shoulders, then slid his hand down her body and curled his fingers possessively over her breast. She tensed, expecting him to be rough, but his palm was warm on her bare flesh, and when he stroked his thumb-pad across her nipple in a feather-light caress she gasped as exquisite sensation arced through her.

'Not just beautiful, but delightfully responsive,' Thanos drawled.

She blushed scarlet at the undisguised satisfaction in his voice, but her body seemed to have a will of its own, and she could do nothing to prevent the dusky nipples from swelling into taut peaks. He moved his hand to her other breast and rolled the swollen nipple between his thumb and forefinger, sending

another lightning bolt of sensation spiralling down to the pit of her stomach. She caught her breath when he tugged her backwards and lowered his head to the slender arch of her body.

He flicked his tongue back and forth over her nipple, building her pleasure to a level that was almost unbearable, and she gave a choked cry when he finally desisted in teasing her and clamped his mouth around the provocative peak. The sensation of him suckling her was so breathtaking that her lashes drifted down and she gave herself up to the storm he was creating, gasping with pleasure when he moved to her other breast and laved the throbbing peak with firm, wet strokes of his tongue.

She was dimly aware of Thanos dragging her skirt over her hips, and he muttered something in Greek in a hoarse tone when he eased away from her and trailed his eyes down from her pouting breasts to her flat stomach, then lower to her black lace knickers and gossamer-fine black stockings. Tahlia held her breath when he placed his hand on the strip of creamy flesh above her stocking-top, and she felt liquid heat flood between her thighs. Was he going to take her here and now? Drag her to the floor and spread her beneath him on the carpet?

Tension gripped her. Until now she had always believed that she would only ever make love when she was in a loving relationship. She had loved Michael, but their gentle romance had still been in its early stages when he had been snatched from her; she had thought she loved James, but he had lied to her, and she was glad she had discovered his treachery before they had become lovers. Maybe it was time she gave up on love, she thought bleakly. There was no love between her and Thanos. Just mistrust and dislike and a searing passion that obliterated every logical thought and demanded to be appeased. She had agreed to have sex with him in return for her parents' financial security and she would not back out

now. But it was only fair that she tell him she was not the ex-
perienced seductress he believed.

Thanos stared down at Tahlia's semi-naked body and drew
a ragged breath, his nostrils flaring as he fought to bring his
raging hormones under control. The delicate skin of her inner
thigh felt like satin beneath his fingers, and the urge to move
his hand higher and slip it beneath her lacy knickers was so
strong that it took every ounce of his formidable will-power
to deny himself the pleasure of touching her intimately. His
brain acknowledged what she had done—how she had hurt
Melina—but his body did not seem to care that she that she
was an immoral slut, and it was on fire for her.

'Thanos... I have to tell you...' Her voice shook, but he
ruthlessly hardened his heart against her.

'But I don't have to listen—and certainly not to more of
your lies and excuses,' he said harshly, disregarding her
startled cry as he swept her up into his arms and strode
towards the bedroom.

Tahlia was shaking so badly she was sure Thanos must feel
the tremors running through her body. Perhaps he thought she
was trembling with excitement? She could not bear to meet
his gaze and see his familiar mocking expression, so instead
she curled her arms around his neck, pressing her face against
his shoulder while he carried her. It was not too late to stop
this, a voice whispered in her head. She could tell Thanos she
would rather sell her soul to the devil than trade her body for
hard cash. But what about her parents? another voice
screamed inside her. How could she allow them to lose their
home and the worry-free retirement they deserved?

Thanos shouldered open the door of the master bedroom,
strode over to the bed, and laid Tahlia down on the peacock-
blue satin bedspread. Her glorious hair fanned across the
pillows in a halo of shimmering gold. He could not resist

winding a long silky strand around his fingers, and heat surged through him as he lowered his eyes to her breasts and feasted on their milky-pale beauty.

Why Tahlia? he asked himself angrily. He had never wanted any woman the way he wanted her. His desire was mindless, desperate, an irresistible force clamouring to be assuaged, and his body shook with need as he stretched out beside her and pressed his mouth to the fragile line of her collarbone. She tasted of ambrosia, her skin as soft as rose petals beneath his lips, and he could not resist tracing them down her body, pausing at each breast to anoint its blush-pink tip, relishing the feel of her nipples swelling inside his mouth before he moved lower still.

Her sweetly puckered navel invited him to explore it with his tongue. He felt the tremor that ran through her, but she made no effort to touch him, and lay passive while he caressed her, as if she were somehow detached from her surroundings—from him. Anger coiled inside him. Did she think she could simply lie there, as unresponsive as a marble figurine while he took his pleasure? When he had finished with her would she wash herself clean of his touch? Believing that the price she had paid for her parents' house had been worth soiling herself for? He did not want a sacrificial offering, he thought grimly. He wanted her warm and willing in his bed, and he was determined that soon she would be begging for his possession.

Tahlia stiffened when she felt Thanos's hand slip between her thighs. Until the moment he had laid her on his bed she had been cocooned in a curious sense of unreality. It seemed impossible to believe that she had actually agreed to have sex with him, that he really would make love to her. But the feel of his hands and mouth on her skin, moving ever lower down her body, had catapulted her back to reality, and now fear churned in her stomach at the prospect of giving her virginity to him.

Hysteria formed a bubble in her throat as she imagined his reaction if she asked him to be gentle. He was convinced that she had been his brother-in-law's mistress, and she could hear his scathing laughter if she told him that this was her first time. He would not believe her. And if he did—if he realised that she was innocent—he might well reject her and call off their deal. She could not risk that happening. She was going to have to put on the act of a lifetime, she thought numbly, and pretend that she was as experienced as he assumed.

His palm felt warm and faintly abrasive on the sensitive skin of her inner thigh, and she forced herself to relax as he hooked his fingers in the waistband of her knickers and slowly drew them over her hips.

'Beautiful,' he murmured, his voice thick with sexual tension. She felt his hand brush gently through the triangle of gold curls, and her heart slammed in her chest when he ran his finger lightly up and down the lips of her vagina, so that they swelled and opened like the petals of a flower, moist and sweetly scented with her arousal, ready for him to explore her. He leaned over her to claim her mouth in a slow, drugging kiss that lit a flame deep inside her and banished her fears. His lips no longer sought to dominate but were gently persuasive, decimating her resistance so that she opened her mouth beneath his and kissed him back with hungry fervour.

Her breath hitched in her throat when she felt him gently part her, and she heard his low growl of satisfaction when he discovered the slick wetness of her arousal. She felt boneless, mindless, and she allowed him to spread her legs wider, excitement cascading through her when she felt his finger probe her velvet folds and slip between them. How could it be wrong when it felt so utterly and exquisitely right? she wondered dazedly. Instinctively she arched her hips so that he could slide his finger deeper into her, and

she could not hold back a moan of pleasure when he stretched her wider and inserted another finger, moving his hand with delicate skill so that she writhed with the pleasure he was creating.

'Undress me.'

The starkness of his command sent a jolt of trepidation through Tahlia, but her apprehension was mixed with irresistible sexual curiosity. His wickedly inventive fingers had aroused her to a fever pitch of desire, and she wanted… She did not know what she wanted, she acknowledged as she shifted her hips restlessly. This was all new to her. Her body felt tense and strung out, and only Thanos could soothe the dragging ache deep inside her.

She fumbled with his shirt buttons, her movements jerky and uncoordinated, but finally she spread the material aside and skimmed her hands over satin skin overlaid with crisp dark hairs. She could feel the heat emanating from him, and her senses flared as she inhaled the sensual musk of his cologne mingled with the subtle perfume of male pheromones. He dominated her mind and captivated her soul so that the world faded and nothing existed but Thanos, and the erotic glide of his hands and mouth over her trembling body.

Her lashes had drifted down, as if she could blot out the reality of what she was doing, but she was aware of him easing away from her as her skin quickly cooled, bereft of the warmth of his powerful body. She opened her eyes to discover that he had stripped down to his underwear. His black silk boxers could not disguise the jutting strength of his arousal, and when her gaze flicked upwards to his face the feral gleam in his eyes caused her heart to miss a beat. There was no going back; the message thudded in her brain, and she licked her suddenly dry lips with the tip of her tongue as he stepped out of his boxers and stood before her, his bronzed, muscle-bound

body as beautiful as a work of art, his powerful erection jutting proudly forward as he strode purposefully over to the bed.

'I want you so badly I'm in danger of exploding,' Thanos said hoarsely, his Greek accent sounding very pronounced. His capacity for logical thought had deserted him and his self-control was non-existent, while his body throbbed with a level of need that he had never experienced before. Tahlia's slender, pale beauty summoned him, and the drumbeat of desire pounding in his veins overwhelmed him. 'I apologise for the lack of leisurely seduction, but I have to have you *now*. And you are ready for me, Tahlia,' he said thickly, his voice deepening with satisfaction as he slipped his hand between her thighs and discovered the drenching sweetness of her arousal.

He could not wait, and swiftly donned protection before joining her on the bed. The mattress dipped as he positioned himself over her and pushed her legs wider apart. He surged forward, rubbing the sensitive tip of his manhood against her until she opened for him. She was tighter than he had expected, and as she tensed he hesitated, confused by the sudden flare of panic in her eyes. He frowned and drew back a little, but already her muscles were stretching to accommodate him, drawing him into a velvet embrace so that he could think of nothing but thrusting into her again, deeper this time, so that he filled her with his swollen shaft.

Tahlia's muscles had clenched at the realisation that Thanos was about to join his body with hers. She had always dreamed that this moment would be special, that she would give her virginity to the man she loved. A wave of intense sadness surged up inside her, but there was no time to think or refuse him, and her eyes widened in shock as she felt the hard length of his arousal push insistently against her femininity. She had no choice but to accept him into her.

To her surprise there was no pain, just an unfamiliar feeling

of fullness, and she released her breath on a shaky sigh as he drew back a little and then eased forward once more, until their bodies were locked together in the most intimate embrace of all. Thanos was part of her. She had given herself to him. In some deep and elemental way she was now his for all time, she thought wonderingly as he moved inside her, setting a rhythm that she knew instinctively would take her to somewhere wonderful but as yet remained frustratingly out of reach.

Thanos slid his hands beneath her bottom and lifted her hips, driving into her with faster, deeper strokes. There was no tenderness in his actions. This was sex at its most basic, Tahlia acknowledged, urgent and hungry, driving them both towards the edge. She was dimly aware that her breath was coming in shallow gasps, and when she opened her eyes she saw that Thanos's face was a rigid mask, the cords on his neck standing out as he drove relentlessly into her.

'Don't stop…don't stop…' She was unaware of her urgent cries, her whole being concentrated on the insistent throbbing deep in her pelvis.

Thanos snatched a harsh breath, fighting for control, but the battle had been lost from the moment he had penetrated Tahlia's body and found her tight and hot and utterly irresistible. To his utter shock he realised that he could not hold back. It had never happened to him before, this complete loss of self-control, but he could not help it. His mind and body were focused on reaching that magical place where he would experience the release he craved, and with one final savage thrust his control shattered. A primal groan of male satisfaction was wrenched from his throat as his whole body convulsed with pleasure.

For a few moments he remained slumped on top of her, his chest heaving as he dragged oxygen into his lungs. He was still stunned by what had happened, by the tidal wave that had

swept through him and demolished his restraint so that he had selfishly snatched his own pleasure.

Shame seared him, and he lifted his head to stare down at her.

'I'm sorry,' he grated harshly.

'For what?' she whispered.

'Don't you know?' He frowned, puzzled by the look of genuine confusion in her eyes. It could not possibly have been her first time, he reminded himself forcefully. He had evidence that she had been James Hamilton's mistress. Her air of innocence was an illusion. Yet he could not forget her expression when he had first thrust into her, the fleeting fear in her eyes that had been replaced by a look of wonderment. Could it be that she had never experienced an orgasm with any of her previous lovers and so did not know what she had missed?

His male pride was hurt by the knowledge that he had been no better than the other men she had slept with. Driven by his overpowering need for satisfaction he had been impatient, had come before she had climaxed. He rolled off her, propped himself up on one elbow, and skimmed his hand lightly over her stomach, down to the cluster of gold curls between her legs. His mouth curved into a small smile when he felt the tremor that ran through her. His hunger for her had overwhelmed him, but now he was sated—temporarily, at least, he acknowledged wryly as his body stirred—and he knew that with patience he could bring her to the peak of ecstasy.

He lowered his head to her breast and flicked his tongue lazily across her swollen nipple, heard her sharply indrawn breath when he drew the reddened crest fully into his mouth and suckled her. She twisted her hips restlessly, and he smiled again against her skin as he moved to her other breast and meted out the same exquisite torture before trailing his lips down over her flat stomach.

'Thanos…? Tahlia murmured uncertainly when he pushed

her legs apart. The knowledge that he was looking intently at the most intimate part of her body was shockingly arousing, and the dragging sensation in her pelvis, which had eased when he had withdrawn from her, uncoiled in a sharp tug of desire. 'No!'

Too late she realised his intention, and gripped his hair, but his tongue was already probing between her silken folds the sensations he was arousing so utterly incredible that her cry of denial faltered.

'Relax, and I will show you what you've clearly been denied by your previous lovers,' he promised thickly.

Mortified, she tried to bring her legs together. But he held them apart and dipped his head once more, the skilled flick of his tongue making her whimper with pleasure. 'You can't,' she pleaded. But he could, and did, and when his lips closed around the tiny, ultra-sensitive nub of her clitoris she sobbed his name and dug her nails into his shoulders, clinging to him as ripples of delight began deep inside her.

He moved swiftly to position himself over her, lifted her hips and drove his powerful erection deep into her, thrusting fast and hard and driving her ever upwards. And now she was almost there, at the place she had sensed the first time he had made love to her. He withdrew almost completely, and then sank into her so deeply that their bodies imploded simultaneously. She gave a startled cry as she experienced wave after wave of ecstasy crashing through her, causing her entire body to tremble with the power of a storm, before slowly ebbing away to leave her spent and utterly replete in his arms.

Dear heaven, she had never known it would be so…so awesome, so astounding. She could not find the words. She curved her hands around Thanos's back, loving the feel of his satiny sweat-slicked skin beneath her palms. He was lying on top of her, his body lax and heavy, but she did not want him

to move. The erratic beat of his heart thundering in unison with hers was strangely comforting. Was it possible that in the shattering moments of his climax he had experienced the same feeling that had swamped her—a feeling that their souls had united and soared to a place that was uniquely theirs?

It was just sex, she told herself—awesome, amazing sex. Although admittedly she did not have any other experience to compare it with. But surely it was nothing more than the pairing of two people who were held in the thrall of a powerful sexual chemistry? It would be stupid to allow her emotions to become involved, yet she felt a bond with him that went far beyond the physical intimacy they had shared.

Thanos finally rolled onto his back and stared blindly up at the ceiling, more stunned than he cared to admit by the power of the passion they had just shared, the feeling of oneness that he had never experienced with any other woman. It made no sense. He despised Tahlia, and his contempt for her had intensified when she had agreed to sell herself to him. But instead of telling her what he thought of her he had succumbed to the temptation of her fragile beauty and taken her to bed. Lust had made a fool of him, and now his hatred of himself threatened to choke him. He was no better than his father, he acknowledged bitterly. Kosta Savakis had fallen for the charms of an immoral woman and had abandoned his family for his mistress. And now he, Thanos, had sacrificed his self-respect and had sex with the woman who had broken his sister's heart.

He had bought her, he reminded himself grimly as he swung his legs over the side of the bed, not sparing her a glance as he strode into the *en suite* bathroom. Tahlia was a whore, and he was paying a fortune for her. It would have been damnably disappointing if the sex *hadn't* been good. He stood beneath the shower, but the powerful spray did nothing to ease

his tension. Sex with Tahlia hadn't just been good, it had been the best he'd ever had, he conceded. He was already hardening again, anticipation licking through his veins as he snatched a towel and roughly dried his body.

But when he returned to the bedroom he discovered her curled up beneath the sheet, one hand beneath her cheek, her long gold lashes making crescents against her flushed skin. Once again he was struck by her air of innocence, and something indefinable tugged in his gut when he saw a single tear slip silently down her face. The sight of her vulnerability shook him to the core, and in moment of absolute clarity his brain finally accepted what his soul had instinctively known when he had joined his body with hers. He was aware of a curious drumming in his ears, and realised that it was the sound of his blood pounding through his veins. His logical mind grasped at straws, recalling all the tabloid stories he had read about her torrid love-life, but when she lifted her lashes and he saw the hurt in her eyes his heart accepted the truth.

'You were a virgin, weren't you?' he said quietly.

She did not reply, but the sudden flare of colour on her pale cheeks filled him with guilt and remorse, and a whole host of other emotions he could not define.

Anger at his crass stupidity swept through him, and his throat felt as though he had swallowed glass as he rasped, 'Why the hell didn't you tell me?'

CHAPTER SIX

THE look of fury on Thanos's face inflamed Tahlia's temper and she sat up, glaring at him as she dragged the sheet across her breasts and pushed her hair over her shoulders. 'What would have been the point?' she demanded bitterly. 'You thought I was an immoral slut who had seduced your sister's husband as well as half the male population of London. Would you have believed me if I'd admitted that I was completely inexperienced?'

Somehow her defiant tone, and the way she hastily dashed her tears away with the back of her hand, emphasised her innocence—an innocence he had taken with all the finesse of a boor, Thanos thought grimly, regret searing him as he recalled his impatience when he had made love to her.

'Probably not,' he conceded honestly. 'But *Theos mou…*' He raked his hand through his hair, his frustration palpable. 'Melina found you in bed with James Hamilton.'

'I told you I didn't sleep with him.'

But he hadn't believed her. He had assumed, as Melina had, that Tahlia and James were lovers, Thanos acknowledged. And during the long hours he had sat at Melina's hospital bedside his hatred of Tahlia had made him determined to seek revenge for the pain he had thought she had caused his sister.

'How do you explain all the stories written about you in the tabloids?' he demanded. 'For the past few months rarely a day has gone by without a picture in the British newspapers of you and one of your seemingly inexhaustible supply of boyfriends at yet another social event.'

'I only went to the parties to promote Reynolds Gems,' Tahlia defended herself. 'My father persuaded me to front an advertising campaign, and then he thought it would give a personal touch if people saw me wearing the company's products. Those men weren't my boyfriends. They were male models hired from an agency. It was all part of the image,' she explained, when Thanos looked sceptical. 'I was photographed by the press wearing couture gowns that were loaned to me by design houses and fabulous jewellery from the Reynolds Gems collection, escorted by a handsome partner. But there was never any romance. Most of the models were too in love with themselves,' she added with a grimace.

'So your party princess image was just a PR stunt?' Thanos gave a harsh laugh. He had certainly been convinced that Tahlia was a good-time girl, and he was still struggling to accept that he had unwittingly stolen her virginity. 'What about the other married actor, Damian Casson? Do you expect me to believe that the photos of the two of you leaving a hotel together were also to promote Reynolds Gems?'

'I don't give a damn what you believe,' Tahlia snapped. 'Damian set me up to make his wife jealous, and as I already told you my solicitor has threatened the papers involved with legal action unless they retract their story of our supposed affair. I hate being in the public eye,' she admitted. 'But I would have done anything to help my father. I just wish all those hours I spent on the PR campaign had done some good.'

'It would have taken a miracle to turn around Reynolds' fortunes,' Thanos told her bluntly. 'Your father had made a

catalogue of terrible decisions in recent years, and with the current economic crisis bankruptcy was almost inevitable.

'It wasn't his fault.' Tahlia sprang to her father's defence. 'My mother has been seriously ill, and Dad was so busy caring for her that he couldn't concentrate on running the company. He was terrified he was going to lose her…we both were,' she said huskily, emotion clogging her throat as she acknowledged how afraid she had been that her mother would die.

That fear had haunted her every day of the past two years, and it was only now her mother was well again that she realised how much of a strain it had been to keep smiling and encouraging her parents to think positively when inside she had been racked with worry. Tears stung her eyes and she blinked furiously to dispel them. She had cried on the day her mother had been diagnosed, but since then she had suppressed her emotions and focused on helping her mother through her treatment. Now it felt as though a dam inside her had burst, and two years' worth of tears were flooding out.

She desperately did not want to cry in front of Thanos, and she stared down at the sheets while she tried to regain her composure. But the weeks and months of worry about her mother's health, and her fears that her father could lose his company, combined with the emotional trauma of giving her virginity to a man who despised her, had shattered her tenuous hold on her self-control, and she buried her face in her hands in a frantic attempt to muffle the sound of her weeping.

Once the storm had begun, it raged out of control. She did not know how long she cried, and was only vaguely aware of the mattress dipping as Thanos dropped down onto the bed beside her. She stiffened when she felt his hand on her shoulder, unbearably embarrassed by her breakdown but unable to check the sobs that still tore through her body. Her chest hurt, and her head felt as though it were about to explode,

but the hand on her shoulder slid up her neck to massage her nape in a soothing motion that gradually calmed her.

'I'm sorry,' she choked at last, scrubbing her eyes with the back of her hand and staring fixedly into her lap, so mortified by her outburst that she could not bring herself to meet his gaze. 'I'm not usually so pathetic.'

The hand on her neck continued its gentle stroking, and when she dared to glance up she discovered that Thanos had donned a black bathrobe and was sitting so close to her that she could see the tiny lines that fanned around his eyes. He was watching her impassively, but she was startled to glimpse the faintest hint of compassion in their depths.

'What was wrong with your mother?' he asked quietly

'She had breast cancer. It was a particularly aggressive form of the disease, and her initial prognosis was not good.' Tahlia took a shaky breath, shocked by the ferocity of the storm that had ripped through her. 'She had surgery immediately to remove the tumour, followed by intensive chemotherapy which left her desperately weak.' She swallowed, wondering why she was confiding in Thanos, but the words kept tumbling out.

'At one point it seemed that she would not survive the treatment, but somehow she found the strength to keep fighting. My father did everything he could to help her; he went to every chemo session with her, and we took it in turns to sleep in a chair by her bed every time she went into hospital. It's strange how those few hours before dawn seem to last for ever,' she said in a low tone. 'You can't sleep, but you dare not move away from the bed, and as the first light glimmers between the blinds you pray that this is the day there will be some improvement, a turning point.'

'Yes.' Thanos's voice was harsh, and she jerked her head up, catching her breath at the agony etched on his face. 'And every

evening, when all hope has gone from that day, you pray that tomorrow will bring the sign you have been waiting for. And so it goes on, day after day. In Melina's case, week after week.'

Tahlia's hand flew to her mouth. How could she have been so crass as to bring up the subject of hospitals when Thanos's sister had been in a coma for weeks? She tensed, expecting him to be angry with her again, and accepted that in all honesty she could not blame him. Since she had learned about the accident she had been tormented by guilt that she should have run after Melina—although it was difficult to imagine what she could have said to the young Greek woman. Even if she had managed to convince Melina she had not known James was married, nothing would have changed the fact that he was a liar and a cheat.

'I can only imagine how awful it must have been,' she said softly, her heart clenching as she pictured Thanos's vigil at his sister's bedside. 'Did other members of your family come to the hospital to wait with you?'

He shrugged. 'I have no other family. My parents died when Melina was five years old, leaving me to bring her up. At first my aunt helped to look after her, but she was elderly and passed away a few months later. Then it was just the two of us.' A nerve flickered in his cheek and he looked away from Tahlia, battling to bring his emotions under control. 'There were times when Melina showed no sign of coming out of her coma and I feared I would be the only surviving member of the Savakis family.'

He must have felt so alone, Tahlia thought gently. As powerless as she had felt as she had watched her mother struggle with the illness that could so easily have ended her life. Instinctively she placed her hand over his, but when he stiffened she realised how stupid her action had been. Thanos now had irrefutable proof that she had not been his brother-in-law's

mistress, but she was sure he still blamed her for Melina's accident. She expected him to reject her sympathy, and she made to snatch her hand back. But to her shock he curled his tanned fingers around her paler ones and held her prisoner.

'How is your mother now?'

'Completely recovered—thankfully. Actually, her recovery is a miracle—even her consultant says so,' Tahlia said with a ghost of a smile. 'Dad was overjoyed when we heard the news.' She swallowed the lump in her throat as she recalled how her father had wept tears of relief when he had phoned her with the news. 'That's why it seemed so…so *cruel* that on the same day Mum was given the all-clear Dad learned that Carlton House was in danger of being repossessed by the bank. He took out a mortgage on the house to finance Reynolds Gems,' she explained when Thanos frowned. 'My mother has no idea of the situation. She thinks they are going to enjoy a wonderful retirement in the house that has been in her family for generations. And that's exactly what's going to happen,' she added fiercely. 'My parents have been through two years of hell, and now they deserve to be happy. Dad was so relieved when he heard that Vantage Investments were prepared to buy Reynolds because it meant that he could pay back the bank loan and the mortgage, and Carlton would be safe…'

'And that is why—after you learned that Vantage is a subsidiary of Savakis Holdings, and I made it clear that I had no intention of saving Reynolds Gems—you agreed to sell yourself to me?' Thanos suggested grimly.

Tahlia bit her lip, sensing his renewed anger. 'Yes.'

'*Theos!*' he exploded, aware of a curious hollow sensation in his stomach. 'Why didn't you tell me your parents were in danger of losing their home?

Tahlia gave him a puzzled look. 'Why would you have cared? You made it clear that you would never help my father.

Time was running out, and I knew I would never find another buyer for Reynolds before the bank seized Carlton. The only thing I had to trade was my body,' she finished huskily.

The silence that fell between them simmered with tension. Thanos could not bring himself to look at Tahlia as guilt at the way he had misjudged her surged through him. Far from being an immoral slut, like his father's mistress, it seemed that she was a devoted daughter who had been desperate to help her parents. Her motivation in agreeing to be his mistress had not been to ensure her own financial security but to prevent her parents from being evicted from their home. And she had made the ultimate sacrifice, he thought bleakly. She had given him her virginity, aware that his motivation for taking her to bed was to seek revenge for a crime she had not committed.

He closed his eyes, shutting out the image of her pale, tear-stained face. In the name of heaven, what had he done?

'How did you meet James Hamilton?' he asked abruptly.

Tahlia shot him a startled glance. 'A friend of mine was starring in a play, and James was a member of the cast. We got chatting when I went backstage after the performance, and he…swept me off my feet.' She shook her head, remembering the buzz she had felt when James had singled her out. 'He was handsome, charming, funny… My mother was desperately ill, and I was sick with worry about her, but when I was with James he made me forget my fears for a few hours. I hadn't dated anyone in the years since Michael died,' she explained quietly. 'I was devastated by his death. He was so young and vibrant. We weren't lovers, but our friendship had been developing into something deeper, and I was heartbroken to lose him. For a long time after he died I blamed myself. I had thought he was suffering from the flu virus that was going around the university campus, and by the time I realised that it was something much more serious it was too

late. Michael died a few hours after being admitted to hospital.' Her eyes darkened with pain as she remembered the horror of that day.

'When I met James, he was so energetic and full of life—just as Michael had been—and I felt that nothing bad could happen while I was with him.' She bit her lip. 'It never crossed my mind that he could be married. He even took me back to his flat a few times, and it was a typical bachelor pad—there was no sign that Melina lived there.'

'She didn't,' Thanos said heavily. 'I bought her and James an apartment in Athens for a wedding present, and she remained in Greece while he went to England for two months to star in that play. When his contract was extended Melina flew to London to join him. She was immediately suspicious that he was being unfaithful, but instead of confiding in me she read the text messages he'd sent you on his mobile phone, discovered that James had arranged to spend the weekend with you at a hotel, and decided to confront you.'

In her mind Tahlia saw Thanos's sister, standing in the doorway of the hotel suite, the look of shock on her face mirrored in James Hamilton's eyes. But where Melina's expression had been one of utter devastation, James had simply looked annoyed that he had been caught out.

'Poor Melina,' she whispered. 'She must have been distraught. I understand why you blamed me. I *would* have become James's lover that night,' she told Thanos, forcing herself to meet his gaze. 'He'd told me that he loved me, and I thought I loved him. Mum's illness had cast a shadow over everything, and James was the one person who could make me smile. I needed him, and I overlooked things like the fact that he always wanted to borrow money from me.' She swallowed. 'I was a fool, and because of my naïveté Melina almost

lost her life. No wonder you hate me,' she said thickly. 'I will always feel guilty that I didn't go after her.'

No one could fake the level of emotion evident in Tahlia's voice, Thanos brooded. The pain she felt at James's treachery was as genuine as her sympathy for Melina. Shame burned like acid in his gut at the way he had treated her. He should not have brought her to Mykonos and forced her to share his bed, and now that he knew what a terrible mistake he had made he should send her back to England immediately. But hard on the heels of that thought came the unsettling realisation that he did not want to let her go.

Guilt filled him with a sudden restlessness, and he stood up and strode over to the window, staring out at the black sky and the silver moonlight dancing on the sea.

'You have nothing to feel guilty about,' he said gruffly. 'James duped you and Melina, and clearly he broke your heart as well as hers.'

Tahlia's heartbeat quickened. 'You believe me?' she asked shakily, shocked by how much his answer mattered.

He swung round from the window, the glow from the bedside lamp casting shadows over his hard-boned face, making his expression unfathomable.

'Yes, I believe you,' he said heavily. 'I'm sorry I misjudged you so badly. But when I first saw Melina in the hospital and learned the extent of her injuries I wanted to kill the two people I believed were responsible for her accident. Now I know you were not to blame, and I bitterly regret forcing you into this damnable deal.'

He walked back over to the bed, his mouth twisting when he saw Tahlia stiffen. *Theos*, he must have terrified her, he thought bleakly, remorse tearing at his insides when he recalled the demands he had made on her untutored body. Her hesitancy should have warned him of her innocence, but she

had responded to him with such intense passion that he had believed she was as sexually experienced as the newspaper stories about her had suggested.

As Thanos came closer Tahlia was startled by the almost haggard expression in his eyes, and she felt a pang of compassion for him. How awful it must have been for him to come so close to losing his sister, who was his only living relative. He had cared for Melina since she was a small child, and she could understand how angry he must have felt that she had been hurt. It was understandable that his anger had turned into a quest for revenge.

'You didn't force me into anything,' she said softly. 'You simply offered me the opportunity to ensure my parents can keep their home and I took it. I knew what I was getting into.'

Thanos gave her a level look. 'Patently you did not,' he murmured, and a feeling he could not define stirred deep inside him when her cheeks flooded with colour. 'I deeply regret that I did not know I was your first lover. My impatience to take you to bed made me brutal, and I probably scared the life out of you.' He paused, and then said in a low tone, 'But, in all honesty, I cannot say I am sorry for making love to you. The sexual alchemy between us was obvious from the moment we met at the art gallery, and despite knowing who you were, the role I thought you had played in my sister's accident, I desired you more than I have ever wanted any woman.

'I still do,' he said harshly. 'The deal we made still stands. I am prepared to buy out Reynolds Gems and save your father from financial ruin in return for your agreement to remain here on Mykonos as my mistress until the end of the month.'

He wanted her to stay with him. Tahlia was shocked by the heady relief that swept through her, but it was quickly followed by a hollow feeling of despair. Making love with Thanos had been an incredible experience that she would

never forget; not simply because it had been her first time, but because the feel of his satiny skin beneath her fingertips and the exquisite brush of his mouth caressing every inch of her body were imprinted on her brain for all time. One night was all it had taken for her to be utterly captivated by him. What would she be like after a month as his mistress—when he dismissed her from his life?

Surely it would be better for her to leave him now? To walk away with her pride restored and forget the deal that had turned her into the wanton creature she had become in his arms? But her father's financial problems still remained, and until the buy-out of Reynolds Gems was completed Carlton House was still at risk of repossession. Nothing had changed—except that Thanos was no longer looking at her with contempt in his eyes.

He sat back down on the bed and trailed his finger lightly over her cheek, the sudden warmth in his eyes making Tahlia's heart lurch. 'The passion we shared tonight was beyond anything I have ever known with any other woman. I was blinded by my anger, and determined to take revenge for the heartbreak I believed you had caused Melina, but I was wrong about you. Can we start over?' he asked quietly. 'Whatever this is between us, it is nowhere close to burning out—not for either of us, is it?'

She wanted to deny it—wished she could coolly thank him for initiating her into the pleasures of sex before she caught the first flight home. But the words would not come, and her breath snagged in her throat as he slowly lowered his head until his mouth was a whisper away from hers.

'Stay with me, Tahlia? Please?'

She must have taken leave of her senses, but she could not resist him. That had been her trouble right from the start, she acknowledged as she sagged against him and parted her lips

beneath the gentle pressure of his. The slow, sweet kiss was like nothing she had ever experienced before, and the element of gentleness tugged at her heart. When he curved his arms around her she slid her hands up to his nape, and the familiar melting warmth started low in her pelvis as he deepened the kiss to another level and desire swiftly built to a crescendo of need.

She was sure he would ease her down onto the pillows, and she slid her fingers into his hair to guide him down on top of her. But to her disbelief he lifted his head, his eyes darkening a fraction as he saw the confusion in hers.

'Wait here.' He dropped a light kiss on her still parted lips and strode into the *en suite* bathroom.

Had he been playing with her? she wondered sickly, clutching the sheet to her. Did he want to demonstrate that *he* would call the shots in any relationship they might have? She must have been out of her mind to have agreed to stay with him, she thought wildly.

But while she was debating whether to get up and pack her suitcase before she informed him that she wanted to leave after all, he re-entered the bedroom.

'What are you doing?' she gasped when he flicked the sheet out of her grasp and leaned over to scoop her into his arms.

'I've run you a bath. I have a feeling you ache in places you didn't know existed,' he murmured, chuckling when she blushed scarlet.

'I can take care of myself,' she muttered, when he shouldered open the door to the bathroom and carried her over to the huge marble bath filled to the brim with fragrant bubbles.

'Humour me, hmm…?' There was a hint of steel beneath his soft tone, and before she had time to argue the point he lowered her into the water.

It felt blissful, Tahlia acknowledged as she leaned her head back against the padded neck support and closed her eyes.

Thanos had been right; she had discovered muscles that were previously unused. But the memory of how he had driven into her over and over again until she had reached the pinnacle of pleasure caused molten heat to unfurl deep in her pelvis. Shocked by the erotic imagery, she let her eyes fly open to discover that he had shrugged out of his robe and was standing naked and unashamedly aroused by the side of the bath. The flickering light from the dozens of candles around the room gave his body a satin sheen, and her gaze moved down, following the path of crisp dark hairs that covered his chest and arrowed over his flat stomach. He was a work of art, she thought shakily, as she dropped her eyes lower still and absorbed the awesome power of his masculinity.

'Look at me like that for much longer and I won't be responsible for my actions,' he warned softly, his slow smile stealing her breath.

How could she ever have thought that his eyes were cold? she wondered, her heartbeat quickening when he stepped into the bath and sat opposite her, drawing her towards him so that she was aware of the muscular strength of his thighs holding her prisoner. Not that she wanted to escape, she acknowledged ruefully, giving a little gasp when he skimmed his hands over her ribs and cupped her breasts in his hands, the delicate brush of his thumb pads across her nipples sending exquisite shafts of sensation spiralling through her.

'How can I wash when you're doing that?' she mumbled, her eyes locked on the sensual curve of his mouth as he slowly lowered his head and claimed her lips in a long, drugging kiss that stoked the fire inside her to an inferno.

'Allow me to help you.' He picked up a bar of soap and smoothed it over her shoulders, breasts, stomach and thighs, with such dedication to detail that she made a muffled sound in her throat.

'I'm sure I'm clean. You can stop now,' she said huskily, her eyes widening in shock when he discarded the soap and slipped his hand between her legs, parting her with gentle skill and sliding a finger deep inside her. Moist heat flooded through her as he stretched her wider and slipped another digit into her, his fingers moving in an erotic dance that drove her higher and higher towards an orgasm.

'Do you want me to stop, *agape*?' he queried gently as he brushed his thumb pad delicately over the tight nub of her clitoris. Sensation speared her and she arched her hips, nothing in her mind now but desperation for him to give her the release she craved.

'No. Don't stop…please…' She groaned when he withdrew his fingers, and clutched his shoulders when he stood and swung her into his arms before climbing out of the bath. Water streamed from their bodies and dripped onto the carpet as he strode into the bedroom, but he seemed unconcerned that her wet hair soaked through the bedspread as he placed her on the bed and stretched out next to her, his mouth capturing hers in a kiss of pure possession.

'This time we'll take it slowly,' he promised, pausing to swiftly don protection before he nudged her legs apart and moved over her.

Tahlia appreciated the care and consideration he showed as he eased the solid length of his erection into her, but as he filled her, inch by tantalising inch, she discovered that she did not want him to be gentle. Her desire for him was as fierce as a forest fire blazing out of control, and she wanted him to make love to her with the same savage passion that had overwhelmed them both the first time he had possessed her.

She was too shy to voice her need for him, but instead she moved with him, arching her hips to meet each powerful

thrust and digging her fingers into his shoulders to urge him to take her faster, harder…

'*Theos*, Tahlia, I don't want to hurt you,' he growled, fighting to retain his self-control.

'You won't. I want you.' Words could not express the depths of her passion, the throbbing ache of her need for him to take her to the heights, but when his lips claimed hers she kissed him hungrily, sliding her tongue into his mouth so that he groaned and tensed before increasing the power of each thrust into her eager body.

Thalia clung to his damp shoulders and tossed her head from side to side, feeling the first spasms building inside her growing, growing until they were an unstoppable force, and she gave a thin, animal cry as her body arched with the explosive force of her climax.

Thanos felt the delicious tightening of her muscles around his shaft and gritted his teeth, determined that this time he would remain in control. He slid his hands beneath her buttocks and tilted her hips, driving into her with deep, steady strokes, taking her higher again, until she sobbed his name and raked her fingers on the silk bedspread. Only when she had climaxed for the third time did his restraint slip, and he paused, savouring the anticipation of the pleasure to come, before he gave one last powerful thrust and experienced the shattering ecstasy of release.

Long moments passed before his breathing returned to normal. He rolled off her and immediately drew her into his arms, frowning when he caught the glimmer of tears on her lashes. 'Forgive me,' he said deeply. 'I was afraid I would hurt you. It was too much, too soon. I should have curbed my impatience.'

Tahlia shook her head, blinking back the tears she had hoped he would not see and giving him a brilliant smile that

evoked a peculiar feeling in his chest. 'I was impatient too,' she assured him, and then to her surprise could not prevent herself from yawning so widely that Thanos chuckled, the sound echoing beneath her ear as he curved his arm around her and settled her against him.

'And now you are tired. Go to sleep, *agape*,' he bade her softly, when she opened her mouth to deny it. Her lashes were already drifting down, and Thanos was shaken by the unexpected surge of protectiveness that swept through him as he watched her fall asleep.

CHAPTER SEVEN

TAHLIA was awoken by the bright sunlight filtering through the blinds. She turned her head and found that she was alone, the faint indentation on the pillow beside her the only indication that Thanos had slept in the bed last night. That and the slight tenderness of her breasts, the ache of muscles never previously used…

She blushed as she recalled in vivid detail the passion they had shared. Sex with Thanos had been a revelation, and in all honesty she did not regret that he was her first lover. The incredible sensuality of their lovemaking was proof that it was possible to enjoy physical intimacy without emotional involvement—because of course her emotions were *not* involved, she assured herself. Sexual chemistry was a powerful force and she had been unable to resist its pull. Yet she was conscious of a dull ache around her heart that had nothing to do with the pleasurable excesses of the previous night.

The most important thing was that Carlton House was safe and her parents would be able to spend their retirement free from financial worries, she told herself firmly as she threw back the sheets and headed for the *en suite* bathroom. It was ridiculous to wonder what would have happened if she and Thanos had simply been two strangers who had met

one evening and been instantly attracted to one another. Perhaps he would have invited her out to dinner or the theatre? Would they have gone the conventional route of dating for a while before their relationship progressed to the bedroom?

It would not have been long before their mutual sexual awareness had exploded into passion, she thought with a rueful smile. But she wished they'd had the chance to get to know one another, to become friends before they became lovers. Instead their relationship was a business arrangement, and although Thanos no longer seemed to despise her, there was no escaping the fact that he was paying for her to share his bed.

The sun was already hot when she stepped onto the terrace, and she was glad of the shade cast by the large parasol as she sat down to breakfast. A note propped up against the coffee pot informed her that Thanos would be in meetings until late afternoon, and, recalling his scathing comments about her lack of clothes, she decided to go shopping in Mykonos Town.

'Yes, there is a bus,' the maid told her, looking puzzled when Tahlia asked her for directions to the town. 'But Mr Savakis would not expect you to take a bus. His chauffeur will drive you wherever you want to go.'

'The bus will be fine,' Tahlia replied cheerfully. She could not rationalise why she did not want to make use of Thanos's personal staff. It was simply important that she retained her independence as much as possible.

Using public transport also meant that she had an excellent tour of the island, she discovered an hour later, as the bus sped along the road. She stared at the rocky hilltops where goats were grazing, and then turned her head to admire the stunning view of the sea. On the horizon she could see the famous windmills, standing like sentinels on the hills above the port, and as the bus wound down into the town centre she

was entranced by the myriad square white, flat-roofed houses, jumbled together in impossibly narrow streets.

Even this early in the season the town was bustling with tourists who strolled along the rows of souvenir shops and sat beneath brightly coloured parasols outside the cafés and tavernas. Mykonos was one of the most cosmopolitan of the Greek Islands, and unfortunately this was reflected in the price tags inside the fashionable boutiques. Determined not to allow Thanos to buy her clothes, Tahlia spent the last of her savings, earmarked to pay her electricity bill, on two evening dresses which she did not particularly like but were the cheapest she could find.

She spent another enjoyable hour window-shopping, had lunch in a charming little restaurant in an area of the town called Little Venice, where the buildings were so close to the sea that the balconies overhung the water, and finally caught the bus back to the Artemis, feeling hot and weary, but satisfied that she had two suitable outfits to replace the blouse that Thanos had ruined.

She was surprised to see him standing by the French doors when she walked into the suite, and his grim expression as he swung round to face her made Tahlia's heart sink.

'Where have you been for the past five hours?' he queried tersely. 'The maid said you went out at eleven this morning,' he added, when Tahlia frowned and checked her watch.

'I can't believe I was out for so long. I went into the town, and there was so much to see. Time just flew,' she said defensively.

'Particularly as you travelled by bus,' Thanos said disapprovingly. 'The maid told me she had explained to you that I have assigned a driver to act as your personal chauffeur. Yianis would have given you a tour of the island—and carried your shopping,' he added, his eyes dropping to the bags she was holding. 'I was

beginning to worry that something had happened to you,' he said tensely. 'You are a stranger to Mykonos, and some of the bars are not good places for you to go on your own.'

Tahlia's temper prickled at the note of censure in his voice. 'I'm a big girl now, and I can take care of myself.'

Did she have any idea how young she looked, with her face bare of make-up and her hair caught up in a ponytail? Thanos mused. He could imagine the interest she had aroused among the male population of Mykonos in her faded denim shorts and a white strap top, beneath which she was clearly not wearing a bra, and he felt a caveman instinct to lock her away in the highest tower.

'During my student days I spent two summers backpacking around Europe. I know the kind of seedy places to avoid. I worked in many of them,' she admitted ruefully.

'Doing what?' Thanos asked curiously.

'Waitressing, mainly—although I did try a brief stint cooking pancakes in a crêperie in Spain. Until I set light to the kitchen and the manager sacked me,' Tahlia told him cheerfully. 'I was better at bar-work, or cleaning. Often I worked seventy hours a week, and saved the money I earned to see me through my next term at university.'

Thanos frowned. 'Didn't your parents support you financially while you were studying?'

'They couldn't afford to. Carlton House suffered serious structural damage in a storm a few years ago, and the cost of the repairs was astronomical. But I was happy to pay my own way. I never expected hand-outs.'

The Tahlia he was getting to know was nothing like the image fostered in the tabloids of a spoilt party-girl, Thanos brooded, trying to picture her waiting on tables. He remembered the exhaustion of working ridiculously long hours as a labourer, struggling to earn enough to pay the bills and feed

and clothe Melina. Memories of those years of poverty were the reason why he now made regular donations to charities supporting the under-privileged, and they had made him appreciate all that he had. Until now he had never met any woman, apart from his sister, who respected the value of money.

'But presumably your parents paid for your flat? You could not have afforded to buy a property in such an affluent area of London on the money you earned as a waitress.'

'Oh, the flat isn't mine, it belongs to George. My aunt Georgina,' Tahlia explained hastily, when Thanos's brows drew together. 'I moved in with her after I left university. She's elderly, and had had several falls. I wanted to take care of her, but sadly she developed dementia and it got to the point where I was terrified of leaving her to go to work because she had so many accidents. After she left a plastic jug on the electric hotplate and the kitchen caught fire my parents and I decided that it would be better for her to move into a residential home where she could have full-time care. I visit her twice a week—' Tahlia broke off at the realisation that she would be unable to visit her aunt for the next month. 'I don't suppose she'll miss me,' she said quietly. 'She doesn't recognise me any more.'

'Yet you still visit her regularly?' Thanos murmured.

'Of course.' Tahlia shrugged. 'Dementia is a cruel illness, but it doesn't define Aunt George. She's still a wonderful person.'

Far from being heartless, as he had once believed, Tahlia clearly possessed a depth of compassion and kindness that he had never found in any other woman, Thanos acknowledged. He did not want to dwell on how he had misjudged her and he strolled towards her, glancing curiously at her shopping bags.

'So, what did you buy?'

'Clothes—as ordered,' she replied brightly. 'Two evening dresses, to be precise.' She pulled a garish pink gown from

one of the bags and held it up for his inspection. 'What do you think?'

'I think you had better show me the other one,' he said flatly.

'If you don't like the pink, I thought I couldn't go wrong with classic black.' Tahlia held the plain black dress against her and gave an impatient sigh when he shook his head. 'What's wrong with it?'

'It's cheap, badly made, and it drains the colour from your face,' Thanos told her bluntly. He lifted his hand and ran his finger lightly down her cheek, watching the soft flush of rose-pink stain her skin. 'If they are the only two choices, then I have to say that I definitely prefer you wearing no clothes at all, *agápe*.'

The sultry gleam in his eyes caused a delicious little shiver to run through Tahlia, and her breath snagged in her throat when he slid the strap of her cotton top over her shoulder. It would be so easy to close the few inches between them and tilt her head in readiness for his kiss, but she was suddenly gripped with shyness. She was here with him to fulfil her side of a business arrangement, she reminded herself fiercely. She had not expected to be so utterly captivated by him—or to feel this lingering regret that their relationship would never be more than sex.

'I think I'll hit the shower,' she mumbled. 'It was hot and dusty in town.'

She quickly made her escape, crossing the lounge to the bedroom and carrying on into the *en suite* bathroom. A long, tepid shower cooled her heated skin and went some way to restoring her equilibrium. When she'd finished she wound a towel sarong-like around her body and blasted her hair with the hairdrier, wondering if Thanos had returned to work.

The sight of him propped up in bed halted her in her tracks, and her heart missed a beat as her eyes travelled down from

his bare muscular chest, covered with whorls of dark hair, to the sheet draped low over his hips. The word handsome did not do justice to his stunning looks and simmering virility. One look at him was all it took for her to melt, she thought despairingly, unable to tear her eyes from the sensual promise of his mouth. The feral heat in his gaze was both an invitation and a demand, and when he wordlessly flicked back the sheet to reveal the awesome strength of his arousal, she swallowed, her eyes locked with his as she walked slowly towards the bed.

Heart pounding so hard she was sure he must hear it, she stretched out beside him, her faint sigh muffled as he lowered his head and claimed her mouth in a slow, drugging kiss that sparked a flame inside her. His tongue probed between her lips, demanding access as he deepened the kiss, and she responded mindlessly, her body quivering with delight. He unwrapped her towel and stroked his hand over her breasts, teasing her nipples into hard peaks before he replaced his fingers with his mouth and laved each dusky tip until she gasped with pleasure.

Passion built swiftly, and when he slipped his hand between her thighs she spread her legs wider, heard his low groan of approval as he parted her and discovered the slick wetness of her arousal.

'You can touch me too,' Thanos murmured, smiling when colour stained her cheeks.

After a moment's hesitation she complied, and tested his restraint to its limit when she stroked her fingers lightly along his swollen length and then grew bolder and encircled him. Her innocence was indisputable, but she was an apt pupil, he acknowledged, his heart racing as he reached for a protective sheath and then positioned himself over her. He entered her with slow deliberation, watching her eyes widen as she felt him slide deeper, filling her to the hilt before he withdrew

almost fully and thrust again, establishing a rhythm that drove them both to the edge and over, as their passion exploded in the glory of mutual climax.

It was just good sex, he reminded himself when he finally withdrew and rolled onto his back, taking her with him and tangling his hand in her hair. He guided her mouth down on his and kissed her with lazy appreciation. Physical compatibility at its best—which left him with a feeling of contentment that he had never experienced with any other woman.

'I need to work for another couple of hours,' he told her as he pulled on his trousers. 'This evening we're attending a reception. The shipping magnate Christos Petrelis is hosting a party on his private island.'

'Which dress shall I wear?' Tahlia mused. 'The black or the pink?'

He gave her a level look. 'Neither.'

'You think I should go nude?' she teased him, her impish smile tugging faintly on his heart.

'It would certainly be an attention-stealer, but I admit I like the fact that I am the only man who has ever seen your naked body,' he told her, frowning slightly as he acknowledged a degree of possessiveness that was unexpected. He reached for his phone and spoke rapidly in Greek before cutting the call. 'Fortunately, I am a much better shopper than you. Come and see.'

Puzzled, Tahlia pulled on her robe and followed him into the lounge. He strode over to the door and opened it, to admit three porters laded with bags and boxes emblazoned with the names of famous design houses.

'What…?' She lifted her eyes to his face and waited for his explanation.

'You need new clothes,' Thanos murmured coolly. 'So I phoned a friend in Paris who is a personal stylist, gave her

your measurements and a description of your colouring, and asked her to send over a selection of suitable outfits.'

'Well, you can just send them straight back.' Tahlia stared around at the dozens of boxes and bags, from Chanel, Gucci, Prada, and felt sick with misery. The laughter she had shared with Thanos a few moments earlier had been replaced with a tangible tension. 'I won't wear clothes paid for by you. I told you—I pay my own way and I won't accept hand-outs. Even though they are haute couture,' she added grimly.

Thanos's smile had faded and his expression was unreadable, although Tahlia sensed that she had angered him. 'You will wear them,' he told her, with a note of implacability in his voice that warned her she would have a fight on her hands if she refused. 'As we discussed before, your sole purpose for the next month is to please me, and I expect you to dress appropriately.'

'I don't need reminding that you are paying for me to act the role of your mistress,' she said stiffly, hurt pride churning in her stomach. In a battle of wills he would be a clear winner, and a dignified retreat was her only option. 'Very well, I'll wear the clothes while I am here on Mykonos. But I shall regard them as a uniform, and I will leave them behind when our contract is over.'

Thanos restrained himself from pulling her into his arms and shaking some sense into her, and ignored the stronger urge to kiss her into submission. 'Suit yourself,' he said laconically, snatching up his jacket from the back of the chair and heading for the door. 'I believe Monique included a Valentino evening gown in the collection. Wear that tonight,' he ordered, and he stepped into the corridor and slammed the door behind him without giving her the chance to argue further.

Tahlia worked off her fury at Thanos's high-handedness by swimming thirty lengths in the private pool. When she re-

turned to the bedroom she discovered that the maid had un-
packed the clothes and hung them in the wardrobe: beautiful
classical evening dresses, elegant trousers, skirts and tops, all
with matching shoes and accessories, and a variety of exqui-
site nightgowns and sets of lacy underwear which were nothing
like the plain cotton bras and knickers she usually wore.

Presumably Thanos believed that as he was paying for her
he could indulge in a typical male fantasy of seeing her in
flimsy scraps of silk and lace, she thought dully as she held up
a low-cut black basque complete with silk ribbons which laced
up at the front. In different circumstances she would have taken
huge delight in a cupboard full of designer outfits, but the
knowledge that Thanos had bought them emphasised the fact
that she was—as he had pointed out—here to please him.

The Valentino dress *was* stunning, she was forced to admit
later, after she had taken a leisurely bath and smoothed
fragrant body lotion onto her skin before dressing for the
party. The heather-coloured silk gown left her shoulders bare
and clung lovingly to her waist and hips, the side-split in the
skirt reaching to mid-thigh. It was the most daring dress she
had ever worn, and as she stared at her reflection in the mirror
she barely recognised the sultry seductress looking back at her
as sensible Tahlia Reynolds.

Thanos walked into the bedroom as she was spraying
perfume to her pulse points. She guessed he must have used
the spare bedroom as a dressing room, because he had
changed into a black dinner suit which emphasised his lean
length and the formidable width of his shoulders. She hated
the way her heart jerked as her gaze skittered over the chi-
selled beauty of his face.

Her heart thudded as his eyes swept over her.

'You look beautiful.' His voice was as deep and sensuous
as crushed velvet, and her senses flared as she caught the drift

of his cologne when he strolled over to her. 'I bought this for you to wear tonight.'

Tahlia caught her breath when he held up a large peardrop-shaped amethyst, surrounded by diamonds and suspended on a fine white-gold chain. Before she had time to argue Thanos fastened the pendant around her neck and stood back to admire the sight of the violet-coloured gem sitting in the V between her creamy breasts.

'Perfect,' he murmured, his eyes gleaming with feral hunger as he traced his finger over the pendant and then slipped it lower and settled it between her breasts. 'It matches the colour of your dress exactly. But whenever I look at you this evening I will be imagining you wearing nothing but the necklace,' he added thickly.

The pendant felt heavy on Tahlia's skin, and she was tempted to tear it off. She felt as though he had branded her—as if every time he looked at her he would be reminded that he had paid for her.

'You think you can buy everything, don't you?' she snapped. 'You have so little understanding of the value of money that the cost of a valuable piece of jewellery is irrelevant to you. I suppose that's what comes of being born into wealth,' she finished scathingly.

Thanos's face had darkened at her outburst, and now he gave a mirthless laugh. 'I wasn't born into wealth,' he said harshly. 'There was no grand mansion house in *my* family to pass down through generations. I didn't enjoy a privileged childhood or have the advantage of a private education. I was born on a small island called Agistri, and I grew up in a tiny stone-built house with no running water,' he explained flatly. 'As a youth I assumed that I would spend my life as a goat-herd. I had no expectations of ever moving away from the island where my family had lived for generations.'

'What made you decide to leave?' Tahlia asked, stunned by his revelation that he had not inherited his vast fortune.

'An English woman called Wendy Jones.' Thanos could not disguise the bitterness in his voice. 'She was my father's mistress—and after he walked out on his family and divorced my mother she subsequently became his new wife. Wendy had already been married and divorced twice when she bought a villa on Agistri. She employed my father to carry out renovation work on her house, but it soon became apparent that she wanted him for more than his building skills. A few months after he began working for her he dropped the bombshell to my mother that their marriage was over.

He continued harshly, 'My mother was distraught, especially when my father stopped all financial support. I was fifteen, and Melina was just three years old. I dropped out of school, lied about my age, and managed to pick up some labouring work, using the skills my father had taught me. My mother wept about the disruption to my education, but I had no choice—I couldn't allow her and my sister to starve, and my father was too besotted with his tart to spare a thought for his wife and children. I lost all the respect I had felt for my father,' Thanos said savagely. 'He made a complete fool of himself. Wendy flirted with him outrageously. She knew he was married, but that little fact didn't seem to matter to her. She'd decided that she wanted him for herself and she deliberately pursued him, uncaring that she had ripped my family apart—'

He broke off abruptly, and in the tense silence Tahlia could feel his barely leashed anger. No wonder Thanos had been so ready to believe that she had stolen James Hamilton from his sister, she brooded. His family had been blown apart by his father's mistress. It must have seemed as though history was repeating itself when his sister had discovered that her husband was having an affair.

'I never spoke to my father after he married again,' he continued grimly. 'Eighteen months after the wedding he was killed in a horrific accident. Wendy had insisted on having a swimming pool, and he was crushed when the mechanical digger he was driving overturned.' He ignored Tahlia's shocked gasp and continued. 'My father had not made a will, and everything he owned—namely the house where my mother, Melina and I still lived—passed to his wife. Within a week of his funeral Wendy demanded that we leave her property. It was the final blow to my mother, to be evicted from the home where she had lived for her entire married life by my father's whore. She died of pneumonia six months later, leaving me to care for Melina, who was then just five years old.'

Tahlia tried to imagine Thanos at seventeen—a boy who overnight had had to become a man and take responsibility for his young sister while he was grieving for both his parents. 'You must feel very protective of Melina,' she murmured.

He turned his head and stared at her, his dark eyes blazing. 'I would give my life for her,' he vowed fiercely. 'I promised my mother as she lay dying that I would always take care of Melina. When I first saw her after the accident and I was told she had less than a fifty percent chance of surviving…' His throat moved convulsively. 'I was haunted by the knowledge that I had failed to protect her.'

Tahlia was shocked by the raw emotion in his eyes. There was no doubt that Thanos adored his sister, and she realised that far from being the hard, ruthless man she had once believed his feelings ran deep. If he ever fell in love he would give his heart utterly, she brooded, aware of a faint tug of envy for the woman who might one day win his devotion.

He had fallen silent, seemingly lost in his thoughts, but after a moment he picked up her stole and placed it around her shoulders. 'Are you ready to leave?'

When she nodded, he escorted her out of the suite. To her surprise the lift carried them upwards, and when the doors opened she stepped out onto the roof of the hotel where a helicopter was waiting.

'The chopper is the quickest way to travel between the islands,' he explained as he assisted her into the cockpit. 'I've held a private pilot's licence for ten years. You'll be quite safe.'

Tahlia had always been nervous in the air, but as they took off she had no qualms about Thanos's ability to fly the chopper. Was there nothing this man could not do? she wondered as she watched him manoeuvre the joystick and the helicopter responded smoothly to his control. She glanced out of the window and watched the streaks of pink and gold which flared from a fiery sun as it slipped below the horizon.

Twenty minutes later they landed on the lawn in front of a huge white-walled villa and were escorted inside by a uniformed member of staff.

There was serious money here, Tahlia mused, glancing around at the stunning array of diamonds and designer gowns worn by the predominantly young and blonde women who were being paraded on the arms of their significantly older male companions. Fortunately she was practised in the art of making small-talk with people she had never met before—or was likely to meet again, and she moved around the room with Thanos, sipping champagne and forcing herself to smile until her jaw ached.

She was aware of the envious glances she received from other women, the thinly veiled speculation in their eyes that she would not remain his mistress for long. Thanos Savakis's relationships were notoriously short-lived, but tonight he only had eyes for her, and he kept his arm around her waist, as if he shared her reluctance for them to be apart for even a moment—although that was surely just wishful thinking, Tahlia told herself firmly.

He dominated her mind: a tall, dark and brooding presence at her side. A man who, in a few hours, would take her to bed and make love to her until he had sated his hunger for her. She would not offer any resistance, she thought wearily as his eyes fused with hers and the flare of heat in their depths sent a jolt of awareness down her spine. He had taken her innocence and awoken her sensuality, and she could not deny the desire that he alone aroused in her.

'Dance with me.' His eyes seemed to scorch her soul, and without waiting for her to reply he drew her onto the dance floor and into his arms.

He swamped her senses, the warmth of his body and the sensual musk of his cologne drifting around her so that she relaxed against him and rested her head on his chest, the ache inside her soothed by the steady beat of his heart. When he lowered his head and claimed her mouth she parted her lips and kissed him back with a fervency that caused him to tighten his hold and pull her closer, so that she could feel the throbbing force of his arousal press impatiently into her pelvis.

At last he lifted his mouth from hers and stared down at her quizzically. 'Ready to go?' he queried softly.

The champagne was flooding through her veins, sweeping away her doubts and inhibitions and leaving her weak and boneless and the slow drumbeat of desire was thudding irresistibly deep inside her.

'Yes.'

His eyes darkened, his mouth twisting in a self-derisive grimace as he slid his hand down to her bottom and pulled her up hard against the swollen shaft straining beneath his trousers. 'You are like a fever in my blood, *agape*,' he muttered thickly. 'I am burning up with wanting you.'

The short flight back to Mykonos seemed interminable. The silence grew ever more intense as the lift carried them

down a floor to Thanos's suite. The moment they stepped through the door Thanos swept her into his arms and strode into the master bedroom, the purpose in his eyes causing anticipation to coil low in Tahlia's stomach.

She helped him remove her clothes and then his, her heart thudding as she ran her hands through the mass of wiry black hairs that covered his chest and felt the erratic beat of his life-force beneath her fingertips. The solid length of his arousal pushed insistently against her thigh, and she felt the familiar melting warmth between her legs as her body grew impatient for him. She wanted him so desperately that her limbs trembled, and when she tentatively stroked her fingers along his swollen shaft and heard his swiftly indrawn breath she expected him to lift her onto the bed, to possess her with the same raw passion of their previous encounters.

Instead he stroked his hands through her hair, before trailing his fingertips in a butterfly caress along her collarbone and then down to cup her breasts in his palms. His slow smile told her that he understood her impatience, but his movements were unhurried as his mouth claimed hers in a deep, drugging kiss that seared her soul.

It was just good sex, she reminded herself. It meant nothing to him, and she would be a fool to open her heart to him. But when he sank down onto the bed and lifted her over him, guiding her gently down so that she absorbed the full strength of his erection, she looked into his dark eyes and acknowledged on a wave of sheer panic that her heart was in serious danger.

CHAPTER EIGHT

THE prickling sensation on Tahlia's shoulders warned her that she would be wise to move out of the sun. It was almost four p.m., she noted, her stomach tightening as she glanced at her watch. Soon Thanos would come back to the suite, and she would go inside, to the cool, shaded bedroom, where he would make love to her as he had done every day of the past week since they had arrived on Mykonos.

She moved her sunbed beneath the parasol and picked up her book—the third paperback novel she'd read this week—but she could not concentrate on the story, and after a few moments she set it down again, looking towards the French doors. Her heart-rate accelerated when she discovered that he had stepped onto the terrace and was watching her, his expression hidden behind his sunglasses. He dipped his head in silent greeting before walking back inside, and, like a puppet controlled by invisible strings, she stood up and followed him.

When she reached the master bedroom she found him naked, stretched out on the silk sheets like a sultan waiting for his favourite concubine. That was all she was to him, she reminded herself despairingly. But he had treated her with respect and consideration since he had made her his mistress, and day by day she had fallen deeper under his spell.

It was ridiculous to still feel shy when he had explored every inch of her body with his hands and mouth, but she could not bring herself to strip off her bikini, and stood watching him, her eyes unconsciously wary, until he held out his hand and murmured, 'Come here,' in the deep, velvet-soft voice that sent a quiver of longing down her spine.

In the sensual feast that followed he aroused her to a fever-pitch of desire, peeling her bikini from her breasts and hips and probing the moist heat of her femininity with his tongue before he moved over her and possessed her with fierce, powerful thrusts that drove them both to the ecstasy of simultaneous release. Afterwards she lay limply beside him, knowing that he would soon stroll into the shower, before dressing and returning to another of his interminable meetings. But to her surprise he propped himself up on one elbow and stared down at her.

'So, what did you do today?'

She shrugged, puzzled by his unexpected interest. 'Sat in the sun before it got too hot, swam, read a book—the same as I've done every day,' she added, unable to disguise the faint note of frustration in her voice.'

Thanos's eyes narrowed. 'You could go shopping. There are some excellent designer boutiques in the town, and I've told you to use the money I left for you.'

'And I've told you I don't want your money,' Tahlia said fiercely. 'Besides, you've already provided me with more than enough clothes. I don't need to go shopping.'

'Most women I know do not shop out of necessity,' Thanos murmured dryly.

'Well, clearly I'm different to your other women.'

Tahlia's tart comment filled Thanos with a mixture of amusement and frustration. He had made love to her every night—and most afternoons—he acknowledged wryly, and he

knew every secret dip and curve of her body. But her mind remained stubbornly closed to him. He was no nearer to understanding what made Tahlia Reynolds tick than he had been a week ago.

He trailed his hand lazily down her body, feeling a spurt of triumph at the sharp catch of her breath as he pushed her legs apart. 'If you are bored, I will have to spend more time… entertaining you,' he drawled.

'It's not possible to have sex any more times than we do already,' she said ruefully. 'But if I spend many more hours sunbathing I'll turn into a crisp.' She pushed her hair out of her eyes and continued hurriedly, 'Isn't there any office work I could do? Filing, admin…? I don't care what it is, as long as I have something to do. I'm a working girl,' she told him seriously. 'I'm not used to sitting around all day doing nothing.'

Tahlia was so very different from the woman he had believed her to be when he had blamed her for his sister's accident, Thanos acknowledged. During the tense hours he'd spent waiting for Melina to regain consciousness his image of Tahlia had fused with his memories of his father's English mistress, and his hatred of her had grown as intense as the hatred he felt towards the woman who had destroyed his family. But over the past week he had discovered that Tahlia was nothing like the callous, cold-hearted woman his father had married. True, she possessed an unexpectedly fiery temper beneath her gentle exterior, but she was unfailingly polite towards his staff, instinctively kind, and the most generous lover he had ever known.

He had not expected to like her, he conceded, but to his surprise he had found himself thinking about her when his mind should have been concentrating on profit margins, and for the first time in his life he resented the hours he spent in the office because he would rather have been with her.

He got up from the bed, retrieved his clothes from the floor where he had carelessly discarded them, and paused on his way to the *en suite* bathroom to look back at her. The sunlight filtering through the blinds turned her hair to pure gold, falling in a silken sheet around her shoulders, and her skin was still flushed from the passion they had just shared. He must be mad to be considering working with her when she was such a serious distraction to his thought process, he thought wryly, but his logical brain insisted that she could be extremely useful to him.

'I've a meeting scheduled for the next hour. Come to my office after that and we'll discuss an idea I've had which I'm certain will alleviate your boredom,' he murmured, smiling at her look of surprise and striding on into the bathroom before she could question him.

Thanos was standing by a window which afforded a spectacular view of the sea when Tahlia entered his office. 'Take a seat,' he invited, the warmth of his smile doing strange things to her insides.

She quickly sat down in the chair in front of his desk, her eyes drawn to his hard profile, and her composure wavered as she studied his chiselled features, the slashing line of his cheekbone and his square chin. An hour ago, that sensual mouth had traced every inch of her body and lingered in her most secret places to wreak havoc. The memory caused liquid heat to flood through her veins, and she knew from the sudden flare of heat in his eyes that he had read her mind.

'You said you have an idea?' she said hastily, aware that she was blushing.

'I have several,' Thanos assured her throatily, conscious of the familiar tug of desire in his groin as he studied her. She had changed into an elegant cream linen skirt and a white

blouse, and looked as chaste as a nun, with her hair drawn back from her face in a neat chignon. But somehow her wholesome, fresh-faced appearance was incredibly sexy. His eyes lingered on her lips, coated in a pale pink gloss, and his heart-rate quickened.

He ruthlessly suppressed the hunger that gnawed in his gut and picked up the folder on his desk. 'However, I think we had better concentrate on the idea I asked you here to discuss. The Artemis is due to open in three weeks' time,' he said abruptly.

Tahlia nodded. 'I'm sure it will be a great success,' she murmured, not sure what the opening date of his new hotel had to do with her.

'I hope so. We're fully booked for the whole of the summer, but it's vital we make an excellent first impression. To that end I have invited tour operators and travel writers to come and enjoy all that the Artemis has to offer, in the hope that they will give a glowing report. If they don't, many of those bookings could be cancelled,' Thanos added tersely. 'I hired a PR company to organise a party for the opening night. Three hundred guests have been invited, including several world-renowned celebrities. I learned yesterday that the PR company has failed to fulfil its promise that the party will be the most spectacular event ever held on Mykonos. In fact I seriously doubt they could organise a kindergarten party,' he added, his irritation palpable. 'And so this morning I fired them.'

Thanos was not a man who gave second chances, Tahlia surmised as she stared at the rigid set of his jaw, and she felt a pang of sympathy for the head of the PR company who must have borne the brunt of his fury.

'Ordinarily my PA would have alerted me to the fact that Cosmo Communications were useless,' Thanos continued. 'But Stephanie is on leave—visiting her family in South

Africa—and I have spent much of the past six months in America with Melina.'

Tahlia felt a pang of guilt for the unwitting part she had played in his sister's accident. 'What will you do? Can you find another PR consultant at such short notice?'

'I've already found one.' He leaned back in his chair and gave her a level look. 'I'm impressed by the work you did for Reynolds Gems, and I want *you* to organise the party.'

For a few seconds Tahlia was lost for words. 'That's an enormous responsibility,' she said slowly. 'Do you really trust that I can meet your expectations?'

'I trust you implicitly, Tahlia, which is why I am awarding you the contract for the Artemis party.'

The words hovered in the air between them, and for some reason Tahlia felt a lump form in her throat. 'Well, that's good to hear,' she said huskily, shocked by how much his opinion of her mattered. 'I'd be honoured to do it.' Panic kicked in as she contemplated the prestigious event he had asked her to organise at short notice. 'But how can I make arrangements for the party when I don't speak Greek?'

'A member of my staff will assist you. Ana speaks English fluently, and she can translate for you when necessary. Your job is to come up with ideas for a party that will be unforgettable and will put the Artemis on the list of the world's most exclusive hotels.'

Thanos handed her a folder.

'This is the guest list. You'll see that many of the celebrities have specific requirements on everything from the size of room they want to the colour of the towels in their bathrooms. It will be your job to ensure that they cannot find fault with the Artemis.'

Tahlia scanned through the file and noted that a well-known actress had given instructions that she was only to be

served foods from those listed on her strict macrobiotic diet sheet. She would have liked six months to organise an event of this magnitude instead of three weeks, and her doubts must have shown on her face.

'I have every faith that you can do this, Tahlia,' Thanos murmured. 'And I will, of course, pay you a salary for your professional expertise,' he added in a tone that brooked no argument. 'Your work for Reynolds has proved that you have talent and a wealth of innovative ideas, which are exactly the qualities I'm looking for.'

After all the misunderstandings between them, and the contempt he had shown her when he had believed she had been his brother-in-law's mistress, the note of respect in his voice was balm to her battered self-respect. She was ashamed that she had agreed to be his mistress in return for him helping her father, but there had been no other way. Now, in offering her the party contract, she felt as though Thanos considered her an equal, and there was a new confidence in her voice when she stood up and smiled at him.

'I'd better make a start,' she said briskly. 'Three weeks will fly past.'

She refused to dwell on the knowledge that at the end of that time Thanos would no longer need her in any capacity, and that she would go home and probably never see him again. Enjoy the here and now, she bade herself as she followed him into Ana's office. She could no longer kid herself that being with him was a hardship. She was drawn to him in a way she did not understand, and she could only pray that her fascination with him would have faded by the time he ended their relationship.

'Why the frown?' Thanos queried, regarding Tahlia across the restaurant table. 'Don't you like the *baklava*?'

'Unfortunately I like it too much,' she replied ruefully, popping the last piece of the delicious pastry made with ground nuts and honey into her mouth. 'I adore Greek food—but it's not doing my waistline any good.'

'You look gorgeous to me, *agape*.' Thanos watched the flush of rosy colour stain Tahlia's cheeks and felt the same curious ache in his gut that had assailed that morning, when he had woken before her and studied her while she slept.

Three weeks in the Mediterranean sunshine had given her skin a light golden tan and added streaks of blonde to her pale red hair, making her eyes appear an even denser shade of sapphire-blue. He felt the familiar flood of heat course through his veins, but he had given up trying to fight his desire for her and instead savoured the anticipation that very soon they would return to the hotel and he would make love to her.

'So, what's troubling you?'

Tahlia gave him an incredulous look. 'The Artemis party—what else? You do realise it's a week from now? I was just thinking that I must phone the pyrotechnic company tomorrow, to check the arrangements for the firework display they're giving as a finale.'

It was one of several dozen items on her 'to do' list, she brooded anxiously. To celebrate the fact that Thanos owned hotels around the world she had decided on an international theme, and she had booked entertainers and chefs from the Caribbean, South America and the Far East to fly out to Mykonos. But, as she had feared, it was proving difficult to make the arrangements at such short notice, and her long days in the office were fraught with problems. Despite being involved in intense negotiations to buy the Ambassador Hotel in London, Thanos was taking a close interest in the party. She just hoped it would live up to his expectations.

'Ana can phone them,' Thanos told her. 'We're going to

Santorini tomorrow. I have another hotel there—the Astraea. It opened a year ago, and has already gained an excellent reputation. I thought it might be useful for you to see a hotel similar to the Artemis in operation.'

That made sense, Tahlia acknowledged. She had planned the various entertainments for the Artemis party while the hotel was empty, and she was having trouble visualising the reception rooms packed with people. 'How long do you think the trip will take? If we're going in the morning I should be able to go into the office in the afternoon.'

'Uh-uh.' Thanos shook his head, and his smile stole her breath. 'We'll be out all day—maybe all night too,' he added, a devilish gleam in his eyes. 'You've worked ten-hour days for the past two weeks and you need a break.'

He did not add that he had planned the trip so that he could spend some time alone with her away from the office, where the predominant topic of conversation between them was the forthcoming party. He could use some relaxation time too, he conceded, running his hand around the back of his neck and feeling the tight knot of tension. In the weeks after Melina's accident his usual coping strategy of suppressing his emotions had kicked in and he had functioned on auto-pilot as he'd combined running a billion-pound company with helping to nurse her. Now Melina was recovering so well that her doctors predicted she would soon be walking unaided. His relief was indescribable, but in the last six months he felt as though he had aged ten years.

He settled the bill for their meal and followed Tahlia out of the restaurant, slipping his hand into hers as they strolled along by the harbour, where fishing boats rocked gently on the calm sea. 'We're travelling to Santorini on my boat. I've a meeting scheduled with the manager of the Astraea, but it shouldn't take too long. After that we'll have the day to ourselves.'

Don't read too much into it, Tahlia told herself firmly. It was true she had worked hard these past couple of weeks. Thanos was simply being kind in offering to take her out for the day. But she could not deny her excitement at the prospect of sharing a whole day with him. Usually they only spent a few hours in the evenings together, when they ate dinner at the Artemis, or walked into Mykonos Town and found a little restaurant, before strolling back to the hotel to make love until they were both sated.

'Would you like to go to a club or head back to the Artemis?' he murmured as they passed the doors of one of the island's many nightclubs.

Would she seem too eager if she said she would prefer to return to the privacy of their suite? The gleam in his dark eyes told her he had read her mind, and she gave him an impish smile. 'I'd like to go back to the hotel.'

His brows lifted quizzically. 'You're tired?'

'Not at all.'

'Ah.' His deep laughter rumbled in his chest. 'Then an early night is definitely in order, *agape mou*. Come on—we'll walk back along the beach.'

They walked down the steps, onto the sand, and kicked off their shoes. Thanos rolled up the hems of his trousers and led her down to the shore, slipping his arm around her waist as they wandered slowly along the water's edge.

She would not be seduced by the moonlit beach, or the myriad stars that studded the velvet sky above them, Tahlia assured herself. Thanos was a charming companion, and they had enjoyed some wonderful dinners together—and of course the sex was amazing—but he meant nothing to her. But when he halted and turned her to face him she felt the familiar weakness invade her bones and knew she was kidding herself. They had become friends as well as lovers over the past

weeks, and had discovered a shared interest in films and authors as well as a mutual love of travel. His dry sense of humour made her laugh, and his desire for her, which showed no sign of lessening, equalled her passion for him.

'Come back,' he murmured, his deep, gravelly voice tugging her from her thoughts. 'You keep leaving me tonight. What are you thinking about?'

About how empty my life is going to be without you, she thought silently. About how afraid I am that I'm falling in love with you.

'I was thinking about Melina,' she told him. It was not completely untrue—his sister had been on her conscience since Melina had discovered her in bed with James. She felt him stiffen, but he said nothing so she continued huskily. 'I would like to write to her and explain...that I never meant to hurt her...that I didn't know about her, and that if I had I would never have dated James. He fooled both of us,' she said sadly. 'I would do anything to change the events of that night, and I would like to tell her how sorry I am about everything.'

No sound disturbed the still air and the darkness seemed to press in on them.

'Have I made you angry?' she whispered, when she could bear his silence no longer.

'No. I'm not angry with you.' His anger was solely with himself, for the way he had misjudged her, Thanos acknowledged bleakly. He had believed the press stories about her and assumed she was a callous bitch. He had given Tahlia every reason to hate him, but during the past weeks he had come to know her, and he seriously doubted that she possessed the capacity for hatred. She had neither judged nor condemned him for the way he had treated her when he had first brought her to Mykonos, and he felt humbled

by her generosity of spirit. Somehow she had slipped beneath his guard, and he wasn't sure what he was going to do about it.

'I have already explained the situation to Melina, but I think she would like to hear from you. She has moved to the convalescent wing of the hospital now. I'll give you the address.'

'Thank you.' Tahlia breathed the words against his lips as he claimed her mouth in a slow, sweet kiss that drew her urgent response. Don't fall for him, her head whispered. But her heart knew that the warning came too late.

The *Leandros* was a ninety-foot luxury yacht, so lavishly fitted out that Tahlia lapsed into stunned silence while Thanos gave her a guided tour.

'Besides the master bedroom there are four additional guest cabins, as well as staff quarters,' he told her as he led the way back through the sumptuous lounge and dining room up the stairs to the main deck. She followed him over to the seating area beneath a white canopy which billowed gently in the breeze. As she sat down a uniformed deck-hand immediately stepped forward and served them flutes of Buck's Fizz.

'It's an amazing boat,' she murmured, taking a sip of her drink and then blinking hard. 'The bubbles have gone up my nose,' she giggled self-consciously. 'I hope there's a higher ratio of orange juice than champagne. I don't usually drink alcohol at ten o'clock in the morning. It'll probably send me to sleep.'

'I will do my best to ensure you stay awake,' Thanos murmured, his eyes gleaming with amusement when she blushed.

He looked more relaxed than she had ever seen him, and utterly gorgeous in close-fitting sun-bleached jeans and a black tee shirt which was stretched tight over the powerful muscles of his chest and abdomen. His black hair was brushed

back from his brow, and he looked lean and fit and so incredibly sexy that Tahlia almost melted on the spot.

His smile made her heart flip, and she grinned back at him. 'Do you take the *Leandros* out often?'

'Not as often as I'd like. Work tends to dominate my life. Melina and I used to invite a crowd of friends and cruise around the islands for a few weeks in the summer, but that stopped once she married. James's idea of fun was to go clubbing every night, and he moaned that the pace of life on the boat was too quiet,' he said grimly.

He had known from the outset that James Hamilton and Melina were not suited, he thought heavily. Given the chance, he would have done his best to dissuade his sister from marrying the brash American actor, but he'd had no opportunity to voice his doubts. Melina had arrived at his house in Athens with a cocky Hamilton in tow and revealed that they had married on the spur of the moment in Las Vegas.

'Don't be angry,' she'd pleaded, when Thanos had muttered his disapproval. 'I know James is the right man for me, and we're going to spend the rest of our lives together.'

But James had quickly grown bored with married life. He had never trusted his brother-in-law, Thanos conceded. In all honesty he had expected Melina's marriage to fail. He had known of James's reputation as a playboy, but in his fury over Melina's accident he had blamed Tahlia and refused to believe her claim that she was innocent.

At his mention of Melina and James, Thanos had fallen into a brooding silence that stretched Tahlia's nerves. 'How long will it take us to reach Santorini?' she murmured, keen to change the subject.

'We'll be there in about half an hour.' He stretched his long legs out in front of him and regarded her from behind his designer shades. 'Have you visited the Greek islands before?'

She shook her head. 'No. I backpacked around France and Spain, but other than that I've always spent my holidays with my parents in Cornwall.'

'You're close to your parents, aren't you?'

'I adore them,' Tahlia agreed. 'I'm their only child, and I guess there was a danger they could have spoiled me rotten, but they brought me up to appreciate the value of love and friendship rather than money, and they encouraged me to work hard at school so that I would have good career prospects. They would have liked more children, but Mum miscarried two babies after me and said she couldn't face the heartbreak of it happening again, so they decided to be thankful that they had one child. They're great people,' she added softly. 'I'd do anything for them—'

She broke off abruptly, wondering if Thanos would make some scathing remark about how she had sold herself to him to help her parents, but he remained silent and she quickly changed the subject again.

'Do you own hotels on any other Greek islands?'

'The Alkimini on Agistri was my first hotel, followed by the Athena on Poros, and my latest project, the Aphrodite, is currently being built on Rhodes and should be ready to open next spring. My aim is to build hotels on all the most popular islands.'

Thanos was not joking, Tahlia realised as she heard the determined note in his voice. 'How did you start your business?' she asked him curiously. 'I mean, what made you decide to build hotels?'

He was silent for a moment, considering the question, and then he said grimly, 'Desperation is probably the best answer. Desperation to keep the promise I had made my mother that I would look after Melina. I had nothing, you see. No money and little education. The only thing I had was some land on Agistri. My mother had inherited it from her family, but I did

not know about it until after her death. I learned that I owned six acres of land and a spectacular view of the sea.' He laughed. 'To be honest I was not overly impressed. The ground was too rocky to farm, and its only use was as grazing land for goats. Meanwhile I was travelling to the nearby island of Aegina every day, to work as a labourer on the dozens of hotels being built there. One evening back on Agistri I watched the sun setting over the sea, and it struck me that if I could build a hotel on my land the view would be a major attraction for tourists.

'It wasn't easy,' he admitted. 'But I managed to talk the local bank manager into giving me a loan for building materials, and I convinced the island's councillors that a hotel would help Agistri's economy. For the next two years I worked on construction sites on Aegina during the day and in the evening I paid a group of labourers to help me build my hotel. The Alkimini is named after my mother. Agistri's close proximity to the mainland and Athens meant that many Greek families came for holidays, and the hotel was soon so successful that I was soon able to repay the loan and buy a prime site on the island of Poros.'

Thanos made light of his route to success, but Tahlia was sure that his life had been incredibly tough, and she felt a surge of admiration for him. 'How did you manage to take care of Melina while you were working all those hours?'

He shrugged. 'She was at school during the day, and then she would sit in the site office and do her homework. On Poros we actually lived in a Portakabin on the site while the Athena was being built, and as she grew older she often cooked for the workers. It wasn't an ideal childhood,' he said heavily. 'In the early days all the money I earned went into the business, and I often felt guilty that she missed out on the things her friends took for granted, like new clothes and school trips. But

she never complained,' he said, his face softening. 'Although she did go through a stage of pestering me to get married. I think her reasoning was that if I had a wife she would no longer have to do the cooking.'

'Did you never consider it?' Tahlia murmured.

He was silent for so long that she thought he was not going to answer, but then he shrugged laconically. 'I was engaged briefly. Yalena came from my village and we grew up together. I suppose I was about fifteen when I first fell in love with her. When my parents' marriage ended, and then they both died, Yalena was the one person I could confide in. I worshipped her,' he admitted, his face hardening, 'and I believed that she loved me. I was overjoyed when she agreed to marry me. She seemed fond of Melina, and I thought we would live together as a family. But a month before our wedding Yalena admitted that she had secretly been seeing one of my closest friends.

'Takis came from one of the wealthiest families on Agistri. His father owned a fishing fleet and Takis had a secure future— whereas I had a scrubby patch of land, a crazy idea, huge debts and an orphaned kid sister.' He gave a harsh laugh. 'Hell, if I'd been in Yalena's shoes, I'd have picked the richer guy too.'

Tahlia caught the note of bitterness in his voice and her heart turned over as she imagined Thanos as a young man, struggling to make a living and care for a young child. 'What did you do when she told you?' she asked curiously.

He gave another shrug. 'What could I do? Takis was the better choice, and I loved Yalena enough that I wanted what was best for her. I released her from our engagement, gave them my blessing, and drowned my sorrows in ouzo on their wedding day,' he finished, with a self-derisive laugh that did not quite disguise the pain he had felt. At twenty he had worn his heart on his sleeve; now he was determined that no other woman would have the power to touch his emotions.

'I'm not surprised you got drunk,' Tahlia said softly. 'You had been deceived by the girl you loved, and your best friend. You must have been hurt.'

Thanos frowned. He had never spoken about his relationship with Yalena to anyone, and he did not understand why he had shared such a personal confidence with Tahlia. Maybe it was because she actually listened—unlike the self-centred women he usually dated, who only wanted to talk about themselves.

'To be honest, I had put Yalena on a pedestal,' he said grimly. 'But six months ago I discovered her true nature. She contacted me out of the blue and suggested we meet up to talk about old times. I assumed Takis would be with her, but she came to my hotel alone and made it clear that, since I was now far wealthier than her husband, she regretted dumping me all those years ago. She offered to divorce Takis, and seemed to think I would jump at the chance to marry her. She was rather put out when I turned her down,' he added sardonically. 'But I was glad I had met her again. It made me realise what a lucky escape I'd had all those years ago, and confirmed my belief that love is an illusion and marriage is an outdated institution.'

'I don't believe that,' Tahlia said quietly. 'My parents have been happily married for thirty years.'

'I guess there are always a few exceptions,' Thanos conceded. 'But my parents' marriage was destroyed by my father's infidelity, and Melina was devastated when she discovered that James was having an affair.'

Tahlia bit her lip. Thanos had told her he accepted that she had been deceived by James Hamilton, but she still felt guilty for the part she had played in ending Melina's marriage. She did not know what to say, and after a few moments she stood up and walked across the deck, leaning against the boat rail as she absorbed the beauty of the crystal-clear Aegean shimmering in the sunshine.

The *Leandros* was heading towards a land mass which rose steeply out of the sea, and as they drew nearer Tahlia saw that the reddish-brown cliffs were topped with hundreds of white houses, which from a distance looked like icing on top of a cake.

'Santorini is on the site of a volcano,' Thanos explained as he came to stand next to her. 'The cliff-sides are volcanic rock and the island forms a bay around the caldera.'

'The cliffs are so high,' Tahlia murmured, staring up at the rugged rocks towering above them.

'I believe the capital, Fira, is over two hundred metres above sea level. The views from the cable-car that you can see running up the side of the mountain are spectacular, but today we are sailing further up the coast. The Astraea is close to the village of Oia, which is reputed to have the most fantastic sunsets in the world.'

'You like your sunsets, don't you?' Tahlia teased him, re-membering how he had said that watching the sun setting on Agistri had given him the idea to build a hotel there.

Thanos's mood seemed to have lightened, and he laughed. 'Sunsets and spectacular views attract tourists. We can travel up to the Astraea by car, or climb the three hundred or so steps up the cliff-side,' he told her, when the *Leandros* had sailed into the tiny port and dropped anchor.

Tahlia lifted her face to the sun and breathed in the salt tang of the sea. 'I'm game for the steps,' she assured him, her pulse racing when he caught hold of her hand. The breeze ruffled his dark hair, and his sudden grin made her heart contract.

'Okay—but don't say I didn't warn you.'

She was panting by the time they reached the top of the cliff, but her lack of breath was not only because of the steep climb, she acknowledged ruefully. Thanos kept hold of her hand as they strolled through the narrow streets of Oia, and waited patiently while she paused to admire the stunning ar-

chitecture of the blue-domed church and the jumble of sugar-cube white houses with their window boxes full of scarlet pelargoniums.

The Astraea was perched on the edge of the cliff, and as Thanos had promised, offered wonderful views over the bay and nearby islands.

'There are one or two problems that need my attention, but I should be finished in an hour,' he told her, after he had given her a guided tour of the hotel. 'Ask one of the reception staff to give you directions to the beach, and I'll meet you there later.'

She had found paradise, Tahlia decided some while later, when she had scrambled down a steep path from the hotel and arrived at a tiny picturesque cove. The *Leandros* was moored out in the bay, and she guessed that one of the deck hands had brought the parasol and picnic rug, which were now arranged on the beach, from the boat. The cove was deserted, hidden from view by the rugged cliffs, and she stripped down to her bikini and stretched out on the rug, wriggling her shoulders in pleasure as the sun warmed her skin. Her eyelids felt heavy. She hadn't had much sleep the previous night, she thought wryly, recalling how Thanos had made love to her with all his considerable skill, so that she had climaxed three times before he had finally lost control and experienced his own shatter-ing release...

'I hope you applied plenty of sunscreen.'

Thanos's deep voice roused her from a shockingly erotic dream in which he was stroking his hands over her naked body. She glanced at her watch and saw that she had been asleep for almost an hour, and then let out a yelp as she felt something cold on her back.

'You don't want to burn,' he murmured, as he began to smooth lotion over her shoulders.

Tahlia's eyes flew open to see him lying on the rug beside her, propped up on one elbow, while he continued to smooth the cream onto her skin. He had stripped off his jeans and tee shirt and looked devastatingly sexy in a pair of navy swim-shorts, his skin gleaming like polished bronze in the sunshine. The rhythmic stroking of his hands on her back was wickedly sensuous, but she resisted the urge to turn over and pull him down on top of her.

'That should do,' she said in a strained voice, blushing furiously when she sat up and saw that her nipples had hardened and were straining beneath her Lycra bikini top. She felt his eyes slide down her body, and when she glanced at his face she was startled by the feral hunger blazing in his eyes.

'We'll spend an hour or so on the beach, and then return to the *Leandros* for a late lunch,' he said idly, brushing her hair over her shoulder and trailing his mouth up her neck.

'Good plan…' Tahlia drew a sharp breath when his teeth nipped her earlobe, sending a quiver of delicious sensation through her. 'How did your meeting go? Did you resolve the problems?'

'Concerning the Astraea, yes. But a new set of problems has arisen in the Caribbean. My hotel on St Lucia was damaged in a tropical storm that hit the island at the weekend. I'm flying out there immediately after the Artemis party.'

That meant that this time next week he would be on the other side of the world—and she would be back in England. Sudden tears blurred her vision, and she turned her head, pretending to stare at the sea while she fought to control her emotions. She had always known that their relationship was a temporary affair. The deal they had struck had been for her to spend one month with him as his mistress and soon their contract would be finished, leaving him free to continue with his own life.

Did he have a lover on St Lucia? Probably, she acknowledged bleakly. Ana, the Greek girl who had been helping her with the party arrangements, had said that Thanos had various mistresses around the world. A week from now he would most likely have forgotten her.

He moved his hands to her shoulders and gently tugged her towards him, but she stiffened, unable to bear the thought of making love with him while she was breaking up inside.

'I've been sunbathing for too long. I'm going to have a swim,' she choked. Tears were falling unchecked down her face, and with a muffled sob she jumped up and raced down the beach.

CHAPTER NINE

THE sea was shockingly cold on Tahlia's sun-warmed skin, but she tore through the shallows and dived beneath a wave so that her tears mingled with the spray. She struck out away from the shore, wanting to put as much distance as possible between her and Thanos, who was watching her broodingly from the beach. She swam until she was out of breath, and then flipped onto her back and allowed the waves to carry her. He was no longer sitting on the sand. She squinted against the sun, trying to spot him, and then gasped when strong arms suddenly closed around her.

'You frightened the life out of me,' she snapped, and she pushed against his chest, trying to force him to release her. But he merely tightened his grip and dragged her closer, so that she was trapped against his hard thighs. 'Let me go,' she cried frantically, hating her treacherous body as molten heat coursed through her veins, undermining her determination to resist him.

'I can't,' he growled savagely, tangling his fingers in her hair and lowering his head.

He captured her lips in a kiss of pure possession, thrusting his tongue deep into her mouth and exploring her with such erotic skill that she instantly melted. She was out of her depth

in more ways than one, she acknowledged, as she tried to stand and realised that the ocean floor was far beneath her. She had no choice but to cling to Thanos for support. And as she curled her arms around his neck she knew she had lost the battle. She wanted him, *needed* him to make love to her. And when she kissed him back with feverish passion and heard the low groan torn from his throat nothing mattered except her desperation for him to possess her.

He waded back to the shallows and lowered her onto the damp sand, not lifting his mouth from hers as he came down on top of her. She was a drug in his veins, and like an addict he could not resist her lure. His hunger for her consumed him utterly, Thanos acknowledged as he stared into her eyes, as blue and crystal-clear as the Aegean.

What was it about this woman that made him wish for something more than simply sexual satisfaction? He had been a fool once before, he reminded himself savagely. Yalena had ripped his heart out, and he had sworn never to open himself up to such pain ever again. He had thought that if he made Tahlia his mistress his obsession with her would eventually fade, leaving him free to continue with a life dominated by work and occasionally enlivened by meaningless affairs with women who meant nothing to him. But as he stared down at her and saw the shimmer of tears in her eyes it struck him that he was tired of his old life.

He kissed her throat, the fragile line of her collarbone, the creamy swell of her breast. Her nipples were jutting provocatively through the wet Lycra of her bikini top, and with a muffled oath he unfastened the strings around her neck and peeled the tiny triangles down, his body tautening as he revealed her breasts in all their naked beauty.

'You are exquisite,' he said hoarsely, and he lowered his head and took first one dusky tip and then its twin into his

mouth, smiling against her skin when she cried out and arched her hips in unmistakable invitation. 'I want you.' The admission was torn from him. His hands were clumsy as he dragged her bikini pants down her legs, and he struggled out of his shorts with an equal lack of finesse, his powerful erection nudging impatiently between her thighs. 'You want me too, don't you, Tahlia? We are both prisoners of the desire that thunders through our veins, and *this* is the only truth between us.'

He entered her with one savage thrust—then instantly stilled and cursed beneath his breath. 'Did I hurt you?' he demanded, his voice rasping with self-disgust at his brutality. But Tahlia's body was aroused and eagerly receptive, and she wrapped her legs around his back to prevent him from withdrawing.

'You couldn't hurt me,' she assured him softly, knowing that physically at least it was the truth. Her body had been designed for him, and she gloried in his wildfire passion that matched her own. She kissed him, telling him with her lips what she could not say out loud: that she was his for all time, and he was the keeper of her heart.

She felt him relax momentarily, but almost immediately his body was gripped with a different kind of tension as he moved, slowly at first, and then with increasing pace and strength, claiming her with a primitive hunger as he drove her higher and higher towards the climax her body craved. The sea lapped gently around them, and overhead the sun blazed in the dense blue sky. The haunting cry of a gull broke the still air, but Tahlia only was aware of Thanos's powerful body, driving into her with deep, steady strokes. She could feel his heart thudding in unison with her own, and she dug her heels into the sand, her body arching as the first spasms of exquisite pleasure ripped through her. Still he thrust, faster and faster, his breathing coming in ragged

groans as he took her to the edge, kept her poised there for timeless seconds and then with one final hard stroke sent them both into freefall.

I love you. She moved her lips over his sweat-slicked chest and breathed the words she could not utter. Soon he would dismiss her from his life, and somehow she would have to live without him. It would be a colourless existence, she thought, her heart contracting painfully. The lonely days and nights ahead would seem unbearable. But he was with her now, and she clung to him as if she could somehow imprint the feel of his body on hers for all time.

'Are you all right?' he asked roughly, lifting his head from her neck and smoothing her hair back from her face with a hand that shook slightly. 'As you may have noticed, you have a disastrous effect on my self-control.' His jaw tightened, and he added in a raw tone laced with self-disgust, 'I regret that with you I become a barbarian.'

Tenderness overflowed Tahlia's heart, and she stroked her hand down his cheek. 'I don't regret your passion. I love the way you make love to me,' she whispered shyly.

He stared down at her, the expression in his dark eyes unfathomable, and she was afraid she had revealed too much. When he rolled away from her and stood up she tensed, waiting for him to make some scornful remark, but he reached his hand out to help her to her feet and drew her into his arms.

'Come to St Lucia with me?'

She must have misheard him. A gull mewed in the sky above her, and her heart hammered in her chest as she stared at him wordlessly, searching for signs that he had been joking. But the expression in his eyes was deadly serious, and her heart beat faster. Why? She wanted to ask him. For how long? A week, a month? Did it matter when her whole being was crying out to agree? she thought

shakily. Nothing in life came with guarantees—losing Michael had taught her that. Why not live for the here and now, and enjoy an affair with him for however long it lasted? Was she brave enough?

'I can't,' she whispered. 'I need to go home, start looking for another job…'

'There would be no need for you to work while you are with me.'

Colour flared in her cheeks. 'I would *never* allow you to keep me. I pay my own way. It was only for my parents' sake that I…' She stumbled to a halt, shame sweeping over her at the memory of how she had sold herself to him.

'The reasons why I brought you to Mykonos are in the past,' Thanos told her fiercely. 'I want us to have a future—to enjoy our relationship for as long as either of us wants it to last.' He could not envisage a time when he would not desire her. She had captivated him like no other woman ever had. But the clichéd happy-ever-after? He'd seen too many relationships fail to contemplate commitment.

What would he say if she revealed that she wanted to be with him for ever? She stared up at his hard-boned face and acknowledged that he was as untameable as she had first thought, when she had looked across the art gallery in London and seen him. His early years had been tough, and had made him into a resolute, independent man who relied on no one, who forged his own destiny, and she doubted he would allow any woman to breach his defences.

'After St Lucia I was planning to take a break for a couple of weeks at my villa in Antigua. It's beautiful there, and we could spend some time away from everyday pressures—chill out and enjoy each other's company,' he murmured persuasively.

His mouth was a whisper away from hers, an unbearable temptation she did not have the strength to resist. 'That sounds

good.' Her breath feathered his lips. 'You work too hard. Maybe I can help you to relax?'

Laugher rumbled deep in his chest. 'The last thing I feel when I am with you, *agape*, is relaxed.' His smile faded and his eyes focused intently on her face. 'You'll come?'

She ignored the feeling that she was about to cast herself off a cliff without the assurance that a safety net would catch her, and nodded. 'Yes.'

The inherent tenderness of his kiss pierced her soul, and she kissed him back with all the emotion she could not reveal in words. When he swung her into his arms she clung to his shoulders and gave him a questioning look.

'You are very lovely, *agape mou*, but also very sandy.' He grinned, looking suddenly like the boy he had been many years ago, before he had been weighed down with responsibility. 'We need to swim.' He carried her into the sea, laughing as he lowered her into the waves, and splashed her until she dived into the crystal depths. The cool water felt sensuous on her naked body, and when Thanos caught her and held her against his chest she curled her arms around his neck, her laughter fading as he captured her mouth in a hungry kiss that revealed the urgency of his need to possess her.

Thanos propped himself up on one elbow and watched the early-morning sunlight dance across Tahlia's hair, turning it into a golden halo on the pillows. Her long lashes fanned her cheeks and her face was serene. His sleeping angel, he brooded, feeling a curious tugging sensation in his chest. But the feelings she evoked in him were far from pious, and he could not resist drawing back the sheet so that the sunlight gilded her slender limbs and her small, firm breasts. Her skin felt like satin beneath his fingertips as he trailed a path over her flat stomach, then moved lower to the triangle of tight gold

curls that hid her femininity. She was unutterably beautiful, and he hardened instantly as he slid his hand between her pale thighs and very gently parted her.

'Thanos?' Her lashes drifted upwards, her eyes still dazed with sleep.

'Who else were you expecting?' he demanded arrogantly.

Her smile stole his breath. 'You,' she whispered softly. 'Only you.'

She opened her mouth beneath his, welcoming the bold thrust of his tongue, and kissed him back with drowsy passion until he eased the pressure of his lips so that the kiss became a slow, sensual tasting, with an underlying tenderness that brought tears to Tahlia's eyes. Her breath hitched in her throat when he trailed his mouth down to her breast and teased her swollen nipple with his tongue, before administering the same delicious torture to its twin.

The feather-light brush of his lips on her inner thigh demolished her thought process—but something was niggling in her brain.

'Thanos! The party!'

'It's not until tonight, *agape*. I promise I'll let you up by then.'

'But there are things to do…'

She caught her breath as he lowered his head and his tongue probed delicately between her velvet folds. Moist heat pooled between her thighs and she instinctively spread her legs wider, gasping when he closed his lips around the sensitive nub of her clitoris. Sensation scorched her, and she whimpered with pleasure, desperate for him to continue his sorcery but unable to dismiss the voice in her head which pointed out that this was the day of the Artemis opening party, and she had planned to get up at dawn.

Frantically she dug her fingers into his luxuriant black hair and tugged. 'But, Thanos, I should…'

He lifted his head briefly and murmured, 'You want me to stop?'

'Yes.' She lifted her hips in mute supplication, groaning when his wickedly invasive tongue dipped between her silken folds. 'No… Don't stop—don't ever stop.'

She was trembling by the time he moved over her, and she sobbed his name as he penetrated her with deep, thrusting strokes, his movements slow and deliberate, demonstrating his complete control.

'This is all that matters, Tahlia *mou*,' he said roughly, his heart pounding so hard beneath his ribs that he felt as though he had run a marathon.

He was shocked to realise that he had spoken the truth. His need to make love to her was a driving force inside him: more important than his business, more important than the forthcoming party to celebrate the opening of his new hotel—even, he acknowledged grimly, more important than his sister. *Theos*, what was he thinking? But his powers of reasoning were slipping away, and he was conscious of nothing but the desperate clamouring of his body as he strove for the release he craved.

He slipped his hands beneath her bottom and lifted her hips, driving into her with faster and deeper strokes until she cried out. The exquisite sensation of her muscles contracting around him threatened to shatter his restraint.

'*Tahlia.*' He threw his head back, the cords on his neck straining as he fought for control. Sex had never been this good with any of his previous lovers. Only with Tahlia did he feel a sense of utter abandonment. With a harsh groan his control splintered and he shuddered, wave after wave of pleasure ripping through him until he collapsed onto her and closed his eyes, wondering why his heart ached every time he made her his.

In the aftermath he held her close, stroking his fingers

through her hair. She could stay here all day, Tahlia thought dreamily. But the Artemis party was important to him, and she wanted it to be perfect.

'Now I'll let you go to work,' he said with a grin, dropping a stinging kiss on her mouth as she gave a languorous stretch.

'Thank you, kind sir,' she teased with an impish smile before she walked unselfconsciously across the room to the *en suite* bathroom, aware of the heat in his dark eyes as he focused on her naked body.

'Have you decided what you're going to wear tonight?'

She paused in the doorway and glanced back at him, feeling the familiar dip in her stomach at the sight of his bronzed, muscular body stretched out indolently on the rumpled sheets. 'I'm not going to the party. I can't,' she continued quickly, when his brows lowered in a slashing frown. 'There will be huge media coverage tonight, and I don't want to risk being photographed with you. How would you explain my presence to Melina? It would be…awkward.' She bit her lip, rattled by his ominous silence. 'I'll ensure that all the preparations are in place, and tonight Ana will be on hand to deal with any last-minute problems.'

Thanos regarded her for a few moments, his expression unfathomable. 'Melina is my responsibility,' he said quietly. 'You don't have to worry about her. You *will* attend the party as my partner. That's an order, Tahlia,' he added forcefully, when she opened her mouth to argue. 'You've put in all the work, and tonight is your night as much as mine.' He jumped up from the bed and strode out of the room, reappearing seconds later, holding a flat box. 'I bought this for you to wear tonight.'

She gave him a startled glance, and then lifted the lid from the box and pushed aside the layers of filmy white tissue paper to reveal an ivory silk gown. With shaking fingers she took it from the box and caught her breath as she held it against her.

'Oh, Thanos…it's beautiful.' Her throat did not seem to want to work and her voice sounded distinctly rusty. The dress was exquisite: a floor-length silk sheath, covered in layers of fragile chiffon and embellished with tiny crystals and pearls on its narrow shoulder-straps and around a sweetheart neckline. 'It's a fairytale dress,' she whispered, dropping her gaze from him so that he would not see her sudden rush of tears.

He slid his hand beneath her chin and tilted her face to his. 'Tonight you will be my princess, *agape mou*.'

Her smile tugged at his insides, and the ache in his gut intensified when she reached up and brushed her lips over his in a feather-light caress that pierced him with its poignant sweetness. They needed to talk, he acknowledged as she walked into the bathroom. There were things he needed to say, to tell her. But he could not forget the original terms of the bargain they had made, and he wondered if he was a fool to hope that his money was not the only reason she gave her body to him every night with a tender passion that stirred his soul.

Tahlia was confident that all the preparations she had made over the past three weeks would ensure that the Artemis opening night party would be a success, but as she had feared there were still unexpected problems which required her attention. She spent the day making last-minute calls, organising media coverage, and attempting to meet the demands of the celebrity guests. It was early evening by the time she returned to the suite, and after a quick shower she blowdried her hair and applied minimal make-up—mascara on her lashes to emphasise the deep blue of her eyes, and a pearly pink gloss on her lips—before she stepped into the dress Thanos had chosen for her.

It was from a well-known design house and must have cost a fortune. She felt uncomfortable that he had spent so

much money on her when he was already paying a huge sum for Reynolds Gems—but he had been adamant that he wanted her to wear it tonight, and she would have worn a wetsuit and flippers if it had pleased him, she acknowledged ruefully.

The door opened and he stepped into the bedroom, halting abruptly when she spun round to face him. 'You take my breath away, *agape*,' he said at length, sweeping his eyes over her in a lingering appraisal which encompassed her amber-gold hair, falling in a silky curtain around her shoulders, and the ivory dress that skimmed her slender figure.

He walked over to her and withdrew a slim velvet box from his jacket pocket. 'This will complement the dress perfectly,' he murmured, lifting out a necklace of creamy pearls inter-linked with glittering diamonds. 'It is a gift in thanks for the hours of hard work you have spent organising the party.'

'Thanos, I can't accept it,' Tahlia said faintly when he turned her to face the mirror. She stared at their twin reflec-tions: the tall, impossibly handsome man in a black dinner jacket, and the woman at his side wearing a couture gown and an exquisite necklace around her throat. 'You don't need to give me presents. I've enjoyed working at the Artemis.'

'Even so, you deserve a break. I will have to spend some time dealing with the problems at my hotel on St Lucia, but our trip to Antigua is purely for pleasure—or impurely,' he murmured wickedly, his eyes gleaming with sensual promise. 'I admit I am impatient to have you to myself, without other distractions, *agape mou*.'

His smile tugged at her heart, and when he lowered his mouth to hers, tears pricked her eyes at the sweetness of his kiss. She'd thought she had imagined the feeling of unity between them every time they made love, and had told herself she was a fool to hope that the Greek words he murmured in the aftermath of their passion meant that she was special to him.

He had once stated that love was an illusion, but the erratic thud of his heart beneath her fingertips was excitingly real.

'We need to talk,' he said quietly, when at last he broke the kiss and stared down at her flushed face. His heart turned over when her lashes swept down a fraction too late to disguise the emotion blazing in her eyes.

'But there's no time now.'

As if on cue, someone knocked on the door of the suite and his mouth tightened.

'That's probably Ana,' Tahlia said huskily. 'I'll just get my purse.'

The phone on the bedside table rang and she picked it up, frowning as the receptionist relayed a message.

'I have a call from my mother,' she told Thanos in a puzzled tone. When she had first arrived on Mykonos she had contacted her parents to explain that she was staying in Greece with a friend for a few weeks, and had given the phone number of the Artemis. An inexplicable feeling of dread coiled in her stomach. 'I hope she's okay.'

'I'll go down with Ana while you take the call,' he said, striding towards the door. 'We're not due to greet our guests for another twenty minutes.'

Tahlia watched him walk out of the room and heard him speak to Ana, followed by the snick of the door as he left the suite. 'Mum?' she gripped the phone as the sound of sobbing met her ears. 'What's wrong?'

'Oh, Tahlia, I don't understand anything,' Vivienne choked incoherently. 'Your father and I arrived back from Cornwall today to find a letter from the bank saying that Carlton House is to be repossessed. Your father admitted that he hadn't paid off the mortgage he took out to finance Reynolds Gems, and we're behind with the payments. He phoned some people— Vantage something or other…'

Vivienne paused and took a shuddering breath. 'He assured me that Vantage had agreed to buy Reynolds, and we would have the money for the house. But when he finished speaking to the CEO he was as pale as a ghost. It seems that Vantage was never interested in Reynolds. The parent company— whatever that is—refused permission for the buy-out. Dad had already assured the bank that Vantage were going to purchase Reynolds Gems, and that he would immediately clear the mortgage. But the bank checked with Vantage, and when they discovered the sale wasn't going ahead they called in the loan on Carlton.' Vivienne's voice broke. 'When your father heard that he collapsed.'

'What do you mean, he collapsed?' Tahlia demanded shakily. 'Mum…?'

'He's all right,' her mother assured her. 'Hobson called an ambulance, and the hospital did lots of checks on his heart, but all the results were fine. They say he's just suffering from extreme stress. Tahlia, I don't know what to do.'

Her mother wept, and the fear in her voice tore at Tahlia's heart.

'The bailiffs are coming at midday tomorrow to evict us, and they will seize any of our possessions that are still in the house. I don't know where to begin with the packing.' Her voice was shrill with panic. 'Our whole life is in this house.'

'Mum, you don't need to pack,' Tahlia assured her mother swiftly. 'There's been some sort of mistake. Vantage Investments definitely agreed to buy Reynolds. I'm in contact with someone at the parent company—Savakis Enterprises.' She paused and closed her eyes briefly, wondering what her mother would say if she revealed just how closely her body had been in contact with Thanos's muscular frame every night for the past month. 'Don't cry. I'll sort everything out— okay?' she said softly. 'And then I'll come home.'

It must be a mistake, she told herself frantically as she dragged out her suitcase and started to fling her belongings into it. A misunderstanding between the bank and Vantage seemed the most likely explanation. She took a deep breath, forcing herself to calm down. She would explain the situation to Thanos, and he would resolve the problem—whatever it was.

Unless *he* was the problem? a little voice whispered in her head. No, of course he wasn't. They had made a deal, and he had promised that the buy-out of Reynolds Gems would go ahead. Her relationship with Thanos was no longer based on his desire for revenge, and there was no reason why he should have reneged on his promise. She trusted him, she assured herself as she snatched up her purse, desperate to hurry down to the lobby where he was waiting for her.

But she could not dismiss the heavy sense of foreboding in the pit of her stomach, and after a moment's hesitation she turned back into the room. The likelihood that Vantage's CEO, Steven Holt, would still be in his office late on a Friday evening was remote, but if she could just speak to him first…

The phone rang several times, and she was just about to cut the call when a woman answered. 'Mr Holt is unavailable,' she said tersely. 'I'll put you through to Mark Lloyd.'

Five minutes later an impatient-sounding male voice interrupted Tahlia's frantic explanation of the reason for her call. 'Miss Reynolds, I am an executive director at Vantage Investments and I assure you I am not mistaken. It is true that we were briefly interested in buying your company, but the idea was vetoed by our parent company on the direct orders of the head of Savakis Enterprises.'

'But Mr Savakis promised me…' Tahlia insisted desperately, gripping the phone so hard that her knuckles whitened. 'You *must* be mistaken…'

'I think you'll find that it is *you* who have made a mistake,'

the voice on the other end of the line said coldly. 'There is not, and never was, any deal to buy Reynolds Gems. Now, it is late, Miss Reynolds, and I would like to go home. So unless there is anything else…?'

'No…nothing else.' Tahlia's throat felt as though she had swallowed glass, and she had to force the words out. 'Thank you for clarifying the situation, Mr Lloyd.'

She replaced the receiver and sank down onto the bed. The room spun alarmingly. Surely she was not going to do something as melodramatic as faint? Bile rose in her throat and she hunched forward so that the blood rushed to her head. She couldn't faint; she had to get back to Carlton House and her parents before the bailiffs threw them onto the street.

Footsteps sounded on the marble floor, and she jerked her head round as the bedroom door opened.

'What's going on?' Thanos demanded, his eyes narrowing on her white face. 'Why haven't you come down? The guests are gathering in the lobby, waiting for the party to begin, and I want you at my side. Damn it, Tahlia,' he said explosively, when she stared at him with dull eyes. 'What's the matter with you?' He could not forget the anguished moan he'd heard as he had entered the suite. 'Are you ill?'

The pain in her heart was sheer agony—but there could still be a simple explanation for the news she had just heard, Tahlia reminded herself. Slowly she got up from the bed and faced him, her eyes locked on his face.

'Tell me, Thanos, did you ever intend to buy Reynolds Gems? Or did you bring me to Greece and make me your mistress—allow me to believe my father's problems would be solved—while all along you *knew* you had told Vantage Investments not to proceed with the buy-out?'

For a split second something indefinable flared in his eyes, before the mask fell and his expression became unfathomable.

But that tiny hesitation had told Tahlia everything—and her heart splintered.

Fool, a voice in her head taunted. Seven months ago she had believed James Hamilton when he had told her that he loved her. She had trusted him implicitly. But he had deceived her as cruelly as he had deceived his wife, and she had vowed never to give her love or trust as easily again. But here she was, with another man, in another hotel bedroom, utterly destroyed by the realisation that Thanos had lied to her. When would she learn that men either abandoned you, or lied and cheated for their own ends, and that they were not worth the heartbreak they caused? she wondered bitterly.

CHAPTER TEN

'MY MOTHER phoned to tell me that the bank has taken possession of Carlton House,' Tahlia told Thanos tensely. 'The bailiffs are due to arrive tomorrow to evict them.'

He frowned. 'Banks do not usually issue a repossession order unless there are serious mortgage arrears on a property.'

'Dad hasn't kept up with the payments on Carlton for months,' Tahlia said heavily. 'All his money has been tied up in the company. I *told* you all this,' she flung at him bitterly. 'You *knew* my parents were in danger of losing their home.'

'I had not realised that it was quite so imminent.'

'No—I suppose you thought you could string me along for a while longer before you revealed what a lying bastard you are.' Tahlia felt a curious sense of detachment as she watched his mouth tighten with anger. 'My father informed the bank that Vantage was buying Reynolds Gems, and that as soon as the sale went through he would pay off the mortgage on Carlton House. But when the bank checked with Vantage they were told that no sale had ever been agreed. Ten minutes ago I spoke to Mark Lloyd at Vantage, who verified that the buy-out had been vetoed by none other than the head of Vantage Investments' parent company, Savakis Enterprises—in other words, by *you*.'

In the simmering silence following her accusation, his lack of denial felt like a knife through her heart.

Tears scalded her throat, but she forced herself to swallow them. 'You've destroyed my parents' lives, and I will *never* forgive you,' she told him, her voice shaking with emotion.

Thanos moved towards her, but halted abruptly when she flinched away from him. 'You're jumping to conclusions,' he said tersely. 'If you would give me a chance to explain—'

'In the same way that you allowed me to defend myself against your accusations that I had deliberately stolen James Hamilton from your sister, you mean?' she interrupted in a brittle voice. 'You refused to listen to me, and in your misguided quest for revenge you demanded that I became your mistress. But worst of all,' she said brokenly, tears slipping down her cheeks, 'you lied to me.'

'Listen to me,' he said urgently. 'I admit that when I first brought you to Greece I had no intention of bailing your father out of his financial mess. My sister had suffered appalling injuries, and as you know I believed you were partly responsible for her accident. The newspapers were full of reports about your wild partying, and your penchant for stealing other women's husbands, and I wanted to hurt you as I believed you had hurt Melina—' His mobile rang. With a muttered curse he answered it, and snapped impatiently, 'I'll be five minutes. Tell the bar staff to serve more champagne to the guests.'

He raked his hand through his hair and stared at Tahlia, frustration etched on his face when she glared at him. 'All that changed when I took you to bed. Sex with you was an incredible experience. I had never known such intense pleasure before,' he admitted harshly. 'And when I discovered that you were a virgin, that I had completely misjudged you...' His voice deepened with an emotion Tahlia could not define. 'I

immediately phoned Steven Holt to tell him that I had changed my mind and wanted Vantage to proceed with the buy-out of Reynolds Gems.'

Tahlia recalled the phone call she'd made before Thanos had come back to the suite, and shook her head. 'I don't believe you,' she said dully. 'Mark Lloyd was adamant that Vantage have no plans to buy Reynolds Gems. One of you must be lying—and I don't think it's him.'

'You're calling me a liar?' Thanos snapped icily, his eyes darkening with anger.

His outrage, after he had refused to believe she was telling the truth about James, was almost funny—but Tahlia doubted she would ever smile again.

'I'm not sure why Mark Lloyd is involved. I left instructions with Steven Holt,' he said tersely. 'There has obviously been a misunderstanding somewhere along the line.'

Tahlia closed her suitcase and reached up to unfasten the pearl necklace that he had placed around her neck earlier. 'Mr Lloyd said that *I* had made a mistake, and he's right,' she said quietly. 'I mistakenly thought you were a man of honour, but you are a liar and a cheat, and I hope I never see you again for as long as I live.'

'*Theos*, Tahlia. You don't really mean that.' Sharp knives were ripping his insides to shreds, and he gripped her arm and swung her round to face him. 'Tell me the truth. Is the deal we made when you came to my hotel in London a month ago the only reason you have given yourself to me so passionately night after night?'

In the silence that trembled between them, Mark Lloyd's voice echoed inside Tahlia's head. *'There is not, and never was, any deal to buy Reynolds Gems.'*

How could her heart still ache for Thanos after the way he had tricked her? Tahlia wondered desperately. She must be the

biggest fool on the planet. But at least she retained sufficient pride to hide her stupidity from him.

'What other reason could there have been?' she demanded coolly. 'I believed you were paying me to be your mistress.'

His eyes were so hard and cold that she took a hasty step backwards.

'I must congratulate you on your exemplary performance every night,' he said, in a dangerously soft voice that sent a trickle of ice down her spine. 'Perhaps you should consider whoring as a new career.'

She closed her eyes briefly as pain tore through her. 'I have to go,' she muttered, grabbing her case and heading for the door. 'I need to get back to my parents.'

Thanos strolled towards her, reminding her of a sleek, dark panther stalking its prey. 'Aren't you forgetting something?'

'I put the necklace on the bedside table. You saw me.'

He smiled pleasantly, like a wolf before it sprang for the kill. 'Not the necklace—the dress.'

'Oh.' She shook her head, feeling an idiot. The old skirt and top she'd left out to travel in—*her* clothes, not the ones he had bought her—were on the bed. 'I'll get changed in the bathroom.'

'I'd like it back *now*.'

The gleam in his eyes warned her that he would have no compunction in stripping the dress from her body. She was breaking up inside, but she would not let him see it. 'What is this, Thanos? Last-minute titillation?' she demanded scornfully, and she reached behind her and slid the zip down her spine. He must have known the dress did not require her to wear a bra, but she refused to drop her gaze from his as she allowed the silk gown to slither to the floor.

Dull colour scorched his cheekbones. 'We both know I could take you right now and you would do nothing to stop me,' he said roughly.

There was little point in denying it when her nipples were

jutting eagerly towards him, begging for the tender ministrations of his hands and mouth. But she tore her eyes from him and managed a nonchalant shrug. 'So you press all the right buttons. You're a fantastic stud, Thanos.'

She swung away from him and clumsily dragged on her skirt and tee shirt, hating the way her breasts were tingling in anticipation. She would *never* allow him to touch her again, would *never* make love with him again and know the indescribable pleasure that she had only ever experienced with him. Her eyes ached with tears as she stumbled to the door, but there was one last thing she needed to know.

'How long had you anticipated our relationship lasting after the trip to Antigua?'

Thanos stared at the streaks of tears and mascara running down her face and felt an overwhelming urge to pull her into his arms and kiss her, until she acknowledged that what they had shared this past month was too good to throw away. But obviously she did not think so, he brooded bitterly. She had come to him in London because she'd needed his money to help her father, and no doubt she had agreed to go to the Caribbean with him because she enjoyed the benefits associated with being the mistress of a millionaire. She was no better than Yalena, and the countless other women who saw dollar signs when they looked at him. He was better off without her.

'I hadn't planned on it lasting at all. I'm not a fan of commitment,' he drawled sardonically. 'A few weeks of sun, sea and sex are all I have ever wanted from any woman, and you are no different.'

'I see.' The tiny flame of hope inside her died, but she could not drag her eyes from him as she committed to memory his sculpted features and his hard body sheathed in the superbly cut black dinner suit—before she turned and walked out of his life.

* * *

By the time Tahlia reached the airport she had missed the last plane to London, but she was so desperate to leave Mykonos that she caught the next flight to Athens and, after spending a sleepless night in the terminal there, managed to book a seat on the first flight to Gatwick the following morning. As the taxi turned through the gates of Carlton House she half expected to see the bailiffs waiting on the drive, but to her relief there was just her father's car parked by the front steps.

'They're not here yet, then?' she murmured, when her mother opened the door and immediately burst into tears at the sight of her. 'Where's Hobson?'

'Unpacking,' Vivienne mumbled, wiping her eyes.

'Unpacking? But…I thought you had to be ready to leave by midday?'

'No.' Vivienne shook her head, looking as dazed as Tahlia felt. 'We can stay. Apparently the money for Reynolds Gems was paid into our bank account late last night, and first thing this morning your father cleared the mortgage. I don't pretend to understand what's going on, but Dad says that everything has been sorted out. Isn't it wonderful, darling?' She gave Tahlia a watery smile. 'The last twenty-four hours have been a rollercoaster.'

'It's brilliant news,' Tahlia said slowly.

Why had Thanos done it? she wondered. Had she damaged his pride when she had proved him to be a liar? She longed to send the money straight back to him, but Carlton House was saved, and her mother was smiling again, and that was really all that mattered, she told herself wearily.

'How's Dad?'

'Relieved—as you can imagine—and resting. He's admitted he hasn't slept properly for months.' Vivienne sighed. 'I wish he had told me about our financial problems rather than going through all that worry on his own.'

'He was trying to protect you,' Tahlia said softly. Her parents' love for each other was as strong as it had been on the day they had married. Some marriages lasted. But Thanos thought that marriage was an outdated institution, and she could not believe she had been so stupid as to hope that he might have begun to care for her a little.

'I have another piece of news,' her mother said gently. 'Aunt George passed away in her sleep two days ago. She was ninety-two, you know. Dear Georgie—she told everyone she was five years younger.'

Charlie stalked into the room, his tail held high, and sprang onto Tahlia's lap, purring loudly when she buried her face in his ginger fur.

Vivienne patted her shoulder and reached for the box of tissues. 'I'm sorry, darling. I know how fond of her you were,' she murmured, unaware that Tahlia's tears were not just for her aunt, but for an enigmatic Greek man who had stolen her heart.

A week later, Tahlia stared at the cheque on the desk in front of her. Then she lifted her gaze to the family's elderly solicitor, Harold Wimbourne, her eyes wide with shock. 'I had no idea Aunt George was so wealthy,' she said faintly.

'Miss Prentice was a shrewd investor on the stockmarket,' the solicitor explained. He cleared his throat and added conspiratorially, 'I believe she also made a fortune from betting on the horses. Your aunt bequeathed to you her flat in Pimlico, and various other assets detailed in her will. She also set up a trust fund which was to mature on your twenty-fifth birthday or on her death—whichever happened first. As trustee of the fund, I have the happy task of handing you that cheque.' He chuckled. 'I can see it has come as a bit of a shock. I don't suppose you have any idea yet about what you'd like to do with the money?'

'A bit of a shock' was an understatement, Tahlia thought numbly as the row of noughts swam in front of her. She gave Harold a faint smile and said steadily, 'Actually, I know exactly what I'm going to do with it. I assume I can spend it straight away?'

'Oh, yes. It's yours to spend in whichever way you choose, my dear. I can advise you on secure investments, and so on, but I'm sure Georgina wanted you to have fun with it.'

Tahlia could not imagine a time when she would ever have fun again, but she was grateful to her aunt for giving her the means to restore a little of her pride. Immediately she sent Thanos a cheque for half the amount he had paid for Reynolds Gems, and an assurance that she would send him the remainder once she had sold the flat.

You paid for my body and treated me as your whore, but now I am buying back my self-respect, she scribbled furiously. *I wonder if you will ever be able to regain yours, Thanos?*

But he had not really treated her like a whore, she acknowledged honestly, as the week dragged into the next and the pain of missing him grew worse with every day. He'd accepted that she had not known James Hamilton was married to his sister, and, with his reason for wanting revenge no longer valid, it did not make sense that he had double-crossed her—especially as the day after she had walked out on him he had paid her father for Reynolds Gems.

Doubt gnawed at her as she recalled his insistence that he *had* instructed the CEO of Vantage Investments to buy Reynolds. Maybe she had been too hasty when she'd refused to listen to him? But she had been so afraid that he had deceived her, as James had done, and so unbearably hurt at the idea that he had tricked her. And then he had revealed that he had only invited her to his villa in Antigua to be his convenient sex partner. She had been kidding herself that their

relationship might develop into something deeper, she acknowledged miserably. She'd known of his reputation as a commitment-phobic playboy, and it was her own fault that her heart was shattered beyond repair.

Thanos watched the rain bounce off the windscreen, and wondered how much longer he would have to sit outside Tahlia's flat waiting for her to return. He would sit here for the rest of his life if necessary, he thought grimly, but when he glanced at his watch and saw that barely five minutes had crawled past since he had last checked his frustration escalated.

He had received her cheque a week ago, and since then it had been burning a hole in his pocket—along with her terse note questioning whether he would ever be able to regain his self-respect. Anger surged through him, but he fought to control it. He had been angry on the night of the Artemis party, when she had accused him of tricking her about buying Reynolds Gems. Fury had burned in his gut that she did not trust him. But later, when his temper had cooled, he'd conceded that he had done little to earn her trust. He had believed every damnable lie the tabloid press had written about her, and forced her to become his mistress without giving her a chance to defend herself. His treatment of her had been unforgivable, he thought wearily. He was probably wasting his time sitting here, but he had discovered over the past two weeks that, as he could neither work nor sleep, he had a lot of time to waste.

A figure came into view, head bowed against the rain, the pale red hair instantly recognizable. The dejected slump of her shoulders tugged at Thanos's insides. She'd lost weight, he noted, his mouth tightening. She looked achingly fragile, and even more beautiful than the woman who had haunted him night and day for the past two weeks. He longed to snatch her

into his arms and simply hold her, but as his eyes lingered on her breasts, clearly outlined beneath her damp top, he acknowledged that holding her would not be enough. His body stirred, but he ruthlessly ignored the sharp clamour of desire. There were things he must say, and this time he was determined she would listen to him.

Tahlia dumped the bag of groceries on the kitchen table and pushed her wet hair impatiently out of her eyes as she unpacked a week's worth of cat food. 'At least one of us still has an appetite,' she muttered, when Charlie wound around her ankles.

The doorbell pealed and she groaned, tempted to ignore it. Although she had not confided the full details of her relationship with Thanos to her friends, they had guessed that she was suffering from 'man trouble' and were running a campaign to drag her out of the depression that some days seemed to swamp her. She knew they meant well, but she seriously doubted she would ever get over him, and she preferred to be on her own.

The bell rang again and, cursing beneath her breath, she walked down the hall and opened the door.

'Hello, Tahlia.'

The gravelly, accented voice was so poignantly evocative that tears stung her eyes. She had experienced the same peculiar rushing noise in her ears on the night she had discovered his deception, but this time she could not control the feeling that she was on a carousel, spinning faster and faster. It was a relief when blackness claimed her.

She opened her eyes to find herself lying on the sofa, Thanos's furious face inches from hers as he crouched beside her. '*Theos*, why haven't you been eating?' he demanded roughly.

'I do eat,' she lied, forcing herself to sit up, relieved that the walls were no longer revolving.

'You're too thin,' he insisted harshly, 'and too pale; there are shadows beneath your eyes.

'So? I haven't been sleeping too well.' She would rather die than have him guess that she was pining away for him. 'I've been having bad dreams,' she told him pointedly, tilting her chin. 'Why are you here, Thanos?'

He stood up, but to her dismay settled himself next to her on the sofa—so close that she was conscious of his hard thigh muscle pressing against her jeans. 'Firstly, I want an answer,' he said coolly. 'Are you pregnant? I did not use protection when I made love to you on the beach on Santorini,' he said, when she gave him a startled look.

She made her decision in a split second. 'No,' she said quickly, praying he had not heard the faint tremor in her voice.

When he made no reply she risked another glance, but his face was expressionless. 'I see,' he murmured at last. 'Then that leads us to the second reason for my visit—which is to return this.' He withdrew the cheque she had sent him from his jacket pocket and held it out to her.

'Keep it,' she said sharply. 'I know you transferred the money for Reynolds Gems into my father's account the day after I left Mykonos, but now I'm repaying every penny. My family are no longer indebted to you.'

He tore the cheque into pieces with tightly leashed savagery and said harshly, 'When I first met you I believed you had seduced my sister's husband as callously as my father's mistress had wrecked my parents' marriage. I could see little to differentiate you from Wendy, and I transferred the hatred I had felt for her onto you.'

She almost preferred his lies to his brutal honesty, Tahlia thought numbly.

A tremor of sheer misery ran through her, causing Thanos to frown. 'You should change out of your wet clothes,' he said

abruptly. When she shook her head he gave an impatient sigh and shrugged out of his jacket, draping it around her shoulders. The leather collar was as soft as butter against her cheek, and the silk lining carried the lingering scent of his cologne. His compassion, when seconds before he had been comparing her to his father's mistress, twisted the knife in Tahlia's heart. She wished he would just say what he had come to say and leave—before she broke down in front of him.

'While we were on Mykonos I was heavily involved with the negotiations to buy the Ambassador Hotel in London,' he said quietly. 'And of course the Artemis party was looming. Vantage Investments *is* a subsidiary company of Savakis Enterprises, but it functions as an independent company. After I had instructed Steven Holt to proceed with buying Reynolds Gems I had no reason to contact him again. I was unaware until the night you left Mykonos that Steven's wife had gone into premature labour the day after I had spoken to him. Their son was born twelve weeks early, and Steven has barely left the hospital since the birth. I understand that the baby is still in the special care unit, but he is now thriving,' he murmured, when Tahlia looked horrified.

'Perhaps understandably, Steven forgot to pass on the message to Mark Lloyd about my change of decision over the purchase of Reynolds Gems. Once I discovered what had happened I immediately transferred money from my personal account to your father's bank.'

Without Thanos's swift intervention her parents would have lost their home, Tahlia acknowledged, guilt sweeping through her when she recalled how she had accused him of being a liar.

He stood up and walked over to the window, staring at the rain lashing against the glass. 'If I am honest, I knew almost from the start that you were nothing like Wendy—or the

vacuous bimbo portrayed by certain tabloids,' Thanos contin-
ued tensely. 'You were gentle and kind.' He glanced dispar-
agingly at Charlie, who was curled up in an armchair like a
fluffy ginger cushion. 'You rescued stray animals. I wanted
to hate you,' he said roughly, 'but you got under my skin and
I discovered that I enjoyed being with you. I wanted to come
after you the night you left, but I couldn't leave Ana to cope
alone at the party—and I was furious that, although the month
that we had been lovers had been the happiest of my life, you
clearly did not feel the same way. You did not trust me. The
next morning I learned that the damage to my hotel on St
Lucia was more serious than I had first realised, and that
several of my staff had been injured in the storm. I had no
choice but to fly immediately to the Caribbean.'

Tahlia could think of nothing to say as she absorbed his
words, and a tense silence quivered between them before
Thanos finally spoke again.

'I'm sorry for the way I treated you when we first met. I
blamed you for hurting my sister, and in my damnable desire
for revenge I stole your innocence.'

The bleakness in his eyes tore at Tahlia's heart, and even
in the midst of her misery she wanted to absolve him. 'Neither
of us could deny the sexual chemistry between us,' she said
softly. 'I wanted you to make love to me.'

She got to her feet and held out his jacket, praying he
would take the hint and go, but he strode towards her, his eyes
blazing, and threw the jacket carelessly onto the sofa.

'I dishonoured you,' he said harshly. 'And the only way I
can try to make amends is to marry you.'

'What?' Tahlia's jaw dropped, and as the room tilted alarm-
ingly she was afraid she was going to faint again.

Thanos was deadly serious, she realised as she stared at his
taut face, his skin stretched tightly over the razor-sharp edges

of his cheekbones. He was impossibly beautiful, and equally impossible to understand—although in a way she did understand his reasoning. At heart he was a traditional Greek male and an honourable man. His self-respect had been badly damaged by what he perceived as the wrong he had done to her. But *marriage*! That was taking contrition a step too far.

'I don't want to marry you,' she said quietly.

Thanos felt as though he had received a hammer-blow to his heart. It was the same pain he had experienced when Yalena had broken their engagement and revealed that she had been sleeping with Takis; the same pain that had ripped through him when he had seen Melina for the first time after the accident, when she had looked so tiny amid all the wires and tubes which had been keeping her alive.

'You must know I would never do anything to hurt you,' he said roughly. 'And I am a wealthy man—you would not want for anything.'

Dear heaven, this was torture. Didn't he realise that her resolve was perilously close to crumbling? That she longed to snatch this chance of happiness even though she knew she would never be truly happy when he did not love her?

'But I would want something that you cannot give me, Thanos,' she whispered, forcing the words past the constriction in her throat. 'I would want love. I don't care about your wealth or the material things you can give me. I would marry you if you were a goat-herd on Agistri if you loved me as much I love you.'

Tears blurred her vision, so she felt rather than saw him move, but she guessed that her admission would have him striding out of the door without a backward glance. She was unprepared for the strong arms that closed around her, and she gave a startled cry when the walls revolved again as he lifted her and carried her down the hall.

'Thanos, what are you doing?' she choked, unable to stem the tears that had been gathering since he had first appeared on her doorstep.

He kicked open her bedroom door and lowered her gently onto the bed. Her heart turned over when she saw that his thick eyelashes were spiked with moisture.

'Thanos?' She raised a trembling hand to his cheek, her eyes widening at the unguarded expression in his eyes as he knelt over her.

'You love me?' he said in a strained tone, all his arrogance stripped away, leaving him achingly vulnerable.

It was small wonder that he sounded disbelieving, Tahlia thought gently. Years ago he had been so cruelly rejected by the woman he had loved. Since then he had shouldered the responsibility of bringing up his sister and building a hugely successful company, and she guessed that deep down he had never come to terms with being abandoned by his both his parents. For most of his life he had felt alone.

Her pride suddenly seemed unimportant—especially when he was staring at her as if her answer mattered desperately to him. 'I love you with all my heart,' she assured him quietly.

He closed his eyes briefly and drew a ragged breath. 'You are my world, Tahlia *mou*,' he said simply, his voice shaking with emotion. 'And I will love you and cherish you until I die. You stole my heart, and now it is yours for ever.' He kissed away the tears slipping down her face. 'Does knowing that I love you make you cry?' he murmured, and the shadow of un-certainty in his eyes tugged at her heart.

'Only because I have wanted you to love me for so long and I can't believe it has happened,' she said shakily.

'Believe it,' he bade her urgently, taking her hand and holding it over his heart, so she could feel its thunderous beat pass through her fingertips into her veins. 'The month we

spent together on Mykonos was the happiest I have ever known, and day by day my feelings for you grew more intense. Now you know that I love you with my heart and soul and everything I am, will you do me the honour of marrying me, *agape mou*?'

She saw the love that blazed in his eyes, and finally began to hope that everything really would be all right.

'Melina...?' she queried anxiously.

'Melina knows how I feel about you and she gives us her blessing. In fact, she says if you don't agree to be my wife she'll catch the next plane to England and try to persuade you herself,' he quipped lightly, his smile not disguising the fierce tension that still gripped him. 'She's looking forward to meeting you and getting to know you properly.'

That left one last doubt, Tahlia acknowledged, catching her lower lip with her teeth. 'I love you, and I would love to marry you.' She pressed her finger to his mouth when he bent his head to kiss her. 'But I have a confession. I lied to you, Thanos.' He held her gaze steadily, and she took a deep breath. 'When you asked if I was pregnant I denied it. I didn't want you to come back to me out of duty.'

She suddenly felt ridiculously shy, and the look of dawning comprehension in his eyes gave no clue to how he felt.

'Tahlia?'

'I going to have your baby,' she said softly. 'Are you...are you pleased?' She watched his smile widen to a grin that made him look almost boyish, and her heart overflowed with her love for him.

'*Pleased* is such an inadequate word to express how I feel, *agape*,' he said deeply, his voice cracking with the emotion. 'Overjoyed is better—and thankful, humbled that I have found you, *pedhaki mou*. And most of all determined that you will never have reason to doubt my love for you and our child.'

He bent his head again and claimed her mouth in a kiss that spoke of passion and desire and a powerful, abiding love that would last a lifetime.

Tahlia responded to him with everything that was in her heart, so that the kiss became a sensual feast that fanned the flames of their mutual hunger. Their clothes were a barrier he swiftly removed, and she cried his name as he cupped her breasts and teased each rosy tip with his tongue. He groaned when she traced her fingers over his body, and fought for control when she encircled him and caressed him until he could not wait a second longer.

'I love you,' he whispered as he gently parted her and discovered the drenching sweetness of her arousal.

She was the love of his life, and he told her so as he entered her and joined their bodies as one, moving with exquisite care until passion overwhelmed them both and they reached the heights together before tumbling back to earth to lie replete in each other's arms, their hearts beating in unison.

EPILOGUE

THEY were married six weeks later, in the village church where Tahlia had been christened, and they held a reception for family and friends in a huge marquee on the lawn at Carlton House.

Melina was well enough to fly over from America, accompanied by a tall, handsome doctor. She revealed that Daniel Sanders had asked her to marry him.

'We've both fallen in love with the right man this time,' she murmured to Tahlia as the guests gathered on the driveway to watch the bride and groom depart for their honeymoon in Antigua.

Tahlia had felt nervous about meeting Thanos's sister, but Melina had quickly assured her that she did not blame anyone but her ex-husband for the collapse of her marriage.

'Do you think Thanos approves of Daniel?' Melina asked anxiously, as Tahlia was about to climb into the limousine next to her new husband.

'He likes him very much,' Tahlia reassured her. 'But I can't believe you want me to be your bridesmaid. My obstetrician has already said that the baby is bigger than average. I'm going to look like a whale in six months' time.'

'What was your whispered conversation with Melina about?' Thanos murmured when the car finally sped away.

Tahlia gave her parents one last wave and turned back to smile at him. 'She wanted to know if you approve of Daniel—I told her that you did.'

'I think he'll make her happy.' Thanos lifted Tahlia's hand to his mouth and pressed his lips to the plain gold wedding band that he had slipped onto her finger, next to her diamond solitaire engagement ring, during the ceremony. 'And I will spend the rest of my life making *you* happy, Tahlia *mou*,' he told her seriously. '*S'agapo*. I love you.'

The raw emotion evident in his dark eyes brought a lump to her throat, and her mouth trembled slightly as she kissed him. 'And I love you. Always and for ever.'

They spent a blissful month in Antigua, before returning to Thanos's stunning villa in a leafy suburb of Athens. Tahlia's parents were frequent visitors, and Thanos refused to be away from home for more than one night, ruthlessly delegating business trips to his executives.

By the end of her pregnancy Tahlia was as big as she had predicted. 'You don't look like a whale. You are my beautiful and very pregnant wife,' Thanos told her softly when she bemoaned her expanding waistline, 'and I love you more than words can say.'

He said those words over and over when she went into labour a week early, and said them again in a voice choked with emotion when she gave birth to their son. They called him Petros. And as Tahlia held her newborn son to her breast, and stroked his shock of dark hair, Thanos claimed her mouth in a lingering kiss.

'You are never going through that again,' he muttered rawly, unable to forget the sight of her pain-ravaged face as she delivered their baby. 'I would have given everything I own if I could have suffered in your place.'

'It wasn't so bad,' Tahlia assured him, her labour pains

already forgotten as she stared in wonder at the precious new life in her arms. 'I always wanted a brother or sister when I was growing up, and I don't want Petros to be an only child. Three children is a nice-sized family, don't you think?'

Thanos stroked a lock of damp hair from her face, and closed his eyes briefly as emotion swept through him. 'I think you are incredible, *kardia mou*, and there are not the words to say how much I love you. You know I'd agree to half a dozen children if it's what you want. But for now we have Petros, and we share a love that will last a lifetime. I could not ask for more, my love, because you are everything.'

* * * * *

THE POWER OF THE LEGENDARY GREEK

CATHERINE GEORGE

Catherine George was born on the border between Wales and England, in a village blessed with both a public and a lending library. Fervently encouraged by a like-minded mother, she developed an addiction to reading very early.

At eighteen Catherine met her husband, who eventually took her off to Brazil. He worked as chief engineer of a large gold-mining operation in Minas Gerais, which provided a popular background for several of Catherine's early novels.

After nine happy years, the education of their small son took them back to Britain and soon afterwards a daughter was born. But Catherine always found time to read, if only in the bath! When her husband's job took him abroad again, she enrolled in a creative writing course, then read countless novels by Mills & Boon® authors before trying a hand at one herself. Her first effort was not only accepted, but voted best of its genre for that year.

Catherine has written more than sixty novels since and she won another award along the way. But now she has come full circle. After living in Brazil and in England's the Wirral, Warwick and the Forest of Dean, Catherine now resides in the beautiful Welsh Marches—with access to a county library, several bookshops and a busy market hall with a treasure trove of second-hand paperbacks!

PROLOGUE

HE STRODE along the top floor of the building towards the double doors standing open at the far end, savouring the moment as he entered the room to smiles of welcome from eleven members of the board. The twelfth member, the only woman present, speared him with eyes like shards of black jet as he gave her a formal bow. The tall windows looked out on a panoramic view of Athens, but inside the boardroom all eyes were riveted on his face as he took the only empty chair and sat, composed, to open his briefcase.

The woman at the head of the table watched his every move like a cat ready to pounce on its prey, but Luke ignored her, supremely confident of success. Due to weeks of secret negotiations held with every man in the room, the meeting today was a mere formality. Once formal greetings were concluded, Luke got to his feet to outline details of his proposal, ignoring the mounting fury of the woman as he brought his bid to a conclusion.

He scanned each face in turn.

'All those in favour?'

Every hand but one shot up in instant approval as Melina Andreadis surged to her feet in furious dissent. Dressed in stark couture black, her signature mane of ringlets rioting in

cruelly youthful contrast around her ageing face, she directed a look of such venom at her adversary he should have turned to stone where he stood.

She swept the basilisk stare over every man at the table. 'You fools think you can turn my company over to this—this playboy?' she shouted, incensed, and shook her fist at the man unmoved by her tirade. 'I vote *against*! I refuse to allow this.'

Luke stared her down, his face blank as a Greek theatre mask to hide the triumph surging through his veins. 'It is already done. My more than generous terms are accepted by the Board by majority vote.'

'They cannot do this. I forbid it. This is *my* airline,' she hissed, enraged.

His eyes glittered coldly as they speared hers. 'No, *kyria*. It *was* my grandfather's airline, never yours. And now it is mine. I, Lukas Andreadis, own it by right of purchase—and of blood.'

CHAPTER ONE

THE smudge on the horizon gradually transformed into an island which surged up, pine-clad, from the dazzling blue sea. As the charter boat grew nearer, Isobel could see tavernas with coloured awnings lining the waterfront, and houses with cinnamon roofs and icing-white walls, stacked like children's building blocks on the slopes above. She scanned the houses as the boat nosed into the harbour, trying to locate the apartments shown in her brochure, but gave up, amused, when she saw that most of them had the blue doors and balconies she was looking for. She hoisted her backpack as the boat docked and picked up her bags with a sigh of relief. She'd arrived!

Isobel's first priorities were lunch and directions to her holiday apartment on this picture-perfect island of Chyros. The taverna her brochure indicated for both was inviting and lively, its tables crammed inside and out with people eating, drinking and talking non-stop. She made a beeline for one of the last unoccupied tables under the awning outside, and tucked her bags close to her feet as she sat to study the menu. With a polite '*parakalo*,' she pointed out her choice to a waiter and was quickly provided with mineral water and bread, followed by a colourful Greek salad with feta cheese. She fell on the food as though she hadn't eaten for days; which wasn't

far off the truth. She enjoyed the arrival part of holidays a whole lot more than the travelling.

'You enjoyed the *salata*?' asked the waiter, eyeing her empty plate in approval.

Isobel smiled, delighted to hear English. 'Very much; it was delicious.' She produced her brochure. 'Could you help me, please? I was told I could collect the keys to one of these apartments here.'

He nodded, smiling. 'My father has keys. He owns the Kalypso. Wait a little and I take you there.'

Isobel shook her head, embarrassed. 'That's very kind of you, but I can't interrupt your work. I can take a taxi—'

He grinned. 'My father is Nikos, also owner of the taverna. He will be pleased if I take you. I am just home from the hospital.'

She eyed the muscular young man in surprise. 'You've been ill?'

'No. I work there. I am a doctor. But at home I help when we are busy. I am Alex Nicolaides. If you give me your name for my father, I take you to the Kalypso.'

She told him she was Isobel James and, by the time she'd downed more water and paid the bill, the helpful Alex was on hand again.

'It is near enough to walk,' he informed her and picked up her luggage, but Isobel hung on to the backpack.

'I'll take this.'

'It has your valuables?' he asked as they walked along the marina.

'In a way.' She pulled the peak of her cap down to meet her sunglasses. 'Some of my drawing materials.'

'You are artist, Miss James?'

Isobel smiled. 'I try to be.'

Her escort was right. It was not far to the Kalypso holiday

lets, but in the scorching sunshine it was far enough for Isobel to feel very hot and travel-weary by the time they reached a group of six white cottages scattered on the hillside on the far side of the waterfront. Offset at different angles amongst the greenery, all of them had blue-painted balconies overlooking the boats bobbing on the brilliant waters below.

Her guide checked the number on Isobel's key tag and eyed her doubtfully. 'Your house is last, high on hill. You will not be lonely?'

She shook her head. Far from it. The peace and semi-isolation of the cottage was exactly what she needed.

The other houses had been left quite a distance behind by the time the young man led the way up a steep path quilted with soft, slippery pine needles. He put the bags down on a veranda furnished with reclining chairs and a table, and with a flourish unlocked the door of Isobel's holiday home.

'Welcome to Chyros, Miss James; enjoy your stay.'

She turned from the view. 'I'm sure I will. One last thing— where exactly is the nearest beach?'

'Next to the harbour. But down here is one you will like better.' He pointed to a path among the Aleppo pines behind the house. 'Smaller, very pretty, and not many people because the path is steep.'

'Sounds wonderful. Thank you so much for your help.' Isobel gave him a warm smile as she said goodbye and went inside to inspect her new quarters, which consisted mainly of one big air-conditioned room with a white-tiled floor and yellow-painted walls. It was simply furnished with a sky-blue sofa and curtains, two white-covered beds and a wardrobe; and through an archway at the end a small kitchen and adjoining bathroom. Everything was so scrupulously clean and peaceful it felt like sanctuary to Isobel.

Her friend Joanna, her regular holiday companion in the past before her marriage, had disapproved of Isobel's choice and had urged her to stay at a hotel on somewhere lively like glitzy Mykonos. But Isobel had opted for quiet, idyllic Chyros, where she could paint, or do nothing at all for the entire holiday, with no demands on her time. Or her emotions.

Isobel unpacked, took a quick shower and, cool in halter neck and shorts, went outside on the balcony. She sent a text to Joanna to report safe arrival and sat down with her guidebook, hair spread out on a towel over her shoulders to dry a little in the warm air before she set about taming it. A fan of Greek mythology from the time she could first read, she checked the location of the island of Serifos, where legend said Perseus and his mother Danae had been washed ashore in a chest set adrift on the sea, but decided the journey there could wait until she'd recovered from this one.

Isobel sat back, content to do nothing at all for a while, but in the end balanced a pad on her knee as usual and began to sketch the boats in the harbour below. Absorbed, she went on working until the light began to fade and sat up, yawning, too tired to go back down to the taverna for supper. Instead, she would eat bread, cheese and tomatoes from the starter pack of supplies provided with the cottage, then, with her iPod and a book for company, she would go early to bed. Tomorrow, as Scarlett O'Hara said, was another day.

Isobel lingered on the veranda as lights came on in the boats far below, and in the houses climbing the slopes above them. Music and cooking smells came drifting up on the night air as she leaned back in her chair to watch the stars appearing like diamonds strung across the dark velvet sky. Contrary to Joanna's worried forecast, she felt peaceful rather than lonely. For the first time in weeks she was free of the dark

cloud she had been unable to shake off, no matter how hard she worked. And there had to be something really special in the air here, because she felt sleepy, even this early. It would be no hardship to go to bed.

She woke early next morning, triumphant to find she'd not only fallen asleep easily, but passed the entire night without a bad dream to jolt her awake in the small hours.

After breakfast Isobel dressed in jeans and T-shirt over a pink bikini, pulled her hair through the back of a blue baseball cap and set out in the cool morning air to find her way back down to the harbour. She strolled past the boats on the waterfront and then turned up towards the town square, returning friendly smiles from ladies in black and from old men already seated outside their doors. She found a little kiosk-type corner shop already open and bought postcards, bread, mineral water and luscious grapes, then retraced her route back to the cottage. Finally, armed with sunglasses and a few basic necessities in her backpack, Isobel set off on the path recommended by Alex Nicolaides.

He was right. It was steep enough to make the descent downright scary in places. But the beach, deserted and utterly beautiful, was well worth the effort when she finally arrived, panting, on the bone-white shingle edging the crescent of sand. Isobel gazed, entranced, itching for paint to capture the way the sea shaded in jewel colours from pale peridot-green, through aquamarine and turquoise into a deep celestial blue. Greenery grew surprisingly close to the water's edge, with tamarisk and something she thought might be juniper among the pines and aromatic maquis-type vegetation. She sighed, frustrated, as a salt breeze rustled the pines. The scene cried out for watercolour. But getting the necessary materials down that path would be tricky. For now she would settle for just

sketching it. Isobel chose the nearest rock formation as a base, took off her jeans and shirt, slathered herself in sun-cream, then pulled the peak of her cap down low, settled herself on a towel with her backpack to cushion her against the rock and began to draw.

No one climbed down the path to join her, but after an hour or so of perfect peace, small boats began discharging passengers at intervals and soon there were people sunbathing and picnicking, and children playing ball, shrieking joyfully as they ran in and out of the sea. So much for peace and quiet. Smiling philosophically, Isobel braced herself for the climb up the cliff to go in search of an early lunch. But while she gathered up her belongings she spotted a gap in the rocks on the far side of the beach and couldn't resist strolling over to investigate. On closer inspection, the fissure was very narrow and dark with overhanging shrubbery. But, by taking off her backpack and hugging it to her chest, she could just manage to squeeze along the rocky passage, which narrowed so sharply at one point Isobel almost gave up. But when the passage widened again curiosity propelled her forward, her sneakers slipping slightly on the wet rock as she emerged at last into a much smaller cove sheltered by high, steep cliffs. With not a soul in sight.

Isobel surveyed her deserted paradise in delight. She would make do with grapes and water for lunch, right here. She stripped down to her bikini again and settled under the over-hang of a rock formation shaped so much like a rampant lion she promised herself to sketch it later. She drank some water, nibbled on her grapes, then took off her cap and moved further into the shade of the rock to catnap.

But her newfound peace was soon shattered by the roar of some kind of engine. Basic survival instinct sent Isobel scram-

bling up on to the steep rock as a man on a Jet Ski shot straight towards her. At the very last minute he veered away, laughing his head off as he went speeding out to sea again. Heart hammering, Isobel cursed the idiot volubly, so furious she lost her footing as she turned to jump down and flailed wildly to avoid falling, her scream cut off as her head met rock with a sickening crack that turned the world black.

Lukas Andreadis was looking forward to a swim followed by a good dinner and an entire evening with no discussion of takeovers, air travel, shipping, or any other form of transport. After working towards it all his adult life, he would celebrate his triumphant defeat of Melina Andreadis alone, in the place he loved best. He began to relax as the helicopter flew over familiar blue waters. When the island finally came into view his spirits rose as usual at the mere sight of Chyros, which stood for peace and privacy in a life which held precious little of either back in Athens. But, as he took the helicopter low on its descent to the villa, Luke cursed in angry frustration. A naked female was sunbathing on his private beach. Again.

He set the machine down on the helipad at the back of the house, switched off the engine and jumped out, crouching low until he was free of the rotating blades. He hurried past the pool to make for the trees lining the cliff edge, and scowled down at the figure lying motionless far below. Why, in the name of all the gods, couldn't they leave him alone? He turned as his faithful Spiro came rushing to greet him, and exchanged affectionate greetings before pointing down at the beach.

'Someone down in the cove again. Where the devil is Milos?'

'He needed time off. Shall I take the boat?'

'No; leave it to me.' Luke collected his bags and strode past the palms and oleanders in the lush garden. Instead of going

through his usual ritual of breathing in the peace and welcome of his retreat, he raced up the curving staircase, threw off his clothes, and pulled on shorts and T-shirt, thrust bare feet into deck shoes, smiling in reassurance at Spiro as the man began to unpack. 'Don't worry, I won't hurt the woman.'

'I know that!' retorted the man, with the familiarity of one who'd known—and loved—his employer from birth. 'Wear your dark glasses—and don't drive too fast.'

Luke Andreadis collected two sets of keys, stopped in the kitchen for an affectionate greeting with Eleni, Spiro's wife, then checked again from the cliff edge, his face grim when he saw the prone figure still frying down on the beach. The stupid woman was risking a bad case of sunstroke at the very least—but not for long.

He ran back through the garden, vaulted into the jeep parked behind the villa and drove up the cypress-lined drive and out on to the road, taking the twists and turns of the tortuous descent at a speed which would have given Spiro a heart attack. Forced to slow down as he reached the town, Luke drove more circumspectly through the main square and on past the tavernas and coffee shops on the waterfront, then parked well out of sight at his secluded private mooring at the far end. He leapt onto the deck of the *Athena*, cast off and switched on the engine and, once clear of the marina, sped across the water past the crowded beach and round the cliffs to his private cove. He moored the boat at a jetty hidden among the rocks, his eyes smouldering. The woman was still there.

'You're trespassing,' he bellowed, storming across the shingle. But as he reached her he realised that the woman was unconscious. Sprawled at an awkward angle, she lay face down and utterly still, a mass of long fair curls streaming over her shoulders. He reached up to turn her face towards him,

but dropped his hand when she opened pain-filled blue eyes which darkened in terror at the look of menace on the face close to hers.

'You had a fall. What are you doing here?' he demanded.

'Sorry—don't understand,' she said faintly, shrinking from him, then stifled a moan, her face screwed up in pain as she tried to back away.

'You fell. Your head is injured,' he said in English, cursing silently as her move brought blood trickling from a gash on her temple.

'Ankle, too.' She swallowed painfully. 'I slipped when you came roaring out of the sea at me on that Jet Ski—'

'Jet Ski?' Luke glared at her. 'You are delirious from your fall, *kyria*. I do not own such a thing. I came by boat.' Scowling, he examined the foot wedged tightly in a crack in the rock. 'I must pull it out. But it will hurt.'

She clenched her jaw stoically and turned her head away.

Luke untied the laces on the blue sneaker but, as he tried to ease the foot out of it, she gasped in pain, beads of sweat rolling down her face.

'Please. Just pull!'

He obliged, but as the foot came free the girl passed out cold again. With a savage curse he yanked his phone out of his back pocket. 'Spiro, the woman's had an accident. She's unconscious. The clinic will be shut at this hour so I'll have to bring her up to the house.' He cut off Spiro's exclamation. 'Find Dr Riga, please. Tell him it's urgent.'

Luke decided against trying to revive the girl. Better she stayed out of it while he manhandled her. Cursing because she was virtually naked except for scraps of pink fabric, he found a towel nearby and shook it free of sand to drape over the girl. He searched in a backpack lying at the foot of the rock, his

lip curling as he found a notebook and pencils. But otherwise there was only a small purse with some currency, and a paperback novel in English. No identity. He hooked his arms into the straps but, as he bent to pick her up, her eyes flew open, wild with fear again.

'You are perfectly safe,' he snapped impatiently. 'I shall carry you to my boat.'

Luke was as careful as possible as he carried his burden across the narrow beach, but she was unconscious again by the time he deposited her in the well of the boat. In a black mood, he cast off and set off across the water on the short trip back to moor the boat at the marina, thankful, not for the first time, that his berth was well away from the tavernas. He secured the boat, then, praying she hadn't fractured her skull, Luke picked up his unconscious passenger who, though slender, was a dead weight. He braced himself, stepped up onto the quay and buckled her in the passenger seat of the Cherokee. Annoyed because he was breathing hard, he tucked the towel around her, shrugged off the backpack and drove back to the villa.

Spiro and Eleni hurried out to meet him, followed by Milos, the gardener, all of them exclaiming volubly over his unconscious passenger.

'My apologies, *kyrie*,' said Milos remorsefully. 'My mother needed me. What happened to the lady?'

'She fell on the rocks,' Luke growled, jumping out.

'Dr Riga is out on a call,' reported Spiro, looking worried.

Luke swallowed a curse. 'Will he be long?'

'Alex Nicolaides is home, *kyrie*. I saw him this morning. I could go down and fetch him,' Milos suggested.

Luke nodded grimly as he checked the girl's pulse. 'Get him here as fast as you can, please.'

'The poor young lady!' Eleni bent to mop the blood from the unconscious girl's temple as Milos rushed off. 'She has hurt her pretty face.'

'Let me help carry her upstairs,' offered Spiro, but Luke shook his head.

'I can manage. But I need you with me, please, Eleni.' As he released the safety belt the girl came round and struggled to sit upright, shrinking away from him in such terror that Luke's patience suddenly ran out.

'You are not in danger,' he snapped. 'I have brought you to my house.'

'No, really—I must get back to my cottage,' Isobel protested, horrified. Before he could stop her, she slid from the car, then gasped in agony as she put her weight on her injured ankle.

With a face like thunder, Luke scooped her up, ignoring Eleni's protests when the towel was left behind. He strode up the curving staircase to a large airy bedroom and deposited his unwilling burden in a chair. 'I will leave you with my housekeeper,' he panted and stalked out of the room.

The woman smiled sympathetically. 'I am Eleni. I speak a little English, but not good.' She took the girl's arm to help her over to the inviting white bed, but Isobel shook her head, a move she deeply regretted when the pain struck so hard the room swam before her eyes.

'Sick,' she gasped, clapping her hand to her mouth, and Eleni acted like lightning to help her hop into the adjoining bathroom. After a painful, humiliating episode, Isobel gasped her thanks and eventually gave in to Eleni's insistence that she remove the bikini, which had suffered badly during the day's various adventures. By this time totally beyond embarrassment, Isobel submitted to Eleni's ministrations as the woman

helped her sponge her face and hot, aching body, then wrapped her in a white towelling robe.

'Thank—you—so—much,' said Isobel, teeth chattering in reaction as the woman helped her lie down against banked snowy pillows on the bed.

Eleni picked up the bikini. 'I wash this. You rest,' she said firmly and went out, closing the door behind her.

The session in the bathroom had rocketed Isobel's headache to hammer-blow dimensions, which almost blotted out the pain of her ankle but only accentuated her raging thirst as she tried to make sense of her accident. She remembered some idiot on a Jet Ski coming straight at the beach from the sea, then hitting her head and nothing else until she opened her eyes on the angry, handsome face of a stranger and assumed he was the culprit. Which had infuriated him. She tensed as the door opened and her hostile rescuer approached the bed.

'How do you feel?' he asked curtly.

'Not too well.' She swallowed. 'I'm so sorry to be a nuisance, but could I possibly have some water?'

Cursing silently for not thinking of it first, Luke nodded stiffly. 'Of course.'

Isobel watched him as he strode out of the room. He was tall, with a fabulous physique, and in a better mood would be very good-looking. Not that she was concerned with his hostility, or with anything else other than how in the world she was going to get herself out of here—wherever 'here' was—and get back to the little cottage she'd paid good money for. And one day of her holiday was already ruined. Tears leaked out of her eyes at the thought, but she knuckled them away, impatient with self-pity as her host returned with her backpack, followed by Eleni with a tray. The woman poured water into

a glass and handed it to Isobel, then, at a look from her employer, went from the room, leaving the door wide open.

'Eleni has looked after my family for years,' he stated.

Desperate to gulp the water down, Isobel forced herself to sip cautiously. 'She's very kind.'

'I am not?'

'Of course.' Her face grew even hotter. 'I'm extremely grateful to you. And very embarrassed for causing so much trouble.'

Luke shrugged negligently. 'Tell me your name.'

'Isobel James.' She drank the rest of the water and held the cold glass to her cheek, eyeing him questioningly. 'And you are?'

He laughed scornfully. 'You do not know?'

She stiffened. 'I'm afraid not. I only arrived on the island yesterday.'

His dark eyes narrowed to a cynical glitter. 'So why were you on my beach? You paid someone to take you there by boat?'

Isobel's knuckles clenched on the glass. 'No. I went down the path nearest the cottage to the beach adjoining yours. But by mid-morning it was crowded, so when I spotted the gap in the rocks I went to explore.'

'That way is blocked!'

'Not quite. I managed to squeeze through.'

'You were so determined to invade my privacy?' His eyes flamed with distaste, which touched Isobel on the raw.

'Certainly not,' she snapped. 'I had no idea it was a private beach, nor who it belonged to. I apologise—*humbly*—for trespassing. And now, if you'll be kind enough to call a taxi, I'll get dressed and leave.'

He raised a cynical eyebrow. 'And how do you propose to walk?'

'I'll manage,' she snapped, praying she was right.

Eleni knocked at the open door and ushered in a familiar figure armed with a medical bag. The two men embraced each other and exchanged greetings before Alex Nicolaides moved to the bed, his eyes wide in consternation as he recognised his patient. 'Miss James! What happened?' He turned to her glowering rescuer, obviously asking him the same question in his own language.

'The lady,' Luke informed him in very deliberate English, 'was trespassing on my private beach when she suffered a fall. She was unconscious when I found her. Thank you for coming, Doctor. Please examine her injuries and tell me what must be done for her.'

'I need Eleni to stay, please,' said Isobel urgently.

Luke motioned the woman to the bed, but stayed at the foot of it, obviously determined to monitor the proceedings.

Eleni patted Isobel's hand comfortingly as Alex bent over her.

'This is very bad luck for you, Miss James,' he said gently.

His sympathy was so genuine tears welled in Isobel's eyes, burning as they trickled down her flushed cheeks. Eleni produced tissues to dry the patient's face so Alex could examine the wound, then he shone a torch in her eyes, held up a finger and told her to follow it with each eye in turn.

'You have vomited?'

'Yes.'

'Does your head hurt very badly?'

'Yes.'

'Examine her foot; she hurt that, also,' Luke said, sounding bored.

Alex frowned as he eyed the swollen ankle. 'It is necessary to examine for fracture,' he told Isobel. 'I will be quick.'

'Careful,' warned Luke. 'She faints a lot.'

A lot? Until today, she'd never fainted before in her life!

Isobel clenched her teeth, determined not to faint again as Alex probed gently, though at one point it was a near thing.

'The ankle is badly sprained only, not broken, Miss James,' Alex assured her. 'I will apply temporary bandage, then report to Dr Riga, who will take X-rays to confirm. I will also put a dressing on your face, and give you mild painkillers. Take with much fluid.'

'Thank you.' She tried to relax as he strapped her ankle. 'Did you come here in a car, Doctor?'

He looked up in surprise. 'No, on back of Milos's motorbike. Why?'

'I was hoping for a lift back to the cottage,' she said, disappointed, and eyed him in appeal. 'Would you be kind enough to arrange a taxi for me?'

Alex shot a startled look at Luke, who showed his teeth in a cold smile.

'Miss James may stay here as long as she wishes.'

Not one second longer, if she could help it. 'How kind,' said Isobel frostily. 'But I wouldn't dream of inconveniencing you. So will you sort out a taxi for me, Doctor?'

Alex looked so uncomfortable Luke took pity on him.

'I will drive you myself, Miss James,' he said impatiently. 'But only when you can manage alone. Demonstrate this for us.'

Isobel summoned every scrap of willpower she possessed to sit up straight. She paused for breath, swivelled round until she could put her good foot on the floor and then took the hand Eleni held out to help her as she struggled to stand. 'You see?' she said through her teeth. 'If you gentlemen will kindly leave, I'll get dressed.'

'Miss James, this is not a good idea,' said Alex, plainly expecting her to collapse in a heap at any second.

'I must try. The cottage is all on one floor. I have food there, so if Mr—'

She glanced at her host. 'I'm afraid I don't know your name.'

'No?' He raised an eyebrow in scornful disbelief. 'I am Lukas Andreadis.'

'How do you do?' She turned to Alex. 'If Mr Andreadis will drive me, I'll be just fine.' She swallowed hard on rising nausea and wavered slightly, her hand tightening on Eleni's.

Luke shook his head. 'I will drive you when you *are* fine, Miss James, but that is most obviously not today. Put her back, Eleni.'

'That is best, Luke,' said Alex, relieved.

Isobel gave up. She let Eleni make her comfortable, then turned her face into the pillows in despair. Her longed-for odyssey had come to a grinding halt before it had even started. She ignored the hushed interchange in their own tongue between the men, wishing they'd just go away and leave her to wallow alone in her misery.

'Miss James,' said Alex, coming back to the bed.

Isobel opened her eyes. 'Yes?'

'If you allow me to have your keys, I will take my sister to your house to pack for you.'

'How kind,' she said unsteadily. 'The keys are in my backpack.'

'I am most happy to do this, but it was Luke's idea,' he added.

She turned unsmiling eyes on her host. 'Then thank you, too, Mr Andreadis.'

'Here in Greece we believe in helping travellers,' he informed her indifferently.

'Unless they invade your beach.'

'True.' He unbent enough to smile faintly. 'Come, then, Alex. I will drive you.'

Eleni closed the door behind them, poured iced fruit juice

into a glass and gave Isobel two of the tablets. 'Drink, *kyria*,' she said firmly.

Isobel obediently swallowed the painkillers and drank some of the juice. '*Efcharisto*, Eleni.' She managed a smile. 'But please call me Isobel.'

Eleni repeated the name shyly, put the glass on the table, then opened the carton of yoghurt.

Isobel eyed it in alarm. 'I'm so sorry, but I really can't eat anything right now.'

'*Ochee*, not for eating. For your face. It is burning, *ne*?'

'Oh, yes,' sighed Isobel, and submitted to an unexpected beauty treatment. Eleni smoothed the blessedly cool, creamy yoghurt over her face, left it there until it warmed up, then gently cleaned it off with tissues.

'I will do it more later,' she promised, 'but now you sleep, Isobel.' She smiled and went from the room, leaving the door ajar.

Eventually the pills took enough edge off her aches and pains to let Isobel take interest in her surroundings. Filmy white curtains stirred at glass doors which led on to a balcony, and the room itself was furnished with the type of elegant simplicity that cost the earth. She groaned in sudden despair. She'd come all this way to Chyros to regain her normal perspective on life, yet one day into her holiday and here she was, stranded in a wealthy—and hugely unfriendly—stranger's house, with no way of escaping until she was more mobile. But why had the man been so sure she'd known who he was? And felt so ticked off about it, too. Perhaps he was some kind of celebrity here in Greece. Her mouth twisted. He needn't worry where she was concerned. He was good-looking enough in a forceful kind of way, but his personality was so horribly overbearing it cancelled out any attraction he might have had for her as a man…

When Isobel opened her eyes again they widened when she found another stranger looking down at her.

'Dr Riga, Isobel,' said Eleni, hurrying to help her to sit up.

The large, bespectacled man gave her a reassuring smile. '*Kalispera*. How do you feel?' he asked in heavily accented English, and took her pulse.

'Not too well,' she admitted.

He nodded, his eyes so sympathetic her own filled with tears again.

'I'm so sorry, Doctor,' she said huskily, and took the tissue Eleni had ready.

'You suffer much pain; you are also in shock and alone in a strange country, Miss James. Tears are natural,' he assured her. 'I must take X-ray at my clinic. Eleni will help you dress.' He smiled reassuringly and went from the room.

'Eleni,' said Isobel urgently, 'will you help me wash again? Did Mr Andreadis bring my clothes?'

The woman nodded and helped Isobel out of the bed, supporting her as she hopped awkwardly to the bathroom. 'I used iron,' she said severely. 'Alyssa Nicolaides packed too quick.'

'You're an angel, thank you, Eleni.' Isobel tried to hurry. 'I mustn't keep the doctor waiting.'

Eleni shook her head. 'He is gone. *Kyrie* Luke will drive you. Not rush,' she warned.

After the hurried bathroom session Isobel felt relatively presentable in a white denim skirt and blue T-shirt, though the effect was marred by wearing only one sandal. Otherwise she felt horribly queasy still, and her head was pounding like a war drum. Eleni helped her to the stool in front of the dressing table, anointed her face with more yoghurt, then wiped it away and handed Isobel her zippered travel pack. Resigned

to see faint bruising under her eye, Isobel used a comb gingerly, decided against lip gloss and smiled wanly at Eleni.

'I'm ready.'

The woman nodded. 'I tell him.'

Isobel would have given a lot to walk downstairs on her own two feet when Luke Andreadis appeared in the doorway in a crisp white shirt and jeans which were obviously custom made by their fit.

'How do you feel now?' he asked, his eyes on the bright hair curling loosely on her shoulders.

'Cleaner.'

'But you are still in pain.'

'Yes.'

He picked her up with exaggerated care. 'I will strive not to cause you more.'

'Likewise, Mr Andreadis,' she returned, holding herself rigid, face averted, as he carried her from the room.

He frowned. 'Likewise?'

'Carrying me around can't be doing your back much good.'

He laughed sardonically as he descended the curving staircase into a marble-floored hall with an alcove containing a striking half-size statue of Perseus brandishing the severed head of the gorgon Medusa. 'I will survive. You are not heavy.'

'As soon as humanly possible, I'll get back to the cottage.'

'When Dr Riga says you are fit to do so,' he said dismissively and carried her through a large plant-filled conservatory to put her in the passenger seat of the Cherokee Jeep parked at the back of the villa. Which, now she had attention to spare for it, Isobel could see was a dream of a house.

'You have a beautiful home,' she said politely as Luke got in beside her.

'*Efcharisto*. I bought it years ago, and altered it to suit my taste. I look on it—and the beach that came with it—as my private retreat.'

'Is that why you were so furious when you found me down there?'

He lifted a shoulder. 'Trespassers are a common occurrence.'

She clenched her teeth. 'Once again, I apologise.'

It was no surprise to find that Luke Andreadis drove with panache. They swerved at speed round one dizzying bend after another on the tortuous descent until at last Isobel had to beg him to stop.

Luke came to a screaming halt, raced round the Jeep and hauled her out, then, to her hideous embarrassment, supported her as she retched miserably over a clump of bushes at the roadside.

'Can you continue now?' he demanded as she straightened.

'Yes,' she gasped, sending up a prayer that she was right.

He put her back in the Jeep and handed her bag over. 'I will drive slowly the rest of the way,' he said stiffly.

'Thank you,' she managed, the pain in her head now so unbearable again she could hardly speak.

The doctor hurried out of the modern clinic building as they arrived, his face anxious.

'You are late. I was worried.'

'We had to stop on the way because Miss James was sick,' Luke informed him. 'I am so used to the road I drove too fast.'

'Ah, poor child. Bring her in, Lukas. My radiologist is waiting, and also Nurse Pappas with a wheelchair.'

Luke lifted Isobel out of the car to transfer her to the wheelchair, his mouth tightening as he felt her shrink from him. 'You will obviously prefer this.'

You bet, thought Isobel, as the friendly nurse wheeled her

away. Later, after X-rays and a trying episode while her wound was thoroughly cleaned and dressed again, she was given painkillers and water, then wheeled back to the reception area.

'There is no fracture to the skull or the ankle, but you are suffering from mild concussion,' Dr Riga reported and smiled encouragingly at Isobel. 'You need light nourishment and much rest. I will give you more medication for the headache, but take no more until bedtime. And Nurse Pappas has a crutch for you.'

'Thank you,' said Isobel gratefully, smiling at both of them.

'Are you ready?' Luke tossed the crutch in the back of the Jeep, then installed Isobel in the passenger seat. His face was so grim as he took the wheel; the drive back to the villa was accomplished in silence so tense until Isobel felt obliged, at last, to break it.

'I'm very grateful for all your help, Mr Andreadis,' she said formally. 'Would you give me Dr Riga's bill, please?'

'I have settled it,' he said dismissively.

'Then I will pay you,' she persisted.

Luke Andreadis, accustomed to women who expected him to foot bills far more expensive than Dr Riga's, shot her a scathing look. 'I require no money from you, Miss James.'

Isobel had no energy to argue, even though the mere thought of owing this man anything at all acted like fire on her skin—which was hot enough already.

Once back at his house, Luke lifted Isobel out, then handed her the crutch. 'Welcome back to the Villa Medusa,' he said formally. 'You can manage with this?'

'Yes, thank you.' Even if it killed her. But, by the time they made it through the conservatory, Isobel felt too exhausted to protest when Luke handed Spiro the crutch and picked her up to carry her upstairs.

CHAPTER TWO

ELENI and Spiro hurried behind, listening closely as Luke reported in their own language on Dr Riga's treatment.

'Eleni asked when you last ate,' he reported, letting Isobel down in the armchair.

'This morning on your beach,' she gasped. No point in mentioning that grapes had been the only thing on the menu. Nor that she'd parted with them and everything else in her system in the guest bathroom, with an encore on the way down to the clinic.

'I bring food to you very soon, Isobel,' promised Eleni.

Relieved to have her catering arrangements decided for her, Isobel smiled wearily. '*Efcharisto*, Eleni. But I'm not at all hungry.'

Luke took the crutch from Spiro and propped it against Isobel's chair. 'You have everything you need?'

Heartily sick of being heaved around by a man who made it so plain it was a tiresome chore, Isobel made no attempt at a polite smile. 'Yes. Thank you. I shan't trouble you again.'

Luke's smile set her teeth on edge. 'You were trouble from the moment I first saw you, on my flight over the beach.'

'Flight?'

'In my helicopter. It is my habit to scan the beach as I come in to land.'

'To scope out trespassers!' She looked him in the eye—or as well as she could with one of her own half closed. 'At the risk of boring you, I apologise once again for my intrusion, Mr Andreadis.' Her mouth twisted. 'Lord knows, I suffered such swift retribution I'll never do it again.'

'Even though you failed in your aim?'

Isobel frowned, her thought processes fighting a losing battle with her headache. 'I don't understand.'

Luke eyed the motionless Spiro, who obviously intended standing his ground until his employer was ready to leave. 'With your permission, Miss James,' continued Luke, 'I will return after you have eaten. I wish to talk to you.'

Isobel inclined her sore head gingerly. As if she could say no!

Alone, she sagged for a moment in relief, then pulled herself together and tried putting her crutch through its paces. To her intense satisfaction she found that, headache and sprained ankle or not, she was now mobile, if not agile. Hallelujah! After the talk with the hostile Mr Andreadis, a lift back to the cottage was all the help she would need from him.

When Eleni came in, followed by Spiro with a tray, Isobel smiled persuasively and pointed to the balcony doors. 'Could I eat out there, please?'

'It is dark,' said the woman, astonished.

'Not with the stars and the light from the lamps in here.'

'Whatever you wish, *kyria*,' said Spiro, and took the tray out to the small table on the balcony. He rearranged the chairs, opened the other door to make it easier for her and bowed to her, smiling.

'*Efcharisto*, Spiro,' said Isobel gratefully and limped out onto the balcony to sit at the table, smiling in such triumph

at Eleni as she parked the crutch that the woman laughed and patted her shoulder.

'You are better. Good, good. Now, eat.' She took a silver cover from an inviting omelette and left Isobel to her solitary meal.

To her surprise, Isobel's taste buds sprang to life with the first mouthful. Once it seemed her stomach meant to behave, she ate all the omelette and some of the salad and bread that came with it, finding that eating alone, with only the stars for company, did wonders for her appetite. Isobel drank some water and then sat back to gaze out over the garden, her eyes fixed in longing on the floodlit pool. She'd love a swim in it before she went back to her cottage. But fond hope of that with Mr Congeniality on the premises.

A knock on the bedroom door brought her out of her reverie. She picked up the crutch and went slowly into the room, smiling at Eleni. 'It was a lovely supper. I've taken some pills and I feel much better now.'

'Good, good,' said the woman, beaming. 'I bring more yoghurt for face. Use before bed. I help you to bathroom now?'

'No, thank you. I can manage myself.'

The woman frowned. 'Then I come back later when time to sleep.'

'All right, Eleni,' sighed Isobel, knowing when she was beaten. 'Before you go, could you put the big chair near the veranda doors? *Efcharisto poli.*'

Isobel eyed her reflection critically in the large bathroom mirror. Her eye was ringed with interesting shades of plum, but at least it was now almost open again, and her sunburn had toned down, thanks to Eleni's yoghurt. Pleased with her new mobility, Isobel limped back into the room to sit in the big, comfortable chair, content just to look out into the night while she waited for her visitor.

'Come in,' she called later, in answer to the expected knock.

Luke strolled in, his eyes on her face. '*Kalispera*. You look better. Eleni tells me you ate most of your supper.'

'Yes. It was delicious.' Isobel sat still and tense, wondering what he wanted to talk about.

'May I sit down?'

'Of course.'

Luke drew the dressing table stool nearer Isobel and stood by it for a moment. 'Shall I fetch your notebook? Since you suffered so much to achieve it, I have decided to grant your interview.'

Isobel stared at him blankly. 'Interview?'

'I collected your belongings on the beach,' he informed her. 'There was a notebook, also several pencils in your bag. Do you deny that you are a journalist, Miss James?'

Isobel took in a deep calming breath, then took the pad from the backpack on the floor beside her and handed it over. 'Look for yourself.'

Luke's mouth tightened as he turned over pages of drawings. 'What are these?'

'I would have thought that's obvious, Mr Andreadis. I drew the boats from the veranda of the cottage when I first arrived, and the other sketch this morning on the beach next to yours. Ideally, I would have used watercolour, but I had no way of getting the materials down such a steep path.' Isobel looked at him coldly. 'Other people take holiday snaps. I make sketches.'

'Which,' he said slowly, leafing through them again, 'are most accomplished.'

'Thank you.'

Luke ran a hand through his thick curls, then looked up, surveying her in silence for so long that Isobel grew restive. 'It is now I who must make apology,' he said at last, as though the words were drawn out of him with pincers.

'Accepted.' She eyed him curiously. 'You dislike journalists and guard your privacy very fiercely, Mr Andreadis, so are you some kind of celebrity here in Greece?'

He shook his head. 'No, just a successful businessman, Miss James. I am in shipping, but also much in the news lately, due to a successful takeover of a private airline.' His mouth turned down. 'And I have no wife. This also attracts interest from the press.'

'About whether you're gay?' she said, secretly delighted by the look of outrage on his face.

'*Ochee*! I may lack a wife, but it is common knowledge that I enjoy the company of women. Did *you* think I was gay?' he demanded.

'Not easy to tell on such brief acquaintance.'

His eyes narrowed to a glitter, which put her on the alert. 'Even though we have been in enforced physical contact from the first moment of our meeting?'

Isobel's face heated. 'I wasn't conscious for most of it. And, now that I am, no further contact is necessary. Not,' she added hastily, 'that I'm ungrateful for your help.'

He shrugged. 'I had no choice but to give it, Miss James.'

She eyed him in disdain. 'You made that very clear—but I'm grateful just the same.'

His eyes softened. 'It has been a bad start to your holiday.'

'It has indeed.' She pushed her hair away from her throbbing forehead. 'So, if you can spare the time to drive me to my cottage tomorrow to get on with it, I'd be very grateful, Mr Andreadis.'

'You cannot manage alone there yet,' he said dismissively.

'I most certainly can. There is absolutely no difference between getting myself around this room and doing the same at the cottage.'

'And how will you feed yourself?'

She'd been prepared for that. 'If Eleni will buy food for me before I go, I'll manage very well until I can walk properly again. My ankle feels better already,' she lied. 'In a day or so I'll be back to normal.'

He eyed her in silence for a moment. 'Before you make your escape from the Villa Medusa, please indulge my curiosity. Tell me something about yourself. From your drawings, your interest obviously lies in art, Miss James.'

'Yes. I have a Fine Art Degree.'

'You teach?'

'No. I manage an art gallery and live in the flat over it as part of a deal which includes putting my work on sale at the gallery, as well as the paintings I sell privately.'

'You live near your family?'

Isobel looked down at the hands she'd folded in her lap. 'No. My wonderful grandparents brought me up, but they're dead now.'

Luke leaned forward slightly. 'And your parents?'

'I never knew them. They were killed in a motorway pile-up in fog when I was a baby.'

'That is a sad story,' he said sombrely. 'But you were fortunate to have grandparents who cared for you.'

'True. They were the only parents I ever knew, and I couldn't have wished for better. But, though I'm short on family, I'm blessed with very good friends,' said Isobel, trying to ignore her headache. 'In the past my holidays were spent with one of them but, since her marriage a couple of years ago, I travel alone.'

Luke got up. 'Have you informed this friend of your accident?'

'I saw no point in worrying her. I'll be fine in a day or two.'

'But you are not fine now. Your headache is bad again, yes?'

'Afraid so,' she admitted.

He looked down at her, frowning. 'I shall send Eleni to help you to bed.' He held up a peremptory hand. 'Yes, I know you can manage without her, but she insisted. Is there anything you would like her to bring you?'

Isobel smiled hopefully. 'I would really love some tea.'

'Of course. You shall have it immediately. *Kalmychta*— goodnight, Miss James.'

'Goodnight, Mr Andreadis.'

Isobel was very thoughtful after he'd gone, wondering why he'd asked so many questions. It made her doubly wary of Lukas Andreadis, mainly because her current opinion of his sex was at an all-time low. But, looked at objectively, from an artistic point of view he was a formidable specimen, with the physique and sculpted features of the Greek statues she'd studied in college. Though more like the Renaissance muscular versions than the androgynous Apollo Belvedere of Ancient Greece. Similar curls, maybe, but Luke Andreadis was very obviously all male, his impressive build a definite plus when it came to carrying her about. His one concession to vanity seemed to be the hair he grew long enough to brush his collar. But she would have expected those curls of his to be black, like his eyes. Instead, they were bronze with lighter streaks, courtesy of the sun. Her mouth tightened. Good-looking he might be, but when she'd first seen him, down on his precious private beach, he'd been so menacing he'd frightened her to death.

Isobel took more painkillers with the tea Eleni brought her, then submitted to her yoghurt beauty treatment and let the kind little woman help her to bed. Isobel thanked Eleni warmly, wished her goodnight, and then settled down against

banked pillows and, though fully expecting to lie awake for hours with her aches and pains for company, eventually drifted off into healing, dreamless sleep.

CHAPTER THREE

LUKE ANDREADIS asked Eleni to take tea up to their guest, then went to his room, but felt too restless for sleep. He made for his balcony with a glass of brandy and leaned against the rail, breathing in the heady nocturnal scents of the garden. After the punishing campaign of the past few weeks he felt anti-climactic, already missing the adrenaline rush of corporate battle. His mouth curled in grim triumph as he relived the victory over Melina Andreadis. She must be incandescent with fury now she no longer controlled the airline acquired by the husband who had once given it to his demanding second wife as if it were a toy to play with. But now, Luke thought triumphantly, she had been rendered powerless. Her ties with the airline had been severed without mercy by the grandson Theo Andreadis refused to acknowledge.

Luke raised his glass to the stars in exultation at the memory of Melina's fury, of her ageing face, scarlet and suffused with rage. It had been worth every minute of his years of hard, unending work just to see the harpy's face when the vote went against her. Whoever said revenge was a dish best served cold was right on target. His long fight to wreak revenge on Melina had left little room in his life for personal relationships. But this mattered very little to him now he had

finally exacted his revenge. His only sorrow was that his mother had not lived to share in his triumph. His face set in implacable lines. That she was not was another sin to lay at his grandfather's door. Theo Andreadis had brought up his motherless daughter so strictly her eventual rebellion had been inevitable. The discovery that she was pregnant had enraged her father so much he'd thrown her out on the street. The desperate girl had fled from Athens to take refuge with her old nurse on Chyros, where Olympia Andreadis, daughter of one of the richest men in Greece, had supported herself by working in the kitchen of the taverna owned by Basil Nicolaides, father of the present owner, Nikos.

Luke's eyes darkened at the thought of his frail, pretty mother, who had escaped from her home in Athens with only the jewels inherited from her mother. These had provided savings hoarded zealously for her child as he grew into a clever, determined boy who soon outstripped his peers academically at school. Young Lukas absorbed knowledge like a sponge and, with the help of a young, enthusiastic teacher early on, became fluent in English, which added to his prowess in all the other subjects on the school curriculum. Fuelled by determination to help his mother, he did odd jobs after school at the taverna to earn money, and at weekends, much to Olympia's disapproval, went out with the local fishermen for the same purpose. He would have done anything to protect his mother from the blandishments of Costas Petrides, the wealthiest man on the island. Costas had been so eager to marry the exquisite, cultured Olympia he had even professed willingness to take her illegitimate son as part of the deal. But she had politely and relentlessly refused, secure in the protection of Spiro, son of her old nurse, and the support of Basil Nicolaides and his son Nikos, who jointly managed the

taverna. But Luke well knew that to this day Costas blamed Olympia's son for her refusal of such a good catch for a husband.

Luke grew up in a home where there was much love, but very little money. As he grew to adulthood he became consumed with the desire to keep his mother in luxury for the rest of her days, to repay Spiro and the Nikolaides family for their kindness, and eventually to wreak merciless revenge on those responsible for his mother's situation, with Melina Andreadis at the top of his hit list.

And he had succeeded. He had rendered Melina powerless with the best weapon of all, the loss of backing from her own board. He smiled with grim satisfaction at the memory of her raging, impotent fury as the vote went against her. For a moment it had seemed likely she would attack him with her own red-taloned fingers as the truth struck home that she was powerless to fight against fate when the airline was torn from her grasp. And now Lukas Andreadis was the power behind Air Chyros, the new name he'd given his grandfather's airline. In the future, instead of making money with as many cheap flights as possible under the grasping Melina's aegis, it would be run with the emphasis on safety, reliability and luxury, the key elements Air Chyros would be offering once the new planes were in operation.

Luke drank down the last of his brandy and turned back into his room, wincing as the odd muscle protested. He smiled a little. He prided himself on his fitness, which he swam daily to maintain, but it wasn't every day he was required to rescue a damsel in distress. A very appealing damsel, he admitted, though tumbling blonde curls and big blue eyes were not female assets which normally appealed to him. He liked his women dark, with fiery temperaments and ample curves—he

laughed shortly, giving thanks to the gods that he hadn't been obliged to carry a woman of that description about, or he might have had more than just a sore muscle or two to complain about. But, even though Miss Isobel James looked the picture of innocence, he still harboured doubts about her reasons for her presence on his beach this morning. Yet her stoicism and independence—and the feel of her slender body in his arms—appealed strongly to him. While she, very obviously, was finding it difficult to be grateful to a man she regarded with suspicion, even dislike. A new experience for him where women were concerned. He smiled slowly. Now he was here for a few days it would be diverting to see how quickly he could break down the barrier she'd erected against him. He must think up ways of keeping her here until he achieved his usual success. His mouth twisted in self-derision as he realised that a great part of the lady's attraction was her immunity to his own—a challenge impossible to resist.

Blissfully unaware of her host's plans for her immediate future, Isobel woke early again next morning and for a moment gazed blankly round the unfamiliar room until a glance at the crutch leaning against the foot of the bed brought the events of the previous day rushing back. She lay quiet for a while as she reviewed them, amazed that she'd survived the night without one of the nightmares afflicting her lately. Perhaps she was cured of them at last. She was so comfortable she was reluctant to move, but at last she had no choice. With a sigh Isobel sat up, carefully manoeuvred herself to the edge of the bed, reached for the crutch and put her good foot to the floor. Twenty minutes later she was sitting by the open veranda doors, hair combed, teeth brushed, face clean and painkillers washed down with fruit juice. And, though both

ankle and head were still making their presence felt, the discomfort was bearable enough to confirm that once she transferred to the cottage she would be able to manage perfectly well on her own.

She looked up with a smile as Eleni appeared with a breakfast tray. 'Good morning.'

The little woman returned the smile shyly. '*Kalimera*. How you feel today, Isobel?'

'Much better,' Isobel assured her. 'Thank you, Eleni. You're a star.'

Eleni carried the tray out on to the veranda, leaving the doors open wide for Isobel. 'Eat well,' she commanded, and left Isobel to the pleasure of breakfast in the fresh air of a Chyros morning.

Thankful to find her nausea gone, Isobel ate one of the sweet rolls and finished off the tea, looking down in longing through the balcony rails at the pool. She sucked in a sudden breath. A bronzed body had appeared in the water, cutting through it like some exotic sea creature as Lukas swam laps of his pool at a speed that tired Isobel to watch. At last he heaved himself out of the water to stand with arms outstretched and face upturned to the sun for a minute or two before he wrapped his spectacular body in a towelling robe.

Isobel let out the breath she hadn't even known she was holding, wondering how to get herself off the balcony without attracting his attention. But before she could move he turned, gave her a mocking bow and strolled into the house.

Face flaming, Isobel did her Long John Silver act back into the bedroom to strip off her dressing gown. Time she moved out. She collected some clothes and a polythene bag used to pack shoes, and then went into the bathroom for a sponge down. It was a messy, unsatisfactory process, but she managed

it without wetting the bandage on her ankle, and felt absurdly pleased with herself when it was over. She slapped on some body lotion, struggled into her underwear, then pulled on a favourite comfortable yellow T-shirt dress and, with the help of the crutch, made it back into the bedroom just as Eleni hurried in.

'I came to help,' said the woman reproachfully.

Isobel smiled in apology. 'I had to see if I could manage on my own. I really must leave today and go back to the cottage. I'm afraid I used rather a lot of towels.'

The woman shrugged this off as unimportant, and went into the bathroom to collect them. 'You sit still now. I bring coffee,' she said firmly, and took the damp bundle away.

Isobel did her sitting still on the balcony, determined not to remain in the vicinity of Lukas Andreadis a moment longer than necessary. When Eleni came back with the coffee she would request a visit from the master of the house, preferably when he was fully clothed, and ask him for a lift down to the cottage. After that she need never see him again. Which would be good because she found his presence disturbing. For one thing, he was a man, and for another she was sure he still believed she'd been up to no good when she invaded his precious beach. While all she wanted from him was a lift back to the cottage so she could enjoy the rest of her holiday alone, in the peace she'd come all this way to find.

When she called in answer to a knock on the bedroom door she heard the slight rattling of a tray and sniffed the enticing scent of freshly made coffee. But, instead of Eleni, it was Luke Andreadis, casual in jeans and T-shirt, who came out onto the veranda to put a tray down on the table.

'*Kalimera*,' he greeted her. 'May I join you?'

'Of course,' she said, hiding her dismay. 'Good morning.'

'How are you today?'

'Much better.'

'Eleni tells me you did not wait for her to help you dress,' he said casually.

'I had to try to manage on my own.'

Luke handed her a cup of coffee, then pulled a chair up to the table. 'I trust,' he said, eyeing her ankle, 'that your bandage is still dry?'

'I wrapped my foot in a plastic bag.' She smiled politely. 'I'm self-sufficient now. So if you'd be kind enough to drive me down to the cottage this morning I'll leave you in peace.'

He shook his damp head. 'Not this morning.'

Isobel's heart sank. 'This afternoon, then?'

'Before you can stay there alone, food must be bought for you.'

'I'll give you money for Eleni,' she said promptly.

'Also,' he went on, brushing that aside, 'I must inspect the place for myself first, to check its suitability for your injury.'

Her chin lifted. 'There's absolutely no need for you to trouble yourself, Mr Andreadis,' she said flatly. 'If I can manage here, I can manage there.'

He raised an eyebrow. 'Also cook for yourself?'

'With a supply of salad vegetables, and bread and cheese, I shan't need to cook for myself for a day or two. And by then I'll be good on both feet,' she assured him, re-senting his tone.

'If you will give me your key I shall go down to the cottage soon,' said Luke. 'And then we shall see.'

Isobel sighed, frustrated. 'If you must. Though I thought you'd be only too pleased to get rid of me.'

His smile set off alarm bells in her head. 'As I told you, Miss James, we revere the traveller here in Greece.'

'You were anything but reverent when you found this one on your beach!'

'Only because I misunderstood the reason for your presence.' And strongly doubted her story of the Jet Ski. His eyes darkened. 'It is by no means unusual for journalists of both sexes to invade my beach, nor for young women to arrange to be stranded there.'

'In the hope that you'll come to the rescue?'

'Their hopes are usually higher—or lower—than that,' he said, his mouth twisting in distaste. 'I do not,' he added sardonically, 'delude myself that they are attracted to me in person. Only to my money.'

'And the power you used to amass it. Isn't power supposed to be the ultimate aphrodisiac?' Isobel smiled politely. 'You Greeks have a word for everything.'

He inclined his head. 'The rest of the world owes much to us.'

'What happens to trespassers when you're not here?'

'Milos deals with them. He is ex-army, and officially works as my gardener. But his main function is security. He had time off yesterday; otherwise you would have been removed before I arrived.'

'Which would have saved a lot of trouble.' One way and another.

Luke gave her the unsettling smile again. 'But it would also have deprived me of the pleasure of meeting you.'

Isobel dismissed that with a shrug. 'You speak very good English.'

'Thank you. I had a very good English teacher in school and, due to his influence, I studied for my MBA in London.' He got up. 'It is good you are not a journalist. I am not usually free with my personal details.'

'I shan't pass them on to anyone,' she assured him.

He looked surprised. 'They are not secrets. I was born here on Chyros. My background is known to everyone.'

'Even so, I don't speak Greek so I'm not likely to talk to anyone about you.'

'Not even to Alex Nicolaides? He speaks English.'

'He hardly knows me! Though he was very helpful,' she added.

'Which cannot surprise you.'

She raised an eyebrow in silent query.

'A look in the mirror will answer your question,' he informed her.

She sighed. Same old, same old. 'I seriously doubt that. I have a black eye, in case you haven't noticed, Mr Andreadis.'

'I could hardly help notice, but it is already fading and detracts very little from your looks, Miss James.'

'Thank you,' she said shortly, and bent to pick up her handbag. 'Here are the keys. Will you let me know your verdict as soon as possible?'

Luke took them, his eyes amused. 'You are so eager to leave my house?'

Her chin lifted. 'I really can't *trespass* on your hospitality any longer.'

'You throw the word at me like a missile!' He chuckled. 'I shall see you at lunch.'

Isobel scowled as he strolled from the room, feeling all at sea. Lukas Andreadis in friendly mode—if you could call it that—was deeply unnerving. Yet hearing something of his background had whetted her curiosity to know more. But Eleni was the only one she could ask, so there was no way she was going to find out any more unless he told her himself. And, since she was hopefully moving out today, and it wasn't

a question she could ask anyway, that was unlikely. But she couldn't leave until Luke Andreadis drove her to the cottage, so she would do what she always did with time on her hands—and far too often when she should have been doing other things entirely.

Isobel established herself at the balcony rail, propped one of her larger pads against it and began to sketch the pool. In the bright morning light it shone like a blue jewel in its setting of palms, oleander and feathery pink tamarisk. And as usual her concentration was soon so intense that Eleni had to clap her hands loudly to gain her attention.

'Lunch, Isobel.'

Isobel closed the sketchbook hastily and turned to smile at Eleni. 'I hadn't realised it was so late.'

'You wash now,' said the woman. 'Food nearly ready. You need help?'

'No, I can manage, thank you.' Isobel spent a few minutes in the bathroom, then went back into the bedroom to find Luke standing outside on the landing.

'Eleni says you must come immediately or the food will spoil,' he informed her. 'I will carry you down.'

Isobel flushed, taken aback. 'I thought I was eating up here again.'

'While I thought you would enjoy lunch on the terrace. Even with the disadvantage of my company,' he added slyly.

Isobel eyed him irritably. If she'd had prior knowledge of the arrangement, out of sheer pride she might have gilded the lily a bit—or as much as she could in her present condition. The swelling on her face had gone down, the bruise was fading slightly below her eye, which she could now open fully, but it was still no pleasure to look in a mirror. 'You don't have to carry me. I can manage with the crutch.'

'That will take too long, and Eleni will be very annoyed if her food is kept waiting,' he informed her and, ignoring her involuntary recoil, picked her up. Isobel tensed, for the first time physically aware of Luke as a man. She felt enveloped in the warmth and scent of him, and wanted to beat him away with clenched fists.

'Eleni didn't warn me,' she said, voice stifled, as Luke carried her down the curving staircase to the hall.

'I told her not to.'

'Why?'

'You would have refused.'

'I hope my manners are better than that, Mr Andreadis!'

He took her through open glass doors to a pergola wreathed with greenery on the section of terrace overlooking the pool. He set her down at a table laid for lunch. 'I think that under the circumstances we can dispense with formality. I am Luke.'

Bad idea. 'I'm Isobel,' she said reluctantly.

'Much better,' he said, and sat opposite her. 'Will you have some wine?'

'In deference to my head, I think I'd better stick with water.'

'Ah, yes—excuse me for a moment.' He went back into the house and returned with a walking stick. 'Borrow this. When you no longer need the crutch you might find it useful.'

Isobel's eyes lit up, winning an arrested look from him. 'I will, indeed. Thank you.' She hooked the stick over the arm of her chair. 'Wonderful. Now I'm completely self-sufficient. What did you think of the cottage?'

He smiled. 'I had already inspected the houses at various stages with Nikos Nicolaides while they were being built.'

Her eyes flashed. 'Then you knew perfectly well mine would be suitable.'

'More or less,' he admitted, and filled her water glass.

'So will you drive me there this afternoon, please?'

Instead of answering, he greeted Eleni with a smile as she delivered a large dish giving off delicious scents. 'Ah, *garides saganaki*, or, for our English guest, prawns with feta in tomato sauce—and probably a few subtleties known only to the cook,' he announced. '*Efcharisto*, Eleni.'

'Eat while hot,' she instructed as she left.

'This smells heavenly,' said Isobel with anticipation.

Luke got up to take the bowl she filled for him. 'You like Greek food?'

'It's only my second experience of it. But,' she said, after tasting the prawns, 'this is just wonderful. I adore seafood.'

'Which is fortunate,' said Luke. 'I did not ask if you were allergic to shellfish.'

'I'm not. Nor to anything else, so far. I have a pretty iron digestive system normally.' She flushed. 'Which is why I was so mortified yesterday on the way down to the clinic. It was a new experience for me.'

'For me, also,' Luke said with feeling, and looked her in the eye. 'You are quite well now in that way?'

'Absolutely. Otherwise I wouldn't be tucking into this delicious prawn dish. Eleni's a great cook. Has she been with you long?'

'All my life. She helped my mother with me when I was a baby. Also her husband Spiro, the son of my mother's old nurse, Sofia. As I told you,' added Luke, 'everyone on Chyros knows my history.'

'That must be rather wonderful—like an extended family.'

He inclined his head. 'Which is why I spend as much time here as possible, when my work allows. In Athens and Thessaloniki many people know who I am, but few know the real Lukas Andreadis.'

'Do you prefer it that way?'

'In some ways, yes. But, like you, I have good friends—in my case, men whose interests are similar to mine.'

'You said your interest in women is well known, too,' she reminded him.

Luke looked her in the eye. 'But they are—or were—just pillow friends, Isobel. I always make my views on marriage—or even commitment—very clear.'

Her hackles rose. Why did he think it necessary to tell her that? She had no designs on him. Or on any other man for the foreseeable future. 'I thought a man like you would want a son to inherit this empire of yours. Not that it's any business of mine,' she added hastily.

'Do you want a husband and family, Isobel?' asked Luke, surprising her.

'Not right now, no.'

'You have never met a man you wish to marry?'

'No,' she said shortly, and smiled as Eleni appeared with a bowl of fruit. 'That was absolutely delicious,' she told her, indicating her empty dish.

The woman looked pleased as she cleared away.

'I saw Dr Riga when I was down in the town,' said Luke casually, once they were alone. 'He thinks it best you remain here at the villa for a few days, rather than manage alone at the cottage.'

Isobel stared at him in astonishment. 'But why? There's nothing wrong with me now, except for the foot. And with my crutch and this wonderful stick I'll be fine on my own.'

'Nevertheless, he advises you stay here until completely recovered.' He shrugged. 'After a fall on the head there can be complications.'

She frowned. 'What kind?'

'A clot of blood on the brain, for one. There was a case only recently of a young boy complaining of head pains after a fall. Lacking the necessary equipment, the doctor performed emergency surgery with an ordinary power drill to release the pressure on the brain and saved the boy's life.'

Isobel blanched, beginning to regret the prawns.

Luke smiled in reassurance. 'Since there was no fracture to your skull, Dr Riga said there is no risk of this in your case. But he thinks you should stay here for a while. So do I.' Though for a quite different reason. 'Eleni thinks so, too.'

Isobel drew in a deep breath, deeply shaken by the idea of blood clots. 'Poor Eleni. I've given her so much extra work.'

'She does not think of it that way, Isobel,' he assured her, peeling an orange. 'In fact, Eleni thinks you are a very lovely young lady, so does Spiro.' The dark, compelling eyes met hers for a moment. 'I agree with them.'

Isobel's eyes fell. 'Thank you. If I had to have an accident I was very lucky to land on your beach for it. You've all been so kind.'

'Including me?' he said, eyes gleaming.

Her chin lifted. 'Once you found I wasn't a journalist, yes, you were—are—kind. Autocratic, too, but I suppose that's second nature to you.'

'If I were truly autocratic,' he said very deliberately, 'I would simply *demand* that you stay here. But, even on such short acquaintance, Miss Isobel James, I realise that this would work against me. So, I repeat my invitation. Stay a little while longer.'

Isobel sighed. 'Now you've planted the idea of electric drills in my head, solitude at the cottage has no appeal right now. So thank you. I will stay for a day or so.'

'Very wise. And when you do leave the villa I shall arrange

for someone to check on you at regular intervals,' he stated, then arched an eyebrow as she smiled wryly. 'What is so amusing?'

'You were in touch with your inner autocrat again, Mr Andreadis.'

'I cannot help who—and what—I am.' Luke smiled. 'I return to Athens shortly, so you may convalesce here in peace, Isobel. And when you are ready to leave, Spiro will drive you to the cottage.'

CHAPTER FOUR

ISOBEL was much cheered by this piece of news. It would be a lot more peaceful at the Villa Medusa without the formidable presence of its owner. But she would miss him from a transport point of view.

'What is going on behind those beautiful blue eyes?' Luke asked, startling her. 'I can almost hear your brain working.' His eyes gleamed. 'Is it possible you might miss my help in carrying you downstairs?'

'Yes,' she said frankly.

'I had thought of that,' he informed her. 'I considered asking Milos to carry you when necessary. But I decided against it.'

'Why?'

Luke looked at her in silence for a while. 'Not a suitable solution,' he said at last. 'Instead, we shall transfer you to a room down here.'

Isobel eyed him curiously. 'May I ask why you didn't put me there in the first place?'

'It had no bed. Now it does. It will be much better for Eleni,' he added. 'It will save her from constant running upstairs to check on you.'

'A definite plus,' agreed Isobel meekly. 'Thank you.'

'Would you like to see the room now?'

'Yes, please.' She picked up the crutch and manoeuvred herself away from the table.

'It would be easier if I carried you,' he said, joining her.

'Unnecessary down here. I'm pretty nippy already with my trusty crutch,' she assured him. 'So lead on, Mr Andreadis.'

He conducted her back into the house and along the hall into a sitting room with glass doors leading on to the terrace and an awning outside to shield the room from the sun. Furniture had obviously been rearranged to allow for the bed to be placed with the best view of the garden.

Isobel looked round doubtfully. 'It's lovely, but isn't this where you sit at night?'

'Rarely. I prefer the conservatory, or my study on the other side of the hall. Sometimes I stay out on the terrace until I go to bed.' Luke smiled. 'Use the room as long as you wish, Isobel. The ground floor bathroom is close by. Eleni and Spiro have one of their own, so you are assured perfect privacy.'

Isobel examined her new quarters in silence. Her belongings were already arranged on the desk, and her clothes hanging on a dress rail beside it. 'I booked my holiday on the recommendation of a client who came here to recover from a divorce,' she said at last. 'She told me that Chyros was the perfect place for peace and quiet, but in my case she was wrong.'

Luke opened the doors onto the terrace. 'Why did *you* need peace and quiet? A love affair gone wrong?'

'No,' lied Isobel. 'My boss recently gave the gallery a huge makeover, and I had my work cut out to make sure it was business as usual during the alterations. At the same time I was working on a commission for a series of watercolours, and setting up an exhibition of paintings by an artist friend at the gallery for its ceremonial reopening.' She smiled wryly.

'Not quite the same high octane stuff as your takeovers, but I was glad of some time off once everything was sorted.'

'Then it is far better you stay here for a while and let Eleni and Spiro take care of you. You have a phone?' he added.

'Yes. At least I hope so.' She limped over to the desk and looked in her bag. 'Still here, thank goodness. In all the excitement yesterday it's a wonder I didn't lose that, too.'

'Give me your number,' he ordered, taking his phone from a pocket. He keyed the number into it, then held out his hand for hers. 'I shall enter mine in yours.'

'I shan't need it,' she said quickly.

'You might. I shall charge this before I give it back.' He gave her a searching look. 'Your head is aching?'

'Yes.'

'I can tell. I shall send Eleni with tea. Take some medication and rest for a while. I shall see you later at dinner,' he added as he left.

When Eleni came with the tea, Isobel asked directions to the bathroom and later, when she was propped up on the comfortable bed, looking out on the garden through the open doors, admitted that now the owner was leaving she had no objection to spending another day or two here. Talk of blood clots had given her quite a fright. On her own in the cottage, the slightest pain in her head would have sent her imagination into overdrive.

She leaned back with a sigh. Here at the Villa Medusa it would be dangerously easy to laze away the days of her holiday in true lotus-eating style, whereas part of her original intention for her trip to Greece had been to produce some watercolours she could put up for sale at the gallery on her return. Joanna had dismissed that idea out of hand, arguing that the idea of a holiday was to have fun as well as take a

rest. But to Isobel painting *was* fun. So tomorrow, once Luke
Andreadis had left for Athens, she would set up her water-
colours, paint the pool in its frame of lush greenery and, if she
considered the result good enough, leave it for him as thanks
for his help. The help had been hostile and reluctant at first
but he'd given it just the same, even though he'd mistaken her
for a journalist, or worse. And, unless she was much mistaken,
he still suspected her of stranding herself on his beach like
some party girl after a good time. But the fact remained that
he had rescued her, arranged medical attention and taken her
into his home to recover. She owed him.

Isobel slept a little, and when she woke just lay there, savour-
ing the pleasure of simply feeling better. But after a while she
sat up and stealthily eased herself out of bed. With the help of
the crutch she would go exploring. Moving with care, she went
out onto the terrace, wishing she had her sunglasses. Hers, pre-
sumably, were still down on that beach somewhere. Pity. With
growing confidence Isobel made her way along the marble flags
edging the pool and stood looking into the water in longing for
a minute or two, then with a sigh turned back towards the arcaded
terrace surrounding the house. But, as she turned, the tip of the
crutch stuck in a crack and with a shriek she fell onto the grass.

Instantly she was swept up in strong, unfamiliar arms and
a flood of anxious Greek poured into her ears. Deeply embar-
rassed, Isobel tried to reassure Milos she was unhurt. Her face
flamed as Luke strode out of the house, holding out imperi-
ous arms, and Milos hastily surrendered Isobel to his
employer and picked up the crutch. He confirmed there was
no damage to it and, with a brief word of thanks to Milos,
Luke carried Isobel along the terrace and out of the sun.

She eyed his stern face warily. 'Sorry for the disturbance,'
she said at last.

'Tell me the truth. Are you really unhurt?' he demanded.

'Yes. I fell on the grass—soft landing this time.' Her smile met with a stony look.

'And yet you are determined to go back to the Kalypso to manage alone!'

'But when I'm there I'll stay in the house,' she protested, and sighed. 'I just wanted to look at your beautiful garden.'

'You could have fallen in the pool!'

She shrugged. 'No problem. I'm a strong swimmer.'

'Excellent,' he said grimly. 'At least I shall not worry that you drown while I am away.' He turned away to the table to pour a glass of fruit juice for her, then perched on the edge of the table, scowling down at her while she drank it.

'Please apologise to Milos for me,' said Isobel.

Luke's mouth curved in a sardonic smile. 'No apology is necessary. Milos was no doubt grateful for the chance to hold you in his arms.'

Isobel eyed him incredulously. 'You think I fell on purpose?'

He gave a cynical shrug. 'Did you?'

She drank the rest of her ice-cold juice to calm down. 'No,' she said when she could trust her voice. 'I did not. Thank you for the drink. Now, if you'll excuse me?' She stood up and limped off to her new room, filled with a burning desire to assault Luke Andreadis with her crutch as he kept pace with her. She gave him a cold little smile as he opened the door for her. 'Thank you. Would you be kind enough to ask Eleni to see me when she has a moment?'

'Of course. Unless there is something I can do for you instead?' Luke eyed her challengingly when she shook her head. 'You are angry?'

'Not in the least,' she lied.

'No?' He arched a disbelieving eyebrow. 'I will fetch Eleni.'

'Thank you so much.'

Isobel stared out into the garden, fuming. Did Luke really imagine she'd fallen over just so that brawny Milos could pick her up? Or, even worse, so that the lord and master himself could come to her rescue again. She ground her teeth impotently. Luke had grabbed her away from Milos as though she were a parcel. Or baggage, from his point of view. She smiled reluctantly, her sense of humour reasserting itself as Eleni came rushing in.

'Isobel? You ill?'

'No, no, nothing like that. I feel fine.'

'Milos said you fell.'

'My crutch stuck in a crack and tripped me up.'

Eleni tutted disapprovingly. 'So what you need?'

'I hate to make extra work for you, but could I possibly have my supper in here on my own tonight?'

The woman looked anxious. 'You did hurt!'

'No, no. I'd just rather eat alone. Please?'

Eleni plumped up the pillows on the bed, eyeing her narrowly. 'You rest. Not time to eat yet.'

'*Efcharisto*, Eleni.'

Although she'd opted out of dining with the lord and master of Villa Medusa, an encounter with him later was no doubt inevitable. To armour herself for it, Isobel washed carefully in the bathroom and zipped herself into a cool cotton shift in her favourite cornflower-blue. With even more care, she combed out her hair, then subsided gratefully against the pillows on the bed. The crutch was a huge help, but getting around with it was tiring just the same. She longed to ring Joanna, but if she did Jo would immediately sense something wrong and keep nagging until Isobel confessed. Time enough for that when she went home. She closed her eyes against a sudden

wave of homesickness. When she opened them again she saw Luke on the terrace, watching her through the open doors.

'May I come in?' he asked.

'It's your house.'

'But this is your room.'

She shrugged indifferently. 'Come in, if you want.' A pity to waste the primping.

Luke came to stand by the bed, looking down at her. 'Eleni says you refuse to join me for dinner.'

'Yes. I'd rather eat alone in here.'

'Why?'

She raised a disdainful eyebrow. 'You were insulting, Mr Andreadis.'

'It was a shock to see Milo holding you in his arms,' he said harshly. 'I thought you were hurt.'

'No,' she corrected. 'You thought I'd engineered a fall just so he'd pick me up.'

'Only for a second.' He smiled persuasively. 'Am I forgiven?'

In his dreams! 'Of course.'

'Then you will dine with me?'

'No, thank you.'

To Isobel's annoyance, Luke drew up a chair and sat down. 'Then I shall also eat here.'

This was silly! 'Eleni wouldn't approve of that,' she told him crossly.

'So join me on the terrace.' He was silent for a moment. 'I apologise, Isobel. My only excuse is my reaction to seeing you in Milos's arms.' His eyes locked on hers with a look which set alarm bells ringing again. 'I was angry when I saw him touching you.'

'How utterly ridiculous,' she said scornfully. 'Milos was just being kind.'

'You will discourage him from such kindness in future!'

Isobel glared at him. 'I will certainly make sure that neither he, nor you, Mr Andreadis, will be forced to pick me up again.'

'No force is necessary,' he assured her, his eyes gleaming, and took her hand. 'To hold you in my arms is a great pleasure, Isobel. Even though you make it so clear the pleasure is not mutual.' He smiled persuasively. 'Change your mind. Dine with me tonight. Otherwise, poor Eleni must serve a meal in two places. Three, if you count the one she shares with Spiro.'

Isobel gave in, defeated. Eleni had been so kind it was hardly fair to cause her extra work. And Luke would be gone soon. Even if he returned to Chyros while she was here, she would be at the cottage, not the villa. She detached her hand very deliberately.

'Oh, very well,' she said at last. 'But only to save Eleni.'

Luke smiled victoriously. 'Good. Rest until dinner time. I shall come for you later.'

Alone again, Isobel lay deep in thought as she gazed through the open doors at the sunlit garden. Luke was giving out signals she identified with misgivings. Was he expecting some kind of return for her bed and board? He was a dangerously attractive man, not least for the inner force so plainly burning behind the impressive physical exterior. But she had no intention of indulging in anything remotely like a fling with him. Or any other man. Had he really been jealous just because Milos fielded her when she fell? She ground her teeth impotently. A very good thing he was leaving tomorrow. Otherwise, he might take her consent to stay on here as willingness to be his 'pillow friend', whatever that meant. It was not impossible. She was far from looking her best at the moment, but in her normal state men were usually attracted to her. With disastrous results in one instance. She shivered.

That there was no significant male presence in her life right now was entirely her own choice. And she was going to keep it that way.

Isobel would have given much to wash her hair, but instead settled for a careful session with a hairbrush, and application of eye-shadow and concealer that worked wonders on her rapidly fading bruise. In spite of all the drama, her headache was surprisingly absent, her ankle less painful and for just moving around the room she could manage with the walking stick. But she would play safe with the crutch to make for the terrace rather than wait for Luke to fetch her.

When he joined her at the dinner table, spectacular in dark linen trousers and a shirt in a shade of pink which looked outrageously good on him, Luke raised a quizzical eyebrow.

'I went to your room, but my little bird had flown away.'

Isobel smiled smugly. 'I needed the exercise.'

'While I had hoped for the pleasure of carrying you,' he assured her suavely, and seated himself beside her. 'Is your headache better?'

'Touch wood,' she said, tapping the table, 'it seems to have gone.'

'Excellent. In that case, will you have a glass of wine? A local label, but I think you will like it.'

'I'm sure I will. Thank you.'

'Thank *you*,' he said very deliberately, 'for joining me tonight after I made you so angry this afternoon.'

She eyed him through lowered lashes, her antennae on the alert in response to Luke Andreadis in charming mode. Why the change of attitude? She raised the glass he'd filled for her. 'You're leaving soon, so let's enjoy the evening in a spirit of friendship.'

Luke raised his own glass. 'We will enjoy the evening, certainly, but I shall return from Athens before you leave.'

'Will you? I thought you'd be too busy with your new venture.'

'I shall be. But I employ clever people more than capable of keeping the engines running when I take time off,' he assured her, and drank some wine. 'Even Air Chyros, my new baby, has a specialist department to look after it and can therefore function without me for short periods. So,' he added, 'should you have a problem, just ring me and I can arrange for whatever help you need. But if you feel ill in any way tell Spiro to contact Dr Riga immediately.'

'I'm sure I'll be fine from now on. But I appreciate the thought.'

'You value your independence very highly,' said Luke indulgently. 'Is there no man at all in your life, Isobel?'

Her eyes shadowed. 'No.'

He shook his head. 'Amazing. Why not?'

Isobel shrugged. 'Because I haven't met anyone remotely suitable lately.'

Luke's eyebrows shot into his hair. 'A cold attitude! A lover must be more than just suitable. Have you never met a man who makes your heart beat faster?'

Yes, but for entirely the wrong reasons. 'I was in a relationship quite recently,' she admitted.

He waited, but when Isobel merely drank her wine he stared at her in frustration. 'So what happened?'

'We broke up due to irreconcilable differences.' She shrugged. 'I wanted his friendship. He was fixated on my appearance. He just couldn't see past it to the personality—and hopefully brain—behind the hair and eyes.'

Luke frowned. 'But surely a man can be attracted by both your looks and your brain?'

'Very few, unfortunately.'

Luke offered her a plate of olives. 'You must eat well tonight to gain your strength. You are too thin, Isobel.'

'I'm sure you were glad of that when you were forced to carry me around so much!'

'Very true. Most ladies of my acquaintance are more generously built,' he admitted, and smiled into her eyes. 'In Athens I will think of you when you are eating alone here.'

Isobel shook her head. 'You'll be too busy.'

'Not too busy to think of *you*, Isobel,' he assured her, a gleam under the heavy, lazy lids she was getting to know. And suspect.

'Amazing!' she said, shaking her head in wonder.

'What is amazing?'

'How you've changed from the man who was so furious at finding me on his beach.' She eyed him curiously. 'If I had been just a sunbathing trespasser, instead of injured and unconscious, what would you have done?'

'My usual treatment is a harsh lecture, after which I give the trespasser a swift passage back to the harbour.' He eyed her thoughtfully. 'I *think* I would have done the same for you, but that is very hard to imagine. Now.'

'I'm sure you'd have sent me packing, just like the rest.'

He smiled indulgently. 'I doubt it.'

Isobel took refuge in her wine. Unless she was mistaken, Luke really was showing signs of fancying her as one of his 'pillow friends'. And because he'd rescued her from his beach and taken her into his home, he probably thought he had the right to expect it. Which would make for a very difficult situation when she refused. As she would.

'You're very quiet,' he commented.

'Anticipation of dinner. And here comes Eleni with it right now,' she added, relieved.

'Which I trust you will eat. Otherwise, you will be too weak to get back to your cottage before you fly home. Right, Eleni?'

The woman nodded vigorously. 'Much better stay here.' She patted Isobel's shoulder as she left.

'Eleni's very sweet,' said Isobel.

'I shall tell her you said so. She will be pleased—she has taken a great fancy to you.' He shrugged. 'I have never brought a woman here. She is enjoying the experience.'

To Isobel's irritation, this information pleased her. How silly was that? His social life was nothing to do with her. 'You keep that side of your life for Athens, I suppose?'

'That side of my life?'

'The pillow friends and so on.'

'By that particular term I mean those ladies who are happy to wine and dine and stay the night occasionally. I make my intentions clear from the start,' he added deliberately, 'so that no one is misled—or hurt.'

She seriously doubted that. Probably they all hoped that wining and dining—and a sleepover—would just be the opening bout for the main event of something permanent with a man like Lukas Andreadis, who possessed physical appeal, success and wealth as the triple layer of icing on the cake. A combination far too overpowering for Isobel.

After the meal Luke suggested she might like to sit in one of the reclining chairs beside the pool.

'I would, indeed—'

Before the words were out of her mouth, Luke picked her up and carried her along the terrace to lay her carefully in one of the chairs. 'Are you comfortable?' he asked as he straightened.

'Yes—thank you,' she said through clenched teeth, irritated to find that, while her brain repudiated physical intimacy with

Luke as total disaster, the fleeting physical contact with him had sent her hormones running riot, damn them.

'What is wrong, Isobel?' he asked, taking the chair beside her.

'Nothing. How could anything be wrong?' she said, getting a grip. 'It's so beautiful here.'

'True—' He groaned as his phone rang. 'Forgive me for a moment?' he asked, identifying the caller. 'I must answer this.'

'Of course.' Isobel watched him stride into the house, talking to his caller in tones which made it obvious, even though she couldn't understand a word of it, that the news he was being given was bad. She sat back in her chair, giving her hormones a stringent lecture as she watched the play of lights on the pool.

Luke looked grim when he rejoined her. 'I must leave for Athens at daybreak.'

'Trouble?'

'Of a kind, yes. During the airline takeover there was one solitary dissenter when the board voted for my acquisition.'

'And he's making difficulties for you?'

'She,' he corrected, with a harsh note in his voice that won him a sharp look. 'The woman previously in charge of the airline. When she found there was no way to stop the merger going through, the lady was so enraged she eventually suffered a stroke. I have just been informed that she died of it today.'

'Do you feel you're to blame?' asked Isobel soberly.

Luke looked at her in surprise. 'No. If the gods struck her down it was her fate.'

'That's very—Greek of you.'

He shrugged. 'Even if I am to blame for her stroke *and* her death, I am merely the instrument fate chose for this.'

Her eyes widened. 'You obviously didn't like her much.'

'Like her?' Luke gave a mirthless bark of laughter. 'It

may shock you to hear this, but I hated her so much I rejoice in her death.'

His brutal honesty sent shivers down Isobel's spine. 'Will you go to her funeral?'

'Of course. It will be expected. Funerals take place here as soon as possible after death, so tonight there will be the *Trisagion*, or vigil, with prayers for the departed. I would not have attended that even if I were there, but I shall put in the necessary appearance at the church tomorrow, complete with black arm band. Unless her husband turns me away at the door,' he added grimly.

'But if his wife had a stroke, it's hardly reasonable to blame you for her death!'

'He has never been a reasonable man.'

'You know him well?'

'I know *of* him well enough!'

'Was he involved in the takeover negotiations?'

Luke smiled coldly. 'For some reason he chose to stay behind the scenes and let his wife Melina do the talking, which was his big mistake. If he had conducted the negotiations himself, things might not have gone so well for me. But from the day he gave her nominal control of the airline, his wife made enemies of every man on the board. The result was unanimous acceptance of my offer.'

'Not a nice lady.'

Luke smiled grimly. 'Not nice at all, Isobel.'

'But her husband must be grieving for her, just the same.'

'Possibly. But he has many business interests to console him. I doubt he will grieve for long.'

'That's cold! You obviously don't like him, either.'

Luke's teeth showed white in the semi-darkness. '*Like* is too lukewarm a word, Isobel.'

'You know him well, then?'

'No. If I meet him tomorrow it will be for the first time. Yet Theodore Andreadis is my grandfather.'

CHAPTER FIVE

ISOBEL'S eyes widened in astonishment. 'Your *grandfather*? And you've never met him?'

'He does not acknowledge the relationship.' The words sounded like pebbles dropped in a dish. Luke shrugged. 'Not that I wish him to, nor do I trade on the fact that I am his grandson. To me, he is just a tyrannical old man I cannot forgive for his treatment of my mother. If I tell you what he did it may help you understand.' He turned to look at her. 'Though normally this is not a subject I discuss.'

'Your confidence is safe with me, I promise.'

'I do not doubt it. So, let me explain the rift. My grandmother, the first wife of Theo Andreadis, left him for a lover when their daughter was a baby, but died soon afterwards. To avoid history repeating itself, Theo brought Olympia up very strictly, educated at home instead of sent to school, and allowed contact with only one friend he considered suitable. In time he remarried and presented her with Melina, the archetypal wicked stepmother. She,' he added harshly, 'made life a living hell for the young Olympia.'

'So that's why you hated her!'

'There was worse to come. Coaxed by her friend to break out and go to a party, Olympia met a man there. Afterwards,

having tasted freedom, Olympia stole out of the house at night to meet him as often as she could. Her absences went unnoticed, due to the discretion of loyal servants who adored Olympia. But I was the inevitable result of these secret meetings. When Melina found out about the pregnancy, she urged Theodore Andreadis to throw his daughter out of the house for disgracing his name, as her mother had done before her. So he did,' Luke added harshly.

Isobel eyed him in horror. 'How did your mother survive?'

'With the help of her faithful friend Chloe, she managed to get to her old nurse, here on Chyros, and begged a job from Basil Nikolaides in the kitchen of his taverna. After I was born she kept her job, saved everything she could for my education, and after school hours and at weekends I worked, too, usually as deck hand on one of the fishing boats. The jewels left to her by my erring grandmother were all my mother took with her from her home in Athens, and sales of these saw me through college and financed my MBA. But, to my great sorrow, my mother died before I began making money with my freighters.' Luke's mouth tightened. 'So you see why I have no love for Theo Andreadis; even less for his harpy of a wife.'

Isobel was silent for a while. 'When did you start thinking about revenge?'

His lips tightened. 'From the day I heard what happened to my mother.'

'It must have been hard for her to tell you.'

Luke shook his head. 'She did not. I had it all from old Sofia, who would have murdered Theo Andreadis with her own bare hands if she could, and Melina with him. I swore I would one day take my revenge. But not with murder, as Sofia thirsted for. I had something more subtle and painful in mind. Taking over the airline was the perfect revenge on

Melina because it was the ultimate humiliation for her. She was so incandescent with fury it is no surprise that she had a stroke afterwards. Nor am I hypocrite enough to pretend regret that she is dead.'

Isobel was silent as she stared out into the starlit night, feeling chilled to the bone.

'You are shocked?' he asked.

'Stunned, rather. It's like a Sophocles tragedy.' She turned to him. 'You've had your revenge on Melina, but what about your grandfather? Is his wife's death enough revenge for you, or do you have something different planned for him?'

'I did not plan Melina's death—fate did that for me. And no doubt it will do the same for Theo Andreadis one day without my help. Even though I have no love for him, I will not seek revenge on someone of my own blood,' Luke assured her and smiled faintly. 'Isobel, you have not asked me the all important question.'

'I wouldn't dream of asking you any questions at all,' she assured him. 'I'm gratified that you told a stranger like me even this much.'

'It is not normal dinner table conversation,' he agreed. 'But you must surely be curious about the identity of my natural father.'

'I'm only human, so of course I am,' she said frankly. 'But only if you want to tell me.'

To his surprise, Luke found that he did. 'Chloe, the friend who took Olympia to the party, had a brother who excelled at athletics. He introduced the shy Olympia to the gold medallist swimmer he brought home from college for the party. It was love at first sight for both of them. After a series of brief stolen meetings, arranged with help from

the faithful Chloe, the secret lover left to train for his next championship, promising to return to marry Olympia straight afterwards.'

'I'm not going to like the next bit,' said Isobel with foreboding. 'He didn't come back, obviously.'

'No. His plane crashed.'

'Oh, Luke, that's so sad!'

He nodded sombrely. 'All she had of him were his gold medals and the son he gave her. Apparently, I resemble him very closely. And,' he added with a smile, 'I have always been a powerful swimmer.'

'I saw you in the pool.'

'I know, Isobel.' He chuckled softly. 'Were you impressed?'

'Yes,' she said honestly. 'Though very embarrassed when you caught me watching.' She gave a sudden yawn, more from nerves than weariness. 'Sorry.'

'You are tired. It is time you went to bed.' Deaf to her protests, he picked her up and carried her along the terrace to her room, finding that his senses were stirred by emotions he normally kept under rigid control—the direct result of sharing such personal information with Isobel. Combined with the scent and warmth of the slender body in his arms, they filled him with a sudden urgent need for the kind of solace only a woman could provide and, instead of setting her down on her feet he sat down in the armchair with her in his lap. 'When a man rescues a damsel in distress he deserves a reward, *ne*?'

She stiffened, pulling away in alarm. 'What kind of reward do you have in mind?'

'Just a goodnight kiss.'

Isobel shook her head vehemently, pushing him away in such frenzied rejection Luke got up, grim-faced, and laid her down against the pillows on the bed.

'Do not look at me like that,' he said harshly, staring down into her ashen face. 'I am not a rapist.'

'Maybe not.' She hugged her arms across her chest, unable to meet his eyes. 'But neither am I applying for the post of pillow friend.'

Luke stood utterly still for a moment. 'A word of advice, Isobel,' he said after a pause. 'Wait until asked to apply for such a post before you refuse.'

She burrowed into the pillows, burning with mortification as he strode through the open doors. Thank God he was leaving tomorrow. Before he came back—if he did come back while she was here—she would be at the cottage. With a gasp, she shot upright again as he reappeared from the terrace with her crutch.

'I will send Eleni with tea,' he said curtly.

'No! Please tell her I don't need anything tonight.'

'As you wish.' Luke gave her a formal nod. 'I leave early in the morning. I shall say goodbye now.'

'Goodbye.' Isobel pulled herself together. 'Thank you again for all your help.'

He shrugged negligently as he made for the door. 'It was nothing.'

Isobel slumped against the pillows, fighting the urge to cry her eyes out. But if she gave in to tears the headache would come back and, threat of blood clots or not, tomorrow she was determined to leave the Villa Medusa. She looked at her watch and groaned. It was still quite early and she was no longer tired. Quite the reverse. The brief episode had sent her into such a spin she would take some calming down if she was to get to sleep any time before morning.

Later, propped up against pillows ready for the night, Isobel felt better, grateful to her head for letting her read. At

least she wouldn't have to lie awake all night, mulling over the mortifying episode with Luke. But she couldn't explain why she'd shied off like a frightened virgin. Although he'd surprised her with details about his background, her own experience was too new and raw to talk about to a man who was virtually a stranger. So if Luke had harboured any idea about a holiday fling it was better to nip it in the bud right now. She sighed heavily. The physical contact of carrying her about so much had been to blame, creating intimacy from the word go.

Isobel steeled herself to concentrate on her book. Then looked up in surprise as someone knocked on her door.

'Come in,' she called, expecting Eleni, her body instantly rigid as Luke came in and closed the door behind him.

'I saw your light.' He approached the bed, something in his eyes pressing her panic button again. 'I knew you were awake, Isobel. I brought your phone.'

'Thank you,' she said stiffly. 'I'd forgotten all about it. I was reading.'

'The phone was just an excuse.' He sat on the edge of the bed, frowning as she backed away. 'Isobel, did you really believe that I would force you? You are a guest in my house, and still recovering from an accident. Do you think I am such a monster?'

'No. I don't.' Her eyes fell.

'Thank the gods for that,' he said dryly. 'Then why such panic?'

She drew in a deep, unsteady breath. 'Bad experience lately.'

'A lover who refused to take no for an answer?'

'Something like that.'

Luke's eyes darkened. 'He hurt you?'

She nodded.

'Can you talk about it?'

'No.'

'Perhaps it would be good for you if you did.' He put a finger under her chin to turn her face up. 'Tell me, Isobel.'

She stared at him in indecision, then sighed wearily. Why not? It was supposed to be easier to confide in a stranger. 'I have this problem,' she began very quietly. 'Due to my lack of relatives, I tend to look for friendship and caring rather than heat and, well, sex, when it comes to relationships. A few months ago I met an artist whose work we put on display at the gallery. He became a regular fixture in my life, good company for meals and concerts and so on. But nothing more than that. But when we got back from what turned out to be our last evening together he asked to see my latest series of watercolours. They were still in my flat, so for the first time I invited him up there.' She pushed the hair back from her face. 'He mistook the invitation for something else entirely. I tried to fight him off, but he's a big man and things got rough.'

Luke's eyes smouldered into hers. 'He raped you, this friend?'

Her hands clenched. 'He had a good try. But I fought him so hard I managed to jab him with a stiletto heel in a place which put a stop to proceedings.' She shivered. 'But not before he hurt me badly. Psychologically as well as physically.'

He swore under his breath. 'It would have been even worse if he had succeeded. You could have been left with child.'

Isobel flushed, and shook her head. 'I have close friends—twin brothers who are both doctors—and, on their advice, I've taken the necessary precautions for years against that kind of accident.' She sighed, depressed. 'Up to that point I'd really thought Gavin was a true friend like the Carey twins. But it was the same old story. He just wanted to get me into bed. And I haven't had a good night's sleep since.' She

shrugged. 'I've given up on men since then. Other than the friends I've known forever.'

'I rejoice to know it is not something I have done.' Luke smiled wryly. 'I was most cast down when you refused to eat with me earlier. My dinner invitations are usually accepted more eagerly.'

She gave a choked little giggle. 'I bet they are.'

His eyes lit up. 'That is better. You are even more lovely when you smile, Isobel. But, if I say so, you will accuse me of appreciating your beauty more than your intellect.'

She smiled. 'Since you've been so kind I'll make an exception in your case, Luke.'

'So we are friends again?' He smiled slyly. 'You said you like men who wish to be friends.'

'I do. Not that it matters. I'll be back in England soon.'

'It is not time for you to go yet. And I shall return here in a few days,' he went on, surprising her. 'After the funeral I will work very hard to make sure I get away. By then,' he added, 'you will be well again. So take care this week. No climbing down cliff paths even when your ankle is better. If you want to sunbathe on my beach, Spiro will take you over in the *Athena*. Spiro,' he repeated significantly, 'not Milos.'

She smiled wryly. 'Actually, I won't bother either of them, thanks just the same. I'll be quite happy to sit on my veranda at the cottage, and when I can I'll stroll down to the taverna to eat.'

Luke frowned. 'It would be more sensible to stay here, Isobel.'

Not if he was coming back. She shook her head. 'It's very kind of you, but I really must get back to the cottage. Before I do, have I your permission for a swim in your pool?'

'Wait until I return. I will swim with you,' he said quickly. 'Dr Riga is coming to check on you tomorrow, and you must do as he says, *ne*?'

'Yes,' she said, resigned.

'And when you return to the cottage, take both walking stick and crutch.'

'Absolutely.' Isobel held out her hand, but her smile faded as her eyes met his. There was sudden taut silence between them, then Luke pressed a kiss on the hand. He leaned nearer, his eyes intent on hers. 'Normally,' he said softly, 'I like my women dark and voluptuous. Unlike you, my little English friend.'

'I definitely don't tick your boxes,' she said, determinedly prosaic. 'My hair is fair—'

'Golden,' he corrected.

'And I'm not in the least voluptuous. Nor,' she said firmly, 'am I one of your women.'

'No? But I saved your life,' he reminded her, his voice deepening. 'In some cultures that means you belong to me now.'

'Not in my culture! Besides, you just wanted to throw me off your island at first. Not quite the same as saving my life, Lukas Andreadis.'

'Was it not? You were unconscious and your foot was caught in the rock. What would have happened to you if I had not found you? I was destined to rescue you, Isobel. It is useless to struggle against the fates.' He smoothed the hair back from her forehead, careful to avoid her wound as he twisted a curl round his finger. 'This hair of yours fascinates me, *hriso mou*.'

'What does that mean?'

'In this instance, golden one.' He smiled into her eyes. 'I would like your friendship, Isobel.'

If only she could believe him. 'Why did you come back, Luke?'

'I had a brainwave, *ne*? Your phone!' He chuckled as he played with her hair. 'It was the perfect excuse. But now I

must go.' Even though he wanted to stay. Whatever her motive for landing on his beach, he had a sudden desire to lie with her like this all night, hold her close and keep her safe, a discovery which shot Luke upright in panic. She was meant to be a diversion, not a complication in his life. Which had complications enough already. 'Goodnight,' he said abruptly, and made for the door.

'Goodnight,' said Isobel, surprised by his sudden hurry.

He opened it and turned, his eyes holding hers. 'Sleep well.'

As he went upstairs to his room Luke smiled wryly. His plan to charm his little golden bird into bed was not progressing according to plan, exactly. But she could not escape the fate that had sent her to him. His mouth twisted. He had spent too much of his life in plotting revenge to have much softness left in his psyche. His relationships with women were always transitory affairs to satisfy his male needs, with no emotions involved. But this English rose touched him in ways new to him. It was surprisingly vital for his peace of mind that she remained safe and well cared for at the villa rather than return to the Kalypso and risk relapse from her injuries. And he was only too willing to be Isobel's 'friend' for the short time they would have together before he let his little bird fly away.

So close a friend that soon he would make love to her with all the subtlety and skill at his command and erase all bad memories of men from her mind forever.

CHAPTER SIX

Isobel had barely closed her eyes before the sound of the helicopter woke her next morning. As she listened to it chop its way up into the sky above the villa she was thoughtful. He'd taken her rejection far better than expected. Not that one solitary 'no' from a woman he'd only known five minutes was likely to upset a man so comfortable in his own skin; especially smooth, bronzed skin that sheathed a muscular body so appealing to women he probably had to beat them off with a stick. And, with the kind of day he had in front of him today, he had probably forgotten her the moment he'd taken off into the sky. Yet now he'd gone the Villa Medusa felt oddly empty.

Eleni brought breakfast earlier than usual. 'Helicopter wake you, *ne*? I go shopping today,' she announced.

Isobel smiled cajolingly. 'Eleni, if I give you money, would you mind buying some food for me to take to the cottage? I'm going back there tomorrow.'

Eleni was dead against this idea and said so in all the English she had at her command, but Isobel was adamant.

'You've been so kind, but I'm giving you far too much work. If Spiro will drive me there tomorrow I'll be fine.'

'Dr Riga comes today,' said Eleni firmly. 'He must say.

Then I buy food. And now you must eat, Isobel. *Kyrie* Luke said I must take care of you.'

This information pleased Isobel more than she cared to admit as she mapped out her programme for the day while she ate her breakfast. Before Dr Riga came she would enjoy a proper shower. And later she planned to settle herself on the shaded part of the terrace to paint, so she could leave the watercolour of the pool for Luke as a permanent reminder of his trespasser.

To begin on her programme she removed the ankle bandage and the dressing on her temple, then turned on the shower. It was wonderful to stand under a warm spray and get totally clean, and she stayed under it so long Eleni was banging on the door before she'd finished.

'Come in,' Isobel called. 'It's not locked.'

Eleni hurried in, frowning in disapproval at the discarded bandages.

'I had to take them off. I just had to get clean, Eleni.' Isobel moved the foot experimentally. 'It feels a lot better. I thought I'd go outside—let the sun dry my hair a bit before it gets too hot.'

Dr Riga arrived soon afterwards. '*Kalimera*, Miss James,' he said, smiling. 'Lukas asked me to check on you before I start my clinic. How are you feeling?'

'Much better.' Isobel indicated her damp hair. 'I had a proper shower for the first time this morning.'

'You have made good progress.' The doctor took her pulse, then examined her face and bent to probe her ankle. 'I shall strap this up again to give support,' he told Isobel, 'but your head wound needs no more dressing; it is healing well.'

When Dr Riga had finished he gave a few more instructions, but agreed that she could return to the holiday cottage next day on condition that she was careful.

When he'd gone Isobel stood up and, with the aid of the crutch, took a few confident steps, delighted with the ankle in its smaller, neater strapping. She collected her bag of drawing materials and went back to the terrace.

'You see, Eleni?' said Isobel jubilantly when the woman brought coffee. 'Dr Riga says I can manage quite easily at the cottage now, so if Spiro will be kind enough to drive me I'll move back there tomorrow.'

The woman sniffed. 'Then I come to cottage every day. Make sure,' she said, eyeing the bag with suspicion. 'What you do with that?'

'I'm going to paint a picture for Luke as a present,' Isobel informed her, and won a broad smile of approval.

'Good, good,' said Eleni. 'Spiro drives me to shop now, Isobel, but Milos will guard you.'

Like the crown jewels, thought Isobel, amused. She drank her coffee while she laid out her drawing materials, then made a couple of trips to the bathroom to fill her water pots, delighted with her new mobility. She set up the light folding easel she'd brought with her and wetted the first sheet of paper. Even in the relatively temperate heat of early morning the paper had dried taut as a drum by the time she'd mixed her first batch of paints, and she was able to lay down her first background wash. The drying time was so much quicker than at home it was exhilarating to put down wash after wash at such speed. By the time Eleni and Spiro returned the background of her painting was well under way, but Isobel was flagging and glad to sit down.

She smiled as the couple came to check on her. 'You were quick!'

Spiro shook his head, smiling. 'We were long time, Miss Isobel.'

'I didn't notice!'

'Milos say he looked from garden, but you worked all the time,' said Eleni, her eyes admiring on the watercolour. 'You are so clever. Kyrie Luke will like very much, Isobel.'

'I hope so. But don't tell him what I'm doing. It's a surprise.'

'You hungry now?'

Isobel nodded with enthusiasm.

'How is your foot, *kyria*?' asked Spiro, picking up the coffee tray.

'Much better. Soon I'll be able to manage without the crutch.'

'Not today,' said Eleni firmly.

Isobel's phone rang as she was about to get back to work after lunch.

'How are you today, little friend?'

'Luke! Where are you?'

'In the car, on the way to the funeral. Has Dr Riga been to see you?'

'Yes. He's strapped my ankle again, and says I'll be fine on my own now.'

'I shall ring you tonight,' he promised. 'Rest this afternoon, Isobel. I wish...' But whatever Luke wished was lost in a burst of static.

Luke's sombre dark suit matched his mood as he arrived at the church shortly after the priest had received the grieving widower and family with the coffin at the front door. Theo Andreadis ignored Luke, but Zena and Zoe Karras, sisters of the dead Melina, eyed him with open venom behind their brother-in-law's back. Luke stared them out, then slipped into the back of the church after the cortege entered and prepared to endure the ceremony, his face a rigid mask as he listened

to the white-robed priests intoning prayers for forgiveness and repose of the soul of the departed. What soul? thought Luke savagely.

When the interminable service was over at last he was the first to leave, in such a hurry to avoid his grandfather that the man who hurtled out of the crowd with upraised knife took him by surprise. Luke's lightning reflexes sent him ducking sideways and the glancing blade pierced the sleeve of his jacket to cut his arm as he slammed his fist into the assailant's stomach, then, with a swift upper cut to the jaw, sent the man sprawling on the ground. Suddenly there were women screaming and police everywhere. Luke caught sight of his grandfather's shocked face, but it was the gloating eyes of the Karras sisters that remained with him afterwards, not least because the gloating changed so quickly to furious disappointment. That he was still alive, obviously. He shot a cold, scathing smile at the women, then turned away to the police officers waiting to question him. Ambulances came rushing to the scene, but he held the paramedics off, determined to give all help possible to the police before he allowed anyone to attend to his wound.

Inspired by talking to Luke, Isobel quickly immersed herself in her painting. The noon light was brighter, more vivid than before, and she spent a long time mixing paints to capture the play of sunlight on the pool. Its frame of greenery was equally challenging. The lush plant life seemed to encompass every shade of green, with overtones of blue and vivid splashes of contrast colour from tamarisk, oleander and geranium; a challenge she responded to with her usual concentration.

When Eleni coughed tactfully, rattling a tray, Isobel looked up, blinking owlishly, and smiled.

'Drinks—wonderful; I'm thirsty.'

'Isobel, you have visitor.'

Isobel stared in surprise. 'Really? Who?'

'Alyssa Nicolaides. No worry. She speak English.'

'How very nice.' Isobel sat back in her chair, rotating her neck as she stretched. 'A break would be good. Could you bring her in while I have a wash?' She waggled her stained fingers and went off with her crutch to change her paint-spattered T-shirt and do something to her face and hair.

When Isobel got back to the terrace a young woman with a mass of dark curling hair spun round from an intent study of the watercolour and smiled warmly.

'Hello. I'm Alyssa. I was speaking to Dr Riga today, and he said you might like some company now Luke's gone.'

Isobel smiled back, delighted. 'I would, very much. How kind of you. Now I can thank you for packing my clothes.'

'I was glad to help. Alex told me about your accident.'

'Your brother was very kind, too. Please thank him when you speak to him again. Is he back at the hospital now?'

'Yes. He was just here for his days off.' Alyssa gestured to the painting. 'I'm impressed. You have enormous talent.'

'Thank you. How about some fruit juice, or water?'

'The juice will be fine. Shall I pour some for you?'

Isobel nodded. 'Please. Do sit down—I've been standing too long.'

Alyssa eyed the strapped ankle doubtfully as she pulled up a chair. 'Will you be able to manage at the cottage on your own?'

'Once Spiro drives me there, yes. The cottage is all on one floor, so with my crutch and the walking stick Luke gave me, no problem.' Isobel eyed her guest with interest. 'You speak very good English.'

'We had a marvellous English teacher here in school. I also

studied it along with my business degree, and went to work in England. I was there for several years.' Alyssa grinned. 'The accent is still strong, but I pride myself I'm fluent.'

'You certainly are. What did you do?'

'I worked in a London bank, with all those hotshot City boys.' She fluttered her eyelashes. 'One of them even tried to persuade me to share his trendy riverside apartment.'

With those eyes and curves and the luxuriant hair, Isobel could well believe it. Alyssa was probably exactly the type of woman Luke usually went for. 'But it didn't happen?'

'No. He was a charmer, and I was tempted, but I was homesick. By that time I had saved a fair sum of money, so home I came. Soon afterwards my baby brother introduced me to a handsome surgeon at his hospital.' She waggled a hand adorned with an impressive ring. 'And in a few weeks I'm going to marry my Dimitri. In the meantime I keep my English up with tourists at the taverna. But that's enough about me. Tell me about you.'

Alyssa listened, fascinated, as Isobel described her painting commissions and her job at the gallery, then bluntly asked her opinion of Luke. 'He's a great guy. Do you like him?'

'Yes. He's been very kind.'

Alyssa gurgled. 'How very British and restrained.'

Isobel felt her colour rise. 'Actually, he wasn't kind at all at first. He was downright menacing when he thought I was one of the paparazzi, lying in wait for him on his beach. But once I put him right about that he's been very—hospitable. But I can't trespass on his hospitality any longer.' She looked up in alarm as Eleni came rushing in, wailing and incoherent, and Alyssa jumped up, firing questions at the woman.

'Grab your crutch, Isobel,' she said tersely. 'There's a

television in Luke's study. Eleni saw an incident in Athens on the news.'

They hurried across the marble hall into a room full of electronic equipment. Alyssa gently pushed Isobel into a comfortable chair and switched on Luke's vast flat screen television.

'I heard Luke's name. Did Eleni say he was involved?' Isobel demanded, breathless from the rush.

'She wasn't making much sense. We'll find out more on here. Ah, here we go. Breaking news.'

The television showed a scene of noisy chaos, with police holding back crowds in front of a church. A reporter at the scene was giving an excited running commentary as paramedics loaded a stretcher into an ambulance. Isobel grasped Alyssa's hand urgently.

'What's happening?'

'Someone attacked Luke as he came out of church after the funeral of Melina Andreadis, his grandfather's wife. You knew about that?'

Isobel nodded impatiently. 'Go on.'

Alyssa listened again, then in rapid monotone translated the reporter's account. 'The grieving widower, accompanied by his dead wife's sisters, watched in shock as Lukas Andreadis, successful entrepreneur, knocked the attacker to the ground even though wounded himself—'

'Wounded?' Isobel swallowed, but forced herself to keep quiet as Alyssa listened intently before translating.

'Luke has been admitted to hospital for treatment. The body on the stretcher was the assailant. Luke obviously flattened him.' Alyssa let out a deep breath, then turned to Eleni, who was weeping in Spiro's arms, her eyes fixed in anguish on the screen. Alyssa patted her hand and soothed her with a

flood of comfort in her own language, then took a phone from the pocket of her tangerine linen skirt.

'I'll get in touch with Dimitri at the hospital, or Alex if not. Don't worry. I'll soon find out about Luke.' She frowned. 'Are you all right, Isobel? You're very pale.'

'Startled, that's all. Never mind me—make your calls.'

Alyssa went off with her phone, giving succinct instructions which sent Eleni hurrying off to the kitchen while Spiro escorted Isobel back to the terrace.

'Do not fear, Miss Isobel,' said Spiro. 'Lukas is very strong man.'

'Yes, of course.' Isobel took in a deep breath and smiled brightly. 'I'm fine. You comfort poor Eleni. She's terribly upset.'

'She loves Lukas like a son,' he said quietly. 'I, also.'

'I know that. So please don't bother about me,' said Isobel guiltily. 'I shouldn't be here, giving you extra work at a time like this.'

'*Kyrie* Lukas told us to take care of you.' Spiro patted her hand for the first time. 'It is our pleasure, not work. Eleni is making tea for you.'

The moment Spiro was out of sight Isobel knuckled tears away impatiently and fished in her bag for tissues. The knock on her head had obviously shaken something loose. She'd cried more since she came to Chyros than she had in years. But any news of Luke would be in Greek, which meant she was forced to wait in frustration until someone told her what was happening. Luke's first meeting with his grandfather had certainly been dramatic.

Isobel stared out at the garden, tense as a drawn bow as she waited for what seemed like years before Alyssa came rushing back to the terrace.

'Sorry to take so long. It took a while to get through to

either of them. Luke is fine!' She seized Isobel's hand in a grasp which made her wince. 'Just a small cut and some grazes and a black eye, according to Dimitri, but it was a text, so I don't have any details. Alex will ring later with more news.' She bent to give Isobel a sudden hug. 'There. Don't cry. Or maybe you should. Do you good. Now I must tell Eleni and Spiro.'

'Thank you,' said Isobel gruffly and blew her nose. 'Lord knows why I'm crying.'

'I can guess!' Alyssa gave her a saucy, knowing grin and ran off down the hall to the kitchen.

Isobel shivered suddenly. If the assailant had a knife, Luke had been very brave—or foolhardy—to attack him. She seized her crutch and made for the bathroom to wash her face, then joined Alyssa on the terrace, smiling ruefully. 'I just wish I understood Greek. It's nerve-racking being unable to understand what's happening.'

Alyssa eyed her challengingly, her big dark eyes sparkling. 'You really like Luke, I think.'

'I do now.' Isobel made a face. 'But I loathed him at first because he was so insulting. He took it for granted I was the kind of female who strands herself on his beach hoping for a fun time with him at the villa.'

'Poor Luke,' said Alyssa, laughing. 'With his looks, women have swarmed around him all his life, and now he's so successful it's even worse. But he never brings anyone with him to the island, Isobel. This is his retreat, and the locals respect his privacy.' She looked round with appreciation. 'You like the house?'

'Who wouldn't?' On impulse, Isobel reached out and touched the other girl's hand. 'I'm so glad you came today. It would have been hell with Eleni and Spiro too upset to

speak English. If you feel like popping in at the cottage once I'm back there, please do.'

Alyssa grinned mischievously. 'I have instructions to "pop in" every day.'

Isobel sat back, startled. 'Who from?'

'Luke, of course. I'm to report to him if you need anything. Luke and I are old friends. We were in school together when we were young.'

Isobel eyed her narrowly. 'Were you and Luke ever more than friends?'

'No.' Alyssa shook her head. 'He was always too busy either studying or earning money any way he could to have time for girls at that stage. He looked me up in London when he was doing his MBA, but my boyfriend at the time took one look at my gorgeous old school pal and created hell. So Luke kept away.'

'But you're the type he goes for.'

'How do you know that?'

'He told me. Blondes leave him cold.'

'Until he met you, obviously.' Alyssa threw out a hand. 'I think he must be pretty hot for *you*, Isobel. Otherwise, why would he order his team to take such care of you?'

'Team?'

'Team Lukas, which means Eleni, Spiro, Milos and me, not to mention Dr Riga. We all have our instructions to take care of you. Talking of which,' said Alyssa, suddenly very serious, 'would you like me to come back this evening in case there's any news?'

Isobel could have kissed her. 'Oh, *would* you? Have dinner with me—but won't you be missed at the taverna?'

'Papa won't mind in the circumstances. He's very fond of Luke. And I won't be seeing Dimitri until the weekend.'

Alyssa looked at her watch. 'I'll go back and talk to my parents, then give them a hand for a couple of hours and come back here about eight.'

'Thanks a lot. I'll tell Eleni.'

'I'll send her to you on my way out. And don't worry. It would take a lot more than a few cuts and grazes to put Luke out of action!'

Once her vivacious visitor had rushed away, Eleni hurried out to Isobel.

'You all right?' she said huskily.

'I'm fine. How are *you*?'

'Better now. Is good for you Alyssa comes back. I make nice dinner.'

'All your dinners are nice—more than nice, they're fabulous.' Isobel reached out her hand and Eleni took it. 'Don't worry. Luke will be fine.'

The woman nodded. 'Spiro said. But I always worry.' She smiled shyly. 'Spiro and I never have children, but we helped *kyria* Olympia with her baby.'

'So he's like the son you never had,' said Isobel softly.

Eleni nodded and brushed a tear from her eye. 'I go now and cook. If any news on TV Spiro will say.'

The light had changed so much Isobel decided against any more work on the watercolour until next day. With an early start in the morning she could easily finish the painting before she left. She saw to her brushes, then sat staring out at the garden, deeply shaken by the thought that Luke could have been killed. Which was worrying. It would be madness to let her emotions get involved when she would never see him again once she left Chyros. But when her phone rang, relief flooded her in a joyous wave at the sound of Luke's voice.

'Isobel?'

'*Luke!* Are you all right? I saw the news. How badly are you hurt? Are you still in the hospital—?'

'Let me speak and I will tell you! Did Eleni tell you what happened?'

'No, she was in such a state she couldn't speak English. Spiro, too. But luckily Alyssa had come to see me, so the four of us watched the TV in your study, with Alyssa translating the newscast. Good God, Luke, you could have been killed!'

'Would you have mourned for me, Isobel?'

'Of course I would,' she said crossly. 'How long will you be in hospital?'

'I am not in hospital. I left straight after treatment. The man did less damage than he intended. I was too quick for him,' he added with arrogance, which made her smile.

'Stitches?'

'No, just dressings. And injections to counter possible infection from the blade.'

'Do you know the man?'

'No—' He cursed under his breath. 'Forgive me, Isobel, Andres wants me. I must go.'

No longer tired, Isobel sat at the desk and, desperate for something other than Luke to occupy her mind, began writing postcards. Picturing the effect on Jo if she gave a truthful account of her adventures on Chyros, she wrote the expected things about the beautiful island and the wonderful weather, then exchanged pen for walking stick and went off to smarten herself up before the stunning Miss Nicolaides came back.

Isobel heaved a sigh as she made for the bathroom. There was such an electric sparkle about Alyssa it was hard to believe that she and Luke had never been more than friends. Though Luke probably knew a lot of women like Alyssa—

vivid, voluptuous Greek beauties far more to his taste than skinny blonde Brits. Isobel laughed at her reflection when she caught herself pouting. Just like Jo's little sister Kitty when she couldn't get her own way. She did her best with her face, pleased that a touch of foundation made the bruise barely noticeable, and her newly washed hair shone, with lighter streaks here and there from the hours she'd spent baking on Luke's beach. Not too bad. How she'd envied Jo's thick straight bob when they were teenagers. And Jo had laughed her to scorn, full of envy for her friend's blonde curls. Barbie doll fixation, she'd teased, then dodged when 'Barbie' started throwing things. Ready at last in a raspberry-pink shift, Isobel went back to the terrace to help Eleni lay the table.

The woman smiled in approval. 'You look very pretty, Isobel!'

'Why, thank you, Eleni. I heard from Luke,' she added as she put out the silver, and the woman nodded happily.

'He ring Spiro. Is bad he not stay long in hospital.'

Isobel smiled. 'He doesn't like hospitals!'

Eleni shot her a knowing look. 'You like him, *ne*?'

Isobel coloured slightly. 'Of course. He's been very kind to me.'

'He likes *you*. He never bring woman here before.'

'He didn't bring *me*, Eleni. He was forced into helping me because I hurt myself.'

'He likes you,' the woman repeated firmly, then hurried away at the sound of a car.

In white palazzo trousers and a sea-green silk shirt which displayed enviable honey-toned cleavage, Isobel's visitor looked even more stunning than before.

'You look a lot better—nice dress.' Alyssa pulled up a chair. 'Recovered from the shock, Isobel?'

'More or less. Luke rang me. He left the hospital as soon as he'd been treated.'

'So I heard.'

Isobel shivered. 'Any news about the man who did it?'

Alyssa shook her head. 'The police are questioning him.'

'Will there be anything on the news right now?'

'The main newscast is on later, after our meal. I'll play interpreter much better once I've eaten.' Alyssa cast an eye over Isobel. 'Are you slim like that because you work at it?'

'No. Metabolism.'

'Lucky you. I have to watch my weight like a hawk.'

'What for?' Isobel eyed her blankly. 'You're gorgeous.'

'Thank you, *glykia mou!* But to stay that way I *do* have to work at it.'

'To please Dimitri?'

Alyssa smiled like a cat with the cream. 'No, he loves the curves. But I want to fit into my wedding dress. I brought a box of pastries with honey and nuts for dessert, by the way, but I'll limit myself to one only.'

'Sounds wonderful.'

'I brought a bottle of wine, too—a gift from my father. He says a glass of wine is good medicine in times of stress.' Alyssa put out a hand to touch Isobel's. 'Don't worry. Luke is a supremely fit man. He'll be fine.'

Isobel flushed. 'I'm concerned, Alyssa, that's all. Luke came to my rescue and I'm grateful to him, and I hate to see him hurt. But there's nothing going on between us. We've only just met.'

'An hour—a minute—is all it takes to fall in love—or lust, Isobel. But I won't tease any more. Here comes dinner.'

Entertained by Alyssa's account of her preparations for her wedding, Isobel ate well enough to satisfy Eleni when she

came to clear away, but by then she could wait no longer. She looked at her guest in appeal. 'Would you check the news for me now, please?'

Alyssa promptly jumped up and handed Isobel her crutch to make for Luke's study. She brought up the required television programme, then patted Isobel's hand as a shot of Luke came on the screen.

'He's been discharged from hospital after treatment, and the assailant is in police custody,' reported Alyssa.

'That's it?' said Isobel, as a shot of schoolchildren filled the screen.

Alyssa nodded and turned the set off. 'If I hear anything more I'll let you know tomorrow. When do you intend leaving the villa?'

But Isobel had taken time to think this over. 'Perhaps I'll wait one more day after all. At the Kalypso I'll be cut off from any news. At least here I've got Eleni and Spiro to keep me up to speed.'

Alyssa nodded in warm approval as they returned to the terrace. 'Very wise. You'd be a bit isolated up there. Take my advice, stay on here until you're really mobile.'

'Et tu, Brute?' said Isobel wryly.

'No use spouting Latin to me, *kyria*, I'm Greek! And,' she added in sudden inspiration, 'you're a Brit so you're bound to like tea. Shall I ask Eleni to make some for us? I'll mention your change of plan.'

Isobel laughed and threw up her hands. 'All right, all right, I give in, *KYRIA* Nicolaides. I'll stay on here for a day or two more.'

'Be sure to tell Luke I was the one who persuaded you—he'll owe me!'

* * *

By Greek standards they'd eaten early. But, after Alyssa left to drive home with a message of thanks to her father for the wine, Isobel got ready for bed, suddenly exhausted. She settled herself against stacked pillows with a book, the usual tray of drinks left beside her by Eleni. But, instead of reading, she kept thinking of how near Luke had come to death that day, and frowned. Why did that matter so much? Just a short time ago she'd actively disliked him, but somewhere along the line her feelings towards him had undergone a sea change. Whatever the reason, Isobel gave a great sigh of relief when Luke rang.

'Did I wake you, Isobel?'

'No. How are you?'

'In terrible pain,' he said promptly. 'I need a friend to comfort me.'

'No, seriously—'

'I am serious. Are you in bed?'

'Yes.'

'I need a picture of you as I lie in my own, so tell me what you sleep in.'

She chuckled. 'A knee-length blue T-shirt. I go for comfort, not glamour in bed.'

'Glamour enough for me—' He drew in a sharp breath.

'What's wrong?' she demanded.

'My various scrapes and scratches making themselves felt. Sleep well, Isobel.'

She closed her phone slowly, then turned out the light and slid lower in the bed, yawning. For some reason, just hearing Luke's voice had been enough to settle her down to sleep. Hoping it had worked the same way for him, she stretched luxuriously and turned her face into her pillows.

* * *

Isobel continued work on her watercolour next day, interrupted at intervals by brief phone calls from Luke.

'I am very glad you decided to remain at the villa. Wait there until I come back. Please, Isobel,' he added, which was so obviously an afterthought she grinned.

'I'll see,' was all she would promise, and said nothing about her intention to complete not only the watercolour of the pool before she left, but another of Luke's beach to go with it. This was more difficult to accomplish when Eleni and Spiro learned what she had in mind, since it meant a lot of argument about working out of doors. But in the end Milos rigged up a canopy to shade Isobel from the sun as she worked at the cliff edge. The study of the pool was for Luke to remind him of her in future. The painting of the beach was for herself, who would need no reminders.

Isobel received a flying visit from Alyssa before the evening rush at the taverna, and added her bit to the concerns voiced by Eleni and Spiro.

'Are you sure you should be doing this? Though it's very beautiful,' said Alyssa, peering over her shoulder. 'Is that for Luke, too?'

'No. This one's for me.'

'How's the ankle?'

'Much better. I'm really speedy with my faithful crutch! It's good exercise, getting in and out of the house for bathroom breaks. And, before you ask, I'm smothered in suncream and I'm drinking gallons of water and eating whatever Eleni puts in front of me. But thank you for coming, Alyssa.'

'My pleasure. Alex sends his regards, by the way. He saw Luke when he was at the hospital and assures you he's fine.'

Isobel raised an eyebrow. 'Why should Alex assure *me*?'

Alyssa fluttered her eyelashes. 'Who knows? Now, be good

and I'll come back tomorrow. We'll have extra help then, so I can stay longer. If you like.'

'I'd like that very much! Thanks a lot, Alyssa.'

After concentrating for hours to make use of the light, Isobel was very tired by the time Spiro helped Milos take down the canopy. 'Time to stop, *kyria*,' he said severely, taking charge of her painting materials. 'Now you rest, then eat good dinner.'

It was a programme Isobel was only too glad to follow. She had a long shower, but felt so tired halfway through the meal she gave up and let Eleni help her to her room, scolding all the way because Isobel had been too weary to eat.

'I bring tea,' said the woman as they reached the room. 'You go to bed now, *ne*?'

'Yes, Eleni,' Isobel promised meekly, startled to feel suddenly cold in the evening breeze coming through the veranda doors. Shivering, she searched in her suitcase for a pair of leggings to go with her vest, and even pulled tennis socks over feet that were suddenly icy.

'Too much sun, work too hard,' said Eleni sternly when she returned with the tea. 'You want blanket?'

'No, I'll be fine now, thank you. Goodnight, Eleni.' Isobel drank the hot tea gratefully and settled back against the pillows.

Luke rang before she had time to wonder if he would. 'How are you, Isobel?'

'I'm in bed now, but I've had a busy day. I've been painting.'

'I heard this. Out on the cliff edge,' he said sternly.

'I wanted a painting of the beach to take home as a souvenir.'

'To remind you of Chyros—and me? I need no reminders,' he said softly. 'I shall never forget my beautiful trespasser.'

Good, thought Isobel, who had painted the watercolour with just that end in view. 'How are your scrapes and scratches?'

'Healing fast.'

'Do you know why the man attacked you?'

'Yes.' His voice hardened. 'After much persuasion, he told the police he was paid to wound me but not to kill. He insists he has no idea who paid him, but I refuse to believe this. The man is obviously too frightened to name names. He said the money and instructions were delivered to him by courier, along with threats to harm his children if he refused.'

'Then, for heaven's sake, take care, Luke,' warned Isobel, startled. 'Whoever paid him might find someone else to hurt you even more. Is there good security where you live?'

'The best. The building I live in has every security device known to man. I have excellent security staff, also temporary police protection. But as soon as I can I shall return to Chyros, where no hurt ever comes to me.'

CHAPTER SEVEN

It was a long time before Isobel slept. She felt worried because Luke was in danger, and even more worried because she felt that way. Don't go there, she warned herself forcibly. She was just about getting over the recent hateful episode. Only a fool would lay herself open to more emotional trauma. Especially with a man who lived his life to a very different set of rules from hers. She tossed and turned endlessly, but when heavy, exhausted sleep overtook her at last she was jolted out of it into a waking nightmare by rough hands which dragged her out of bed, her terrified scream smothered by a pungent cloth clamped over her face.

When Isobel opened her eyes again she felt icy-cold as she stared up into a starlit sky. She could hear an insistent put-putting noise, but instead of fear her knee-jerk reaction was sheer bloody-minded anger when she found she was tied up. Other people had nice package holidays, uneventful except for lost luggage, plane delays and sunburn, while so far hers had been one disaster after another. But burning resentment swiftly morphed into the cold chill of fear as she identified the noise. It was an outboard motor and she was not only in the bottom of a boat, but trussed up like an oven-ready chicken. How long had she been unconscious? And where on

earth was she being taken? Even more frightening, what would happen when she got there? At least the smothering cloth had gone. Chloroform, probably. She swallowed down on a wave of nausea, thankful she hadn't been gagged, then clenched her teeth in anguish as she prayed hard that nothing had happened to Eleni and Spiro. And, instead of howling in anger at fate, she forced herself to lie perfectly still. Better to pretend she was still unconscious than risk the chloroform treatment again.

But why had she been snatched? If ransom was the motive, she had no money so she was no earthly use to a kidnapper. She shivered, feeling cold for all kinds of reasons. And hideously helpless. Then her heart lurched as the engine died and the boat grated against shingle. Now what? She kept her eyes tightly shut, playing dead as she was heaved over a burly shoulder. Her nostrils were assaulted by unwashed wool and sweat and tobacco as she was carried over what appeared to be rocks, by the way she was jolted. The rough handling had started up the throbbing in her temple again and her ankle was joining in. When I get home, Isobel promised herself bitterly—*if* I get home—I'll never leave it again.

She heard a door creak, then she was dumped on some kind of bed, pungent with the smell of wet wood and fish. She opened her eyes a crack to see a nightmare shape outlined by the moonlight shining through the small window of some kind of hut, and swallowed a scream as a huge hooded figure bent over her. He spoke to her roughly in Greek very different from Luke's, but when she stared at him in speechless horror he took her by the shoulders, obviously demanding a reply.

Isobel cleared her throat. 'I—I'm British. I don't understand Greek.'

This was seriously bad news to him by the stream of what

were obviously curses as he yanked her upright until her bound ankles hung over the bunk. He'd wrapped her in some kind of rug before trussing her up, which made it hard to keep her balance.

'Do you speak English?' she asked hopefully.

A negative grunt was the only response.

'Could you possibly untie my hands?' she asked without much hope. 'My wrists and shoulders are hurting.'

To her surprise, he did as she asked, then removed the rug and retied her wrists in front of her. Isobel forced herself to sit as upright as possible, horribly conscious now of how little she was wearing on her top half as he lit a lantern suspended from a hook on a roof beam. As the light fell on her the man cursed again, his eyes glaring through the slits of the hood. Isobel backed away in terror, her skin crawling as he ran his fingers through her tousled curls to frame her face. What was he going to do? Then she found out. He pushed a newspaper between her tied hands and took photographs of her with his phone, and for a finale took her breath away by flicking a knife open to slice off a lock of hair. Determined not to show fear, she glared at him defiantly as he pointed to a box which held a package and bottles of water. He fetched a metal bucket and placed it at the end of the bunk, then turned out the lamp and left the hut. The door slammed shut behind him and bolts rammed home, and shortly afterwards the outboard motor roared into action as the boat took off, leaving Isobel limp with relief because rape had not been part of the plan. Not yet, anyway.

As the moonlight faded, instead of the total darkness she'd dreaded, the first faint light of dawn took its place. Isobel's spirits rose as the light gradually increased enough for a look round her prison. She was in some kind of fisherman's hut,

and a primitive one at that. The bunk was the only seating, and the mattress was damp and smelly.

The man had tied her wrists more loosely than before, which was good news. Otherwise, using the bucket would have been tricky, so would the eating and drinking part. How long was the man intending to leave her here? And who would be the lucky recipient of the hair and the candid camera shots? Luke? The kidnapper now knew she was British and obviously not some relative of Lukas Andreadis, so was he banking on the fact that she was his lover and worth ransoming? But in most cases kidnappers tended to get rid of their victims, whether the money was paid or not, didn't they? Isobel batted that thought away and set about solving more immediate problems. She had to get her hands free as the first step to getting herself out of here. There was no way she was just going to curl up in misery like a victim and wait for rescue or rape, whichever came first.

Fired with new determination, she tested the ropes. She'd deliberately tensed her wrists as the man retied them to gain a little leeway, and once she could see clearly she began tugging at the knots with her teeth. Ignoring the oily taste of the hemp, Isobel kept at it until the knot loosened and her teeth ached, but with freedom in sight she worked frantically, ignoring the soreness of her wrists until after what seemed like hours the knot finally gave and the rope fell away. Bingo! Triumphant, she smoothed her sore wrists for a while as she took a breather, then after some wriggling swung her feet up on to the bench to get to work on the ankle restraints. By some miracle, the support bandage was still in place though the ankle was aching. But with two hands instead of teeth for tools, unravelling this set of knots was marginally easier. After an endless, muscle-straining interval she managed to

free herself and collapsed back on the bunk, panting but jubilant, as the ropes fell away.

The morning sun was revealing her primitive surroundings in all their glory now she had attention to spare for them. Isobel smiled sardonically as she reviewed her dramatic change of circumstances. Just a short time before she had been enjoying the luxury of Luke's villa, waited on hand and foot and coaxed to eat. Today, she was in a rude hut odorous with fishing tackle and nets, with only herself to rely on and her own two feet to get her anywhere. And, in spite of fright and the oily rope she'd been gnawing on, she was hungry. Wishing she'd eaten more last night, Isobel stood up gingerly and limped over the dank plank floor, the ankle hurting enough without her crutch to make her sweat as she grabbed her supplies. The bag contained bread, a chunk of hard cheese, a container of the inevitable olives and a few tomatoes. Panting as she got back to the bunk, Isobel eyed her haul thoughtfully. Exactly how long was the food, what there was of it, intended to last?

She ate some bread and a tomato, gnawed on a bit of the cheese, then packed the rest away for later. She drank the water thirstily, but stopped after a few needy mouthfuls. Who knew how long that had to last, either? Tired after her labours, Isobel decided a rest was only practical to sharpen her wits, and fell into such an exhausted sleep she woke to find more than an hour had gone by. Furious about taking a nap instead of looking for an escape route, it was some consolation to find she at least felt better for the rest. But now it was time to take action. She was heartily sick of being victimised by a man purely because he was bigger and stronger, like her kidnapper. And Gavin.

Isobel knelt up on the bunk to look out of the window. The

hut was in a narrow cove with rock formations and shingle edged by pines and shrubs, but hemmed in by cliffs so steep and sheer it was a dark, forbidding place. She limped over to inspect the door, which was made of solid wood planking. The memory of bolts going home confirmed that there was no possibility of opening it, so she returned to the bunk and sat down, determined to stay positive at all costs. Cheering herself on with the prospect of Joanna's reaction when she got home to describe her adventures, she reminded herself that this was a fisherman's hut. Its owner might return and help her. She rolled her eyes. In fiction, maybe. But this was reality. The only one around to give her a helping hand was herself.

Isobel leaned her forehead against the glass, then moved back, eyes narrowed. The window was small, but if she smashed the glass she might just about wriggle through. But first she had to break the window. Isobel inspected the fishing paraphernalia stacked against the wall. Nothing there to break glass. Back at the dirty window, she used a corner of the rug to wipe a section of window clear to survey her section of the beach. And made an exciting discovery. The windowpane was made of hard, opaque plastic, not glass, which was why she could barely see through it. Her eyes lit up. If she heaved the metal bucket at the window it should do the trick. She gave a hysterical little chuckle. It was a good thing she'd thought of it now, before using the bucket for its intended purpose. Steadying herself on her good foot, Isobel picked up the bucket, stood back and heaved it at the window with skill retained from her netball-playing days in school. She checked the result. The window showed a few cracks but remained disappointingly intact. Damn!

Isobel drank a little more water, then resumed her window battering. It was tiring, noisy work, but she kept on doggedly

until her entire body ached with effort. Then at last she gave a yell of triumph as the window gave and shards of plastic showered outside. Covered in sweat, her breath heaving through her chest, she wrapped her hand in the rug to hammer out the remaining bits, then shook more fragments out of the rug and sat down, head bowed and hands on knees while she heaved air into her lungs. After a minute or two she straightened to assess her escape hatch. It would be a tight fit, but she would manage. No choice. She had to. And her provisions had to go with her. She knotted up the bag of food and bottles of water in the rug and scrambled up on the bunk, wincing as her ankle protested. Stop that, she ordered. Cooperate. I've got to get myself out of here. She hoisted up her makeshift bundle and lowered it outside, then let it go the short distance to the ground, praying that the bottles wouldn't burst on impact, but, to her relief, the bundle touched down quietly on the sand between the rocks.

Isobel took a deep breath, then began to wriggle her way backwards through the opening. When she was halfway out she managed to get her good leg free, tearing her leggings in the process, then clung to the window frame, breaking a fingernail as she manoeuvred the other leg out. She hung there for a moment, gasping, then let go and landed on her bottom and fell flat on her back in the sand. Good. She stayed there, panting, pleased to find she was still in one piece. Isobel sat up and slowly got to her knees, and then to her feet. Her ankle was doing its usual throbbing thing but the rest of her was in reasonable working order. She could stand if she put most of her weight on the good foot.

Isobel stood on it to lean against the wall of the hut and size up the situation. If she hung about here, hoping to catch the attention of a passing fisherman, she was far more likely

to attract the attention of the kidnapper, who was bound to return sooner or later, either to exchange her for money, or… She blanked out the alternative and concentrated on a survey of the beach and the belt of greenery edging it. Beyond it, the cliffs rose even more steeply than those leading to the Villa Medusa, but her eyes lit up as she realised that what looked like a ribbon winding up the cliff was actually a path leading from the far side of the beach. It looked more user-friendly for a mountain goat than a human, but even if she climbed up it on her hands and knees she had to try rather than stay here like a sitting duck.

Isobel picked up her unwieldy bundle and, with the help of a sharp pebble, made a jagged tear in the cloth and ripped the thin rug in two. She tied one half round her shoulders for protection like a shawl, finished off the half empty bottle of water, then tied up the remaining two with the food and fastened the ends of the rug round her waist. She limped across the sand as far as she could go, then picked her way over the shingle, glad to leave the scorching sun for the shade of the pines. She winced as needles caught in her socks. Shoes would have been nice. So would a hat and sunglasses. But when she finally reached the foot of it the path was a crushing disappointment; far narrower than she'd thought, and so vertiginously steep she had no hope of climbing up it, hands and knees or any other way. She regrouped. Time to do some serious thinking. Thankful that her watch had survived intact, Isobel saw it was later than she'd realised. It had taken her far too long to get free of the ropes, and the nap had been a big mistake.

She stiffened suddenly, her heart in her throat as she heard an engine out to sea. Panting in panic, she dropped to the ground, dispensing with her bundle to wriggle under cover as

the sound grew louder, and scrabbled around until she found
a tree branch sturdy enough for a weapon. Just in case. She
fought to lie still, ignoring the spiny plant pricking at her as
the engine noise grew louder, then had a sudden change of
heart. No more victim nonsense, Isobel! She scrambled to her
feet, squaring her shoulders as she brandished her weapon. If
it was the kidnapper she'd face him on her own two feet and
put up a fight, rather than burrow into the ground like a
coward. Her heart began pounding like a trip hammer as the
boat came nearer; then, to her overwhelming relief, a familiar
voice shouted her name and Luke leapt from the boat as it
reached the shingle.

With a cry of joy Isobel dropped her weapon as he came
racing towards her; the most beautiful sight she'd ever seen
in her life, villainous black eye included. He swept her up in
his arms, hugging her hard enough to crack her ribs as Spiro
came hurrying to wring her hand in passionate relief before
excusing himself to ring Eleni with the wonderful news.

'Are you hurt, Isobel?' demanded Luke roughly, slacken-
ing his hold to look her up and down.

'Not really,' she gasped. 'Please! Can we just get away
before he comes back?'

'Just one man?' demanded Luke as he carried her to the
Athena.

'Yes.'

'Can you describe him?'

Isobel shook her head. 'It was dark and he wore a hood.
But he was very big, and spoke Greek with an accent very dif-
ferent from yours.'

'He was definitely strong,' said Luke grimly. 'He carried
you down the cliff path to the beach to get to the boat. And I
have made sure that path is difficult to discourage trespassers.'

She smiled valiantly. 'Good thing I was unconscious for that part!'

Luke deposited his burden very gently on a seat in the boat and, ignoring her protests that she was hot, wrapped her in a light rug very different from the one provided by the kidnapper. Luke gave her wonderfully cold water to drink and then held her close as Spiro untied the boat and jumped aboard to restart the engine. Something unclenched inside Isobel as the boat headed out into the sea and she leaned against Luke in the cool salt breeze of their passage, savouring his warmth and strength, hardly daring to believe she was safe.

'The hut was locked,' he said hoarsely, holding her close. 'You actually climbed out through that window?'

'With enormous difficulty, yes. I had to break it first.' Isobel gave him a brief account of her labours, and her idea of climbing up the cliff to escape. 'But the path was too narrow and steep, and my ankle hurt,' she finished. 'My wrists, too,' she added, and Luke swore volubly as he examined them. 'How did you know where to find me?'

'When I was young I spent half my life on these waters.' He hugged her closer. 'When the photograph came through to me from my people in Athens I was mad with worry. But once I calmed down I realised I recognised the hut, even though it is many years since I worked for the old fisherman who owned it. There are probably countless others like it but, thank the gods, I was right about this one.' His voice roughened. 'Tell me the truth, Isobel. Did this animal hurt you?'

She shook her head, knowing he meant far more than just the marks on her wrists. 'No. He put a cloth over my face with something like chloroform on it, and trussed me up. And in the hut he cut off some of my hair—did you receive that, by the way?'

'Not personally,' he said, in a tone which sent shivers down

her spine. 'I was already on my way back to Chyros after Spiro rang in a frenzy to report that you were missing.'

Isobel smiled comfortingly at Spiro as he shook his head in mute remorse. 'The man left food and water with me, so I suppose he was going to come back at some point. Did he ask for money?'

'Yes. I have until ten tomorrow night to pay. My people in Athens relayed the message.' He drew in a deep, unsteady breath. 'Spiro heard something in the night and went out into the garden to investigate, but could see nothing in the darkness. Then he heard a boat start up in the cove below and went to check on you. The doors to your room had been forced and you were gone. So was the intruder, or Spiro would have been a casualty, too,' said Luke grimly.

'Thank God he didn't run into him! The man would make two of him.' Isobel shuddered at the thought.

'Even so, Spiro is deeply ashamed that he failed to keep you safe.' Luke's arms tightened. 'So am I.'

Isobel shook her head firmly. 'It's no one's fault. I'm all right. Really. Where was this place, by the way?'

'A small, uninhabited island just a short distance to the south of Chyros. Probably chosen so he could get you there quickly without being seen.'

'Uninhabited?' She rolled her eyes. 'So if, by some miracle, I *had* managed to climb that path up the cliff, it would have been for nothing?'

Luke nodded grimly. 'No beach on the other side, just rocks. Old Petros was a loner and spent a lot of time there. He kept a goat or two at one time, hence the path. But fishing was his main pastime. He used to bring his catch in to Chyros to sell to the tavernas, which is how I met him. He liked me, for some reason, and gave me a job in the school holidays. I

was often there on the island, sharing food with him in that hut, which is why I recognised it from the photograph.' His arm tightened painfully. 'Otherwise—'

'Let's not think of otherwise,' said Isobel firmly, then sighed with relief as a familiar smudge appeared on the horizon. 'Chyros!'

CHAPTER EIGHT

TO ISOBEL'S surprise, Spiro kept well out to sea instead of making for the familiar harbour. Luke smiled at her in reassurance and held a finger to his lips as he pulled the rug up to cover her head when Spiro finally steered the *Athena* into a narrow, steep-sided cove on the far side of Chyros. He secured the boat close to the waiting Cherokee on the jetty, and jumped out to hold the Jeep's passenger door wide as Luke stepped on to the jetty with his tightly wrapped burden.

'Forgive me; I must do this,' Luke whispered as he laid Isobel on the floor between the front and back seats. 'I cannot risk someone seeing you. Just a few minutes more, and you will be safe.'

Isobel had to concentrate hard on keeping still in her wrappings as Luke drove at breakneck pace up a steep helter-skelter of a road. She relaxed a little as the Jeep eventually stopped climbing and began to descend, and when it finally turned down the drive to the villa she heaved a heartfelt sigh of relief. The instant it came to a halt Luke plucked her out to carry her inside the house, where Eleni, hysterical with relief, hurried behind as he bore Isobel upstairs to the guest room on the upper floor.

Luke unwound the rug and set her down in the big chair in

the familiar, beautiful bedroom, then stood back to look at her over Eleni's head as the little woman knelt to grasp Isobel's hands, pouring out remorse and apologies it was hard to understand with only one word in five in English.

'I'm all *right*, honestly, Eleni,' Isobel assured her unsteadily. 'Just dirty and thirsty. I'd kill for some tea.'

Luke spoke kindly to the woman in her own language and she got to her feet, scrubbing her face with the corner of her apron.

'*Me synchoreite!* I get tea.'

Luke turned to Spiro. 'Be careful, *ne*? If someone rings or calls here, we failed to find our guest.'

Spiro nodded grimly and led his wife from the room.

'Did the police get involved?' asked Isobel, eyeing the dressing on Luke's arm.

'When Spiro rang I contacted them in Athens.' Luke looked down at her with an intensity which made Isobel suddenly conscious of her sweat-stained clinging vest and torn leggings. 'Now, tell me how you feel. Truthfully.'

'As I told Eleni, I'm dirty and thirsty and my ankle hurts a bit, but I'm not too bad, all things considered.' She held out her chafed wrists. 'Do you have anything I can put on these after I shower?'

Luke's mouth twisted as he raised her hands to his lips. 'Isobel, this is all my fault. The man orchestrating this campaign thinks I will pay whatever he wants to get you back.' He looked up into her eyes. 'He is right. But I would give much to lay my hands on the scum who put you through this. And I cannot even call Dr Riga out to you yet for fear that word gets out that I have you.'

'I don't need Dr Riga,' said Isobel firmly. 'And you look battered enough already, so keep well away from the man who kidnapped me. He's a big brute.'

'Are you sure he didn't hurt you?' demanded Luke fiercely.

'Yes, though when he carried me to the hut he wasn't exactly gentle.' Her eyes flashed. 'And he went raving mad when he saw my hair.'

To her surprise, Luke looked uncomfortable. 'It was the colour. He was expecting dark hair.'

'What?' Her eyes narrowed. 'He thought he was kidnapping someone else?'

'Yes. A friend of mine. Granddaughter of the industrialist Denis Stratos—who received a ransom note this morning, also.'

All this had happened due to mistaken identity? Isobel felt a sudden violent urge to hit someone. 'No wonder the man was furious. Could you ask Eleni to fetch some clothes up here for me, please? I'm utterly desperate to get clean.'

'All your belongings are back in this room again,' he said quickly. 'You sleep here tonight and every other night, where I can keep you safe.'

'But once the kidnapper's caught it won't matter where I sleep; I can go back to the Kalypso,' said Isobel, though secretly she was not at all keen on the prospect after her adventure.

'No,' said Luke flatly. 'Until your flight to the UK, you remain here. I have rescued you twice. A third time you might not be so lucky.'

She glared at him. 'It was hardly my intention to trouble you, either time.'

'I know; I put that badly—' He broke off as Eleni came in with the tea. 'You must drink your tea in here, not on the veranda. With a telescopic lens someone could see you.'

Wonderful. 'Whatever you say,' she said wearily, utterly shattered now her adrenaline rush had receded.

'I shall leave you for a while,' said Luke, eyeing her narrowly. 'Are you really all right, Isobel? You look exhausted.'

'Hardly surprising, after my labours.' She smiled doggedly as Eleni poured tea. 'A cup of tea and a long hot shower and I'll be fine.'

Once Luke had gone, Isobel sagged in the chair, tears suddenly streaming down her face, and Eleni went on her knees beside her, rocking her in her arms as she made comforting noises. But after a while the little woman pulled away, her eyes fierce as she examined the rope marks on Isobel's wrists.

'The pig did this?'

Isobel nodded dumbly.

'Tell truth. That all?'

'Yes. Nothing worse.' Isobel gulped and scrubbed at her eyes with the tissue Eleni handed her. 'Stupid to cry now I'm safe.'

'Is natural! Now, drink tea, then shower. Want help?'

'No, I can manage.' Isobel hugged her hard. 'Oh, God, Eleni, I was so terrified that you and Spiro had been hurt.'

At which point the woman's English deserted her and she rocked Isobel in her arms again for a while before letting her go.

When Isobel finally stood under the spray, wincing as it caught her various scrapes and bruises, her mood was a long way short of the elation it should have been. She had expected Luke to make rather more fuss of her. They'd agreed to be friends, after all, so a comforting cuddle or two would have been nice. But once the first violence of his relief had abated he seemed to have switched off. And tonight she couldn't even eat with him. The terrace was as public as her bedroom veranda.

Isobel had to work hard to get her damp hair in shape with a chunk of it missing at one side. Her first priority would obviously be a haircut once she got home. She smiled wryly. How wonderfully tame life would be back at the gallery. She fought down a sudden wave of homesick-

ness at the thought of it and went to work on her face, then covered her array of bruises with a white long-sleeved shirt and soft blue cotton jeans. But went barefoot rather than subject her tender feet to shoes. And she felt vulnerable without the ankle support, which had been so filthy she'd had to bin it. When she left the bathroom Eleni was patting the pillows invitingly on the bed, but Isobel shook her head, smiling.

'I'll just sit in this lovely comfortable chair and read.'

It seemed like hours before Luke, with a perfunctory knock on the open door, came in carrying the crutch. He was obviously fresh from a shower, with a clean dressing on his arm.

'You look better, Isobel,' he said in approval. He propped the crutch at the foot of the bed and drew up a chair.

'Cleaner, certainly. You were a very long time,' she added, then regretted it when his eyes gleamed.

'You missed me?'

'I thought you might want to know more about my miraculous escape,' she said tartly.

'I do. Every last detail. But first I had to drive down to the boat. I took the *Athena* over to the harbour while Spiro drove the Cherokee back up the hill and then down to the town to meet me in full view of the public as I docked. The object,' he added patiently, as though explaining to a child, 'was to give the impression that you were still missing.'

She flushed. 'Oh. I see.'

'As soon as I docked, Alyssa came running from the taverna to demand news,' he went on. 'I clasped her dramatically to my chest so I could whisper in her ear that you were safe, and ordered her to keep it totally secret. Then I said very loudly that I had failed to find you.' He grinned suddenly. 'She began wailing and crying, and made such a scene that she col-

lected a crowd. At this point, apparently overcome with despair at my lack of success, I joined Spiro in the Jeep and he drove me home past a sympathetic audience.'

'Wow,' said Isobel, impressed. 'I wish I'd been there. Sorry I was cross,' she added contritely.

'It is not surprising. But you missed a wonderful performance from Alyssa. I told her not to ring the house because I need all lines open, but she will be here tomorrow, whatever happens.' He took a tube from his pocket. 'Give me your hands.'

She held them out for him to squeeze cream on her rope burns. 'Thank you. That feels good.'

His eyes held hers. 'Are there any hidden injuries that need attention?'

'No. Just the odd scrape and bruise. And my feet are a bit tender. Nothing a night's rest won't put right.'

He frowned. 'You have removed your ankle support.'

'No choice. It was dirty.'

'As soon as I can I will ask Dr Riga to replace it. In the meantime, take great care as you walk, Isobel.'

'I'll be fine now you've brought the crutch,' she assured him. 'After all, I didn't even have that when I managed to get myself out of the hut and across the beach.'

'Which still amazes me.' He breathed in deeply. 'But it is my fault that such effort was necessary. You were kidnapped not just to extort money from me, but to cause me maximum pain. My one piece of luck was the location. The kidnapper was obviously a stranger; otherwise he would have taken you somewhere more remote. Have you remembered anything else about him?'

'No.' She shrugged. 'Not that I was in any condition to take much note at the time. He grunted and swore more than he actually spoke. But when he retied my hands he did it loosely enough for me to undo the knots eventually. With my teeth,'

she added in distaste. 'It was horribly oily rope and tasted foul, but I won in the end.'

Luke looked down at the hands he was still holding. 'Can you imagine,' he said without expression, 'how I felt when Spiro rang me to say you were missing?'

She thought about it. 'Guilty, maybe, because your wealth was the motive for ransom? Also because kidnappers rarely let their victims live.'

Luke looked up, his eyes glittering. 'All this and more flashed through my mind. I felt such despair and frustration—and sheer rage—that I burned to kill whoever had done this.'

Isobel felt suddenly a lot better. 'Did it matter so much to you, then?'

His dark brows shot up in disbelief. 'Can you doubt it?'

Her eyes fell as she tried to think of some kind of response.

Luke smiled crookedly and released her hands. 'You find my feelings so hard to believe?'

'Other than the guilt part, yes,' she muttered. 'I'm just a passing stranger in your life.'

'I feel I know you very well, Isobel,' he said softly, his eyes hot with a look that made her own fall again.

'That's probably because the circumstances have been so unusual.'

'Holding your delectable body in my arms so much certainly accelerated the process,' he agreed with relish.

'At least you don't have to do that any more,' she retorted. 'I'm mobile now.'

His eyes fastened on hers. 'But I still want to hold you in my arms, little friend.'

Battening down a leap of response, Isobel took in a deep breath. 'Luke, next week I'm going home. So, although I'm deeply grateful to you for saving my life—'

'Twice!'

Her eyes flashed. 'Even so, I'm afraid I have nothing to—to offer in return but my grateful thanks. I may be jumping the gun again, but holiday romances are just not my thing.'

Luke got to his feet, irritatingly unperturbed. 'I will try hard to remember that, Isobel.' He looked at his watch. 'Rest now until Eleni brings your dinner. I shall be in the study, keeping in touch with my people in Athens. Is there anything you need?'

'No, thank you,' she said, subdued, and with a formal little bow he turned away.

'Luke.'

'Yes?' He turned at the door.

She smiled shakily. 'Thank you again for rescuing me. But I'm worried. What if the man makes off with the money without being caught?'

'Then he does,' he said, shrugging.

'In which case I'll owe you a lot more than mere thanks.'

'You owe me nothing,' he retorted, suddenly grim. 'You were a guest in my house. I should have taken better care of you. This, in some small way, I can remedy now.' He strode back to her and picked her up to place her against the stacked pillows on the bed, then handed the book to her. 'Read if you must, but sleep would be better.'

Isobel smiled her thanks, but she had a lump in her throat. Again. She had to kick this crying habit. Not her style, normally. But then, nothing quite so momentous as kidnapping had ever happened in her life before. What a tale she would have to tell when she got home.

Luke ran down to the study to check with his assistant in Athens. Andres, as usual, was concise and efficient, with news that the money was ready and would be left the follow-

ing evening, packaged according to instructions, in the alley alongside the indicated *kafeinion*, which was already under covert surveillance by the police. There had been no communication from the kidnapper since the original statement that the goods would be returned once he had the money.

Not right, thought Luke. 'I don't like this, Andres. Something smells wrong. I want him caught. And I need to know who's behind this. Someone's after my blood, one way or another. It has to stop.'

'I agree, *kyrie*. And with police help, and our own people watching, we shall catch him and make it stop.'

'I'll be back in the morning,' said Luke decisively.

'Better you are not! You would be an obvious target.'

'All the more reason for me to return. I am the one he wants. No argument, Andres. I have to do this.'

'Then I will cover your back, *kyrie*,' said Andres promptly.

'I was counting on that,' Luke assured him. 'Ari has his team ready in support?'

'Ready and waiting. How is the lady?'

'Doing remarkably well after her ordeal. Thanks, Andres. Keep me informed.'

Luke went outside to prowl round the garden. Given the choice, he would have returned to Athens immediately, to be right at the heart of things well in advance of zero hour. Luke's fists clenched at the thought of Isobel helpless in the kidnapper's hands. His blood ran cold at the thought of what he might have done to her before killing her. Because whoever was behind all this knew that the perfect way to make him suffer was to threaten the woman they assumed was his. But a fatal mistake had been made in choosing a kidnapper. The man had taken it for granted that the guest staying in his house on Chyros was Arianna Stratos, the woman most recently linked with him.

Luke stalked restlessly through the garden. His feelings had been indescribable as the *Athena* approached that barren little island—hope and gripping fear and then overwhelming, engulfing relief as he spotted the bright gleam of hair against the undergrowth and saw Isobel, dirty and defiant, brandishing her weapon as she prepared to do battle. One look, and all his original suspicions of her had vanished, consumed in the fire of his rage at the thought of losing her, of another man touching her, or worse. Luke smiled crookedly. How polite Isobel had been, making it plain that if he was expecting anything more from his little friend than gratitude for his trouble he was out of luck.

CHAPTER NINE

ISOBEL woke to a hand patting hers gently and smiled into Eleni's hovering face. 'What time is it?' she asked.

'Dinner time.'

'Already?' Isobel yawned as she sat upright. 'You should have woken me sooner.'

'*Kyrie* Luke said leave you rest.'

'Right. Just give me a few minutes.'

'Spiro put paintings in room downstairs,' the woman informed her.

Isobel thanked her warmly. So much had happened since painting them, she'd forgotten about her watercolours. Ten minutes later, her hair and face were as good as she could make them, but her shirt was badly creased. Not that it mattered if she was eating alone. Though she would have appreciated some company after her adventure. But, as had happened in the past with other men, maybe Luke wasn't interested in her sparkling conversation if it was the only thing on offer. Isobel's thoughts skidded to a halt. Why, exactly, was she so adamant about that? After her brush with possible death, would it be so terrible to enjoy a brief love affair with a man who appealed to her on every possible level? She leaned back in the chair with a sigh. Not terrible, at all,

which was the problem. A love affair with Luke might—
would—be a thing of glory for a few days. And nights. But
she had to think outside the box, to the time when she flew
home to the real world. So she'd pushed him away, even
though every instinct had been screaming at her to celebrate
life by making love with the charismatic man who'd saved that
life for her. Twice.

Luke suddenly appeared in the open doorway as though her
thoughts had conjured him up. 'You look very serious, Isobel.'

'I was contemplating the mysteries of life,' she said lightly.
'Is there any news?'

'Only that all arrangements are in hand.' Luke drew up a
chair beside her. 'My assistant is keeping me up to speed.'

'Is she super-efficient?' And probably beautiful, too,
thought Isobel glumly.

'The best. Andres Stefanides has been my right-hand man
since I bought my first freighter. I would trust him with my
life, Isobel,' said Luke and got up, still too restless to sit. He
went over to the glass doors to open them wide and brought
in the veranda table. He set it in front of Isobel, then closed
and locked the doors.

'Do you *really* think there's a danger he might come here
again?' she asked.

'It is best to guard against the possibility.' He slammed one
fist into the other in frustration. 'I will not rest until the police
have him in custody and I can find out who is pulling his
strings. From your description, he sounds like another hired
thug, so there must be some mastermind behind him.'

She hesitated. 'It couldn't possibly be your grandfather?
Because of his wife's death?'

Luke shook his head. 'Even if he did the unthinkable and
hired a man to kill someone of his own blood, Theo would

not have arranged the abduction. Arianna's grandfather is a lifelong friend.'

'You mean the kidnapper thought I was this Arianna?' said Isobel, eyes narrowed.

'Yes. She is a good friend of mine.'

'Pillow variety?'

'No. We share the kind of relationship you say you yearn for, Isobel. She is an intelligent, handsome woman whose company I enjoy when we get together, but—'

'But she's not the type you take to bed.'

'No.' Luke lifted an expressive shoulder. 'She is proof that it is possible for a man and woman to be just friends, Isobel.'

'I just wish more men felt the same. When I was in the hut, wondering if the man was going to come back and finish me off, I wondered if I'd ever see any of my friends again, Joanna most of all. It was an extra spur to get myself out.' Isobel smiled. 'And then you came, so all's well that ends well.'

'You should not have been forced to endure such treatment,' said Luke bitterly.

She shrugged. 'I survived. By the way, when he found he had the wrong woman, surely whoever's behind this must have wondered if you'd pay to get me back?'

'You were a guest in my house, whoever you were,' said Luke with emphasis. 'He knew I would pay. Though he made a big mistake with old Denis Stratos. Arianna was actually there in the room with her grandfather when the ransom demand arrived.'

Eleni beamed at them both as she came in to lay the table. For two, Isobel noted, brightening, as Spiro followed with a tray of steaming dishes.

Luke thanked them and smiled at Isobel as the couple left them to their dinner. 'You look surprised.'

'I am. I was expecting to dine alone tonight.'

'You would prefer that?'

Isobel shook her head irritably. 'Of course I wouldn't.'

'Then you must eat well tonight,' he urged. 'You must be very hungry, Isobel.'

'Oddly enough, I wasn't when we arrived home. I was just dirty and thirsty—' She broke off at the look he gave her. 'What is it?'

'You said "home".'

She flushed. 'I suppose the villa felt like that after my adventures.' She went on eating for a moment, then met his watchful eyes. 'In the hut I thought I might never live to eat another meal of any kind.'

Luke's mouth twisted as he put out a hand to cover hers. 'Do not think of it any more, Isobel. I have you safe now. And I swear I will keep you that way.'

'Right. Let's talk about pleasanter things.' She raised a quizzical eyebrow. 'Tell me about this Arianna of yours.'

'She is not mine!' Luke grinned. 'Arianna is an attractive, intellectual woman who refuses to marry any of the men her family keep bringing out for her.'

'Are you one of those?'

He shook his head. 'Due to the circumstances of my birth, I am not considered eligible.'

'Even though you're the grandson of Theo Andreadis?'

'Since he refuses to acknowledge the relationship, yes.'

'Would you like him to?'

His mouth tightened. 'Would you, in the same situation?'

Isobel gave it some thought. 'If he was the only relative I had it's possible I might make some kind of move towards détente, yes.'

'I do not possess your capacity for forgiveness. Also your

experience of grandparents was very different from mine,' he reminded her.

'True.' She smiled fondly at the memory. 'I was very lucky. But tell me more about Arianna.'

'We dine together occasionally, and if she needs an escort for some function her family insists she attend, I help her out. Which is no hardship. She is good company and I am fond of her.'

'Is she fond of you?'

'Of course,' he said, grinning. 'But she is in love with someone else.'

'So why doesn't he escort her?'

Luke smiled wryly. 'Arianna is a follower of Sappho. Her lover is a woman. But, other than me, and now you, no one knows that.'

'That kind of secret must be hard to keep,' said Isobel. 'But at least she has one thing going for her—she didn't get kidnapped.'

Luke laughed and seized her hand to kiss it. 'She would have been more of a handful for the kidnapper than you, Isobel. Arianna is built on heroic lines.' He eyed her challengingly. 'So, I have told you about the woman in my life. Now tell me about the men in yours. There must have been other men in your life before the swine who tried to force you.'

She winced. 'There were several in college, of course, but the ones who remain constant in my life are Leo and Josh Carey. Their family lived near my grandparents, so we grew up together. When they were teenagers they had a party. Joanna, the new kid on the block at the time, was invited to it, and the four of us have been firm friends ever since. Jo and I had boyfriends, of course, and the twins, who are doctors now, attract women like magnets, but Jo and I have a special relationship with them. Though Jo is married now.'

'And does her husband approve of these men?'

'Of course. But it wouldn't matter to her if he didn't. Jo is fiercely loyal.'

Luke smiled. 'I think you are, too, Isobel.'

'I try to be. Besides, I've known the twins since nursery school. To me, they're like brothers.'

'Ah, but do they look on you as a sister?'

'Of course they do.' She looked at the straight-backed chair he was sitting on, legs outstretched. 'You can't be comfortable on that. If I lie on the bed you can have the easy chair. Unless you have things to do.'

'What could be more important than spending the evening with you, Isobel?' He stood up. 'But first I shall go down to the study and check again with Andres. Though there can be no real news or he would have contacted me. Then I shall come back and take advantage of your offer. Unless you need sleep?' he added.

'*No.*' She shook her head so emphatically he frowned.

'You are nervous about sleeping?'

'Not exactly. But I'd like to be a lot more tired tonight before I try.' She smiled ruefully. 'It was a bad move to sleep before dinner.'

'Rest was vitally necessary after your ordeal.' His eyes darkened as he looked down at her. 'I would give much to have spared you that.'

'But you rescued me—again,' she pointed out.

'For which I have not been suitably rewarded,' he said casually and strolled to the door, slanting a glittering smile over his shoulder. 'Is there anything you need when I come back?'

'Nothing, thank you.'

Isobel wondered what Luke meant by a suitable reward. Who was she trying to kid? What would any man expect

under the circumstances? She piled the pillows against the headboard and propped herself upright against them.

When Luke came back she eyed him expectantly. 'Any news?'

'No. Just that all is in readiness for tomorrow night, and I shall leave early in the morning. I shall be there on the scene when the ransom money is claimed.'

'*What?* Are you mad?' Isobel stared at him, horrified. 'Surely it's best to leave the police to deal with that! You've already escaped a stabbing; you might not be so lucky a second time.'

His face set into lines which made argument futile. 'Then that is my fate and cannot be avoided. This is something I must do, Isobel.' He sat on the edge of the bed and took her hand. 'Surely you can understand this.'

'Oh, I do,' she said with hostility. 'It's all down to testosterone. But I don't approve.' But, if he was taking off in the morning, maybe this was a good time to give him her present, just in case… She pushed the thought away. 'I should have asked you to fetch something for me.'

'I will fetch it now. What is it?'

'The watercolours I was working on. Spiro put them safe somewhere, in the room I was using downstairs.'

Isobel felt tense as she waited for him to bring the paintings. A man like Lukas Andreadis could buy whatever expensive artwork he fancied. Would he consider her efforts amateurish? The pool painting was no Hockney, but she hoped Luke would like it as a keepsake just the same.

He came back quickly, holding a large package. 'Spiro wrapped them up very carefully,' he said, handing it to her.

'He's such a star, your Spiro,' said Isobel warmly. 'Eleni, too. You're lucky to have them.'

'I know this.' Luke gestured at the package impatiently. 'Open it.'

Isobel removed the wrapping paper carefully, then handed him the painting of the pool.

Luke stood looking down at it, his face inscrutable, and then said the last thing she expected to hear. 'So. You really do paint.'

Isobel's eyes blazed as she realised what he meant. 'My sketches didn't convince you, then. You still suspected me of wanting a story for some tabloid—or, worse still, that I was a tourist out for a holiday thrill.'

'However beautiful and appealing you were, past experience made me suspicious,' he admitted, and gave her a long, unsmiling look. 'I soon discovered that you were neither of those things.'

'But you still doubted that I could paint!'

'If I did, I doubt no longer. This is exquisite.' He was so obviously sincere she calmed down. 'You are not only an artist, but a very gifted one, Isobel. You create atmosphere. I feel both the cool of the water *and* the heat of the day in your painting.'

'It's a present for you—a very small way to thank you for all your kindness,' she said with formality.

He bowed, equally formal. '*Efcharisto poli*, Isobel. I am honoured.' He put the painting very carefully on the dressing table. 'I shall have it framed in Athens and hang it in my bedroom there.' He watched closely as she unwrapped the painting of the beach. 'This also is wonderful.'

'It's *my* keepsake. To take home to look at and convince myself that all this really happened.'

Luke took the painting to join the other one, then sat beside her on the bed. 'As I said before, Isobel, I shall need no reminders of my trespasser. But I shall treasure the painting because it is not only beautiful, but a gift from you.'

'Now you know I really am an artist!' she said acidly, then looked at him in appeal. 'I wish you wouldn't go there tomorrow, Luke.'

'You are afraid I shall be killed?'

'Of course I am!'

'I was brought up in a hard school. I can look after myself. And I am not fool enough to go there alone. Andres and my security team will be in the background in support.' Luke looked into her eyes, as though assessing her mood, then drew her into his arms and held her close. 'Do not worry, Isobel.'

'I can't help it. I'll have nightmares tonight.'

'I know a remedy for that,' he whispered.

'Cocoa?'

He let out a smothered crack of laughter. 'I tasted that once in England, but I doubt that we have any here. My remedy is even sweeter, Isobel,' he added in a tone which sent her pulse racing. 'I must go down and tell Spiro what hour I intend to leave.' He kissed her fleetingly on the lips and brushed a hand over her hair.

Isobel lay frowning at the door he'd closed behind him. Had that been a *goodnight, sleep well* kind of kiss? She slid carefully off the bed to collect the beautifully laundered nightgown Eleni had left ready and limped to the bathroom, impatient with herself. He probably thought his doubts had made her angry. Maybe normally they would have. But tomorrow he was going to risk his life to hunt down the man out for his blood. She shivered, knowing she had no hope of any sleep tonight, for more reasons than one. She should have been more blunt and simply asked Luke to sleep with her. Best cure of all for nightmares—and probably a good many other things. Surviving kidnap had put things into perspective, teaching her that life was not only short, but could also be very sweet if she let it.

Isobel went over to the veranda windows, tested them to see that they were locked securely, then returned to the bed, picked up her book and sat up against the pillows. If Luke wasn't coming back, insomnia would be her fate. But she could at least read, and leave her bedside lamp on as her candle in the dark. The story was by one of her favourite authors, but the intricate mediaeval mystery, though gripping and beautifully written, failed to hold her attention. Then her eyes flew up in surprise as Luke came in and very deliberately locked the door behind him.

'As I thought, we have no cocoa,' he said, his eyes holding hers as he walked slowly to the bed. 'So we must try my remedy instead.'

Isobel licked the tip of her tongue over suddenly dry lips. 'You didn't say, exactly, what that was.'

Luke smiled as he sat on the edge of the bed. 'It is very simple, *hriso mou*. I just hold you in my arms all night and keep you safe.'

Isobel's heart turned over. 'Sounds most effective,' she said shakily.

'It is. There is just one problem. Or possibly more than one.'

'Oh?'

'If I hold you in my arms I will not sleep.' His eyes blazed. 'But I will gladly endure insomnia to guard you from nightmares, Isobel.'

Her eyes fell. 'I seem to be constantly in your debt. How will I ever repay you?'

'I can think of a way.' Luke smoothed a hand over her hair. 'Can you?'

'Yes,' she said, burning her boats. 'Is it the same way as yours?'

Luke growled as he pulled her into his arms. 'You are tor-

menting me, Isobel *mou*,' he whispered, his lips a tantalising inch from hers. 'I want you. Tell me you want *me*.'

Of *course* she wanted him. At this moment she wanted him more than anything or anyone she'd ever wanted before. After all the trauma, she *deserved* this. It would be her reward equally as much as Luke's. And if things went wrong tomorrow… She shivered and Luke's arms tightened, his victorious smile hidden in her hair.

'Talk to me, *hriso mou*. You said your thanks were all you had to give. Have you changed your mind?'

'Yes,' she muttered into his chest. 'So stop talking and make love to me, Lukas Andreadis—before I change it back again.'

He let out a shout of laughter and leapt up to strip off his clothes. But as he moved naked to the bed she held up her hand.

'No. Just stand still for a moment, as you did by the pool.'

She let her eyes move slowly over the burnished bronze curls, and the eyes that glowed like coals in his taut face. She lingered over the broad shoulders, the torso that tapered into a lean waist and long muscular legs, and the stirring masculinity between them. To Isobel's delight, colour rose along his sculpted cheekbones.

'I refuse to just stand here while you look at me.'

'Why not?'

His eyes flared. 'Because my body is betraying me!'

'So I see,' said Isobel, suddenly reckless as she took her nightgown over her head and pulled the covers back for him.

Luke slid in beside her and with a groan of pleasure held her close, his hands smoothing down her back to mould every curve and hollow of her body to his. 'I have dreamed of this,' he said into the angle where her neck met her shoulder.

Isobel sighed and wriggled closer, delighting in the tremor she felt run through him. 'I refused to let myself dream of it.'

'Because you did not want to make love with me?'

'No, because I did.'

He growled in triumph and kissed her fiercely. His lips were warm and skilled and now they were naked together the first touch of them on hers sent her so dizzy with delight she surged against him. And with her breasts crushed against his chest she found his heart was pounding in unison with hers as his kisses sent her blood rushing through her veins, and her body turned into one entire erogenous zone.

He raised his head and smiled in triumphant possession. 'You are so lovely, Isobel. It is impossible to believe, now, that I was angry with you that first day on the beach.'

'You frightened the life out of me.'

He tensed. 'Are you frightened now?'

'No.' She moved closer. 'Make love to me, Luke. Make me glad to be alive!'

He obeyed with such fervour Isobel's pulse raced as the heat from his kisses ran through her like a jolt of electricity. She pressed closer, glorying in the feel of his skin against hers until he moved her away a fraction so that his lips could move down her throat in a string of soft, sweet kisses, and her breasts grew taut in anticipation as she felt the heat of his breath on her skin. He made love to each breast in turn with lips and tongue and gently grazing teeth, his caresses flooding her with hot, liquid arousal as her body filled with an urgency so new and overwhelming she shook with the force of it.

Luke stiffened. 'Do not tremble. I will stop if you wish.'

'I don't wish. Go on—*please*!' She gloried in his renewed caresses, making a little relishing sound deep in her throat as his hands moved lower to stroke the satiny curve below her waist. But she gasped as his fingers aroused turbulence with the most intimate caress of all, his mouth devouring hers with

a kiss so possessive and overwhelming her blood seemed to turn to steam. He looked deep into her eyes, asking a question she answered with such an impatient little nod he smiled in triumph and surged inside her, filling her to such capacity Isobel's heart lurched with the shock of it. For a long, throbbing moment they lay utterly still, then her inner muscles clenched around him in fierce invitation and he took her with him on a surging, accelerating climb towards some fiery, longed for peak he reached at last before her, then held her tightly until her body arched against him, convulsed in throbbing waves of release.

Luke stayed still for a long, silent interval while their hearts slowed, pinning her to the bed with his weight. At last he rolled over onto his back, drawing her close against him as he smoothed the damp curls away from her forehead. 'Look at me, Isobel.'

Reluctantly, she opened heavy eyes to meet the possessive black gaze.

'Did I hurt you, *hriso mou*?' he asked softly.

'No.' Isobel heaved in a deep, unsteady breath. 'But you surprised me.'

'Surprised?' He frowned. 'Why?'

'After the episode with Gavin, I was sure I'd never want to make love again, ever.' Isobel met his eyes squarely. 'But with you it was as if we were climbing together, and I'd die if I didn't reach the summit.'

His eyes glittered in triumph. 'But you did reach it, *glykia mou, ne*?'

'Not only reached it, I soared off it in free fall!'

Luke threw back his head and laughed in unashamed male satisfaction. 'It is so good for a man to hear that.'

Isobel smiled wryly. 'You sounded very Greek just then.'

He nodded with sudden arrogance. 'Because that is what I am, and proud of it. And you are an English rose, Isobel, and so beautiful and intelligent I find it hard to believe no man has wanted to marry you.'

'One did a couple of years ago. But when he started talking about mortgages and urging me to get a proper job it put me off marriage permanently.'

Luke laughed scornfully. 'The fool wanted to make you into someone else.'

'Exactly,' said Isobel, delighted he understood. 'So we broke up.' She sighed. 'But not without a fight on his part. He wanted Isobel the woman, but not Isobel the artist.'

'I want them both,' said Luke, and flipped her over on her back to lean over her, his handsome face intent with an expression that made her pulse race. 'Forget all other men; you are mine now,' he whispered and kissed her, and Isobel wreathed her arms round his neck and drew him closer. She *was* his. For now. But now was all they had together. In a few days she would be leaving Chyros to go back to the real world, where there was no place in her life for someone like Lukas Andreadis. But that life seemed very far away and unreal as he made love to her in the hot reality of the present, taking infinite pleasure in the responses he wrung from her. His lips moved over her face and throat, then continued slowly down until she felt those crisp bronze curls against her skin as he kissed her in a place unused to such attention. His lips and tongue caressed her so skilfully they sent her climbing to a different peak of pleasure she experienced alone. And in triumph Luke held her close as she gasped in the throes of it.

CHAPTER TEN

ONCE again Isobel heard the helicopter chop away at first light, and said a swift, fierce prayer for the pilot. She slid down in the bed, intending to lie there for a moment, but when she woke again a glance at her watch catapulted her out of bed in such a hurry to snatch up her nightgown she tripped as she pulled it on and only just managed to stop from falling as Eleni came in.

'You hurt?' she demanded, coming to help.

'No, no, I'm fine. I was just in a hurry for the bathroom,' said Isobel, embarrassed. 'I want a shower before breakfast.'

'*Kyrie* Luke left early,' said the little woman glumly. 'You heard?'

'Yes.'

'How you feel today?'

'Pretty good, Eleni. I'm none the worse for my adventure.' She smiled. 'And for once I really fancy some breakfast this morning.'

Isobel raced through her shower, then eyed herself critically in the steamed up mirror, surprised to see she looked much the same as usual. What had she expected? Evidence of sin? But it had been bliss, not sin. The dreamy look in her eyes soon changed to apprehension. She hugged the towel

around her, suddenly cold at the thought of Luke acting out his *High Noon* scenario later.

Determined to stay strong, no matter what happened, Isobel got dressed and did her hair and face, and limped as fast as she could into the bedroom when her phone rang.

'*Kalimera*, Isobel. How are you today?'

'Luke, are you back already? I'm ashamed to say I've slept half the morning away. But I feel good. Even my eye is back to normal.'

'Unlike mine!'

'Yours is *very* sexy.' She chuckled. 'I really go for the pirate look.'

'I am so happy to hear that. I would have given much to stay and kiss you awake this morning. But I have news, Isobel. When I arrived at my apartment I found a hand-written note among my mail giving the location of Petros's island. Like the man who attacked me, your kidnapper was probably threatened in some way, but he has a conscience, it seems, and could not leave you there to perish. Even so, be careful today. Stay close to the house.'

'Yes, Luke.'

'I so like to hear you say that. When I come home I shall ask more questions that require the same answer.'

Isobel's eyebrows rose. What did he mean by that? 'Luke, I'll be desperately worried. So ring me tonight after—afterwards.'

'I will. But do not worry, *hriso mou*. I will take no chances, I swear. Now, eat.'

Worried or not, hot rolls and butter, followed by cup after cup of coffee, tasted wonderful to Isobel. At the same time yesterday she would have sold her soul for even part of the meal. She was about to ask Eleni for more coffee when she

heard a car coming down the drive and, soon afterwards, Alyssa came running from the kitchen, beaming.

'*Kalimera*, Isobel. After your ordeal you should be shattered, but you look wonderful.'

'I feel fine.' Isobel smiled warmly. 'I was just about to ask Eleni for more coffee.'

'Unnecessary, *glykia mou*. She's on her way with it right now.'

By the time Eleni left them to their coffee, Alyssa was vibrating with impatience.

'So, Isobel! Did Luke tell you about my masterly performance when he returned on the *Athena* without you?'

Isobel laughed. 'He certainly did. He said you're a terrific actress.'

'Drama queen, he means!' Alyssa grinned, flipping back a lock of shining dark hair as she struck a pose. 'I rather fancy myself as Medea. Or possibly Elektra. But never mind that. Tell me what happened—every last detail.' She sobered abruptly. 'You must have been so terrified, Isobel.'

'Oddly enough, when I woke up in the boat my first reaction was fury. But the fright soon kicked in when I found I was tied up. I hated feeling so helpless.' Isobel gulped some coffee, then told Alyssa what happened, right up to the moment Luke arrived in the *Athena* to rescue her.

'For the second time!' Alyssa's lips curved in a wicked little smile. 'I trust you rewarded him generously?'

'Absolutely,' said Isobel, returning the smile in kind. 'I gave him the watercolour I painted.'

Alyssa rolled her eyes. 'Surely you can think of something more exciting than a painting?'

'Luke liked it.' Isobel's smile faded. 'I hope it will remind him of me after I leave.'

Alyssa snorted. 'He will never forget *you*, Isobel!'

'You're probably right. I've been nothing but trouble to him from the moment we met.'

'I doubt that. What man thinks of a gorgeous blonde as trouble?'

Isobel coloured. 'Luke told me he likes his women dark and curvy.'

'He has changed his mind since he met you, *glykia mou*.'

'What does that mean?'

'My sweet, more or less. Does Luke say that?'

'We're not on those kind of terms.'

'If you stayed, you soon would be,' said Alyssa firmly. 'So stay. Please. I would love you to come to my wedding.'

Isobel smiled wistfully. 'I would love it, too, but I must get back to my job. I've used up all my holiday allowance for this year.'

Alyssa sighed, then rummaged in her bag and handed over a card. 'These are my telephone numbers. Ring me if you change your mind.'

'I will.' Isobel smiled warmly. 'Thanks for coming to see me.'

'Nothing could have kept me away! It amazes me that you survived such a horrible experience so bravely. Me, I would have nightmares.' Alyssa touched the uneven lock of hair over Isobel's ear, then glanced at her watch with regret. 'I must go. Since Luke is away, why not come down to the taverna tonight? I could fetch you, and my parents would love to meet you.'

Isobel was touched. 'It's a lovely thought, Alyssa, but I'm not quite up for that right now and I'm not sure I should be seen yet. Can I take a rain check?'

'Of course. Ring me if you need me. Any time. Take care.' She kissed Isobel's cheek, then rushed off to talk to Eleni on

her way out and a moment later her car roared away up the cypress-lined drive, leaving Isobel feeling restless and on edge, and wondering what to do with the rest of her day.

After trying to read for a while, Isobel gave up and got out her drawing materials. As a change from watercolours she would try a pencil portrait of Luke. Portraits were not normally her area of expertise, but the forceful, handsome features of Luke took shape on her drawing pad with such ease and speed that by late afternoon Isobel had achieved a strikingly accurate likeness. When Eleni was allowed to see the finished sketch she called Spiro to marvel at Isobel's skill, and it was so obvious that both of them lusted after the drawing Isobel promised to do another to keep herself occupied as she wondered what was happening to Luke.

At that particular moment Luke was in his office, in a meeting with Andres and various members of his staff and security force, all of whom were arguing that one of them should take his place at the designated ransom drop, a *kafeinion* in the Psyrri district of Athens.

Luke heard them out until the hubbub showed signs of abating, then held up his hand. 'I appreciate your offers, but this is personal for me. To wreak vengeance on me, this man has caused harm to a lady who is a visitor to our country, also a guest in my house. Therefore, gentlemen, I must confront this man myself before I hand him over to the police. Who,' he added, 'agreed to my keeping out of sight until the man actually tries to take the money.'

'But the criminal knows you,' said Ari Constantinou, Luke's massive head of security. 'You've survived a stabbing already, *kyrie*. You might not be so lucky a second time.'

'The intention was never to have me killed. To get the

money, he needs me alive.' Luke's eyes hardened. 'But he made a big mistake in kidnapping a lady under my protection.'

There were loud exclamations of assent from everyone present.

'So this is the plan I have worked out with Ari,' said Andres, after a nod from Luke. 'I shall go early and drink coffee at a table by the window looking out on the alley. Two of you will occupy another near the door. Another will keep watch from the men's room which overlooks the back of the alley. The boss will keep out of sight until nearer the time, and the rest of the team will be with Ari in the bar opposite. The police surveillance team will stay out of sight as *kyrie* Andreadis requested.'

'They were happy with this arrangement?' asked a voice.

'No,' said Luke. 'They wanted me to keep well away.' He smiled grimly. 'I refused.'

Later, in the stiflingly hot night, obeying an instinct that prodded him like a goad, Luke was an hour early when he began strolling amongst Athenian café society in the warren of streets that comprised the Psyrri district. He made for the designated *kafeinion* and paused on the corner opposite, smiling a greeting at one of his security men, who took his cue like a casual bystander enjoying a chat while they kept secret watch on the alley.

'You are early, *kyrie*,' said the man softly, then swore violently as a fire alarm blared in the *kafeinion*, sending everyone streaming out into the street. Luke shot through the scattering throng into the alley and launched himself in a flying tackle to ground a big, burly figure about to snatch the ransom bag. Luke fought to keep the man on the ground until help arrived, and in seconds Luke's security team closed in on them and the man was pulled to his feet to face the police, eyes

rolling in fear as he was secured and hustled into the police van now blocking the alley.

'I was allowed to observe while he was being questioned later,' Luke told Isobel when he rang for the second time to give details. 'Once in custody, the man begged protection for his family against Zena and Zoe Karras, twin sisters of the dead Melina Andreadis. As I suspected, they were the driving force behind this all along. Just like the man who attacked me, your kidnapper's wife and children had been threatened by the two harpies. But he swore he was no killer, which is why he sent me the note giving me your location.'

'And he never actually hurt me,' added Isobel.

'But he tied you up and left you in that hut,' said Luke grimly, then continued to tell her that the police went straight to the Karras house to question the sisters, who promptly went berserk with fury at the failure of their plan and poured everything out in a flood of venom against him, which shocked even the battle-hardened detectives. Luke laughed cynically. 'But the sisters' vendetta against me was more for the loss of the generous allowance Melina had made them, than for her death. I was informed later that they blamed me for her death and everything else wrong in their lives.'

'They meant to have you killed?'

'No. Just to wound and harm me in any way possible, out of pure venom. As a source of money, I was no good to them dead.'

Isobel shivered, her knuckles white on the phone. 'What was to happen to me?'

'They were too hysterical to make any sense by the time they were taken into custody, but Andres is related to one of the policemen interrogating them, so I shall know more even-

tually.' His voice dropped a tone. 'But, no matter what they intended, you are safe now, *hriso mou*. You can sleep tonight.'

'I'll probably have nightmares!'

'If I were there with you I could provide a cure for those,' he said softly.

The mere thought of it made her weak at the knees. 'When will you be back?'

'As soon as I can, Isobel. I must work with Andres for a while first today. Even without all this drama I have been neglecting my business interests since you came into my life, Miss Isobel James!'

'So sorry about that. Never mind. I'll soon be gone.'

'I know this very well,' he assured her darkly. 'When I get back we will spend every possible moment together before you leave.'

Isobel put her phone on the bedside table, limp with relief now it was all over and Luke was safe. But she was very thoughtful as she settled into the pillows. If Luke intended to spend every moment possible with her before she left, did he mean in as well as out of bed? And, if so, what would Eleni and Spiro think of the arrangement? Isobel bit her lip. She had become so fond of the couple the thought of losing their respect was painful. She hugged a pillow to her chest fiercely. If she'd known beforehand that she'd be in danger of falling madly in love during her holiday she would have steered clear of these magical Greek islands. The holiday had been intended as a recovery programme, both from working overtime for weeks and from the hateful episode with Gavin. But now she would need all the hard work she could get once she was home to help her recover from her Greek odyssey. And from Luke. She sighed. If she wasn't her sparkling self for a while, at least Jo would assume that

her hair-raising adventures were the reason. Whereas the real problem would be that she was pining for the man who'd rescued her from them.

The next day seemed endless. Luke rang twice in snatched moments between meetings, but he was too busy for more than a word or two. And when Alyssa rang later she apologised because the taverna was short-staffed and she had to work all day rather than drive up to the Villa Medusa as she'd intended. To occupy herself, Isobel finished the drawing of Luke for Eleni and Spiro, ate the lunch put in front of her and in between took walks in the garden with her stick at regular intervals to exercise her ankle and pass the time until Luke got back. After that, her time with him would be so brief she was determined to make the most of every minute—once he tore himself away from his empire to fly back to Chyros.

When Eleni apologised because dinner would be served an hour later that evening Isobel assured her it was fine with her and went carefully up the stairs, supporting herself on the carved banister rail as she went. In preparation for Luke's return tomorrow she would use the hour for the kind of top-to-toe beauty treatment she rarely had time, or inclination, for at home.

Isobel was sitting on the veranda as the sun set, waving her newly painted toes around to dry the polish, when her heart leapt at the sound she hadn't been expecting until the next day. Tense with excitement, she leaned out over the balcony rail as Luke's helicopter circled round to land, then forced herself to wait for him to come to her. She went barefoot into the bedroom, listening to the sound of greetings downstairs as Luke brought Spiro up to date, her pulse racing in time with his footsteps as Luke ran upstairs, and at last he was there in

the doorway, arms outstretched. She flew into them and he buried his face in the fragrant mass of her newly washed hair, holding her close against his thudding heart.

Luke raised his head at last, smiling down into her eyes. '*Kalispera*, Isobel.'

'Hi,' she said, smiling radiantly. 'You forgot to tell me you were coming home today.'

'I did not forget. I wanted to surprise you.'

She wagged a finger. 'But you let Spiro know, because Eleni asked to put dinner later tonight. She never said a word.'

'On my orders,' Luke said, and put her away from him to look down into her eyes. 'I wanted to see your face when I arrived, and now I have seen it and know you are glad to see me I want to kiss you very badly. But if I do I might not stop, and I need time to make myself worthy of my beautiful dinner companion.'

'Thank you, kind sir. I'll wait for you on the terrace.'

'Wait up here and I shall carry you down,' he said promptly, but she shook her head.

'With care, I can manage without my crutch now if I go barefoot and carry these to put on downstairs.' Isobel grinned at him as she picked up her sandals. 'Don't be long. I'm hungry.'

Isobel had felt no enthusiasm for dining alone, but with Luke for such unexpected company she did full justice to the celebration meal Eleni and Spiro took such pleasure in serving them, both of them blazingly happy now that the man they loved like a son had faced down his enemies and returned to them safely.

At intervals Luke left the table to answer the phone to well wishers who had seen the news, among them Alyssa Nicolaides, who apologised for disturbing him but had been

instructed to convey her parents' relief, along with hers, that he had survived yet another dangerous encounter unscathed.

'The gods must be watching over you, Lukas *mou*. Give my love to Isobel,' Alyssa added sweetly as she said goodbye.

'That was Alyssa,' said Luke as he resumed his place at the table. 'She sent you her love. I shall leave all other calls to the machine. If there is anything urgent from Andres he will use my private line.' He yawned hugely. 'Forgive me, Isobel, I had very little sleep last night.'

'I'm not surprised.' She abandoned the pomegranate she'd been toying with. 'Do you want to go to bed?'

Luke jumped up to pull out her chair. 'Zeus, yes, I do. I will tell Spiro he can lock up.'

'Thank Eleni for a wonderful dinner, Luke, but don't be long,' said Isobel, then flushed hectically at the look he gave her.

As Luke strode off towards the kitchen Isobel slipped off the sandals and began her usual careful ascent of the stairs but, before she was even halfway up, he caught up with her and carried her the rest of the way and along the landing to her room. Once inside, he kicked the door shut and laid her on the bed, then cast himself down beside her and took her in his arms, his face buried against her neck.

'Last night,' he said, his breath hot against her skin, 'I thought of this when I was watching that alley, waiting to seize the man who had kidnapped you.'

'I thought of it every minute of the day,' she admitted huskily. 'Then you rang me to say you were safe, and I could breathe again.'

Luke raised his head to look in her eyes. 'You cared that much?'

'Yes.' She wriggled closer. 'Now tell me about it again. Was it a shock to learn the Karras sisters were behind the vendetta?'

'No. After their behaviour towards me at Melina's funeral it was no surprise at all.' Luke kissed her with sudden heat. 'Now forget them, *agapi mou*, and concentrate on me.'

Isobel woke alone the next morning and had showered and dressed before Luke came to find her.

'*Kalimera,*' he said, taking her in his arms.

'Good morning.' She smiled up at him. 'How are you today?'

'Now there is no longer danger to you, I feel as though a great weight has rolled from my shoulders, Isobel. I also feel hungry,' he added, and kissed her. 'For breakfast also, you understand. And while we eat you shall tell me what you would like to do today.'

They had reached the coffee stage when Isobel made her request. 'I'd love a swim.' She laid a hand on his, smiling at him cajolingly. 'You're here now, so you can hardly refuse me a second time.'

Luke raised the hand to his lips. 'Of course you can swim. Milos is not here today so this is a good time.'

Isobel eyed him narrowly. 'Is Milos the reason why you wouldn't let me use the pool before?'

'Yes,' he said bluntly. 'I had seen what you wear to swim, remember.'

'My bikini is perfectly respectable,' she retorted.

He snorted. 'When I first saw you on my beach I thought you were naked.'

'Only because the bikini's pink—at least it was.' She made a face. 'Not that I'll ever wear it again.'

After breakfast they went upstairs together, Luke's arm in support after an argument about carrying her.

'Give me ten minutes,' she said at her bedroom door, then hurried to change into a sleek gentian-blue swimsuit; her only

alternative to the bikini. Isobel eyed the various bruises which had now matured into multicoloured glory, then shrugged philosophically. Luke had seen them all before. She put a filmy tunic on top, collected a bath towel and opened the door to Luke. 'That was a lot less than ten minutes.'

'Why waste time apart?' said Luke and bent to pick her up, but Isobel shook her head.

'If you just hold my hand I'll manage the stairs perfectly well.'

'No matter. I need to hold you in my arms. Indulge me, *ne*?'

Luke set her down on one of the reclining chairs at the pool's edge, then took off the T-shirt and jeans he was wearing over his swimming gear. 'Shall I help you take off this pretty thing?' he asked, eyeing the tunic.

'That I can do myself!' She slipped the garment over her head and stood up unaided.

His eyes narrowed to a hot gleam as they moved over her. 'That is even more alluring than the bikini!'

'I thought you'd be pleased that I'm more covered up,' she said primly, and he laughed and scooped her up to run along the pool, ignoring her frantic protests as he jumped in the water with her.

Spluttering and laughing as she surfaced, Isobel pushed him away, then took off down the pool in the stylish crawl which had won races in school. But Luke followed her with the grace and power she'd so much admired from her balcony and passed her easily, thrusting his wet curls back as he waited at the end for her. She gave him a challenging grin as she did a racing turn and swam off again, and with a shout he gave chase to swim beside her for a few lengths. When Isobel called it quits he hoisted himself out of the pool and lifted her out to wrap her in a towel.

'You are like a mermaid in the water, Isobel. Do you want to go in, or will you wait for me while I finish my swim?'

'I'll sit here in the sun for a minute or two,' she panted. 'I'm out of condition. I haven't done this for a while. Besides, I want to watch you.'

Luke gave her a quick kiss and dived into the pool. Isobel watched, transfixed, for once wishing she had a camera to preserve the moment as he powered through the water for several lengths of the pool. At last he swung himself up beside her, breathing hard.

'I think you should go in now, Isobel.' He startled her by casually stripping off to towel himself down before pulling on his jeans. He handed the filmy tunic over and bent to pick her up.

'You can't feel like carrying me after all that exercise,' she said severely, but Luke merely chuckled and carried on through the hall, not even out of breath, she saw, impressed, as Eleni came hurrying to offer coffee. He nodded and gave instructions in her own language as he carried on up the stairs.

'I said to give you time to dress,' said Luke as he set Isobel down in the bedroom. He frowned suddenly, his eyes dark as they lingered on her bruises as she discarded the towel. 'I was too dazzled by your swimsuit to see those by the pool—and too desperate to make love to you last night,' he said, and dropped to his knees to set his lips to the marks. 'The man did that?' he demanded harshly.

'No. Wriggling out through the hut window did most of the damage.' Isobel brushed a hand over his wet curls. 'I must have a shower.'

He stood up to pull her close. 'I wish we were alone in the house,' he whispered.

She felt guilty for secretly agreeing. 'But we're not, and I'd love some coffee.'

Isobel rushed through her shower, then towelled her hair,

scrunched her fingers through it and left it to do its own thing while she got dressed again. Glowing after her swim, she collected her walking stick, determined to make it downstairs under her own steam. She was halfway there when Luke came out of his study to catch her in the act.

'You see?' she said defiantly and, with her hand on the intricate lacework of the carved banister, limped carefully down the last few stairs.

'You are a very determined woman,' he said, laughing, and, before she could prevent him, picked her up again. 'But I am a very determined man. You must take care until your ankle is bandaged again,' he informed her as he took her back to the reclining chairs. He sat down beside her and took her hand. 'So how do you really feel, *hriso mou*?'

Isobel gave him a straight look. 'Do you mean after my swim, or after making love with you last night?'

He frowned. 'I meant the last part. Because in my desire to celebrate life I think I was too demanding, *ne*? Did I hurt you?'

'No.' She flushed a little. 'I felt the same urge to celebrate, Luke.' She eyed him uneasily. 'Do you regret what happened between us?'

He raised the hand and pressed a kiss into her palm. 'How could I regret something so sublime, *kardia mou*?'

'But you were gone this morning.'

'For a very good reason. I woke up wanting to make love to you again, but exerted much self-control and let you sleep. Also, I thought you might not like Eleni to find me in your bed.'

'Very true,' she said with feeling, and shot a troubled look at him. 'Luke, will she think less of me for sleeping with you?'

'No,' he said emphatically. 'I told her—also Spiro—that I shall keep you with me night and day until you leave, to keep you safe. They agreed with great fervour. Spiro cannot

forget the horror they felt the night you were stolen.' Luke smiled. 'They believe that fate sent such a lovely young lady to me.'

'Oh, dear,' said Isobel, mopping her eyes with a napkin. 'That's made me cry again. You won't believe this, but normally I hardly ever cry.'

'There is no sin in showing emotion, Isobel.' His eyes kindled. 'As you did in my arms last night. So dry your eyes, *agapi mou*. We must go down to Dr Riga now and ask him to strap your ankle.'

Isobel pulled a face. 'Is my hair a mess? I didn't do much to it after I washed it.'

'Those wild curls are very sexy. Leave them like that.' He handed her the stick. 'Be careful. I have worked hard—and braved much danger—to keep you safe.'

'I did some of the heavy lifting myself by getting out of that hut on the island,' she reminded him, laughing, then sobered suddenly. 'All the time I was praying for a miracle, and it happened. You came, Luke.'

'I did some praying myself on that boat trip,' he said grimly, and snatched her back into his arms to give her a hard, fleeting kiss. 'When I saw your hair as we came in to land I knew my prayers were answered.'

The trip to the clinic was made without incident and, after greetings with Dr Riga and the thorough check-up he insisted on, Isobel's ankle was strapped up and she was able to walk normally as she left, feeling secure in yellow espadrilles.

'I shall miss carrying you everywhere,' he said as he lifted her into the Cherokee.

So would she, Isobel admitted secretly. 'And I appreciated it,' she assured him, 'but it's good to feel independent again.'

'How you value your independence! But do not imagine you can go climbing down to any beaches,' he warned.

She pulled a face. 'No hardship there. I've rather lost my enthusiasm for beaches just now.'

'Good. Keep to peaceful strolls in the garden. When we get back I must ring Andres, and you can drink the tea Eleni is certain to have waiting for you. Ah,' he said, stopping the car. 'Alyssa is waving us down.'

Alyssa ran to lean in at the open window. *'Kalispera.'* She grinned at Luke. 'Just can't keep out of trouble, can you!'

'I do not seek it,' he assured her.

'You never try to avoid it either.' Alyssa smiled in apology at Isobel. 'Sorry I couldn't come up last night. Did you know what was going on?'

'Yes, I did.' Isobel exchanged a look with Luke. 'It was a huge relief to hear it was all over.'

'Come down to the taverna for a meal tonight and celebrate. My parents would love to see you both. Give Eleni the night off, Luke,' she coaxed.

He glanced at Isobel. 'Would you like that?'

With Alyssa waiting, there was only one answer Isobel felt she could make. 'I would, yes.'

'Are you sure about this?' said Luke as they drove off. 'I was hoping to have you all to myself this evening.'

'We needn't stay long,' she consoled him, and smiled up at him as she stroked a finger along his muscular thigh. 'We can go to bed early when we get home.'

As soon as the car stopped, both Eleni and Spiro hurried to hear the doctor's verdict.

'I hope you weren't cooking anything special tonight, Eleni,' said Isobel anxiously. 'Alyssa is keen for us to dine at the taverna.'

Eleni shook her head, smiling, and led Isobel indoors to sit on a chair at the veranda table. 'I not even shop yet. Spiro take me now.'

Isobel poured herself a cup of tea as Eleni hurried off, but she'd managed only a sip before Luke bent over her. 'How fast can you drink that?'

'Why?'

He smiled persuasively as the car started up outside. 'We shall be alone in the house for hours, and you look tired. You need a rest. So do I.'

'In that case, pour my tea on a flower bed or wherever. I'm hot, anyway.'

'So am I, *hriso mou*,' he said huskily, and picked her up.

'I can walk now,' she protested, but he shook his head and hurried up the stairs with her.

'Too slow. Why waste time?'

There was so little of it before she left, Isobel was in full agreement as Luke carried her into her cool, airy bedroom and immediately began undressing her.

'You're in a big hurry,' she protested breathlessly as he flung their garments in all directions.

'Only over this part,' he said, and knelt naked on the bed to lean over her, his eyes gleaming down into hers. 'I promise to love you as slowly as possible.'

The words spoken in that husky, irresistible voice, coupled with the knowledge that they were alone in the big house in the hot languor of the afternoon, created an aphrodisiac effect new to Isobel. As with so many other things since her arrival on Chyros.

'It's so quiet, we could be alone in the world,' she whispered, quivering at the touch of skilled, inciting hands.

'Just the two of us, *hriso mou*, like Adam and Eve. But with

no serpents in our paradise any more.' He caressed her breasts, kissing her softly and nibbling gently on her lower lip, then as her lips parted his kisses became fierce and his hands more urgent and she threaded her fingers through his hair, holding him closer, responding with heat and fire which brought him to full, triumphant arousal. At last, when they were both trembling with the desperation to mate, he reared up over her, his face stern with the desire he was trying to hold in check.

'I can't keep my promise,' he panted, and she gave him a smile the original Adam would have recognised.

'Break it, then,' she whispered, and gave a gasp of pure, unadulterated pleasure as he obeyed.

This time there was no gradual acceleration of their loving. Isobel was as wild as Luke from the start, and all too soon found herself throbbing in the throes of a climax which overtook her several seconds before his body collapsed on hers in his own convulsive release. She lay stunned as her heart began to slow down, but at last, when oxygen became a necessity, she pushed at Luke's shoulders and in one movement he lifted himself from her and rolled so that she lay on top of him instead.

'Better?' he asked, smiling at her, lazy-eyed, as he held her in place, skin to skin.

'I liked having you lie on me, but in the end I couldn't breathe.' She bent her head to kiss him. 'Will you be able to hear when the car comes back?'

'Spiro will gun the engine down to the house, making as much noise as possible,' he assured her, grinning.

'You told him to do that?'

'No. Spiro is a man, and Greek. I had no need to tell him.'

Isobel sniffed. 'I suppose he's used to it.'

His eyebrow arched. 'And what, *kyria* Isobel, do you mean by that?'

She felt suddenly very vulnerable, sprawled naked, and by the sudden tightening of his arms, with no hope of getting free. Her eyes fell, unable to meet the look of hot possession in his.

'I have never brought a woman to the Villa Medusa before,' he said with emphasis. 'This is my private retreat. Or it was—'

'Until I trespassed,' she finished for him. 'Let me up, please.'

'No,' he said flatly. 'Not until you atone for doubting me.'

She eyed him stormily and tried to wriggle free, but he held her fast and too late she realised that her attempts to escape had such an inflammatory effect on him she was suddenly flat on her back again and Luke was holding her prisoner in an entirely different way.

'All—right, I—believe you,' she said with difficulty.

'Too late. You must pay the penalty,' he said roughly.

And, sooner than she would have believed possible, Luke was making love to her again, with an added edge that sent delicious thrills through her body as he claimed it with mastery which sent them both rocketing to another climax even more powerful than the first.

'So do you believe me now?' he panted as he pulled away, holding her so close against him Isobel could feel his heartbeat as his taut body began to relax.

'Yes. I do. But you have other women in Athens—'

'In the past, yes. But there is no one in my life now, I swear. I was brought up to tell the truth, Isobel.' He turned her face up to his. 'And so were you, *ne*? So tell me, *agapi mou*, are your feelings warmer to me now?'

'Warmer than what, exactly?'

'You were very hostile towards me at first.'

She sniffed. 'Only because you were so hostile to me, Lukas Andreadis.'

He smoothed the uneven lock of hair back from her forehead. 'When you return, will you tell your friend Joanna about me?'

'Of course. She'll be only too glad that I met someone who could make me forget the Gavin episode. Joanna never liked him. Neither did March, her husband.'

'You like your friend's husband?'

'Very much. Seeing them so happy together almost changes my mind about marriage.'

His eyes narrowed intently. 'But not enough to want it for yourself.'

'Never. As I told you before, marriage doesn't appeal to me in the slightest. I enjoy my independence too much—' She tensed as she heard the Jeep approaching the house. 'Luke, hurry, they're back!'

CHAPTER ELEVEN

THEY were late leaving for the taverna. Isobel had taken a shower as soon as Luke left her, and then collapsed on her bed to sleep for a while, while Luke spent the time in consultation with Andres before standing lost in thought under his own shower.

So Isobel disliked the idea of marriage. Which was good, because so did he. But there was nothing to keep them from being lovers. He smiled as he lay on his bed, which was a lot larger than the one in the guest room. He made a note to bring Isobel here to sleep with him once he had persuaded her to stay for a while. The heat and pleasure of lovemaking was something he'd experienced often enough in his life, but in the past it had soon died away, leaving nothing to replace it other than fond regret when the parting of the ways arrived, as it always did. But Isobel was different. Making love with her surpassed all other experiences in his life to such an extent it seemed to touch his soul. But he also took great pleasure in her company as they talked and ate and swam and simply spent time together. He would make her see that leaving him was not an option yet. But his persuasion must be subtle. He must accustom her to the idea by degrees, paint an irresist-ible picture of what they could have together. But it was best to wait until the agonising moment of their parting when her

only answer could be yes. Miss Isobel James must be convinced beyond all doubt that fate had not only sent her to him, but meant her to stay here with him for the foreseeable future.

The evening at the taverna was lively. Luke and Isobel were welcomed with open arms, with much admiration for Luke's part in the dramatic rescue of the beautiful Miss James. Nikos Nicolaides, in particular, felt a proprietorial pleasure about this, since Lukas had met the lady because she came to spend a holiday in one of his properties.

The evening was a further celebration of life for Isobel, a time to rejoice with people who so obviously thought the world not only of Luke, but had felt the same about his mother.

'They're all very fond of you,' Isobel told him on the way home.

'And I of them. This is why Chyros is such a special place to me. People here remember how hard I had to work to achieve my success; therefore no one resents it.' His voice dropped a tone. 'And you, Isobel? Has your experience here turned you against my island?'

'No, of course not. I'll always treasure my memories of Eleni and Spiro, and Alyssa and her family. And you.' She drew in a deep breath. 'I'd planned to do so many things while I was here, take a trip to Serifos and some of the other islands, also paint a few watercolours I could put on sale back home in the gallery.'

'But the only trip you made was against your will, to a barren island with no legends of any kind. So I shall take you wherever you want to go,' he promised as they turned down the tree-lined drive to the villa. 'I spoke to Andres earlier, by the way. The Karras sisters finally confessed in their more lucid moments that they hired both men, who are workers on the Karras family estate up north.'

'Did the women order the kidnapper to kill me once they got the ransom?' asked Isobel as he lifted her out of the jeep.

Luke held her tightly for a moment, kissed her fiercely, then set her on her feet. 'If they did, they chose the wrong man to commit murder for them. Which is why he told me where to find you. Not that it mattered, because I had found you first.'

'Thank God,' said Isobel, and buried her face against his chest. 'I confess that I was bit frightened, Luke.'

'Enough to give you nightmares,' he agreed as they went into the house. 'I think I should guard you from them again tonight, *ne*?'

'Yes, *please*,' she said fervently as Luke bent to pick her up. 'I can walk now.'

He slid an arm round her waist. 'Like this, then.'

Isobel leaned against him happily. 'Like this,' she agreed with a sigh. 'I had such a good time tonight, Luke.'

'So did I, *hriso mou*. Are you tired?'

'Just pleasantly so.'

'Where would you like to go tomorrow?'

'I'd like to explore Chyros properly,' she said eagerly. 'Since I've been here at the villa I've seen only quick glimpses of it. And the day you rescued me I travelled back to the villa rolled up in a rug like Cleopatra.'

Luke closed her bedroom door behind them and took her in his arms. 'You shall do whatever you want tomorrow, Isobel, I promise. But tonight we do what I want. Tell me you want it, too, *kardia mou*.'

'You know I do,' she said honestly, her eyes falling before the blaze in his as he picked her up to put her on the bed.

Later, when Isobel was quiet at last in Luke's arms, he lay with his face buried in her hair for a long time before he raised his head to look into her heavy eyes.

'It was never like this for me with others,' he said in a tone which melted her bones.

She heaved in a long unsteady breath, wanting passionately to believe him. 'Nor for me, either.' She raised an eyebrow. 'Though there have been fewer *others* by far in *my* life, Lukas Andreadis.'

'I can tell,' he said with satisfaction.

'How?'

'Because you are so plainly—and enchantingly—surprised by the joy we find together, *ne*?'

Surprised seemed hardly the word. Luke's caresses had been revelations, not only in themselves, but in her wildly uninhibited response to them. 'I said it was different with you,' she reminded him.

'Because I am a good lover?'

'You want marks for your performance?' she demanded, laughing, and he smiled smugly.

'No. Your response was accolade enough, *agapi mou*.'

Isobel laughed again, and Luke rolled over, hugging her to him.

'Now we sleep. Tomorrow we explore my island.'

And soon after that she would be leaving. Secure in Luke's arms, Isobel firmly shut all thought of the future away and concentrated on the blissful present.

The programme Luke had mapped out was everything that Isobel could have wished for except that it made the time go by far too quickly. He took her on a tour of Chyros the next day, as promised, and drove up beyond the villa, following a road which wound up through olive groves and stands of pines. They passed a monastery, with a white dome glimmering like a pearl in its crown of cypress, and soon afterwards Luke halted on a promontory of rock near the highest point

of the island, with a view of such beauty spread out below Isobel wished she had brushes and paint to capture it.

'You can make a painting from here next time you come,' said Luke, reading her mind.

Her face fell. 'I won't be coming back.'

He shook his head, the sun catching glints of gold in the bronze curls. 'You will return for Alyssa's wedding, *ne*?'

'No, Luke. I can't expect my boss to let me take more time off. And I need the job.'

He gave her a long introspective look, then started the car without further argument. Which left Isobel more forlorn than ever. A touch more coaxing would have been nice.

Over dinner Luke gave Isobel details of the conversation he'd had with Andres while she was reading on the veranda earlier. 'I am sorry it took the entire afternoon, but there was much to catch up on with the airline, also with my freighters. And,' he added dramatically, 'Andres had more news of the Karras sisters. Loss of the ransom money, added to claustrophobia at being locked up separately, tipped them over the edge into insanity. They have been committed to a secure mental institution.' He leaned to grasp Isobel's hand. 'So you can sleep easy now, *agapi mou*.' His eyes narrowed suddenly as he gazed out over the pool. 'Do you want a trip in the *Athena* tomorrow?'

'Why? Is there something you'd rather do?'

'Zeus, yes,' he said with feeling, and smiled into her eyes. 'I think Eleni and Spiro should take the day off tomorrow to visit family.'

Isobel frowned. 'I thought they didn't have a family.'

'No children, but they have numerous relatives all over the island. They must be anxious to bring them up to date on what happened here at the villa. Eleni can leave food for us and Spiro can take the Cherokee.'

She felt her colour rise. 'Won't they want to know why?'

Luke got up and drew her to her feet. 'They will think I want you to myself for the last day before you leave. Which is the simple truth. Do you want that, Isobel?'

'Of course I do.'

'Not,' he said very deliberately, 'that I mean to spend the whole day in bed, you understand. It will be enough just to be alone with you by the pool, and walk in the garden, and simply spend every minute possible together. Though I hope—need— to spend *some* of those minutes making love with you. But,' he added nobly, 'we can still go out in the boat if you prefer.'

Isobel stood on tiptoe and put her arms round his neck. 'I prefer your plan,' she assured him.

And a whole day spent this way, thought Luke as he rubbed his cheek against her hair, was all it would take to convince Isobel that she must stay, to ensure many more such days together.

Isobel's last full day on Chyros with Luke would have been perfect, bar one inescapable element—that she would be leaving the next morning. As he wanted, they spent almost every minute of the day together. As the sound of the Cherokee's engine dwindled into the distance, taking Spiro and Eleni away, Luke smiled at Isobel with deep satisfaction.

'Alone at last!'

'So now we talk,' she said firmly. 'Tell me all about your life, Luke.'

'Not all of it is exciting, Isobel,' he warned, and began with the freighter which had been his starting point, out of which he'd built up a fleet so commercially successful it enabled him to take over the airline Melina Andreadis had considered her own personal property. Now it was his, he informed Isobel, it would soon have a very different reputa-

tion for luxury and dependability instead of the cheap, too frequent flights of her day. 'I have an apartment in Athens, also one in Thessaloniki. You would like it there. Visitors rate it as a very hip, cool city. And from there you can explore the mountains, go to the oracle at Delphi and to Mount Olympus, the home of the gods.'

'I'd love to do that one day,' said Isobel wistfully, getting to her feet.

'You want to go back to bed?' he said, kissing her.

'No way, *kyrie*,' she retorted, laughing, and stripped off her sundress. 'Let's swim.'

They swam and sunbathed, ate the salad lunch Eleni had left for them, then Luke got up, holding out his hand. 'Now we go to bed.'

A long time later, when they were holding each other close in the sweet, languorous aftermath of passion, tears trickled down Isobel's cheeks.

'Why are you crying?' demanded Luke, kissing them away.

'Because I'm happy,' lied Isobel, and concealed a sharp pang of pain with a yawn.

'Sleep, *hriso mou*,' he said in a tone like a caress.

It seemed a wanton waste of the time left to them, but Isobel was so tired she obeyed, and woke later to find him tickling her nose with a lock of her own hair.

'I will leave you to your shower, then we take a walk in the garden while the sun goes down. And after that we drink a glass of wine while we watch the stars come out to play.' He kissed her swiftly. 'Ten minutes, *ne*?'

Isobel was pleased in one way that Luke hadn't wanted to share her shower. It was not the most graceful of procedures for someone balanced on one foot. Though it would have been something to look back on, she thought wistfully. Also

a first for her. With Luke she wanted to experience everything possible between a man and woman in love… Her breath caught. Love, the four letter word. It was pointless to pretend she wasn't madly in love with Luke. But did he feel the same? Their time together had been packed so full of incident there had been an inevitable greenhouse effect on their relationship. Luke left her in no doubt that he wanted her physically. But whether love was part of his equation was hard to tell. Not that it mattered. Tomorrow she was going home and would never see him again.

Luke was waiting outside on the landing when Isobel emerged in a brief, filmy slip dress the colour of her eyes. He gave her a look which brought a blush to her face, and took her hand as they went downstairs together.

'Why didn't you just come in to wait for me, Luke?'

'Because I would have wanted to lay you down on that bed again,' he informed her huskily. 'And you would have objected because you look so perfect in that delightful dress.'

Isobel smiled at him as they reached the veranda. 'I'm glad you like it. I've been saving it for a special occasion.'

'Every night with you is a special occasion,' he said, and took her hand to stroll out into the garden. 'How is the foot, Isobel?'

'It's fine now, really. Which is good, because it has to get me home tomorrow.'

'Let me fly you to the airport in the helicopter,' he urged, but she shook her head.

'No, thanks. I'll go back on the boat, the way I came. The journey will get me back to normal by degrees.' She smiled wryly. 'Life at home is going to seem very humdrum from now on.'

'Who will meet you at the airport?'

'Joanna. I'll send her a text just before I board the plane.'
Isobel breathed in the scent of the flowers as they skirted the
pool to make for the row of Aleppo pines lining the cliff edge.
She gazed down on the sunset-gilded beach. 'It's such a short
time since you found me down there, yet in other ways it
seems as though I've known you forever.'

'I believe we met in another life,' said Luke, and put his
arm round her. 'Come. We shall go back and toast the setting
sun with a glass of wine.'

Later, Isobel had little appetite for the *mezedes* Eleni had
left them; though the appetizers were as delicious as all her
food. 'I'm not so hungry tonight,' she said apologetically.

'Nor I.' He raised her hand to his and kissed it. 'Isobel, I
need to talk to you. And the best place for that is bed.'

'Pillow talk?'

He shook his head. 'Vital, important talk.'

Isobel disliked the sound of this; her misgivings intensi-
fied when Luke opened the bedroom door for her, but
remained outside. 'I will join you in a few moments,' he said,
surprising her. 'Tonight, it is better you undress yourself.'

His tone left Isobel so uneasy that, after undressing quickly,
she put a nightgown over her head. Nudity was inappropriate
for a serious talk. She went back to sit on the bed, and while
she waited for Luke sent a text to Joanna to confirm that she
was returning tomorrow on schedule, and would ring just
before boarding the plane.

Luke arrived as she closed her phone. 'Who were you tele-
phoning?' He was wearing a towelling robe for once, and
added to Isobel's misgivings by taking the chair beside the bed
instead of joining her on it.

'Just a text to Joanna, to confirm the travel arrangements.'
Isobel eyed him narrowly. 'Is something wrong, Luke?'

He scowled. 'You are leaving tomorrow and you ask me if something is wrong?' When she said nothing, he leaned forward, his face urgent. 'It is necessary that I talk to you like this, without touching, so you know that my words are not said in the heat of the moment.'

She stiffened. 'Could you just get on and say these words, Luke. You're worrying me.'

His eyes softened. 'That was not my intention. In fact,' he added heavily, 'I think I have made a mistake. It would have been better to talk after making love.'

'For heaven's sake, Luke,' she said in desperation. 'Tell me what's wrong!'

'Nothing wrong, *agapi mou*. If we had more time together I would have waited longer to lead up to this, but you are leaving tomorrow. What I have to say is very simple. I want so much more of you than your holiday has allowed me,' he said with emphasis, his eyes urgent on hers. 'Listen to my plan, Isobel. I shall buy you a house in Athens, or Thessaloniki, whichever you prefer. You can paint there as much as you like. I will give you anything your heart desires, and spend as much time with you as I can.' He leaned nearer. 'Think of all the happy days—and nights—we could enjoy together, Isobel.'

She thought of them in silence so prolonged he grew restive. 'Are you serious?' she said at last.

Luke's eyebrows shot together. 'The idea does not please you?'

Isobel took in a deep breath. 'Luke, we come from different cultures, so I don't know quite where I stand on this. Are you asking me to be one of your pillow friends?'

'No! There will be no one else in my life when you come to me, Isobel.'

'So my official job description would be mistress?'

He smiled indulgently. 'Not my mistress, Isobel—my lover!'

Same thing. 'And what would happen when you marry?'

'There is no fear of that. Like you, I do not want marriage. But I want *you* so much it is agony to part with you, *hriso mou*.' His eyes locked with hers. 'Say yes, Isobel. Say you will come to me.'

She sighed and shook her head. 'I'm sorry. The answer's no.'

Luke leapt to his feet, his eyes incredulous, as though he couldn't believe she'd refused. Then they hardened as his face set into the familiar blank mask. 'I have made a most humiliating mistake. I believed you had come to care for me, and shared my pain at the thought of parting. Neither of us desires marriage; therefore my plan seemed the perfect solution. I was obviously wrong.' His mirthless smile sent shivers down her spine. 'In time I shall be able to laugh at myself for such hubris. But not yet. Goodnight, Isobel.'

She stared in anguish as the door closed behind him, then burrowed into the pillows feeling as though her world was breaking in pieces around her. At last she went into the bathroom to wash her tear-stained face. She had expected to spend their last night in bed together but, as that wasn't going to happen, she might as well pack. She took her bags from the wardrobe and began folding clothes and rolling up underwear, putting shoes in what polythene bags she had left, and reminded herself that her drawing materials were downstairs and would have to be packed in the morning.

She worked like an automaton, her brain still reeling from the shock of Luke's proposition. She might be madly in love with him, but Luke's offer—or demand, more like it—would mean uprooting herself from her life, and parting from her friends and everything familiar. And for what? Marriage was

a tricky enough relationship, but the insecurity of living as Luke's mistress, lover, or whatever, was out of the question. He obviously intended her to lack for nothing, which probably meant an allowance of some kind. And, with money involved, the whole idea left a nasty taste in her mouth. Besides, what would happen when the arrangement came to an end? She might love Luke with a depth and passion which almost frightened her, but she valued her independence—and her self-respect—too highly to agree to such a dubious arrangement. Even with Lukas Andreadis.

Not that there was any point in beating herself up about it because none of that was going to happen. Right now, she just had to go home, back to her old life, and learn to live without Lukas Andreadis as part of it. But to part from him this way, like enemies instead of lovers, was cutting her to the heart. If they were never going to see each other again she desperately wanted—needed—one last memory to look back on when she was home, alone and lonely.

Before she could change her mind, Isobel limped as fast as she could out onto the landing to knock on Luke's door. When there was no answer she turned away blindly but ran into a hard, familiar body and Luke snatched her up in his arms, kissing her tears away as he carried her back to her room.

'What did you want, Isobel?' he demanded as he laid her on the bed.

No point in lying. 'I couldn't bear to leave without making up.'

'Nor could I.' He shrugged off his robe, took her nightgown over her head and covered her body with his, devouring her with hot, desperate kisses she responded to with such impassioned fervour they surged together at once, their emotions running so high after their quarrel they achieved cul-

mination so swiftly Isobel shook in Luke's arms with the force of it.

Luke looked down into her swollen eyes. 'Does this mean you have changed your mind?' he panted.

'No.' She sucked in a deep breath. 'Though you could be forgiven for thinking I had by the way I—I—'

'Participated so joyously in our loving?'

She gave a choked little laugh. 'Shamelessly, you mean.'

'There is no shame in a man and a woman giving each other such rapture, *agapi mou*,' he assured her and held her close, rubbing his cheek against hers. 'Think of the joy we can give each other in future, Isobel. You may run away tomorrow, but I shall not give up. We were created to be together. When you were stolen from me I was in hell thinking I had lost you.' He kissed her fiercely. 'Fate sent you to me, and what I find I keep. It is useless to fight fate, *hriso mou*. You are mine.'

CHAPTER TWELVE

As THE first light of dawn appeared Luke propped himself on one elbow to look down into Isobel's face.

'I will give you six weeks,' he said imperiously. 'At the end of that time you will come back to me, or I will fetch you.'

'You're very sure of yourself, Lukas Andreadis.'

'It is the way I succeed in life.' His eyes glittered. 'I want you, Isobel. You are clear on this?'

She smiled wryly. 'Yes. But what happens if I say no again at the end of six weeks?'

'You will not,' he said simply, and drew her down into his arms. 'I will not allow it.'

It was a day of painful partings, starting with Eleni and Spiro, and even Milos, who came to say goodbye. Before boarding the boat there was a brief stop at the clinic for Isobel to say her goodbyes to Dr Riga, then more at the taverna, to Alyssa and her parents. By the time Luke carried her bags onto the boat, Isobel was desperate for him to leave her alone with her misery. But, to her surprise, Luke sat beside her, his arm very firmly around her waist.

'I shall come to the airport with you,' he said in a tone that told Isobel not to argue.

'But how will you get back?'

'I shall stay in Athens.' He tightened his arm as the boat moved out to sea. 'I will need much work to fill my days once I am without you, *kardia mou*.' He smiled crookedly. 'Did you really think I'd let you go to the airport alone? You need someone to carry your bags, *ne*?'

Isobel leaned against him, her heart already wanting her to change her mind and tell him she would come back and do, and be, anything he wanted. But in the end her head took over and kept her emotions firmly under wraps, even through the torment of parting with Luke at the airport.

The flight home gave Isobel much-needed time to think. Although Luke had given her six weeks to get used to the idea, she already knew that she could never agree to the role of part-time playmate. If he'd simply asked her to live with him, share his life in his Athens flat, or in Thessaloniki, or anywhere else, she would have said yes without hesitation. But languishing alone in some house in either city, waiting for him to spare time for her, was out of the question, no matter how much she loved him. Which she did, passionately. The wrench of parting from Luke had been so painful she felt as though she'd left her heart behind with him.

Isobel's spirits rose at the airport as she saw Joanna waiting for her. Glowing and vital, chestnut hair gleaming, her friend was waving madly as Isobel steered a luggage trolley towards her. After a brief explanation of the walking stick, Isobel stayed put as ordered while Jo fetched the car.

'Now then, Isobel James,' said Jo, once they were on the motorway heading for home. 'The one time you cut loose on your own on holiday you come back injured. Give me every last detail, please.'

But Isobel shook her head. 'I'd rather you weren't driving when I do. Are you in a hurry to get back to Arnborough?'

'No.' Jo shot her a worried look. 'March knew we'd want to catch up. I'm yours for the evening.'

'Great. Let's buy some food on the way home and talk over supper.'

The gallery was closed for the day by the time they arrived. Isobel unlocked her private side door, gritting her teeth as she confronted two flights of steep stairs. She hooked the walking stick through the straps of her backpack and picked up her tote, but Jo insisted on making two trips to carry the shopping and the rest of the luggage up to the flat. She even took over the unpacking while Isobel first sent a text message to Luke to announce her arrival, and then sat down at the kitchen table to make sandwiches. When they were ready Jo planted herself in the chair opposite and fixed Isobel with a steely eye.

'Right. Talk,' she ordered.

Isobel told her tale as dispassionately as possible. Other than the occasional exclamation, Joanna heard her out in silence, then sat staring at her friend, stupefied.

'What a *story*,' she said faintly and reached out a hand to touch the ragged lock of hair beside her friend's ear. 'Thank God I didn't know what was happening.' She looked Isobel in the eye. 'And this man—'

'Lukas Andreadis.'

'Yes, him. He wants you to be his *mistress*?'

'Don't sound so shocked!'

'Well, it's a hell of a cheek,' said Jo impatiently. 'I thought only married men had mistresses. So what was your reaction?'

Isobel smiled ruefully. 'When he first brought it up I turned him down flat, and he stormed off in a temper. Luke is used

to women throwing themselves at him, so to have one say no to him was quite a shock.'

'That type, is he! So is your answer still no now you've had time to get used to the idea?'

'He's given me six weeks. After which I am to overcome my qualms about leaving everything familiar and dear to me, and let him install me in some love-nest in Athens or Thessaloniki, my choice. There I am to paint my pictures and wait around until he has time to visit me.'

Joanna's jaw dropped. 'Which century is he living in? So what happens if you say no again?'

Isobel heaved a sigh. 'He has this Greek thing about fate. Because he found me stranded on his beach he believes fate handed me to him on a platter, so to speak. He's so certain of this he swears he'll never give up on me.'

'Wild!' said Jo, impressed. 'So, if women throw themselves at him, I take it the man's no turn-off in the looks department?'

Isobel smiled as she took the portrait of Luke from her luggage. 'There he is. Like no other man I've ever met. And I'm so much in love with him it's going to be hell to say no when he wants his answer.'

The weeks that followed Isobel's return home were taxing in multiple ways, over and above the almost physical pain of missing Luke. Working in the busy gallery was tiring enough normally, even with the help of the art student who came in part-time, but with a weak ankle still in the mix she was exhausted by the end of her working day. And before her holiday she had thought nothing of living in a flat over a gallery full of valuable paintings. But now, even though the high-end security system was allegedly burglar-proof, she was nervous at night and found it hard to sleep. Even when she did she

sometimes woke in fright from a new nightmare, fighting to remove an imaginary cloth from her face. With no Luke in the flesh to keep her safe in the night, his phone calls were the high points of her life. And, as he never ceased to remind her, the six weeks he had given her would soon be up.

Luke passed on messages from Alyssa, who ordered him to give Isobel all the news of the island and to do his utmost to persuade her to come back there for her wedding. Strange, thought Isobel, how she could be homesick for a place where she'd spent such a short time. She gave Luke messages to pass back to Alyssa and felt a pang when she heard that he was returning to Chyros for Eleni's birthday, which, he said with significance, would also mark the end of the six weeks.

Isobel posted off a cashmere shawl to Eleni as a birthday gift. Then, after spending hours over composing a painful letter to Luke, she sent it off, got rid of her mobile phone and bought a new one.

'Why on earth have you done that?' demanded Joanna.

'My time's up, but I just couldn't face telling Luke my answer's no, so I wrote to him instead. I left the address off the letter and then ditched the phone so he can't contact me,' she said wearily.

'You've made up your mind, then?'

'Yes. It was never on, really.' Isobel gave a mirthless little chuckle. 'Deep down, it seems, I'm the product of my grandparents' upbringing.'

Having made her decision, Isobel hid Luke's portrait away, but she hung the watercolour of his beach in the gallery with a 'sold' sticker on it. The painting aroused such interest it resulted in new commissions Isobel welcomed with open arms, both from an extra income point of view and as a means to fill time, which hung heavy since her return from holiday.

Jo came into town once a week to take her out to a meal, a ritual she'd kept up since her marriage. One evening her husband March came with her, and on another occasion Isobel managed to catch Josh and Leo Carey with rare matching time off from the hospital, which resulted in a hilarious evening, as always when the four of them were together. Jo also passed on an invitation from her parents to spend an entire day at their home one Sunday. 'March is coming, too, and you can play with the children as much as you like,' she said firmly.

Isobel accepted only too happily, glad of the chance to see young Kitty and Tom, Jo's irresistible little siblings. The working week she could manage. But when the gallery was shut on Sundays she had too much time for the burning question of whether she had made the biggest mistake of her life in cutting herself off from Luke.

Two months after her return from Greece, Isobel was about to lock up for the day when a car drew up right outside the gallery. She went out to say that it was a no parking zone, then froze, the colour draining from her face as the driver got out and stood looking at her over the top of the car.

Oh, God. Isobel's mouth dried and her heart began to pound as the familiar black eyes locked with hers. Her gut reaction was to run inside and lock the door. Instead, she stood her ground and smiled brightly. 'Why, hello. This is a surprise.'

'And not a pleasant one, I think,' said Luke, locking the car. He wore beautiful suede boots, heavy sweater and jeans, all very different from his usual garb on Chyros. But his face was the handsome mask she remembered only too well. Whatever Luke was thinking, he was giving nothing away as he crossed the kerb to join her. 'But surely you expected this after the letter you wrote, Isobel?'

'No, I didn't,' she said truthfully. How on earth had he found her?

'Have you finished for the day?'

'Yes. I was just about to lock up. Would you like to come in?'

Luke followed her inside, watching as she closed the door. Conscious of the black eyes following her every move, Isobel punched in the numbers on the security pad beside it and shot bolts home at the top of the door and again at the base.

'Perhaps you'd care to look round the paintings while I make coffee,' she said brightly. 'Or would you prefer a drink? I have some wine—'

He shook his head. 'I would like to look at the paintings. Is any of your work here, Isobel?'

'Yes. I have a little section all to myself.' When she made no move to direct him, Luke strolled away on a tour of the artwork she prided herself she displayed to the best advantage with subtle lighting against the contrast of the gallery's dark red walls.

Luke paused when he reached the far end of the room and looked in silence at a collection of Isobel's watercolours. 'You have sold your painting of my beach.'

'No. I put a sold sticker on it to show it wasn't for sale.'

'You intend to keep it?'

'Yes.'

'Why?'

She looked at him steadily. 'As a souvenir of my holiday. I once told you—though you didn't believe me at the time— that where others take holiday snaps, I sketch or paint.'

Luke's mask slipped a fraction as he walked back to her. 'Spiro showed me the drawing you made of my face. It flatters me.'

She shrugged. 'I thought it was pretty accurate, myself.

Though I rarely do portraits. Not my field.' Lord, this was painful. Why didn't he yell at her, or at least tell her why he'd come?

'Your hair is shorter,' he remarked. 'I prefer it long.'

Her eyes flashed. 'So do I. Losing a chunk of it was hardly my fault.'

'No, it was mine,' he agreed grimly and moved closer, his eyes softening. 'You look tired, Isobel.'

'I've been busy today.'

'You have no help here?'

'I have an assistant, but he left a short while ago.' Tired of small talk, Isobel cut to the chase. 'I didn't put an address on my letter, so how did you find me?'

Luke's smile set her teeth on edge. 'For a while I was so furious I had no wish to find you. But, after seeing your painting of my pool, my faithful Andres, who found working with me very difficult after I received your letter, suggested that you might sell your work through a website. The rest was easy. Had you forgotten the power of the Internet, Isobel?'

'No. I just took it for granted that once you received my letter you'd be so angry you'd just put me out of your life and forget me.'

'It was my first reaction,' he admitted. 'Out of all the emotions that besieged me, the most violent was anger because you were a coward, Isobel. You rejected me by letter. But my fury soon gave way to a desire to hear you say no to me, face to face. And to give me your real explanation.' He moved closer. 'So here I am.'

Isobel looked at him in silence for a moment, then crossed to the control panel. 'I leave the security lights on for the paintings in the windows, but at this hour I switch off the rest.' She turned with a polite smile. 'Perhaps you'd like to come

up to my flat. I'm desperate for a cup of tea.' Inane, but the truth. Her mouth was so dry it was hard to swallow.

'*Efcharisto*, Isobel. Then later I will take you out to dine.'

She made no response to that and opened the private door leading to her stairs. 'Two flights up, I'm afraid.'

'Is your ankle better? These stairs must have been difficult for a while when you first returned,' he commented, following her up.

A lot of things had been difficult. Most of them still were. 'My ankle's fine now,' she said politely. When she reached the small landing at the head of the stairs she opened the door of her sitting room and waved him inside. 'Do sit down while I make tea.'

Left alone to inspect them, Luke eyed his surroundings with interest. The artist in Isobel had a flair for the dramatic. A peacock-blue throw draped a jade velvet couch, and ruby and gold silk cushions glowed on a leather armchair. At strategic points around the room small tables of varying design held piles of books and lamps with vivid shades.

A jewel box of a room, thought Luke, then turned as the jewel who lived in it backed into the room with a tray. 'Let me,' he said, and took the tray from her. 'Where shall I put it?'

Isobel cleared a space on a table alongside the sofa and Luke set the tray down with care, feeling very male and clumsy in the feminine room. 'Try the chair,' she invited. 'I made coffee for you, by the way.'

'*Efcharisto*.' He took the cup from her and put it safe on a table alongside the couch, afraid that if he moved too suddenly he would knock something over. 'So. Why would you not come to me, Isobel?' he said baldly.

She sipped some tea before she answered. 'I did consider it—I thought about it long and hard. Then something happened which made it impossible. So I wrote the letter.'

Luke snatched up his coffee cup, ignoring the sting as the liquid scalded his mouth. 'You met another man?'

'No.' Isobel took in a deep breath, wishing her heart would stop banging around in her chest. 'I found out I'm pregnant—I'm having a baby, Luke.'

He looked as though she'd punched him in the stomach. 'Is it mine?' He sat very still, every muscle in his body tense as he watched the colour leach from her face.

'No,' she said after a taut pause.

'Whose, then?' he demanded, his pallor outdoing hers.

'Mine.'

His jaw clenched. 'You told me you took care of birth control yourself.'

Isobel stabbed him with a glacial blue glare. 'I did. But I was kidnapped, remember. The man didn't give me time to pack my pills.' Suddenly she sprang up to run to the bathroom and stayed there until she was sure her stomach meant to behave. She would have given much to remain locked in the bathroom for the foreseeable future, but eventually she went out in answer to Luke's urgent knock on the door.

He barred her way as she made to brush past him. 'You are sure of this?'

'Yes. But don't worry; I'm not asking *you* for anything.' Her eyes blazed like sapphires into his. 'Your knee-jerk reaction to my glad news only confirms how right I was to finish things between us.'

Luke seized her by the wrists. 'I apologise, Isobel. I said such a bad thing because the thought of you with another man's child was a stab to my heart.'

'How melodramatic,' she said dully, and detached her hands. 'Perhaps you'd be good enough to leave now, and go back to wherever you're staying. I'm very tired.'

'But we have much to discuss,' he said hotly. 'How do you expect me to sleep after such news?'

She shrugged indifferently. 'Frankly, Lukas Andreadis, I don't care a toss whether you sleep or not. Just *go*.'

'Of course,' he said stiffly. 'I will burden you with my presence no longer. But,' he added in a tone which made her toes curl, 'when I return, Isobel, we shall talk.'

After the menace in Luke's parting shot Isobel decided to postpone supper for a while. 'I'll eat something later,' she promised, patting her stomach. 'Sorry about your dad. I'm afraid it's just you and me, babe.' But even if she managed some supper she had little hope of getting any sleep later with the prospect of Luke's return visit hanging over her. Hopefully, he would come at a reasonable enough hour the next day to allow recovery from her daily date with morning sickness.

The bell on Isobel's door rang later while she was drying her hair after her bath. She frowned. She wasn't expecting Jo, or one of the Careys. And her boss, the owner of the gallery, was sunning himself in Mauritius. When the bell rang again she picked up the receiver on her intercom.

'Let me in, Isobel,' said Luke's unmistakable tones.

'I didn't expect you back tonight,' she said coldly.

'Nevertheless, I am here. And attracting attention. Open the door,' he ordered.

Isobel pressed the release button, cursing because she had no time to dress. She ran into the bedroom for her old blue velour robe, tied the sash tightly, raked her fingers through her damp curls, then took a deep breath and opened her sitting room door to Luke's knock.

He was wearing different clothes, he was newly shaved and his hair, like hers, was damp.

'Have you eaten?' he demanded, eyeing the robe.

'No. We weren't hungry.'

A pulse throbbed at the corner of his mouth at the 'we'. 'You must eat,' he said disapprovingly. 'I will take you to my hotel for dinner.'

She shook her head. 'I'd rather not be seen with you in public.'

Colour flared along his cheekbones. 'Why? Am I not dressed suitably?'

'This is a small town. People know me here. Questions would be asked.'

'That you would not care to answer,' he flung at her.

'Why are you so angry? I'm the one expecting the baby!'

Luke controlled himself with visible effort. 'Come,' he said, taking her by the hand. 'Let us sit down and talk like reasonable people.'

'By all means.' Isobel let him lead her to the sofa. She curled up in a corner and waved Luke to the chair.

He looked so overpoweringly male in her feminine room Isobel's heart started thumping again as his eyes locked with hers.

'If,' he began, 'I had not come here to see you, would you have told me about the child? Ever?'

'I don't know,' she said honestly. 'I intended to wait until after she arrived and see how I felt.'

His eyebrows rose. 'You know it is a girl?'

'Not officially. I just feel it in my bones.'

There was silence for a while. 'It is a bad thing for a child to grow up without a father,' he said at last. 'I have experience of this.'

As Isobel well knew. She sat still, waiting for him to go on.

'We must marry,' he said at last.

Oh, must we? 'No,' she said flatly.

Luke sprang up to loom over her. 'You cannot say no this time, Isobel. We have another life to consider, not just yours, or mine.'

She glared up at him. 'Are you seriously expecting me to marry you and acknowledge you as the father of a child you don't believe is yours, Lukas Andreadis?'

'I know the child is mine,' he said impatiently. 'Are you going to make me pay for the rest of our lives, and our child's life, because I am human, and in my shock I said words I regretted the moment they were uttered?'

'They hurt, Luke.' Isobel hugged her arms across her chest. 'Not least because, before I knew about the baby, I was going to put a different proposition to you when the six weeks were up.'

'What was it?' he said quickly.

'I didn't fancy being some sort of playmate you visited when you had time to spare—'

'It would not have been like that!'

'That's how it seemed to me. Anyway, I was going to suggest that we just lived together, as people do. In your apartment in Athens, or your house in Thessaloniki, or wherever. In basic terms, I wanted to share all your life, not just small doses of it, Luke.'

He gazed down at her in disbelief. 'Is this true?'

'Yes.'

He drew in a deep, unsteady breath. 'If you had, I would have agreed with much enthusiasm after several weeks apart from you. So what changed your mind?'

Isobel patted her stomach. 'I found out about her. I couldn't come asking to live with you once I found I was pregnant.'

'Why not?'

'You would have thought that was the only reason for my

suggestion. Besides, I was afraid you might question my baby's parentage. And I was right,' she added with rancour.

'I refuse to believe that you would be cruel enough to keep our child from me.'

Isobel's heart did a little skip at the 'our'. 'I suppose not,' she said quietly.

Luke raised her hand to his lips and kissed the palm. 'Our child was conceived in love, *ne*? So he—'

'She!'

He laughed unsteadily. 'So it is only right that our child should grow up secure in the love of parents who are husband and wife.'

'That's emotional blackmail,' she protested thickly.

'Call it what you wish. But you must agree, Isobel. We have both suffered from the lack of family in our lives. If you marry me, you will never suffer such lack again.' He gave her the rare smile that always stopped her heart. 'You cannot fight fate, *kardia mou*.'

Luke drew her to her feet with infinite care, his eyes intent on hers, and with a deep, shuddering sigh Isobel surrendered to his arms as his mouth met hers in a kiss that went on and on until neither could breathe. Luke picked her up and sat down with her in his lap, cradling her close.

'Tell me you love me, Isobel,' he commanded thickly.

She gave an unsteady little chuckle. 'There you go, ordering me about as usual. Not that it matters because I do love you, Lukas Andreadis.'

His eyes blazed. 'Then why did you put me through hell? When I read your letter I was like a madman. You did not give your address, and you told me you had destroyed your phone. Andres saved my sanity, Isobel, when he suggested a way to trace you.'

Her lashes were suddenly wet with tears. 'I wasn't doing too well in the sanity department myself. Hormones. I really thought it was the right thing to do at the time.'

Luke smoothed a hand over her hair. 'But now the right thing is very obvious to both of us, *ne*? Even though you never wished for marriage, I swear I will make ours happy for you!'

'But you never fancied marriage either!'

He bent his head to kiss her. 'Then I met you, *agapi mou*, and changed my mind.'

'But you asked me to be your mistress—'

'Lover, not mistress,' he said with tender violence. 'I was afraid you would never agree to marriage, Isobel. I was trying to keep you with me in the way I thought you would like best.'

Her stomach gave a sudden audible rumble and they both laughed.

'Was that my baby saying hello to Papa?' said Luke in a tone which brought a lump to Isobel's throat.

She gave him a wobbly little smile. 'I think she was telling me to say yes this time!'

Normally, Isobel enjoyed the short helicopter flight to Chyros, but this time she sent up a prayer of thanks as Luke set the machine down behind the Villa Medusa.

'Are you all right?' he said tightly as he helped Isobel out.

'Fine,' she lied, managing a smile as Eleni and Spiro came hurrying to meet them.

There was a flurry of greetings, then Eleni frowned as Isobel caught her breath on the way into the house. 'It has started?'

'I think so,' said Isobel through her teeth.

'What did you say?' demanded Luke, catching up with them.

'Your daughter has decided it's her birthday.'

Luke swore long and volubly, his face haggard as he helped

her up the stairs to the master bedroom they shared. 'I should not have given in to you. We should have stayed in reach of the hospital in Athens.'

'Not a chance,' she panted. 'I wanted our child born here on Chyros, like her father.'

And twelve hours later, by which time Isobel was exhausted and Luke demented, their child came into the world protesting loudly. Dr Riga shook Luke's hand in congratulation as Nurse Pappas passed the tightly wrapped bundle to Eleni, who proudly handed it over to Isobel.

'You took your time,' she told her baby drowsily when she was alone with a very pale, haggard husband. She smiled as Luke knelt on the bed to kiss her. 'Isn't she beautiful, darling?'

'Almost as beautiful as you, *hriso mou*,' he said huskily, and smiled as he touched a finger to the baby's cheek. 'But our child is a boy, Isobel. We have a son, not a daughter.'

She stared at him blankly. 'Are you sure?'

Luke nodded, laughing. 'He is most definitely male.'

'Just like his papa.' She chuckled weakly. She cuddled the little bundle to her breast, smiling down into the crumpled sleeping face. 'Oh, well, son, we'll just have to try for a sister next time.'

'*No!*' Luke shook his head vehemently. 'No next time. Ever.' He raised her hand to his lips and kissed it passionately. 'I could not bear it.'

'You don't have to bear it. I do that part.'

'I am not joking!' he said sternly and bent to kiss her. 'I must go. Nurse Pappas says there are things to be done for both of you. Is there something you need first, *glykia mou*?'

'A huge pot of tea and my phone, please,' said Isobel promptly.

'You may have the tea, but I shall ring Joanna and Alyssa

myself, also Andres, who can spread the word in Athens.' He smiled proudly. 'It is the father's privilege, *ne*?'

Her sleepy blue eyes fastened on his. 'Are you proud of your son, Lukas Andreadis?'

'I do not have the vocabulary to say exactly how much, though I would have been just as proud of a daughter,' he assured her and stroked her hair. 'But I am most proud of my wife. You did not complain once.'

She laughed unsteadily. 'No breath to spare for complaints. Besides, all women go through the same process, Luke.'

'But I am not married to other women. Only to you, Isobel.' He smiled as the baby stirred. 'What name shall we give our son?'

She stared at him blankly. 'I was so settled on Olympia for a girl, I never thought about boy names.'

'What was your father's name?'

'Paul. Is there a Greek version?'

'Pavlos. But Paul is used also.' Luke nodded in approval. 'I like that. It sounds good.'

'Now I have given you a son, Lukas Andreadis, I would like something in return,' she said, surprising him.

'Anything your heart desires,' he said huskily and stroked her damp hair. 'What do you want, *hriso mou*?'

'When we've both recovered from this, I want to give a party here to celebrate Paul's birth—and to send your grandfather an invitation.'

Luke eyed her in shock. 'You ask me this at a time when you know I can't refuse, *ne*?'

'That's right.' Isobel smiled at him lovingly. 'You said anything my heart desires, and I desire this very much, darling.'

He sighed heavily. 'Then of course I shall agree. After all, it is not so great a thing. He may not come.' He bent to kiss

her gently. 'And now I must go. While Nurse Pappas and Eleni are making you comfortable I shall offer Dr Riga a brandy in libation to the safe arrival of Paul Andreadis.' Luke turned at the door to smile at her, looking so pleased with himself Isobel blew him a loving kiss. 'But I shall make a secret toast of my own. To fate, who gave me the gift of the most beautiful wife and son in the world.'

THE GREEK
MILLIONAIRE'S
MISTRESS

CATHERINE SPENCER

Some people know practically from birth that they're going to be writers. **Catherine Spencer** wasn't one of them. Her first idea was to be a nun, which was clearly never going to work! A series of other choices followed. She considered becoming a vet (but she lacked the emotional stamina to deal with sick and injured animals), a hairdresser (until she overheated a curling iron and singed the hair off the top of her best friend's head the day before her first date) or a nurse (but that meant emptying bedpans!). As a last resort, she became a high-school English teacher and loved it.

Eventually she married, had four children and, always, always, a dog or two or three. How can a house become a home without a dog? In time, the children grew up and moved out on their own and she returned to teaching, but a middle-aged restlessness overtook her and she looked for a change of career.

What's an English teacher's area of expertise? Well, novels, among other things, and moody, brooding, unforgettable heroes: Heathcliff, Edward Fairfax Rochester, Romeo and Rhett Butler. Then there's that picky business of knowing how to punctuate and spell and all those rules of grammar. They all pointed her in the same direction: breaking the rules every chance she got and creating her own moody, brooding unforgettable heroes. And that's where she happily resides now, in Mills & Boon® novels, of course.

CHAPTER ONE

FROM his position at one side of the orchestra rostrum, Mikos swung his gaze over the crowded ballroom and brought it to rest on the woman edging closer to the table where Angelo held court. Who was she? And how come he hadn't spotted her before? The party had been in full swing for almost three hours, yet only now, with midnight approaching, had she come to his attention.

She seemed to be alone and, like him, giving the impression she preferred to remain an observer, rather than a participant, of the festivities. The difference was, he was very good at what he did, and only a handful of those present knew that he was more than just Angelo's executive vice president and most favored confidant.

She, on the other hand, was trying too hard to be inconspicuous. If you wanted to disappear into the background, *koritsi mou*, he thought, taking in the daring cut of a dress the same shade of misty mauve as the Aegean at dawn, you should have worn something less eye-catching.

Surveying the room one last time, he exchanged a nod with the security guards posted at the doors, then stepped down from the dais and casually made his way to where she stood half-concealed by the ornate drapery in a window alcove. Dark haired and dark eyed, she could have passed for Greek, but he'd

been around the international social set long enough to recognize a European when he saw one, and this woman didn't fit the mold. American, he decided, and addressed her mostly in English. *"Kalispera.* I don't believe we've met."

If she was startled at being accosted by a stranger, she didn't let it show. "I believe you're right," she said, her gaze locking fearlessly with his. "But then, I've met very few people here tonight."

He couldn't quite place her accent, and knew for a fact that he'd never seen her before. Hers was not a face a man would soon forget. "Then allow me to remedy the situation. I'm Mikolas Christopoulos." *And it's my job to find out everything there is to know about you.*

"Very nice to meet you, Mr. Christopoulos," she said composedly. "I'm Gina Hudson."

"And you're not American."

"No," she replied, with a laugh more melodic than anything the orchestra could hope to produce. "I'm Canadian. Is that okay with you?"

He ran a mental check of the guest list, pretty sure no Canadians were on it. "Of course it's okay. Who did you come with?"

"No one. I'm alone, and here on assignment."

A working woman? Possibly. But one thing he knew for certain: she was not on the Tyros payroll. Apart from anything else, Angelo didn't believe in hiring women, except as domestics, although he was happy enough, even at eighty, to occupy them in other ways. If this one happened to take his fancy...

Mikos shuddered inwardly at the thought. "To do what?" he inquired, steering her out of Angelo's line of vision.

"Write an article for a magazine published in Vancouver which, in case you're not aware, lies on the West Coast of—"

"I'm familiar with Vancouver," he said, stopping her dead in her attempt to sidetrack him. "I work for Hesperus

International which, as I'm sure you know, is owned by the man being honored here tonight. Two of our cruise ships sail to Alaska from Vancouver during the summer season. It's a beautiful city."

"Yes." She smiled. "Spectacular, in fact."

As are you, he thought. If she'd appeared lovely from a distance, up close she was exquisite. A stunningly beautiful brunette with an hourglass figure, and skin the color of honey. And that smile!

He couldn't remember the last time a woman's smile had hit him with such a shock of sexual awareness. Or if he'd ever felt such a compelling urge to run his hand over her skin to discover if its texture matched the satin silk of her dress. Forcing his attention back where it belonged, he remarked, "I'm surprised the residents of Vancouver even know of this event, let alone care about it. How did it come to your notice?"

"We might strike you as people living at the back end of beyond, Mr. Christopoulos," she said evenly, "but we're actually quite in touch with the rest of the planet. Angelo Tyros is a world-wide celebrity, and his birthday party has aroused quite a bit of international attention. Considering Vancouver's large Greek community, plus the fact, as you already pointed out, that his cruise ships sail out of our harbor, it shouldn't surprise you that we find him newsworthy."

A beaded bag, dangling from her shoulder by a long silver chain and just large enough to hold a notepad or mini tape recorder, lent some credence to her story. "Well, it's true that he can make headlines just by blinking," Mikos allowed. "But for you to travel so far, for so little…"

"I quite agree, which is why, once I'm finished here, I plan to combine business with pleasure and spend a week or two discovering the Greek islands."

She sounded so convincing, he almost believed her. But he didn't get paid to be "almost" anything; he had to be one hundred percent sure. Angelo expected no less, and there'd been enough attempts on the old man's life, as it was. No way was Mikos going to risk exposing him to another, even if the threat this time did come swathed in silk and sex appeal. *That* kind was the most dangerous of all.

Ignoring the blinding dazzle of camera flashbulbs intent on recording every moment of the evening, Mikos indicated the mob of couples gyrating under the dim lights to the orchestra's insistent beat, and adopted his most persuasive tone. "But this is a party meant to be enjoyed by everyone, including those, like the two of us, not strictly here for pleasure. So I say, let's put work aside for a moment, and dance."

"You're sure your boss won't mind?"

He shot a quick look at the head table where Angelo was ogling the cleavage of the woman draped over his shoulder. "I doubt he'll even notice."

Following his glance, Gina compressed her lips, apparently not impressed by what she saw, and thereby heightening his suspicion of her. "You're right. He won't."

"Then let's not waste any more time."

Just briefly, she hesitated, then, inclining her head, smiled again. "All right. I'd love to."

"You can leave this here. It'll be perfectly safe." He took her little beaded bag and secreted it behind the window drapery. Then, after trading significant glances with Theo Keramidis, a plainclothes security guard stationed a few meters away, he slid his arm around her waist, whisked her onto the dance floor and quickly maneuvered her into the middle of the crowd.

The music pounded, its message one of throbbing, primitive urgency calculated to stir a man's blood. The heat and press of

the bodies surrounding them enforced an intimacy she'd probably have found offensive under any other circumstances. As it was, there was no avoiding physical contact—a fleeting touch here, a dangerously erotic brush there. Not that he minded. With business taken care of, he was more than ready to enjoy the moment for however long it might last, and honest enough to admit that, if he had any say in the matter, it would not end anytime soon.

Plainly put, the second their eyes had met, a very elemental, male-female recognition had arced between him and her. He'd had his share of women. Was well acquainted with the mild exhilaration of a brief affair. But his visceral response to this particular woman was different and spoke of a deeper connection that went beyond the ordinary. Gina Hudson was different, too. So different that, in acknowledging her allure, he knew he ran the risk of compromising his professional integrity.

Since that was something he never permitted himself, no matter how tempting the distraction, the smart thing would be to pass her off to a more impartial member of his team, and let them keep her occupied. Yet when the orchestra swung into a slower, more sultry tempo, he pulled her into his arms and held her close.

She was so petite that his splayed fingers spanned an area from the slight swell of her hip, and past the indent of her waist to the upper edge of her gown. Spread them a centimeter farther apart, and his thumb could test the soft skin between her shoulder blades. Slide his arm more snugly around her, and he'd graze the outer curve of her right breast. The realization shot a surge of heat to his groin and cast a death blow to the caution that was his usual trademark.

Blithely unaware of her effect on him, she glanced up from beneath long, silky eyelashes. "Are you from Athens, Mr. Christopoulos?"

"No," he said, making a valiant effort to rein in his overactive libido. "I was born in a village in the northwest corner of the country. And I wish you'd call me Mikos."

"Is that Greek for Michael?"

"A regional variation of the same. My full name is Mikolas." To avoid collision with a large elderly couple bent on cutting a wide swath through the crowd, he swung her into a sudden reverse turn. From the unhesitating way she followed his lead, they might have been dancing together for years. But the satin whisper of her gown flirting with his trousered thighs, the soft resilience of her breasts against his starched dress shirt, left him fighting to control his breathing.

The music came to an end. "So what else should I know about, Ms. Gina Hudson?" he inquired, forcing himself to concentrate on his prime objective. "How do you spend your time when you're not covering high society events for your magazine?"

A fleeting uneasiness crossed her face before she was able to camouflage it with another breathless little laugh. "Nothing very exciting, I'm afraid."

But *you* are, he thought. Exciting…and more than a little evasive.

Keeping his hand in the small of her back, he led her to where her bag lay exactly as he'd left it. She slipped the silver chain over her shoulder again and deftly steered the conversation away from herself. "So how long have you lived in Athens?"

"Ever since my teens, when I came here to work." He smiled bleakly at the memory of those grueling years. "In other words, a very long, and different, lifetime ago."

She looked out the window at the traffic streaming along Vassillissis Sofias, and grimaced. "You don't mind the frantic pace? The noise and pollution?"

"Not as long as I can escape it once in a while. Am I right in thinking you're not much for city life yourself?"

"I was, once. Now, I live at my family's home in the Gulf Islands."

She surprised him with that. He judged her to be in her early to mid-twenties. A tad old, he'd have thought, still to be living at home, but definitely too young to shut herself away on an island. "I have a small place a few kilometers offshore, too," he remarked conversationally, sparing Theo an inquiring glance and receiving a barely discernible nod in reply, "as well as an apartment here, on Lycabettus Hill."

To reply, she had to raise her voice over the sudden eruption of laughter from a nearby table. "I'm afraid that doesn't mean anything to me. I'm not at all familiar with the layout of the city."

He hadn't expected she would be. Bringing his mouth close enough to her ear to catch a faint whiff of her perfume, he said, "Then what do you say to my ordering us something cold and re-freshing to drink, and I'll take you up to the hotel roof garden for a bird's-eye tour of the area? Quite apart from anything else, it'll be much quieter up there and we can talk without having to shout."

"Well…" She tilted her head and pursed her lips thought-fully. "This ballroom is rather noisy."

"Wait here, then, and I'll be right back."

Theo joined him at the bar a few seconds later. "So, what did you find in the bag?" Mikos asked.

"Nothing untoward," the security guard replied. "A valid Press pass, a little cash and the usual girly stuff—comb, lipstick, mirror, breath mints, that sort of thing." He patted his jacket pocket. "Oh, and the key to her hotel room. The old-fash-ioned kind, with the room number engraved on it."

"Press pass, hmm? She did say she was here on assignment for a magazine."

"Looks as if she told the truth then, doesn't it?"

"Certainly does." His rush of elation was premature, to say the least, but telling himself so didn't quell it one iota. "Nice work, Theo. Think you can manage without me for a while?"

Theo made no attempt to hide his smirk. "For as long as it takes, and whatever it takes, to find out which hotel she's staying at."

The view from the roof of the Grande Bretagne was no doubt impressive. The elegant old hotel, she quickly learned, occupied the most prestigious block in the city center, overlooked Syntagma Square, the House of Parliament and National Gardens, and lay within easy walking distance of such popular tourist spots as the Agora, Plaka, Monastiraki flea market, Acropolis and Presidential Palace.

All very interesting, she was sure, and normally she'd have soaked up the information but, in this instance, she found it difficult to concentrate. Even the ancient, floodlit columns of the Parthenon failed to hold her attention for more than a second or two. And all because, much closer—and far *too* close for comfort—the sleeve of Mikos Christopoulos's immaculate dinner jacket repeatedly brushed against her bare arm. His warm breath ruffled her hair. His voice, darker than midnight and more seductive than chocolate, mesmerized her with its foreign intonation. Most disturbing of all, his exceedingly masculine aura enveloped her in a web of sexual awareness that left her trapped like a hapless butterfly pinned to a collector's mounting board.

Oblivious to his effect on her, he directed her attention to a block of real estate just east of the hotel. "Down there is Kolonaki, one of the most sought-after areas in Athens. Often referred to as Embassy territory, it's also home to the business

district, as well as some high-priced apartment buildings and many trendy coffee houses where the social set likes to hang out."

"But that's not where you live, is it?" she asked weakly, less because she really gave a hoot where he lived than because she felt she had to say something to indicate she still had a working brain. "When we were downstairs, you mentioned an apartment in Lika-something Hill."

"Lycabettus, that's right." He cupped her shoulders in his big, warm hands, and turned her slightly to the north. "You can see it quite clearly from here. But I work in Kolonaki, in the Tyros office complex."

Mention of Angelo Tyros's name served as a stark reminder of why she was in Greece to begin with. Fighting to keep her tone neutral, she said, "How long have you worked for him?"

"Almost half my life, though not always in my present capacity."

"So you know him well?"

"As well as anyone does, yes."

"What kind of man is he—besides rich and famous, that is?"

Mikos gave the question some thought before answering. "Indestructible," he finally replied. "As you know, he just turned eighty, but he's still very much a hands-on chairman of the board, at his desk every morning by nine and expecting everyone else to be at theirs. He takes enormous pride in the fact that he's never missed a day's work in his life, not when his wife died, nor even when his son and only child was killed in an auto racing accident, some thirty years ago."

That figures, Gina thought bitterly. What does family matter, compared to the amassing of more wealth? "And you admire such a man?"

"I respect him, I'm grateful to him, and yes, I'm fond of him. Deeply so. I might not always agree with him or the choices

he makes, but I wouldn't be where I am today if it weren't for Angelo Tyros."

Nor would my mother!

How she kept the words from flying out of her mouth, she'd never know, but something of her contempt must have shown on her face because Mikos tilted his head to one side, the better to observe her. She'd noticed earlier that his eyes were not the dark brown she'd have expected of a man so classically Greek in every other respect, but a light, clear green. Framed by thick, black lashes, they made an arresting statement in a face already blessed with more than its fair share of masculine beauty. But more than that, they were sharply observant and full of keen intelligence. He wouldn't be easily fooled.

She'd do well to remember that, she thought, glancing away before she lost herself in the depths of that alluring gaze. If she played her cards right, this man could introduce her to Angelo Tyros, but not if she gave him reason to be suspicious of her motives. Without his help, a journalistic nonentity like herself hadn't a chance of getting within spitting distance of the old brute. His army of sycophants would see to that, as she'd realized the moment she set foot in the ballroom.

Interpreting her silence as disapproval, Mikos said, "If I've given the impression that he's cold and unfeeling, and more concerned with power than people, let me balance that by saying with absolute sincerity that he's also capable of great generosity and kindness."

"I'll try to remember that when I write my article."

His voice sank lower, rolling over her skin with the soft abrasion of velvet dragged against the nap to bring every nerve ending in her body to tingling life. "And I will never forget this night, or this moment."

"Why's that?" she whispered haltingly.

Again, he brought his hands to her shoulders, but this time ran them up her neck and along the underside of her jaw until they cradled her face. "We both know why, *calli mou*."

Well, she didn't. Not really. Oh, she knew he was going to kiss her. Had known it from the moment they'd stepped out onto the deserted roof garden, just as she'd known she was going to let him because, quite apart from any other consideration, he happened to be handsome as the proverbial Greek god, and so charming that his smile alone was enough to set her entire body vibrating right down to her toes, and it had been such a long time since she'd felt desirable. But in no way did any of that answer the real question, *why?*

The ballroom had been overflowing with beautiful women clad in the very latest, most sumptuous designer fashions. She had on a dress she'd last worn five years ago, and even in its prime, it hadn't exactly qualified as being on the cutting edge of haute couture.

Those other women had diamonds threaded through their hair, and draped around their necks and wrists, and swinging from their ears. Her only adornment consisted of a piece of costume jewelry—a big old purple-colored pendant, studded around the perimeter with grimy crystals, which she used to wear when she played dress-up as a little girl. Although its chain had long since been lost or broken, she'd scrubbed its paste gems in ammonia until they sparkled, then attached it to a wide band of black velvet, which she now wore at her throat. It was a pretty enough bauble to suit the occasion, especially in the subdued light of the ballroom, but it didn't compare to the real thing.

Which brought her back full circle to her original question: *Why* had Mikos Christopoulos singled out her, a social nobody from Canada, with neither pedigree, position nor money to make her stand out from the crowd?

Grabbing at the remnants of her vanishing sanity, she stammered, "That hardly answers my question, Mikos."

"No? Then perhaps this does," he murmured, and lowered his mouth to hers in a kiss that redefined the meaning of the word, at least as it applied to her experience.

She clutched at him, then, because it was either that or slither to the ground in a heap of molten hormones. How was it possible for fire to torch her senses, yet leave behind no scar? How could a man turn the most elementary tool of seduction into an instrument of such exquisite sensory torture that spasms of pleasure shot to the pit of her stomach and left her most secret flesh humming and aching and drenched?

Oh, this was madness! But telling herself so did nothing to stop an inarticulate moan from rising in her throat. Or keep her hands where they properly belonged, planted firmly at his shoulders to ward him off. Instead she wilted against him and wound her arms around his neck, and tunneled her fingers through his smooth, dense hair, and opened her lips to his persuasive tongue and let him do as he pleased with her mouth, and just generally behaved like a trollop.

Remember why you're here! the dim voice of reason beseeched. *You didn't have to travel all the way to Greece, if all you wanted was sex!*

Not even if this is sex transformed into something rare and wonderful? her other, shameless self inquired.

Not even then, you idiot! What kind of woman abandons her cause, the moment a handsome foreigner spares her a second glance?

But this is about more than exotic good looks. It's about chemistry—alchemy, even. It's about looking into a man's eyes and seeing my future written there. It's about trusting my instincts and recognizing destiny when it comes calling.

Tell that to the mother you left in the care of strangers!

The words slapped her in the face like a dash of cold water.

"Mmm…oh!" She tore her mouth free. Forced her hands to stop their exploration of his hair and pushed them hard against his chest. "I can't do this! It isn't right!"

His eyes smoldered in the gloom, primitive green fire warring with civilized restraint. "How can it be wrong, *agapiti mou*, when I find you so irresistible? We are free to follow our hearts, are we not—or is yours promised to someone else?"

"Of course it isn't!" she responded heatedly. "If I were involved with another man, I would *never* cheat on him. But this…what we're getting into here, well, it's…!"

She floundered into silence, knowing she could not confide in him. Although he didn't realize it, he was on the enemy's side, and when he discovered her true reason for coming to Athens, *he'd* become her enemy, too. He wouldn't find her quite so irresistible then.

"Moving too quickly. I understand. We met less than an hour ago, and have tomorrow and as many days after that as you are willing to spend with me, before we must say *adio*. There is no need to rush so pleasurable a prospect."

His voice caressed her. Soothed her uneasy conscience. He was neither making nor demanding promises for anything beyond what either was willing to give. The way he saw it, the most they had to offer each other was a week or two of their otherwise separate lives. After that, he would move on to his next conquest and she would return home, possibly a little heart sore, but definitely more fulfilled as a woman than she had been when she left—and hopefully having achieved her covert objective. One of those win-win situations, in other words.

Pack your bags and get on that aircraft, Sam Irving, her doctor, had ordered when he learned she was following his

advice after all, even if it wasn't entirely for the reasons he thought. *You're a young woman in her prime, Gina, and it's long past time you had a little fun. Discover Greece, have a fling and leave me to take care of things on the homefront.*

Good advice, Sam, she decided, a little bubble of happiness erupting inside her.

Smiling at Mikos, she said, "No need at all. I'm enjoying just being up here with you, although I'm surprised we have the place to ourselves. I didn't think Athenians ever went to bed before dawn."

"You're right. As a rule, we'd be just two of many enjoying the night. But for this occasion, the public rooms of the hotel are off-limits to all but those officially invited to attend the birthday celebration."

"Then can we just sit and get to know one another better? You said earlier that you wouldn't be where you are today if it weren't for Angelo Tyros, and I've been wondering what you meant by that."

He shrugged his impeccably tailored shoulders regretfully. "Much though I'd prefer to watch the sun come up with you at my side, I'm afraid I must deny myself the pleasure. I'm officially working and shouldn't be gone from the party too long."

Well, so much for finding her irresistible! As long as she was willing to let him seduce her, he had all the time in the world to spare, but the minute she called a halt to the physical side of things, duty called him elsewhere—probably to one of those women she'd earlier noticed salivating over him as if he were a particularly mouthwatering slice of baklava!

"Thanks for reminding me that I'm slacking off, too," she said, not quite able to keep the sting out of her voice. "I'm being paid to produce an article about the rich and famous, and could be missing all kinds of delicious goings-on downstairs."

He started to speak, but she was in no mood to listen because her little bubble of happiness had burst and left her flat with disillusionment. She'd been out of circulation too long, that was the trouble. Adopting the role of parent to her poor, lost mother had blunted her social skills, and left her so hungry for a touch of glamour, a soupçon of romance, that she'd lost all perspective the very second Mikos had spared her a second glance.

How could she have been so naive? Sophisticated men like him weren't interested in cosy chats by moonlight. She ought to be grateful he hadn't laughed in her face at the mere idea!

Swallowing the absurd lump in her throat, she swept to the elevator and pressed the call button. Mercifully the doors slid open promptly, offering a fast escape. But not quite fast enough. Mikos was right on her heels, ushering her into the car with such charming continental gallantry that it took every iota of will-power for her to maintain a stony-faced mask of indifference.

"I have offended you," he observed ruefully, as the doors ghosted shut.

"Don't be ridiculous," she retorted, and wished he'd stop staring at her. Didn't he know that people in elevators were supposed to look at the illuminated numbers on the directory panel, and never at other passengers?

"If that is true," he replied, after a lengthy pause, "then once things start to quieten down a little, perhaps you'll join me for a late snack?"

She covered her mouth with her hand and faked a long yawn. "Oh, I doubt that. I'm pretty tired already, and won't be hanging around once I've collected enough material to complete my article."

"I see." Another silence followed, this one more protracted, then, "You have a room here, at the Grande Bretagne, do you, Gina?"

She thought of the Grande Bretagne, newly restored to its nineteenth century grandeur, and laughed, a brittle humorless sound that echoed harshly in that confined space. "Hardly! I'm a working woman, remember?"

"But you have adequate accommodation in a decent neighborhood?"

"I'm at the Topikos, just a couple of blocks from the Hilton." It was nothing splashy, and certainly didn't compare to the Grande Bretagne, but her room was clean and comfortable, came with its own bathroom and was affordable.

"Then I'll arrange for a car to take you home when you're ready to leave."

"No need," she said. "It's not far. I can walk, or take a taxi."

"I will not allow any such thing. Please let me know when you've had enough of the party."

Fat chance! she almost told him. Fortunately the elevator sighed to a stop and the second the doors slid open, the din from the party swam through, drowning out any possibility of further conversation.

Once inside the ballroom, she waggled her fingers in farewell. "See you later," she mouthed, and promptly put as much distance between him and her as possible.

Sadly he made no attempt to stop her. Instead, with the careless elegance only the very rich and self-assured dared assume, he sauntered across the imposing lobby and struck up a conversation with a man seated in an alcove.

Well, if Mikolas Christopoulos wasn't going to give her access to Angelo Tyros, she'd have to do it on her own. Refusing to admit the bitter taste in her mouth sprang from a disappointment that had to do with more than thwarted ambition, she made her way unimpeded to the head table, only to suffer another setback. There was no sign of the Greek billionaire.

"Excuse me, do you speak English?" she asked a woman still seated there.

"A little, yes."

"Then can you tell me where I might find Mr. Tyros? I was hoping he'd grant me an interview."

The woman's eyebrows rose in amusement. "You're too late, *Kyria!* Even if he'd have agreed to speak to you, which is doubtful, Angelo left some time ago. He is eighty, after all!"

Oh, great! Just wonderful!

No denying her letdown this time. It burned her throat raw.

She'd started out on such a high note. Been greeted on her arrival at the Grande Bretagne by a cloaked doorman who'd ushered her into the lobby as if she were royalty. Somehow caught the eye of the most attractive man in the room, who'd singled her out for his undivided attention, only to dump her as soon as he realized she wasn't up for a quick grope between the potted palms. And matters had gone steadily downhill ever since. All in all, the evening had been a complete bust.

Discouraged and exhausted suddenly, she circled back to the ballroom's exit, grateful to see that although the faithful four continued to stand guard against gatecrashers, Mikos was nowhere in sight.

At least, that was her assumption until, when she was halfway across the Persian carpet adorning the lobby, a hand closed over her shoulder and that dark, rich voice that had so nearly seduced her on the roof, murmured in her ear, "And just where do you think you're going, Ms. Hudson?"

CHAPTER TWO

SHE'D thought she was tired, that falling into bed and sleeping without fear of what she might wake up to was exactly what she both needed and wanted. But the sun was well-risen and already flushing the tall buildings of downtown Athens with color when she finally arrived back at her hotel room, just after eight o-clock the next morning.

"Not that it's any of your business," she'd told Mikos, pushing aside yet another pesky photographer and making her determined way through the rotating doors of the Grande Bretagne to the street outside, "but I'm heading back to my hotel."

Undeterred, he'd followed her. "We decided you'd let me know when you were ready to do that."

"No," she corrected him stonily. "*You* decided, not I."

He raised his left hand and snapped his fingers imperiously. That, it seemed, was all it took for a small black Mercedes limousine to materialize from the shadows and cruise to a stop at the curb. "Just as well one of us has some sense then, isn't it?" he said, and held open the rear door in refuse-me-at-your-peril invitation.

Although she'd have loved to defy him and stalk haughtily off into the night under her own steam, in truth she was glad of the excuse to be off her feet. Strappy rhinestone sandals

might exemplify the ultimate in elegant evening accessories, but they didn't lend themselves to hiking. Not only that, she hadn't worn three inch heels in years, and her feet were aching unmercifully. So she swallowed her pride and slithered into the back seat in a flurry of violet silk chiffon. "Thank you," she said stiffly. "I appreciate your consideration."

"*Parakalo!* Don't mention it," he returned.

Assuming she'd seen the last of him, she leaned forward to give the uniformed chauffeur the name of her hotel, then realized that Mikos had also climbed into the car with every sign of remaining there.

Rattled, she gasped, "What do you think you're doing?"

"Putting an end to this nonsense," he replied, then switched to Greek in a brief conversation with the driver, at the conclusion of which the man nodded compliantly, raised the smoked-glass panel between him and his passengers and eased the car into the traffic still clogging the road.

Gina wasn't familiar with the layout of Athens, but one glance out of the dark-tinted side window was enough to tell her they weren't headed toward her hotel. "In case you're not aware, your driver's going the wrong way," she informed Mikos.

"He's going precisely the right way," he drawled, unbuttoning his dinner jacket and stretching out his long legs. "I suggest you relax and enjoy the ride."

For a moment, she was tempted. What woman wouldn't be, especially one who'd been deprived of the so-called "finer things in life" for far too long? She was ensconced in black leather upholstery as plush and soft as polished marshmallows, in a limousine that purred like a well-bred cat and traveled over the surface of the road as smoothly as a sleek length of satin floating on air.

The neck of a bottle of champagne—Bollinger, she

noticed—poked out of a silver ice bucket in the built-in bar. Crystal flutes sparkled in the subdued glow of the rear interior lights. The man seated next to her was sexy and gorgeous. Tall, dark and handsome. Worldly, sophisticated and charming.

Then it occurred to her that she was headed toward an unknown destination, in a car with a comparative stranger, and could be in very serious trouble. Women traveling alone in foreign lands had been known to disappear without trace, never to be seen again, precisely because they'd behaved as rashly as she just had.

"If you're thinking of kidnapping me," she said, sounding distressingly terrified, "you should know that you won't be able to raise a ransom worth spit. I have no value, monetary or otherwise, to a living soul." *Except,* she added silently, *to my mother who hasn't a clue where I am, or what sort of trouble I might be facing. And if even if she had, she couldn't do a damned thing about it.*

"Kidnap you?" He stifled a grin, though not quite soon enough for it to pass unnoticed. Teeth like his, she thought sourly, were a dentist's worst nightmare. Straight, white and flawless, they'd push the poor man to the brink of bankruptcy before he'd find reason to tamper with them. "The thought hadn't crossed my mind, but now that you mention it, it might not be such a bad idea."

"I'm glad one of us finds this amusing!" she spat.

He angled a long, assessing glance her way. "I find you many things. Amusing, certainly, *agapiti mou*, but also intriguing, ingenuous—"

"I find you insufferable!"

This time, he laughed out loud, an eruption of sound rumbling rich and low as an earthquake from deep inside his chest. "At least I've made some sort of impression," he said dryly, removing the champagne from the ice bucket.

His hands, darkly tanned against the white cuffs of his dress shirt, were well-shaped, with long, capable fingers. Spellbound, she watched as they stripped the foil from the neck of the bottle and removed the cork with the kind of negligent ease that suggested he was no stranger to the task. The wine foamed in the flutes, tiny volcanoes of bubbles exploding to the surface in effervescent glee.

"What shall we drink to, Gina?" he asked, offering a glass to her.

Exercising a mind of their own that was completely at odds with how common sense dictated they should respond, her fingers reached out and circled the slender stem. "You decide."

"How about, to getting to know more about one another?"

"When I suggested that, little more than an hour ago, you claimed you had more pressing matters to attend to."

"I've changed my mind since then."

"You're not the only one! I now know more than I care to about the kind of man you are," she replied, "and if you think that by getting me in the back seat of this…this *sexmobile*, I'm going to lie down and let you have your way with me, you're in for a rude awakening."

At first, he seemed bereft of speech. He covered his mouth with his hand, and from the way his champagne trembled in its glass, it was plain enough that he was convulsed with more laughter, albeit silent this time. Finally making an effort to control himself—and not very well at that, judging by the amusement quivering in his voice—he said, "I assure you, I have far too much respect for you to entertain any such notion."

"Oh." She digested that for a second, then turned to him, puzzled. "Well then, what *do* you want?"

"To explain myself to you."

"You didn't have to go to such extreme lengths to do that."

"Really? Are you saying that if I'd tried to speak my mind as
you left the hotel, you'd have stopped in midflight and listened?"

"Probably not," she had to admit. "I was pretty ticked off
with you."

"Exactly! And that's what encouraged me to spirit you away
like this. If you hadn't cared that our rendezvous on the hotel
roof came to such an abrupt end, I wouldn't have bothered
wasting any more of your time, or mine. But…" He fixed her
in his gaze and shrugged his broad, beautiful shoulders. "You
did care, didn't you? You felt it, too—that spark of attraction
between us, so powerful it defies all reason?"

Mesmerized, she nodded, such a maelstrom of emotion
rushing through her at the message she read in his eyes that it
took her a moment to pose the question that had gnawed at her
for hours. "But in that case, why did you suddenly—?"

"Put an end to things, before they went too far?"

She nodded again.

"Because," he said, removing her glass before she dropped
it, and placing it beside his on the built-in shelf at his side, "I
pride myself on being a civilized man who is long past the age
where hasty fumbling in a public place is an acceptable way to
treat a lady. But you, Gina, you aroused such a hunger in me
that I wasn't sure I could control myself if I remained alone with
you any longer."

At that, a lovely warmth spread through her. "I thought it
might be because you're married."

"I am not, nor have I ever been married."

"Oh," she said, those same bubbles which had streamed so exu-
berantly in her champagne flute chasing now through her blood.

"Nor," he continued, "do I plan to seduce you in the back
seat of this car. If we are to make love—and that is by no means
certain—it will be at a place and time of both our choosing."

His teeth gleamed in another smile. "But if you'll permit it, I'd very much like to kiss you again."

Heart stammering with pleasure, she whispered, "I think that can be arranged."

He took her face between his hands and very slowly let his breath feather over her closed eyes, and her lashes, and down her face to her jaw, before making his deliberate way to her mouth. Once there, his lips closed over hers lightly, decorously even, yet spoke a silent language that promised a depth of passion completely foreign to anything she'd known before.

How easily he made her ache and want and need! Desire gnawed at her, raw and merciless. She felt herself melting, as she had when he'd kissed her on the hotel roof. Heat swirled through her blood. Pooled hot and heavy in the pit of her stomach. Sprang moist as dew in the secret folds of her femininity.

Stop being such a gentleman! she almost begged aloud. *Stop holding back!*

She was ravenous for him. Wanted him to touch her all over. Wished he'd lower her dress from her shoulders, raise its hem to her waist. Slide his hand inside her underwear. Cup the fullness of her breasts in his palms. Discover the tight buds of her nipples, the hot, tingling flesh between her legs.

More, she wanted to touch him. Run the tips of her fingers down his chest and past the flat planes of his belly. Stray lower into forbidden territory and explore the aroused shape of him. Test its smooth, naked weight in her hand. He would be big and powerful, just like the attraction flaring between them. He would be like no other man she'd ever met. She knew it as surely as she knew her own name.

Her realizing the direction of her thoughts was the only thing that prevented her from acting on her impulses.

Horrified at how close she'd come to embarrassing herself, she pulled away, shocked to the core.

What was wrong with her, that she was behaving like a…a *floozy* and practically throwing herself at a stranger? Had she been bitten by some exotic foreign bug and contracted brain fever? Admittedly she wasn't a complete innocent where sex was concerned. She'd lost her virginity at twenty-two to Paul Johnson, her then-fiancé, who'd eventually changed his mind about marrying her when he'd realized it meant taking on her mother, too. But she'd never been "easy," never cheapened herself with loose behavior.

Of course, some people might say she hadn't had much choice in the matter because, after Paul broke things off and she went back to the island for good, her social life had pretty much hit rock bottom, especially when it came to dating. The limited number of eligible men she'd met there weren't interested in a woman forever preoccupied with the doings of a sixty-year-old child.

But this was Athens, Greece, and incredible, beautiful Mikos Christopoulos had kissed her twice, and in doing so had awakened all the pent-up female needs and yearnings she'd suppressed for over five years, and set them free with a vengeance.

It had nothing to do with attraction, although Mikos surely was the most attractive man to walk the earth. It had to do with hunger; with the basic need to be acknowledged as a woman who amounted to more than a daughter and caregiver. But for her to give in to it like this? Never!

"Oh, my…!" she gasped, putting more distance between him and her, and sitting on her hands to keep them from wandering where they most definitely didn't belong. "I think that's enough for now."

He didn't attempt to dissuade her. If anything, he seemed

almost relieved that she'd called a halt to things. "I'll drink to that," he said, reaching for the bottle and topping up their champagne.

Bewildered by the mixed messages he was sending—so hot for her one minute, yet able to cool his ardor so effectively the next—she gestured at the luxurious appointments of the limousine. "This isn't exactly how I expected the evening to end, when I came to the party tonight."

"Exactly what did you expect, Gina?"

"Why, that I'd go back to my hotel as soon as I'd gathered enough information."

"Information?"

"For my magazine article."

"Ah, yes, the magazine article," he echoed suavely.

Too suavely.

"Yes," she said, brought up short by the veiled cynicism she detected in his voice. "Don't you believe me?"

"Is there any reason I shouldn't?"

"Not that I'm aware of," she lied, taking umbrage at his answering her question with one of his own. "But you sound awfully suspicious suddenly."

"Do I?" He flicked a glance her way, then turned his attention to the bubbles rising in his glass as if they were the most fascinating things he'd ever come across.

"Yes," she said again, and when he made no attempt to deny the fact, continued, "*Are* you?"

He deliberated at length before replying, "Let me put it this way. I'm not a man easily swayed by a beautiful face or an alluring body. It takes more than that to capture my interest. But I'm so strongly drawn to you that I'm at a loss to know how to deal with it."

"You don't strike me as the type to be at a loss about anything or anyone."

"Normally I'm not. But I'd be lying if I said I find this situation normal. In truth, I consider it to be quite extraordinary."

"And you don't like not being in charge."

"No, I don't," he said. "I am, as you say in your part of the world, a control freak. It's what makes me so good at my job."

"Which is what, exactly? You told me you work for Mr. Tyros, but you never said what it is you do."

"I'm in management. An executive vice president, in fact."

Which told her precisely nothing. Well, I didn't think you were a janitor! she almost retorted, struck by the sense that he'd edited his answer very carefully.

Realistically she supposed it wasn't surprising. Likely no employee of a high-powered tycoon like Angelo Tyros, was at liberty to share top-level information with an outsider, and she only had to remember his imperious commandeering of the limousine to recognize that Mikos was very top-level indeed. "Do you like your job?" she asked him instead.

The interior car lights were dim, but not enough to hide the grimace that passed over his face. "Not always," he admitted. "But then, who does? Take you, for instance. Are you entirely happy with what you do every day?"

She turned and looked out of the window, her reasons for coming to Greece suddenly back in the forefront of her mind where they rightly belonged.

Ms. Hudson…Gina, this is very awkward, but I'm quite sure I left my earrings on the dresser before we went out this morning, and they're not there now….

Gina, is that you? I just caught your mother down on the beach, waist-deep in the water…in November, Gina…!

Seen Maeve? Not since this morning, Gina, no. When did you realize she was missing…?

How did one rate a labor of love, she wondered, leaning her

forehead against the cool glass. She hated what had happened to her mother. Hated the slow slipping away of the woman who'd once been the mainstay of her life. So, to answer his question, no, she wasn't happy with what she had to do every day. But not for the reasons he might think.

Turning to face him again, she said, "Some days are better than others. I guess that's true of every job."

"Tell me about that."

"What?"

"Your job. You said you live on one of the Gulf Islands."

"That's right."

"Isn't that rather inconvenient? If my memory serves correctly, they lie quite some distance from the mainland. I'd have thought that rather limiting for a writer interested in covering the international social set."

"Many people commute from the islands to Vancouver. I can make it by seaplane in twenty minutes, if I need to."

"But what made a young woman like you decide to live at home again?"

"How do you know I live at home?"

"You told me so, when we were dancing."

Oh dear! She'd have to keep a tighter rein on her tongue or he'd definitely become suspicious. Or was it just that he was killing time in idle conversation and hoping she wouldn't notice that they'd left the city behind and were approaching a bridge spanning a stretch of dark water? A lake? The sea? And if the latter, which one?

Her earlier fears resurfacing suddenly, she said, "Why don't you tell me where you're taking me?"

"To a place where we can be alone."

"We're already alone."

"Not quite." He glanced meaningfully at the smoked glass

partition separating them from the driver. "My work is such that I'm seldom able to escape it, but tonight…" He traced the tip of his forefinger lightly over her lower lip, leaving it throbbing for more. "Tonight, I'm playing hooky. With you."

Soon, they'd crossed the bridge and were passing through a fair-size town where lamps still shone from many houses. "Are we still on the mainland?"

"No. We're on Evia, our second largest island after Crete. Many Greeks consider it to be the most beautiful, but because it lies so close to the mainland, it's often overlooked by tourists and, as a result, has retained much of its traditional customs and charm."

"Is it where you have your weekend place?"

He folded his fingers around hers. "No," he said again.

The blood raced through her veins, not only because the simple touch of his hand on hers electrified her senses, but also from growing apprehension. Too soon, the lights of the town faded into the night. About fifteen minutes later, they passed through a village. Not long after that, the car cruised to a stop on a deserted stretch of coast road far from any sign of civilization. "Come," Mikos said, drawing her out of the vehicle, the very second the driver raced around to hold open the door.

She stepped onto the road, stumbling a little in her high heels. Steadying her, Mikos spoke to his chauffeur who, to her dismay, climbed back into the Mercedes, turned the car around and sped back toward the village they'd left behind.

Within seconds, the night was filled with nothing but starshine, the swish of the restless sea and the erratic thud of her heart. At her side, Mikos stood tall and dark as a monolith, his grip still firm on her elbow. Struggling to keep her tone even, she said, "I'm really not very comfortable with this situation. Exactly what do you have in mind?"

"A walk on the beach. What did you think?"

"That it's almost three o'clock in the morning, and most people are in bed at this hour."

He laughed softly. "Are you saying you'd rather be in bed with me, Gina?"

The thought had crossed her mind often enough over the course of the evening that she was glad the night hid her blush. "No," she snapped. "I'm saying that I don't understand why we're here."

"Well, look around you." He looped his arm over her shoulders and turned her to face the water. "See how the reflection of the stars dances over the sea. Feel how softly the air caresses your skin. Breathe in the scent of the pine trees and oleanders. Then tell me that you'd rather be alone in your hotel room in Athens, a city that never sleeps."

How could she, when every word he spoke was the indisputable truth? "It *is* beautiful here."

He drew her closer so that the rough velvet of his voice rasped intimately against her ear. "Then put your doubts to rest and come with me."

Did she have any other choice? Did she *want* one? That she risked breaking both ankles as she tottered behind him down a narrow path to the shore, was answer enough. "I'm wearing high-heeled sandals," she panted, when at last she reached the beach, "and they don't lend themselves to navigating rough terrain like this."

He shrugged. "So take them off," he said, and before she knew what he was about, he squatted in front of her, his fingers warm around her right ankle. "Lean on me."

Such was his effect on her, it simply never occurred to her to refuse. Pathetic, docile fool that she was, she complied without protest, resting a hand on his shoulder to keep her balance and raising first one foot, then the other.

"There," he said, swiftly completing his task. "How's that?"

The sand drifted cool and soft as flour against the soles of her feet and between her toes. "Heavenly," she admitted on a sigh of relief. But oh, how disturbing, that he could so easily bend her to his will!

Releasing her left ankle, he grasped the full skirted hem of her dress and slid it up her calf. "Be careful not to trip over this. It would be a pity to see such a lovely thing damaged."

He sounded matter-of-fact enough, but there was nothing the least bit matter-of-fact about the way she turned limp with pleasure as his fingers whispered impersonally against her leg. "What next?" she asked faintly, bunching the yards of filmy fabric in her fist.

"We'll walk along the water's edge and make our way back to the village. It's only about three kilometers, and won't take more than half an hour."

In fact, it took close to two. How did it happen that, during that time, she found herself holding hands with him? That she frequently caught him looking at her as if he couldn't get enough of the sight of her? That, every once in a while, he grazed his mouth over hers in a fleeting kiss?

When did she abandon the dry sand and decide instead to let the waves splash cool around her ankles, and not care that they sometimes soaked the bottom of her dress? At what point did he remove his shoes and socks, roll his trouser legs up to midcalf and join her?

She couldn't say, nor did she care. It was enough that, for a few short hours, she believed in fairy tales; in a handsome prince discovering Cinderella and freeing her, just for a little while, from the cares of real life.

Even when the tile roofs of the village rose up against a horizon faintly touched with the hint of dawn, the magic didn't

end. Mikos led her past a fleet of fishing boats rocking against a wooden pier, to a *kafenion* set right on the beach itself. Its window shutters stood open, releasing the aroma of strong Greek coffee, and spilling yellow light onto several small iron tables and chairs set on a cobbled terrace.

"Have a seat," Mikos invited, pulling back one of the chairs.

She sat and gave an involuntary shiver. The metal struck cold through the thin stuff of her dress, and now that she wasn't moving, the morning air struck unpleasantly against her damp legs and feet.

Noticing, he removed his jacket and draped it around her shoulders before taking his place opposite. Like her, he was barefoot still. His bow tie hung loose around his neck, his shirt collar open at the throat. Damp and salt-stained, his trouser legs hung in wrinkles about his ankles, their former knife-sharp crease washed away by the sea, but although he might have ruined what was surely a thousand-dollar dinner suit, he still carried himself with that leisurely self-confidence that made him stand out from the crowd.

Just then, the coffee shop owner appeared. "This is probably stronger than what you're used to," Mikos remarked, after the man had served them each a glass of water and a thimble-size cup filled with a black, evil-looking brew topped with a light layer of brownish foam, "but it's how we Greeks like our coffee, especially when we've been up all night."

"It's fine," she said, controlling a grimace as it ate a corrosive path over the lining of her stomach. "Um…do you have to work today?"

"No. My weekends are mine to do with as I please. What about you?"

My time's my own, as well, she thought, swallowing half the contents of the water glass in one gulp. Then remembering

why she was supposed to be in Athens, said, "I'll go over my notes and get started on my article."

"After you catch up on your sleep, of course."

"Of course," she echoed, her fairy tale morphing into reality when he didn't follow up by suggesting they meet later on in the day.

Instead he cradled his demitasse in his hand—the cups hadn't come with saucers, she noticed—settled his big frame on the uncomfortable little chair with the casual grace of a cat lounging on a cushion, and gave her his undivided attention. "Were you able to get enough material to satisfy your editor?"

You don't have to bring me back anything, Gina, you know that, Lorne MacDonald, her former boss had told her, when she appealed to him for a press pass to get her into the Tyros birthday bash. *I'm happy to help you out any way I can. But if it clears your conscience any, give me something I can publish—names of the rich and famous, what the women wore, what they were eating and drinking, who was cosying up to whom. You know the drill. You did it well and often enough in the old days.*

"Not really," she told Mikos. "I was hoping I'd get the chance to interview Mr. Tyros in person, but I suppose that was expecting too much."

"Definitely," he said. "Angelo seldom grants private interviews anymore. But if you have questions, I can probably answer them, so fire away."

Oh, she had questions, although she seriously doubted he, or anyone but Angelo Tyros himself, could provide the answers! But this much she did know: one way or another, she'd find a way to corner the miserable old goat and force him to meet her demands. She hadn't depleted her savings account and come all this way, just to go home empty-handed. There was too much at stake.

CHAPTER THREE

HE WATCHED her closely, veiling his scrutiny behind dark, reflective glasses as the sun conveniently inched above the horizon just enough to warrant his wearing them. "Don't be shy, Gina," he said. "Ask me anything. Anything at all."

She took another sip of coffee and shuddered at its taste. "You mentioned he was a widower. Was he married just the one time?"

He couldn't hold back his grin. His employer's appetite for women was legendary. At the same time, it struck him as odd that she'd been sent on foreign assignment and not bothered to do her research beforehand. Five minutes on the Internet would reveal that Angelo had definitely been to the altar more than once. "Make that five times," he told her. "His first wife, the mother of his son, died in her forties. He divorced the second and third within a year of marrying them, the fourth after six months and outlived the fifth who passed away eight years ago."

"Is he likely to marry again, do you think?"

"It's entirely possible. Angelo doesn't like being alone, and he does very much like beautiful women."

Gina's laugh, brittle as ice cracking under pressure, struck a discordant note. "In other words, he uses them."

"No," he said flatly. "That is not what I said, and I caution you to exercise great accuracy when quoting me."

Bright spots of color stained her cheeks. Clearly stung by his rebuke, she turned to study the fishermen tending their nets. "I apologize. Rest assured I shall treat my subject with all the respect he deserves," she replied stiffly.

His jacket had slipped to reveal her long, graceful neck and sweetly rounded shoulders. She wore her hair in a chignon, but several strands had fallen free and curled loosely at her nape.

Finely carved against a background of pale morning sky, her profile could have served as the model for a cameo brooch of matchless delicacy and beauty. Pure Anglo-Saxon elegance— except for the lush, passionate mouth and huge, dark eyes. Those, he decided, curbing a visceral tug of arousal, she must have inherited from some long-ago ancestors of Mediterranean origin.

"I apologize also," he told her, and meant it. "I'm sorry if I spoke too harshly."

"Don't be sorry. You were merely doing what you're paid to do, and you already told me that Mr. Tyros has earned your undying loyalty. I should have remembered that before I made such a thoughtless remark. Are the fishermen's nets usually that orange color?"

"That or a deeper terra cotta," he said, recognizing her question for the deliberate shift of topic that it was, and finding it odd that she'd so easily abandon the subject she claimed had brought her to Greece. "But what has that to do with your assign—?"

Anticipating his question, she cut him off before he could complete it. "Local color," she said shortly. "It adds credibility to the article. Do they stay out all night—the fishermen, I mean?"

"A good part of it, yes."

She shook her head, apparently mystified. "Doesn't anyone in this country sleep at night?"

"Not so much in the summer months, no. Instead we sleep

several hours during the day. That way, we avoid the worst of the heat."

"So it's quite normal for a little café like this to be open at dawn?"

"Certainly. Any time now, the villagers will come down to buy fish. Once they've sold their catch and cleaned up their boats, the men will crowd in here to drink coffee and talk. But I say again, none of this has anything to do with Angelo Tyros. Why have you suddenly lost interest in him, Gina?"

"Oh, I haven't lost interest in him," she said, with unexpected fervor. "I'm quite, um, fascinated by everything about him."

Something didn't ring true in her reply. Her peculiar little pause wasn't lost on him, nor the fact that she settled on "fascinated" as if it were the least offensive word she could come up with at short notice. "You almost sound as if you have reason to dislike Angelo," he remarked, eyeing her intently, "but that hardly makes sense, does it, since you've never met him? Or am I wrong to assume that?"

Stooping, she picked up a puppy that had wandered out of the *kafenion,* and snuggled it on her lap. "Not wrong at all," she said, without the slightest hesitation this time. "Perhaps what you hear in my voice is disappointment that I've not had the pleasure. But that does bring up an interesting point. If he's so reclusive, why did he authorize such a very public birthday celebration?"

"'Reclusive' isn't the word I'd use to describe him. As I mentioned before, he dislikes being alone and loves to be surrounded by friends. But like other very rich men, he's made his share of enemies over the years. When he was younger, he took that in stride but, understandably at his age, he's more cautious now and avoids strangers unless he's assured they intend him no harm."

"To the point that he's afraid to speak to someone as innocuous as me?" Too ladylike to snort with derision at such an idea, she did the next closest thing and wrinkled her elegant little nose. "What does he think I might do, stab him with my pencil?"

"Anything's possible," he said, envying the puppy that was pawing at her breasts and trying to lick her neck. "Money is a powerful aphrodisiac to those who don't have any, and that makes him a target of unscrupulous individuals wherever he goes."

She put the dog down and picked up her cup again. "What kind of target?"

"Three attempts at extortion in the last month alone. Kidnapping. And, of course, he's always being hounded by amateur entrepreneurs who come creeping out of the woodwork claiming to be long-lost relatives. If they were all to believed, he'd have sired at least five hundred sons and daughters in the last sixty-six years."

She choked on her coffee.

"Sorry," he said, when she managed to regain her breath. "I didn't mean to make you laugh at the wrong time."

Except, he belatedly realized, she wasn't laughing at all. If anything, she was thoroughly rattled, enough that she knocked her bag off the table. It fell open and spilled most of its contents over the terrace. A fortuitous accident, he thought, bending to retrieve a runaway lipstick before the pup ran off with it. When she found her room key was missing, he'd know exactly how to explain it.

Apart from a facial tissue, which she used to mop up the tears pooling at the outer corners of her eyes, she rammed everything back in the bag, and favored him with a bloodshot glare. "Actually," she wheezed, "I didn't find it funny. In fact, nothing I've so far learned about Angelo Tyros strikes me as amusing. Don't ask me why, because I can't give you an answer."

"Perhaps it's simply that you're on overload and exhausted. You might see him in quite a different light after you've caught up on your sleep."

She smothered a yawn. "I am very tired, suddenly."

"In that case, we'll head back to the city. The car's on the road, but it's a bit of a climb to get up there. Do you want to put on your shoes before tackling it?"

She got up from her chair and made a face. "No, thanks! My feet are still in recovery and probably will be for the next week."

Stuffing his socks in his trouser pocket, he shoved his feet into his own shoes and reclaimed his jacket. "I guess that leaves me with only one option then," he said, and ignoring her squeaks of protest, picked her up, tossed her over his shoulder and made his way to where his driver, face betraying no expression, stood holding open the car door.

"That," she huffed, landing on the back seat in a flurry of silk and indignation, "was completely unnecessary!"

He averted his gaze, dangerously aroused by the shapely length of leg exposed as she tried to put her skirt to rights again. "Not from my point of view, Gina," he said obliquely.

She didn't remember curling up against him. Had no recollection at all of his slipping his arm around her and drawing her head down to rest against his shoulder. Only when the blare of traffic horns penetrated her drowsy haze did she become aware of the smooth starched cotton of his shirt against her cheek, the muscled contours of his chest beneath her hand—and everywhere, *everywhere* that his body touched hers, the velvet heat of his skin.

Opening her eyes, she ventured a glance up at him. He was staring out the window, his expression preoccupied. "I'm not very good company, am I?" she croaked, her voice rusty with sleep.

He swung his gaze to meet hers and a smile lightened his face. "Do you hear me complaining?"

"No."

But she wished he would. Wished he'd say something along the lines of, *We wasted precious time while you slept.* Instead, as the car turned into the forecourt of her hotel, his only comment was, "I kept you out too late. You look weary."

That was reassuring! Straightening, she fiddled self-consciously with her hair; wondered if her mascara had run, or her lipstick smudged. Had she drooled in her sleep? Worse yet, had she *snored?*

The possibility sent a wash of embarrassment through her. As far as she knew, she didn't snore, but who was there to tell her differently, when no one shared her bed?

Angling a surreptitious glance at Mikos, she saw that even without socks, with the laces of his shoes untied, his trouser legs all creased, and his shirt not quite as pristine as it had been a few hours before, he still managed to look elegant. Even with the shadow of new beard growth darkening his jaw, and his black hair decidedly mussed, he was still the picture of unparalleled masculine beauty. It wasn't fair.

The driver snicked open the car door. Mikos swung his long legs out and unfolded to his full six feet plus. Extended his hand. "Gina?"

She nested her palm in his. Felt his fingers close warmly around hers. In one smooth move he had her standing barefoot beside him on the forecourt's cool paving stones, with her skirt falling in disarray around her ankles. Aware that the window of opportunity was rapidly closing, she searched his clear green eyes for a hint, a shred of hope, that he'd ask to see her again.

"Thank you for a wonderful time," she said.

He smiled. Stepped closer. Bent his head. Dropped a swift, sweet kiss on her mouth. *"Parakalo.* Sleep well," he murmured.

So let down it was all she could do not to burst into tears, she nodded, turned away and was almost at the hotel's front doors when he suddenly called out, "Gina, wait!"

She spun back to face him, hope percolating through her blood. Her rhinestone sandals dangled from his hand. "Don't forget these," he said.

Like a cake taken too soon out of the oven, her moment of optimism sank into a leaden weight in the pit of her stomach. Accepting the benighted shoes, she muttered a listless "Thanks," and quickly entered the hotel before she made a complete fool of herself.

Before the wide glass doors had swung closed behind her, Prince Charming and his limousine had been swallowed up by the noxious fumes of the traffic roaring down the narrow street. So much for fairy tales!

Feeling pathetically sorry for herself, she rode the elevator to her fourth-floor room, only to discover when she got there that she'd lost her key. She had no idea where or when or how it had happened, but she did know it was the last straw and, giving vent to her frustration, she let fly with a solid kick at the door.

The only thing that suffered was her big toe. She hopped on one foot as agonizing pain knifed through the other, and yelped loudly enough to bring a maid scurrying out of the room next door. Taking in the situation with a single glance, she muttered sympathetically in broken English, and used her master key to open Gina's door. Then, after helping her to the small armchair next to the window, the woman hurried away, and returned a short time later with a large plastic bowl half full of ice cubes.

"You grow big, *Kyria*," she announced, eyeing the rapidly swelling toe mournfully. "Better you do this!" And to make sure

her message had come across loud and clear, she plunked Gina's foot in the bowl.

Whether she burst into tears because of the shocking crunch of ice against her injured toe, or because someone was looking after *her* for a change, or simply from the culmination of a fatigue that had been building for months, was anyone's guess. All Gina knew was that, one minute she was smiling gamely, and the next she was sobbing against the matronly breast of the chambermaid who stroked her hair and murmured Greek words of comfort that somehow transcended the language barrier.

"I'm so sorry," Gina hiccuped when she finally gained control again. "I don't know what's gotten into me since I arrived here, that I'm so emotional all the time."

"Neh, neh," the maid crooned. *"Neh, katalaveno.* I understand."

Gina smiled wistfully. No, you don't, she thought, but your saying so makes me feel better anyway.

The maid smiled, too, and poked herself in the chest. *"Me lene Apostolia.* You?"

Understanding, she replied, "Gina."

The maid nodded. "You okay now, Gina?"

"Yes. Much better, thanks." She made a shooing motion toward the door. "You should go. I don't want you to be in trouble because of me. But thank you again, Apostolia. You've been very kind. *Efkharisto!"*

"Parakalo." Apostolia gave a final nod and left, closing the door softly behind her.

Gina sat for a few minutes, staring out the window at the looming hulk of the Acropolis. In the blazing light of morning, with her toe throbbing and her eyes gritty from lack of sleep, she saw everything to do with the previous ten hours for what they really were: a glamorous, romantic interlude as ephemeral

as stardust. She'd met a man who'd made her feel like a woman again. He'd flirted with her, and shown her a time she'd never forget. But he was no more part of her real world than she'd ever be part of his.

Not only that, she'd sensed an ambivalence about him at times, caused, not as he claimed because he didn't trust himself, but as if he wasn't sure he could trust her. It showed in the way he suddenly drew back when everything else about him indicated he wanted more, far more, than he felt able to take.

Why? What was it about her that had made him withhold himself? Had she been too eager? Too transparently hungry? Because heaven knew, nothing frightened a man off faster than a woman so desperate that she might as well have gone after him wielding a net.

I should have been the one applying the brakes, she thought dismally. Pity I didn't ram my head against the door. It could use having some sense knocked into it.

A glance at the bedside radio clock showed it was eight on Saturday morning, Athens time, which made it nine on Friday evening on Canada's West Coast. A good time to call home. Her mother would be in bed, leaving Lynn O'Keefe, the temporary care giver, free to talk. Hobbling to the desk, Gina picked up the phone.

Lynn answered on the first ring. "I expected it would be you," she said. "How's Athens?"

"Hot, noisy, exotic and exhausting," Gina replied. "How's my mom?"

"She had a good day. We walked on the beach this morning and collected shells, then went into town after lunch and ate ice cream in the park."

"Does she realize I'm gone, do you think? Does she miss me?"

"I don't think so," Lynn said kindly. "She's off in her own world most of the time. You know how it is for her, Gina."

"Yes," she said, flooded with sudden guilt at the realization that she hadn't spared her mother more than a passing thought in the last twelve hours. "But she doesn't handle change well, and I'm afraid—"

"Don't be. I've had a lot of experience with Alzheimer's patients. I'll take very good care of her, and if I need it, help's just a phone call away."

"You won't forget to give her medication?"

"Of course I won't! Listen, she's not the only one under doctor's orders. You're supposed to be making the most of your time off, not worrying about what's happening on the home-front. If an emergency arises, you'll hear about it. Otherwise, you may assume everything's under control. So stop worrying, and just enjoy yourself. Please."

"I'll try," she said.

But she knew it wouldn't be easy. Worrying had become as much a part of her daily routine as brushing her teeth, and her being thousands of miles away did nothing to change that.

"You don't need to worry," Theo Keramidis said. "She's clean."

"You're sure?"

"Mikos, I went over that hotel room with a fine-tooth comb. Trust me, if she had anything to hide, I'd have found it. Everything's in order, from her passport to her luggage tags. She's who she says she is. I Googled her magazine and pulled up past articles she's written. She's legit, right down to her little cotton panties."

The idea that Theo had pawed through her underwear left a bad taste in his mouth. "I trust you left everything exactly as you found it?"

Theo scowled. "Come on, Mikos! After all the years we've worked together, you know better than to ask a question like that."

"*Sighnomi*," he muttered. "You're right, of course. It's just that—"

"I know what it is, boss. You're so hot for this woman, you're about ready to blow a fuse, and can't wait to get her in the sack."

Succinctly, if crudely put, Mikos thought, annoyed. It wasn't like him to be so transparently obvious. He *never* allowed pleasure to interfere with business. With him, work always came first. Until now. "I'll pretend I didn't hear that," he said. "Thanks again, Theo. I'll handle it from here."

"I don't doubt that for a minute!" Grinning, the security guard made his way to the door, then stopped at the last second. "By the way, there was one discrepancy, but slight enough that I doubt it's significant. She calls herself Gina, but her full name is Angelina Maeve Hudson, and if it matters any, she'll turn twenty-nine on August the fifth."

Filing the information at the back of his mind, Mikos stepped out to the penthouse terrace. Although it was still early June, the midday temperature had risen close to thirty. Unusually hot, even for Athens, and under normal circumstances he'd be off to the island for the weekend. But Theo had hit closer to the mark than even he realized. It had been all Mikos could do to let Gina walk away from him that morning.

He'd seen the disappointment in her beautiful brown eyes when she'd said goodbye, and knew he'd put it there. But he'd had little other choice until he'd known for sure that her story checked out. The pity of it was, he'd seen no other way to verify her credentials except by having Theo violate her privacy.

That, as Angelo was fond of reminding him, was the price of doing business, and when it came to security, Mikos knew

he was right. Too bad it sometimes left him feeling so dirty that no amount of soap and hot water could quite rid him of the smell.

The sun was casting long shadows across the wall when a knock awoke Gina. Surprised, she saw the radio clock read ten after seven. She'd slept for nearly twelve hours.

Bleary-eyed, she crawled out of bed, thrust her arms in the sleeves of her cotton robe and tied the belt snugly at her waist, them made her gingerly way to the door. Although no longer quite as swollen, her toe still throbbed a little when she put weight on it, but she'd definitely live. At least, she thought so until she happened to glance in the mirror on the dresser. Smudged mascara, puffy eyes and bed head didn't make a pretty sight.

"Just a sec," she called out, making a quick stop in the bathroom to swipe a wet cloth over her face and rake a brush through her hair.

But either whoever had knocked didn't understand, or couldn't spare the time to wait for her to answer because, when she peered through the spy hole, no one appeared to be waiting in the hall. Instead a massive flower arrangement had been left at her door.

Roses, she discovered. At least three dozen long-stemmed, blood-red beauties, arranged in a tall crystal vase among a feathery mass of baby's breath. "In memory of an unforgettable night," the card read. And if all that wasn't enough to set her heart soaring, Mikos's signature surely was.

She carried the flowers inside and had barely set them on the dresser when the phone rang. "So," the voice she'd never thought to hear again purred, "are you feeling more rested now?"

"Oh, much," she said, giddy with an elation that defied everything her common sense had dictated earlier.

"Enough to spend another evening with me?"

This, on top of red roses? It was more than she'd dared hope for. "I'd love to, as long as you give me an hour to get ready." She ventured another glance in the mirror. "Actually better make that two."

"Then I'll call for you at nine."

"Perfect. And Mikos, thank you for the flowers. They're beautiful."

"As are you," he replied huskily, and hung up.

She replaced the phone in its cradle and, sore toe notwithstanding, danced a little jig around the room. Her mother was coping without her. She had a date with the most exciting man she'd ever met. For a little while at least, her world turned in complete harmony. She found it a heady experience, and one she intended to enjoy without fear for what tomorrow might bring.

CHAPTER FOUR

"THE owner of this place," Mikos told her, walking her to a tiny restaurant tucked in the corner of a quiet square near the top of Lycabettus Hill, "serves the best ouzo in Athens—perhaps in all of Greece."

Gina didn't care if plain old tap water was all the owner served. She was too enchanted by her surroundings. Remnants of the lemony-gold sunset lingered over Homer's "wine dark sea" which, that evening, was more twilight purple than red. It didn't matter; the ambience was what counted.

All of Athens lay spread at her feet, decked out in a million different-colored lights and, as always, dominated by the dramatic silhouette of the Acropolis. Behind her, flowering vines sprawled over pastel-colored walls. Palm trees towered over red tile roofs. And best of all, there was Mikos, bathing her in attention, his smile disarming, his gaze more potent than a kiss.

After his phone call, she'd spent quite some time debating what to wear. Under the best circumstances, her choices were limited since she hadn't anticipated any sort of social life beyond the birthday party. Bearing in mind that her bruised toe limited her to flat-heeled sandals, she'd finally settled on a three-tiered skirt made of filmy white cotton threaded with silver, and a matching scoop-necked top. Teamed with a wide

red leather belt, the outfit struck a cool, comfortable balance between dressy and informal.

The hotel had replaced her lost key, but the manager had cautioned her against being careless with it a second time. "One never knows, *Kyria,* who might find it, and we have our share of thieves and pickpockets here in Athens. Small, older hotels like ours don't offer the kind of in-room security you find in newer establishments. You wouldn't be the first to discover valuables missing from your room."

A sobering prospect! Not that she owned anything of real value except for her passport and travel tickets, but their loss would be catastrophic, especially if she was called home without warning. Bearing that in mind, she'd left herself enough time to stop by the front desk and arranged for them to be kept in the hotel safe. Then tucking the receipt in the zippered pocket inside her bag, she'd stepped out into the forecourt.

Almost immediately, Mikos had arrived, driving a late model Jaguar XJ. At that, she'd known a moment's panic. Handsome and sleekly powerful, the car hinted at an evening of sophisticated glamour she hadn't expected. If he took her someplace where all the men wore suits and ties, and the women were decked out in designer cocktail gowns, she'd be pitifully underdressed.

Her concern, though, was short-lived. As he climbed out to greet her, she saw he was as casually dressed as she, even if his superbly tailored taupe linen trousers and short-sleeved cream shirt probably cost more than she'd ever earned in a month.

Now, seated across from her, with a flickering candle casting alluring shadows over his sun-bronzed skin, he looked good enough to eat and certainly better than anything the restaurant had to offer. A woman could easily lose her head over such a man.

Gina didn't realize she'd been staring avidly, and probably

close to drooling, as well, until he glanced up from the menu, caught her at it and asked, "You're hungry?"

And how! But not for food! Containing herself with difficulty, she uttered a nonchalant, "I suppose I am, a little."

"*Eksertikos!* That makes for a more interesting meal. We'll start with a little ouzo and some *mezedes*. You like octopus, calamari, zucchini?"

"All of the above," she said, although she wasn't quite as sure about the ouzo, which she'd tried only once, years before, and not cared for.

"An easy woman to please." Mikos nodded approvingly. "I like that."

And I like you, far more than is good for me!

Oblivious to her state of mind, he signaled their waiter who brought ouzo and a metal pitcher of ice water to their table. The two men then launched into an animated conversation that, although completely beyond her understanding, made it plain they knew each other well.

"You must come here often," she remarked, when they were alone again.

"At least once a week," Mikos said. "My apartment is close by."

"And Mr. Tyros?"

"He has a place in Kolonaki for when he's in town, and a house on Evia, overlooking the Aegean." He added ice water to their ouzo, which turned it milky white. "At one time, he spent the week in Athens and went to the island only on weekends, but lately, he's taken to staying on Evia more often, especially during the summer."

She nodded thanks as he pushed her glass toward her. "You mentioned you have an island getaway, too."

"*Neh*, Petaloutha, which means butterfly. A magical spot, farther south, in the Cyclades."

"Do you spend much time there?"

"Every chance I get, which means most weekends."

"But not this weekend."

"No." Yet again, his heavily lashed gaze roamed over her, warming her from the toes up and leaving her awash in tingling awareness. "This weekend, I found myself lured by a different kind of enchantment."

It was as well their waiter returned with a loaded tray just then, because when it came to cloaking a few words with a wealth of sexual promise, Mikos had it down to a fine art, and she wasn't sure she could respond coherently. To cover her disarray, she pretended an interest in the variety of appetizers placed on the table.

Olives, sun-dried tomatoes, tzitiki and calamari she recognized and, of course, the wonderful bread fresh from the oven. Others she wasn't sure of, among them little sautéed chunks of some meaty substance.

"*Spetsofai,*" Mikos explained. "It's a *loukanika*—Greek blood sausage made from both lamb and pork, flavored with black pepper and orange rind." He clinked the rim of his glass against hers. "Here's to an evening of discovery for both of us. *Isiyian!*"

"Cheers," she replied, and bravely downed a mouthful of her drink.

"Sip it slowly," he cautioned, a smile playing over his mouth when she almost choked on the stuff. "The night lies ahead, *agape mou*, and I'd rather you were sober enough to enjoy it with me."

"Me, too." She laughed ruefully. "I probably should have warned you ahead of time that I'm not much of a drinker."

"You don't have to tell me anything, Gina," he said quietly. "I already know everything I need to know about you, and that is that you please me very much, in every way."

Oh, dear heaven! He was intoxication enough, and never mind the alcohol!

"Actually," she began, prompted by conscience to divulge at least part of the truth, "you really don't know much about me at all. There are always hidden layers to people—motives and impulses and...*mysteries* that don't show on the surface. In my case, I came to Greece because—"

"Stop!" He covered her hand with his. Laced his fingers possessively around hers. "I already know why you came to Greece. More than that, I know you are beautiful from the inside out. I see passion in your lovely eyes. I hear music in your voice. I sense generosity and kindness in your spirit. For me, they are enough. The only mystery is why no other man has staked a claim to you before now, and for that I am deeply grateful."

"But, Mikos—"

"No. If you wanted to discourage me, you shouldn't have agreed to have dinner with me. You shouldn't have let me kiss you."

"Well, you haven't. Not tonight, anyway."

He laughed. "Not yet!" He clasped her hand more tightly. "Wipe away that anxious frown. I'm thirty-five, Gina. Old enough to know what I want. Experienced enough to see past the surface of the people I meet. Smart enough to recognize a gift when I'm presented with one."

"That might be, but—"

Again, he interrupted. "Do you think you know all my secrets?"

"No, of course not."

"Then why should I know all yours? Everyone has a past, *karthula mou*, and we have to live with the mistakes that are part of it. But today and tomorrow are ours to shape as we will."

She should have stopped him then. Explained that her circumstances didn't allow for much future planning. But somehow the difficulties and worries waiting for her at home seemed very far away just then, and in that respect, he was right.

Now, at this very moment, in this charming little restaurant with its flickering candles competing with the rising moon, and the metallic plink of a bouzouki drifting on the flower-scented night air, she did have choices. She could ask him to take her back to her hotel and forget he ever met her, or she could stay and let the man-woman nature of things run its course, limited though that might be.

She risked another glance at him. He was so handsome, so sure of himself; so completely at ease with her, with his world and his life. She knew she wasn't the first woman he'd pursued, and she wouldn't be the last. When she left to go back to Canada, he would kiss her goodbye with his heart intact. Was it then so very wrong of her to carve out a few indelible memories of her own now, to keep her going when the future seemed impossibly grim?

"Tell me the thoughts that make you look so solemn," he murmured, stroking her fingers.

Her decision made, she met his glance and smiled. "You called me *karthula mou*, and I'm wondering if I should take offence."

"I called you 'sweetheart,'" he said, his voice rough and deep. "My Gina. My sweetheart."

She knew it was anatomically impossible, but at that, her own heart seemed quite literally to turn over. Everything inside her swelled with emotion and filled her to overflowing. "You know," she said shakily, "I'm suddenly not very hungry, after all."

"You ate earlier?"

"No. I haven't had anything since last night."

"Then you will eat now. A glass of ouzo is no substitute for food." He took a chunk of bread and dipped it in the tzitiki. "Here, begin with this."

He was taking care of her, she realized, and it had been so

long since anyone had done that, that she found herself swallowing a sudden lump in her throat. Willing her emotions under control, she focused on the food.

"Well?" He eyed her sternly as she sampled the tzitiki.

"It's good," she said. "Better than good, in fact. The bread is wonderful."

"*Neh*. We Greeks love our bread. Now try a little calamari."

"What about you? Or are you just going to sit there and watch me eat?"

"Both," he told her, his eyes glinting with humor. "We are going to feast at leisure."

And feast they did, for the next three hours. Following the appetizers came Greek salad, made a little differently from the kind she was used to. Mikos ordered a bottle of excellent Boutari Moschofilero to go with their entrée, a pasta crayfish dish with a fabulous tomato sauce.

For dessert, he insisted she try the apricot and pistachio cake, which he claimed he was too full to enjoy, but he stole it anyway and fed her little bites in between those he took for himself. They had only one fork, and she found the intimacy of his drawing it slowly out of her mouth, then using it to spear another piece of cake for himself, incredibly erotic.

Finally they lingered over espresso and metaxa, the atmosphere between them simmering with the knowledge that although the meal might be drawing to an end, their night had only just begun.

"Will you come with me?" he asked, when at last they left the square.

She knew what he was asking. "Yes," she said, and placed her hand in his.

He drove the few short blocks to his apartment, except *that* was something of a misnomer since he occupied the entire top

floor of a handsome old building, which had been modernized without sacrificing any of its original charm.

From his foyer, painted cool white with framed abstract paintings providing the only splashes of color, she could see straight through the main living area to wide glass sliders beyond which lay a huge roof garden with its own small swimming pool. Tubs of ornamental lemon trees and flowering plants were scattered around the perimeter of the terrace, with two sun chaises set under a striped canvas canopy.

The interior of the place was elegantly finished with lovely old marble floors, and antique oak moldings around the doors and windows. The decor he'd chosen, eclectic and a reflection of flawless, expensive taste on his part, blended perfectly in these surroundings, as she discovered on closer inspection when he excused himself to answer the phone.

In the living room, deep, dark green leather couches were grouped around a heavy plate glass coffee table. A large screen television and stereo unit filled most of one wall. On either side, built-in shelves were crammed with books. Strategically placed brass reading lamps shed pools of warm amber light.

Through an open archway to the right, a glass dining table, eight high-backed chairs, and a wall cabinet filled with exquisite crystal stemware gleamed in the soft glow of recessed ceiling lights. And at every turn, magnificent panoramic views of the city and moonlit sea gave the sense of an aerie hovering midway between earth and sky.

Yet despite the luxury, the penthouse bore signs that it was a home as well as a high-rent address. A newspaper had slipped to the floor and spread its pages in disarray over the marble tiles, with a pair of black leather shoes abandoned next to it. A lightweight sweater hung over the back of one of the couches. A stack of opened mail filled a side table, which also held the pho-

tograph of a woman. From the clothes she wore and her hair-style, the picture was probably about thirty years old. Mikos's mother? Gina wondered, picking it up to examine it more closely, even to the extent of turning it over to see if anything written on the back might give a clue.

Almost as bad as looking under your hostess's teacup to see if she owns good china, her mother would have reproved, back in the days when such things had mattered to her.

Embarrassed at finding herself so blatantly cataloging the details of his private life, Gina replaced the photo and turned to the glass doors and the less personal aspect of the roof garden. What an idyllic retreat in the heart of the city! If she lived here, she'd never want to leave.

She wasn't aware that Mikos had come up behind her until he slid his arms around her waist and said, "The pool's not much good for swimming laps, but if you like, we can go for a cooling dip later on."

"I didn't bring a swimsuit," she said, her heart so aflutter, she could barely draw breath.

"And you wouldn't be wearing it, even if you had." He lifted her hair, which she'd worn loose, and trailed his lips over her nape. His nearness electrified her from head to toe and left every inch of her suspended in quivering expectation. Noticing, he murmured against her ear, "Are you afraid of me, Gina?"

"No," she whispered. "I'm afraid of myself, of the way you make me feel."

"And how is that, *karthula mou*?"

"Absolutely certain that I'm precisely where I want to be. When I'm with you, the rest of the world ceases to exist."

"I know," he said hoarsely. "I know. It is the same for me. It's been that way from the moment we met. Until now, I have been marking time, waiting for you, even though I knew neither

your name nor your face. Yet when I looked into your eyes, I recognized you immediately and, just like that, I felt complete."

Her breath caught. He'd found the words to capture exactly something that evaded logical explanation and yet was as real and tangible as the ground beneath their feet.

His arms tightened around her waist, drawing her body more snugly against his. He was powerfully aroused, pressing hard and big and strong against the softer contours of her bottom. "Will you let me love you, Gina?"

This is wrong, that damnably prudish voice of conscience chided. *You don't sleep with a man on a first date.*

But the truth was, wrong had never felt so right or good or wonderful.

Shut up! she retorted and turned within the circle of his arms to face Mikos. "Yes," she sighed. "Oh, yes please…."

They didn't talk after that, because there was no need for words when lips and tongues and hands spoke a different, more eloquent language. There was no awkwardness as they undressed each other. No hesitation in the way they discovered one another's bodies. Just a reverence that bordered on the spiritual. A familiarity that seemed to owe its roots to another time, another life together, long before this one began.

He was perfect. Impressively endowed in all the right places. Broad across the shoulder, deep in the chest, narrow in the waist and hips, magnificently erect and virile. His legs were long and smoothly muscled, the dark hair patterning his chest silky to the touch.

The first orgasm ripped through her as they stood amid their discarded clothes in the living room. He dipped his head and took her nipple gently between his teeth. At the same time, he touched her between her thighs, and she exploded. Sagged weakly against him and clung tight as the tremors shook her unmercifully.

He picked her up then and strode down a wide hallway to where he slept. Another space separated from the night by a wall of glass that flooded the room with moonlight. His bed, high and wide, stood in the middle of the floor, draped in white linens and piled high with pillows.

The mattress received her with a gentle sigh. Gave more distinctly when he joined her. He did then with his lips what he'd done with his fingers a moment before. Ignoring her faint murmur of surprise, he parted her legs, buried his mouth at her core, and played his tongue over her sensitized flesh. A second orgasm assaulted her then, this one so intense, she couldn't suppress a tiny scream.

He soothed her, running his hands over her flanks with long, easy strokes until she could breathe again, then pleasured her a third time, drawing her relentlessly to the brink of delirium. She heard herself begging him to come to her. Felt herself clawing at his shoulders, raking her fingernails over his back, thrashing her head from side to side in an agony of impatience that refused to be satisfied until he buried himself in her hot, clinging depths. Which he did, but not until he reached into the drawer of the bedside table and sheathed himself in a condom.

The minute he drove into her, the magnetic attraction that had brought them to this point arced and sparked and exploded around her. In a nanosecond, the entire universe was recreated. He possessed her so completely, with such unparalleled finesse, that she shattered again and again.

Locked in his embrace, she tasted the salt of sweat on his skin as he gave unstintingly to her what he labored to withhold from himself, and when, without warning, he brought her to another explosive climax, she thought she might die from the shock of it.

Whipped to a frenzy, she wept, she moaned, she cried out

his name. She wrapped her legs around his hips and held him fast against her. Finally, with an instinct foreign to anything she'd ever done before, she delivered the coup de grace, sliding her hands between their joined bodies to caress the heavy pouch of flesh between his legs.

At that, he let out a fractured groan. His body tensed briefly, then jerked uncontrollably as he drove into her again and again and again.

The calm that followed must be, she thought dazedly, like that which came after an earthquake that knocked the world slightly off its axis. Deafening in the silence of its aftermath. Numbing in its density.

Yet astonishingly, nothing had changed. The moon still beamed through the glass slider. The furniture remained exactly as it had stood before the upheaval. The pool still sent water reflections dancing over the ceiling.

But she was different.

She would never be the same again. Not just because he was a masterful, unselfish lover who'd taught her more about her body than she'd learned in her previous twenty-eight years and nine months, although he was certainly all that and then some, but because he didn't play games. He looked her straight in the eye and laid bare his desire without embellishing it with promises he couldn't keep. He used protection, and made no bones about the fact that he kept condoms beside his bed. He was what her ex-fiancé had never been: decent enough to recognize the truth, and strong enough not to hide from it.

How Paul had blatted on about *doing the right thing for you, Gina,* when what he really meant was he didn't want her mother cluttering up his marriage.

It wouldn't be fair for me to hold you to our engagement, he'd mourned, his saintly expression so transparently false that

she'd almost thrown up on the spot. *You have to put Maeve first. I can't ask you to commit to me, as well. It's breaking my heart, but I'm going to set you free from your promise to marry me.*

Thank you, Paul! she thought now. You'll never know the favor you conferred on me.

Sighing with pure contentment, she turned her head and looked at the man lying next to her, just to make sure she hadn't imagined him.

He was real enough, and staring right back at her, his eyes dark as jade. *"Itan katapliktiko!"* he said softly. "That was amazing!"

"Amazing," she echoed, burning his image forever in her heart.

She wasn't so naive as to think that they could be in love on such short acquaintance, or that what they shared could continue indefinitely. This was an interlude only, a rare and precious gift loaned by kindly gods. When it came time to give it back, Mikos's life would remain here, while hers lay on the other side of the world. But for however long it lasted, she would live every moment to the fullest. Savor every drop of sweetness, every moment of passion, every tender glance and quiet touch.

It would be enough, she told herself drowsily. It had to be. She'd rather know perfection for a little while, than settle for second best over a lifetime.

She had drifted off. Watching the even rise and fall of her breasts, Mikos marveled at how young she looked, with that little worried frown she sometimes wore softened by sleep.

Careful not to disturb her, he drew up the sheet to cover her. He'd rather she was awake. Time was precious and they had much to learn about one another. But the sweet thing wasn't used to the rhythm of Athens in summer, when sunset marked the start of evenings that frequently didn't end until dawn.

For himself, sleep was out of the question. The taste of her still lingered on his tongue. Her desperate, breathless little cries still echoed in his ears. When he closed his eyes, he could see again her slim, pale thighs, the triangle of silky hair at their juncture, the trusting way she opened for him.

Easing himself off the bed, he made his swift, silent way to the bathroom, turned on the shower and adjusted the water temperature until it almost ran cold. Watching her sleep had left him so painfully close to taking her again that just soaping himself almost made him come.

But it wasn't just her physical loveliness, or the sex, that he found irresistible. The fact was, everything about her enchanted him. Too much for him to dismiss her as just another romantic fling, quickly entered into, and just as quickly forgotten.

He loved her sometimes sharp tongue, and the way she unsheathed her claws when she felt under threat. It still made him laugh when he remembered her spitting out that she wasn't going to lie back and let him have his way with her in the back seat of what she'd so colorfully referred to as the *sexmobile*.

He loved how she'd scooped up the dog at the *kafenion* on Evia, and not given a damn about her evening gown dragging in the dust. He loved the look of concern he'd caught on her face when a young boy had run unsupervised down the docks at the crack of dawn, and how she'd relaxed only when she saw his grandfather following behind. Her beautiful body housed a beautiful heart and soul, the kind a man might learn to love if he wasn't careful.

Thee mou, could he be falling in love with her?

Shocked, he stood motionless, waiting for the sharp needles of the water to pummel his brain back to sanity. He was not on familiar terms with the word "love." "Like, respect, admire and lust after"—those he recognized and could deal with. But

apart from the first few years of his life, "love" had always eluded him. Not once since his mother's death had he known it. Not as a child, and not as a man. And except to her, never had he given it. The closest he'd come had been his devotion and gratitude to Angelo, the man who'd stepped in as father figure when no one else wanted the job.

So what the devil had come over him now, that he was suddenly ready to say "I love you," to a woman he'd had to have investigated before he could trust her enough to seduce her?

CHAPTER FIVE

GINA awoke to purple shadows lurking in the corner of a room she didn't immediately recognize, and a soft, persistent hum she couldn't identify. She ached all over, but pleasurably. Running her tongue over her lips, she found them slightly swollen, enough to bring back the memory of another mouth on hers. The skin on her face, her neck, her breasts and thighs burned a little, as if they'd been lightly scraped by very fine sandpaper. The cool cotton sheet covering her bore the unmistakable scent of a man and a woman and sex.

It came back to her then, all of it: Mikos carrying her to his bed, both of them naked; his voice vibrating deep and hypnotic in her ear; his hands bringing her to ecstasy; his jaw rasping over her in places she'd never thought to have a man put his tongue.

Her body's response to the memories was immediate and unmistakable. Heat uncoiled deep inside and shot the length of her. A spasm clenched low in her womb, sent aftershocks quivering over her nerve endings, and left her so wet and eager for him that she moaned his name aloud.

He didn't respond, and rising up in the bed, she realized she was quite alone. But a crack of light visible under a closed door, coupled with the sound she now recognized as the muted rush of a shower running full blast, told her where she'd find him.

His bathroom was huge. Larger than the bedroom in her first apartment. Luxuriously appointed with sparkling white fixtures, including a sunken soaker tub set in a windowed alcove that overlooked a private corner of the roof garden. A slab of polished black granite formed a long vanity. Everything else was finished in ivory marble, except for the walk-in shower stall's curved glass enclosure which, oddly, was free of steam at that moment, allowing her an unimpaired view of Mikos.

Unaware he had an audience, he faced away from her, standing under the pulsing jets with the water flattening his dark hair to his scalp, and sluicing over his shoulders to run in rivulets down his torso. Following their path, her gaze slid from his taut buttocks to his sculpted thighs.

She swallowed and drew in a sharp breath, the hunger that had driven her to spy on him so brazenly growing more voracious at the sight of such perfect symmetry of shape and structure. Dreamy as a sleepwalker, she stepped into the shower and announced herself by slipping her arms around him and pressing an openmouthed kiss to a small, star-shaped scar just above his left shoulder blade.

For a brief, electric second, he tensed, every bronze, muscled inch of him so motionless that she instantly regretted her audacity. But then he swung one hand behind him to cradle her bottom and pin her tight against his. With the other, he shoved her hand past his waist to his penis, risen hard and urgent against his belly.

Even though the water ran so tepid it was almost cool, he was hot to the touch. Hot and silky and throbbing, and so close to ejaculating that when she increased the pressure of her fingers just slightly, he started to come.

At that, he let out a deep-throated, primitive groan. In one swift, smooth move, he swung around, slid his hands under her

bottom, and hoisted her legs around his waist. Then, plastering her spine against the glass enclosure, he drove into her, hard and fast and repeatedly, spilling furiously the whole time.

At first, she felt his seed searing the tender skin of her inner thighs. Then all she felt was him, inside her where he belonged, invoking in her such blind, blissful oblivion that caution and possible consequences ceased to matter.

She contracted around him, her body racked by the explosive force of the spasms convulsing her. Her lungs burned. The blood thundered in her veins. She sank her teeth into his shoulder. And burst into jagged sobs from the torrent of emotion tearing her apart.

"Hush, *mana mou. S'agapo*," he panted, covering her with his big body as if to protect her from further assault. "Don't cry. Everything is all right."

She clung to him, tighter than a barnacle on a rock, too dazed to ask him to translate. Too shocked by the depth of her attraction to him. *Twenty-four hours is all it's been!* a distant, barely functioning part of her mind whimpered. *Don't let him matter this much. Stop caring about what he says.*

But she did care. More than just about anything else in her life. "I'm afraid," she said raggedly, sounding like a child confronted by the dark, and how could that possibly be, when the future had never been clearer? Her life didn't allow for this kind of diversion. She could not afford to forget that, even for a moment.

"Afraid of what, *karthula mou*?"

"That we're moving too fast. You're drawing me too deeply into your world, and I don't belong here. We need to talk, Mikos."

"Neh." He lowered her gently to the tiled floor, turned the control until the water ran hot, and when they'd showered, plucked an oversize bath sheet from the stack piled on a high glass shelf at the far end of the stall. "I'll make coffee, and we'll

watch the sun come up and say all that has to be said," he told her, wrapping her in the towel. "But this you must know. You don't need to be afraid. I am here. I'll take care of everything."

She knew it wasn't that simple and never would be, but he spoke with such authority that, for a little while, she was willing to suspend disbelief. Enough that she dried herself off, put on a thick terry robe like the one he wore, rolled back the sleeves, which hung a good six inches below her hands, and followed him to the kitchen.

Like all the other rooms, this one, too, gave access to the roof garden by a French door. All stainless steel efficiency, it was a bachelor's kitchen and showed little sign of use. The espresso machine was top-of-the line, as were the toaster, three-burner cooktop and large refrigerator. But if a woman wanted to roast a turkey, she'd have to find another place to do it, because he made do with a microwave oven which, she suspected, he used rarely and, even then, only to heat commercially prepared frozen foods.

"Don't you like to cook?" she asked.

He laughed. "Not in the least. Do you?"

"I've learned to like it. I've had to, and I think it's important that I tell you why."

"I want to hear, Gina" he told her. "Come sit with me in the garden and let's continue our mutual journey of exploration."

He pulled two chaises close to the edge of the pool. Already, the sky was turning from midnight-blue to dusty-mauve. Soon, early sunlight would glitter on the sea, and another day begin. Drawing up her feet and tucking them under the hem of her robe, she leaned back in her seat, her coffee cup nestled warmly between her hands.

"So," he began, lounging next to her, "where do we start? With you, or with me?"

"With me," she said, so anxious to spill the truth about herself that she couldn't get the words out fast enough. "The thing is, Mikos, I've sort of...misled you. I *am* here to write an article, but it's a one-time assignment only. I no longer work at the magazine, and haven't for several years. So I'm not exactly who you think I am. I tried to tell you this at the restaurant last night, but you didn't want to hear and I confess I was relieved. I wanted nothing to spoil the evening."

"I see," he said.

But he didn't. She knew from the sudden reserve in his voice, and from the way he stared out at the view, that the distance between him and her stretched much farther than the few inches literally separating them. If a cool breeze had sprung up out of nowhere, she could not have felt its chill more keenly.

He drained his coffee cup and set it down with a staccato click on a glass-topped side table. "This truth you speak of appears to weigh heavily on your mind. If so, you should have insisted on revealing it, regardless of whether or not I might like what I heard."

"I didn't think you'd understand."

"Try me," he said, ice chips coating the words.

She gulped, swamped in all kinds of useless regret. It wasn't fair that her mother had been struck down by such a wicked disease. It wasn't fair that money played such a critical role in the decisions she had to make. It wasn't fair to be blindsided by such a powerful attraction to this man, and not be able to run with it and see where it led. Plainly put, life wasn't fair! "I hardly know where to start."

"The beginning is usually a good place."

Not in this case. She wasn't going to earn sympathy or understanding by going back to the real beginning. That would have to wait until she'd laid the groundwork for her motives.

"Okay," she said baldly. "I'm not a magazine reporter anymore because I run a small bed-and-breakfast operation."

Clearly expecting something much more nefarious, he spared her a quick, surprised glance. "By yourself?"

"Yes."

"Isn't that a lot for one person to take on?"

"Yes."

"But you enjoy it?"

"No," she said.

"Then why continue with it? More to the point, why try to hide what you really do?"

"Because of a promise I made to my mother," she said.

"What sort of promise compels a grown woman to lie about the way she earns a living?" he asked harshly. "It's not as if you're operating a whorehouse."

"I might be a grown woman, but my mother…isn't. Not anymore." She stopped, her throat thick suddenly. Sharing the details of her mother's deterioration seemed the ultimate betrayal of the woman whose dignity had been eroded by a vicious illness until she'd been left with nothing.

I can't do this, Gina thought, flinching mentally at the prospect. *Then get out of this chair, find your clothes, and walk away from this man and don't look back,* her conscience invoked. *At least then, your integrity will remain intact, even if your heart is shredded. But stop playing both ends against the middle. Either he's every bit as wonderful as you think he is and will take what you tell him in stride, or he isn't. Make up your mind which it is.*

She closed her eyes, a brief and bitter war raging within her. She'd given him reason not to trust her. Did that make it right that she not trust him, when he'd given her no reason to doubt him? "The thing is, Mikos," she said in a low voice, "my mother is in the advanced stages of Alzheimer's disease."

He uttered a shocked murmur of sympathy and reached for her hand. "And *that* is your secret? Ah, Gina, how could you think I wouldn't understand?"

"Not everyone does."

"I'm not 'everyone,' *agape mou*. Indeed I'm probably better able to appreciate your sad situation than most. Through no fault of her own, my mother became an outcast among the people who'd known her as a child. A lawyer, living here in Athens when Greece was under the rule of the dictator Papadopoulos, she was openly critical of the regime and ended up in prison where she was raped by one of the guards."

"Dear God!" Gina clapped a hand to her mouth in shock. "Was the perpetrator held to account?"

He shook his head. *"Ohi.* Shortly after, she was released and returned to her ancestral village, but was ostracized by her neighbors when it became clear she was pregnant. With the help of an old midwife, she gave birth to me in the little house she'd inherited from her parents. As a child, I remember seeing her work from dawn to dusk at menial tasks to make enough money to put food on our table. When I grew older, I helped after school by cultivating the patch of land around our house. I was fourteen when she died, and I left that village without a single backward glance, so much did I hate the people living there for what they'd put her through."

"Then you *do* understand."

"Completely." He stroked her arm, his touch warm and reassuring. "When did your mother's illness start?"

"We don't know for sure, but probably about six years ago. I was living in Vancouver at the time, in a loft in Yaletown, but I loved the island where I grew up and went back often to visit. My grandmother, who lived with us all my life, had died the year before, and when I first noticed my mom wasn't quite

herself, I put it down to loneliness and delayed grief. In fact, we laughed together at some of the things she did."

She stopped, engulfed in memories of a time when laughter had been such a big part of their lives.

You're wearing your shoes on the wrong feet, Mom!

So I am! No wonder they don't feel right....

Be careful, Mom, you'll burn your hand! Use an oven mitt to take the cake out of the oven.

Well, for heaven's sake, of course! What was I thinking...?

"She lived alone after your grandmother's death? Your father—?"

"Was a commercial fisherman and drowned at sea off the northwest coast of Vancouver Island, the winter I turned eighteen."

"Thee mou! Your family has seen its share of trouble and heartache!"

"Yours, too," she said. "At least my mother's enjoyed more good years than bad. She and my father had a wonderful marriage. I grew up in a very happy home, with two terrific parents and a grandmother I adored. I can't imagine the horror of what your mother went through, or how it must have been for you, growing up without a father."

"It was better that I didn't know him. I would have killed him for what he did to her."

"Even so, a boy needs a father figure, but it sounds as if no one in your village was willing to step forward and take on the job."

He laughed, a sound rich with amusement and not a little irony. "Have I turned out so very badly, *agape mou*?"

"You know that's not what I mean. I think you're amazing in every way, and the credit lies with you and your mother."

"Not entirely," he confessed. "In fact, I did have a mentor. After my mother died, I left our village and came to Athens. I was big for my age, and looked much older than fourteen, so I

was able to find work helping paint offices. That's how I met Angelo Tyros."

Oh, please! she thought, revulsion skittering over her on hearing the man's name. *Please* don't tell me *he* stepped up to the plate on your behalf!

Not privy to her reaction, Mikos continued, "He took an interest in me. Thought it a shame that a bright boy was working with his hands when he should be working with his brain. We struck a deal: he would give me a place to live, and in return, I would complete high school, and in my spare time, help out with maintenance and gardening at his house. At that time, he lived with his third wife in Kiffisia, a very pleasant area with lots of trees, several kilometers from the city center. Until I saw it, I had no idea such opulence existed."

"How long did you stay with him?"

"Several years. Much longer than I'd anticipated when I agreed to his terms. I took the school leaving exam that summer and started classes at the university in the autumn."

"Which he paid for?"

"He didn't have to. In Greece, university is free, provided you're an outstanding student and know the right people. I was lucky. My marks were good enough, and Angelo had the connections. But I still needed a place to live, and he was a generous benefactor. I stayed in his home and was treated like one of the family, until I completed my degree."

"Is that why you work for him now?"

"Yes, and no. After I graduated and completed a tour of duty in the air force—national service is still compulsory in Greece—he took me into his business and taught me well. If I'm successful today, it's thanks to him. "

"So you feel obligated to him?"

He shrugged. "There's no question that I owe Angelo more

than I can ever hope to repay. In effect, he took the place of the
father I didn't know as a child, and perhaps in some measure, I
filled the emptiness in his heart left by his son's death. But it's
also fair to say that, for the most part, I find my work stimulat-
ing and fulfilling, and have no wish to seek other opportunities."

His words left her numb with dismay, and something of it
must have shown in her expression. Misunderstanding the
reason, he brushed his hand down her cheek and said, "But
enough about my life. Tell me more about yours."

More, yes. But now that she fully understood how much
Angelo Tyros meant to him, she could never tell him every-
thing, and the knowledge filled her with such despair that, for
a moment, she simply stared at him, bereft of words.

"How long before you learned something more serious was
wrong with your mother?" he prompted.

Pulling herself together, she answered, "Almost a year. We
both realized her forgetfulness was past being a joke when her
telephone was cut off because she hadn't paid the bill for over
four months."

"What did you do then?"

"Consulted our family doctor, who ran some preliminary
tests, then sent us to Vancouver for confirmation of what he sus-
pected. The results were conclusive and, as you can imagine,
totally devastating."

"Especially because she had no one to turn to but you."
He nodded understandingly. "And this, in turn, led to the
promise you made?"

"Yes. It had to do with our house, which sits right on the
beach, looking across Georgia Strait to the mainland moun-
tains. Every good thing that ever happened to her, happened
there. She was born in the big bedroom facing east, in the iron
bed her great-grandmother brought with her from Ireland in

1896. She married my father on the lawn, under the wisteria pergola. His ashes and my grandmother's are scattered in the rose garden.

"At the time I gave her my word, she was still able to understand the progression of the disease, and knew the day would come when she couldn't live alone, but the thought of having to leave her home and her beloved island, and be placed in a residential facility under the care of strangers, terrified her. 'I'd rather be dead,' she told me, and it wasn't just a melodramatic turn of phrase. She meant it."

"So you promised her you wouldn't allow that to happen."

"Yes. Apart from all the other considerations, it's thought that keeping Alzheimer's patients in familiar surroundings, among familiar things and faces, might slow down the rate at which the disease takes over their lives."

"And so far, you've honored your word?"

She went to answer, but the stark reality of the situation crept up on her unawares and, as it so often had in the past several weeks, slapped her hard in the face. She choked on the words struggling to emerge, and burying her face in her hands, burst into tears.

His arms came around her, warm and solid and strong, and lifted her bodily out of the chaise and onto his lap. *"Min cles, glikia mou,"* he murmured, stroking her hair. "Don't cry, my Gina. Tell me, instead, how I can help you."

"You can't," she sobbed. "Only God can do that, and He's not listening anymore!"

He lifted the hem of her bathrobe and mopped her face with it. "You're afraid you must renege on your promise?"

She nodded and started crying all over again.

"Why is that, *agape mou?"*

"I can't keep her safe anymore. I'm going to have to do the

one thing she begged me not to do and put her in a home, and it's killing me."

"You're sure this is your only option?"

"I'm afraid so. Not today or tomorrow, perhaps, but very soon. Our doctor spelled it out very succinctly. She's only going to get worse from here on, and looking after her is more than I can handle alone."

What Sam Irving had actually said was, *What you're trying to do is humanly impossible, woman! Cooking, cleaning and running a B&B is already a full-time job, and never mind the hours you spend maintaining that rambling old house of yours. You can't be up a ladder, cleaning out gutters or painting siding, and look after your mother as well. She's a full-time job in herself—even for a trained professional.*

"Then it would seem clear you need round-the-clock help," Mikos reasoned. "Hiring a team of private nurses would ease the burden on you, and give you peace of mind."

That takes money which I don't have, she could have told him, but she wasn't about to make such an admission to a man she'd just slept with, especially not one as obviously well-off as Mikos. It smacked too much of soliciting in return for sexual favors.

"Yes, that was the other choice our doctor mentioned, but when I said I didn't think my mother would accept a stranger in our home, he thought the only way to find out was for me to step out of the picture for a while, and give it a try." She grimaced self-consciously. "He thinks I'm too stressed out to make any major decisions right now. *Take a break or risk a breakdown,* were his exact words."

"So that's what persuaded you to come here on assignment? For the chance to occupy your mind with something else, and try to view the situation more objectively?"

No, Mikos! My intentions are much more devious than that.

"More or less," she replied evasively.

"Well, your doctor's right. Whatever your next move, it has to be something you can live with for the rest of your life. So I propose to follow his advice and take your mind off your troubles for a few hours. Today, Athens is yours to discover." He hoisted her off his lap and slapped her playfully on the bottom. "Get yourself dressed, woman, before my good intentions are overcome by baser instincts."

"I'd feel better if I could phone home first, just to make sure everything's running smoothly over there."

"Mana mou," he replied soothingly, "you may call home as often as you please. While you are my guest, my telephone is yours to use whenever you need it."

After such painful self-revelations, she wouldn't have thought she could put aside her worries, but Mikos was as good as his word. Once reassured that all was well on the homefront, she put herself entirely in his hands.

Although he drove to the bottom of Lycabettus Hill, they walked the rest of the way. Central Athens, she discovered, was easily covered on foot. They began with fruit and toast and coffee at an outdoor café under the looming hulk of the Acropolis. After, they wandered the tiny, winding streets of the Plaka, which were full of street musicians, flower sellers and photographers.

A knowledgeable and entertaining guide, he showed her famous landmarks no tourist should miss: the Tower of the Winds, the Mosque on the grounds of the Roman Agora, the doorway of Medrese, which was all that was left of a theological school founded in 1721, the Monument to Lysikrates, and of course, the Acropolis itself and the Parthenon.

When she began to wilt from the heat, he steered her to a *kafenion* in a little park, with tables set out under the trees, and bought her a *frappeh meh trio,* iced coffee with milk and sugar, although he settled for his usual potent espresso.

They lazed in the shaded heat, sipping their drinks and watching the people strolling by.

"See the old men at the next table?" he said, with a wink. "They're complaining that it's a public disgrace for young women to show off so much skin, but what they're really doing is ogling the short skirts and tight jeans, and wishing they were young enough to chase after those girls over there."

But Gina only had eyes for him. His face, touched by the sun, seemed cast in ancient copper. His smile, by comparison, dazzled her with its brilliance. She felt like the luckiest woman in all of Athens that he'd chosen to spend his Sunday with her.

Toward noon, they followed the crowds to the Monastiraki Flea Market, a colorful mix of small shops catering to tourists and locals alike, and an old-fashioned flea market selling everything from antiques to plain old junk. And all the time, he held her hand and flirted outrageously with her. Most of all, he made her laugh.

At one point, they turned into a narrow alley where very poor people were buying and selling from piles of rags on an open stall. Nearby, a group of barefoot gypsy children played with a beaten-up soccer ball. One boy gave it kick and it landed at Mikos's feet. Without missing a beat, he kicked it right back and, for the next ten minutes, joined in their game. At the end, he flung a handful of euros on the dusty ground, which they fell on with cries of delight.

"Poor little beggars," he said soberly, coming back to where Gina waited. "They have nothing, but right now, they're on top of the world. It takes so little to make them happy."

* * *

"If you could have just one wish—one that has nothing to do with your mother or her illness, what would it be?" he asked, as the afternoon drew toward evening.

With an impulsiveness rare in her, she said, "That this day might never end."

For a moment, he was silent, his gaze solemn, his expression thoughtful. "Well, it must, of course," he finally replied, "but that's no reason for there not to be a tomorrow, or a day after that."

"I'm not sure I follow you," she said, not daring to believe what she thought he meant.

"You're here for a few weeks only, *mana mou*, and the time will pass soon enough. Why waste them apart, when we can spend them together? Give up your room at the hotel and move in with me, Gina. Let me give you a holiday you'll never forget, something to sustain you when you go back home. I can't make your troubles disappear, but I can make you forget them for a little while. What do you say? Will you take a chance on me? On us?"

CHAPTER SIX

SHE stared at him, appalled. "How can you even suggest such a thing? No self-respecting woman moves in with a man she's known less than forty-eight hours."

"Isn't it a bit late in the day to be worrying about propriety? We've already—"

"I know what we've already done," she said, cutting him off before he spelled it out in colorful detail for everyone else at the park to hear, "but there's a big difference between that and setting up house together, even if it is just a temporary arrangement."

"There is?" He feigned wide-eyed astonishment. "Explain it to me, then, because your point escapes me."

"For a start, we don't know one another well enough."

"How much better can a couple get to know one another than in the raw honesty that comes of sharing the most intimate experience possible between a man and a woman?"

She glanced around furtively. "If you insist on talking about sex," she hissed, "at least have the decency to lower your voice!"

"I'm not talking about sex," he retorted in tones resonating with enough conviction to keep the whole of Athens informed. "I'm talking about making love. Sex doesn't engage one's emotions, and is soon over and done with. A man moves on to the next conquest—a woman, too. Can you look me in the eye

and tell me that, after all we shared last night, you're prepared to walk away from me?"

"N-no," she stammered, the truth emerging despite the fact that she was dying of embarrassment. If the people sitting at the next table understood English...!

"Then where's the problem?" Mikos persisted. "Why can't we continue to enjoy one another?"

If she told him she was afraid, he'd ask why, and how could she possibly explain without sounding like a naive fool? How to tell him that, in the space of two short days, she'd experienced greater joy with him, a more profound sense of fulfillment, a more binding emotional connection, than anything she'd known in the two years that she'd fancied herself in love with her ex-fiancé?

Obviously, with Mikos, it *wasn't* love. It couldn't be, not this soon or quickly. Love didn't strike out of nowhere like sudden, random lightning, without regard for its victims.

Or did it?

She slewed a glance at him, forcing herself to rationalize the irrational. That she was unquestionably intoxicated by him spoke for itself. But why? What made him so compelling and irresistible that the more she saw of him, the more potent his appeal?

Yes, he was about as perfect a male specimen as ever walked the face of the earth, but surely she wasn't so shallow as to be bowled over by a handsome face and hot body? And yes, he was strong and self-assured and overwhelmingly masculine, but so were a lot of other men. He might have been blessed with a voice as dark as sin and smooth as whipped cream, but that didn't account for her being equally besotted with him when he wasn't saying a word. So precisely what *was* it that made him unique?

The answer struck, swift and straight as an arrow finding its

target. He acted as if he cared about her. About *her!* When she talked about her mother, he paid attention and didn't try to minimize the gravity of the situation or its outcome. He understood her concerns and responded to them with kindness and compassion. And in doing all that, he struck right at the most vulnerable heart of her.

She was entirely too susceptible to his particular brand of charm. Was it any wonder the word "love" crept past her defenses, despite her best efforts to reject it?

"I see the wheels spinning in your mind, Gina," he said, bathing her in the warmth of his gaze. "Talk to me. Tell me what you're thinking."

"That you're the nicest man I've ever met," she said impulsively.

"Prove it. Spend your holiday with me."

She went to sigh, more tempted than he could begin to guess, and ended up smothering a yawn instead. "I'll think about it, but right now what I most want is to lie down for an hour or two. The heat is really getting to me, and I'm suddenly very tired."

"Okay." He ran the pad of his forefinger up her arm with devastating effect. "But don't take too long to reach a decision, *karthula mou*. Time isn't on our side."

As it turned out, the decision was pretty much made for her because, when he took her back to her hotel, they learned that her room had been flooded by a guest on the floor above who'd let his bathtub overflow. The ceiling had collapsed in places, the room was uninhabitable, just about all her clothes had been ruined and stuffed in a plastic garbage bag, with what had been salvaged dumped in a cardboard box because her suitcase was unusable.

Worse, "We have no other rooms available," the manager explained, wringing his hands apologetically. "As you're already aware, we are a small hotel, Ms. Hudson, and fully booked for

the next two weeks. As it is, I must turn away guests expected tonight. But I will gladly phone around and try to find you other accommodation, if you wish."

Not bothering to consult her, Mikos took over. "No need," he declared. "Ms. Hudson will stay with me."

Visibly relieved, the manager pushed a sheet of paper toward her. "Then please, before you go, be so kind as to put a value on the list of items destroyed, and our insurance company will send you a check to cover their replacement. And we will, of course, arrange to reimburse you for the remaining time you expected to be here."

"That's all very fine and dandy," she replied, dismayed. "But what do I do in the meantime?"

"You let me take care of you," Mikos put in. "We'll go shopping and I will buy you what you need."

"You certainly will not!" she snapped.

Her decision to fly to Greece had been spur-of-the-moment, the action of a woman left with so few other options that she couldn't afford to be proud. Money was tight, and she'd come prepared to do whatever she had to—for her mother. Beg, browbeat, blackmail, as long as she could provide well for her parent, it was all the same to her. But not for a minute was she willing to accept hand-outs for herself.

"Be sensible, Gina," he said. "You need a few essentials to see you through your holiday, and I can well afford it."

Did she have any other choice? she wondered savagely, examining the meager contents of the box the manager retrieved from a back room. Either she did as Mikos suggested, or she walked around in nothing but what was left of her underwear, one soggy evening sandal and her jewelry. The remainder of her stuff, including her evening gown, was past saving. At that point, about the only thing she had to be

grateful for was that her airline tickets and passport were stashed in the hotel safe.

The magazine had prepaid her hotel, she'd used air miles points for travel. She'd stopped using credit cards when she couldn't pay off the balance each month and was stuck with exorbitant interest charges.

Even if she'd brought her checkbook with her, which she hadn't, the balance in her account was down to a couple of hundred dollars because she'd had to pay Lynn up-front to take care of her mom. Granted, Lorne had given her an advance on the magazine article, but she was loath to dip into that until she knew she'd earned it.

She'd have to cancel her planned tour of the islands, but that she could handle. What she couldn't and wouldn't do was abandon her main reason for coming to Greece in the first place. Not until she'd exhausted all possibilities.

"Come on, Gina," Mikos urged, glancing impatiently over her shoulder as she noted the value of the items she'd lost. "Stop making something out of nothing. The only problem here is the one you're concocting in your mind. We've got better things to do than waste time standing around arguing over the trifling matter of a few hundred euros."

Heaving a disgruntled sigh, she said, "All right. I'll accept a loan, but only for the amount I'll get back from the insurance company—plus interest. I absolutely insist on that, Mikos, or there's no deal."

"As you wish." Collecting her box of possessions, he strong-armed her back to the flea market. "Nothing much else is open on Sunday, but we'll find something here that'll see you through until the boutiques open tomorrow."

"I don't shop at boutiques," she informed him. "They don't exactly fit my lifestyle, these days."

Guiding her to a little shop selling a variety of fairly cheap clothing, he said, "We'll see about that."

If she could have summoned up the energy, she'd have challenged him on such an ambiguous remark, but realistically, she could afford to splurge a little and still stay within the amount she'd receive from the insurance company, and she was frankly too tired to go another round with him. Their exchange at the hotel might have been brief, but it had been enough for her to realize that he didn't take kindly to being opposed.

Rummaging among a rack of broomstick skirts, he selected one in vibrant shades of red, orange and yellow on a black background, and held it up for her inspection. "What do you think of this? Will it fit you?"

"Probably. These are usually one-size-fits-all items."

"How about this to go with it?" He removed an embroidered black cotton blouse from a hanger and draped it over her shoulder.

"It's…nice."

In fact, she found it strange having a man pick out clothing, especially one showing such a good eye for what suited her. Her father had been away much of the time when she was growing up, so the time he had spent at home hadn't been wasted on shopping sprees, and Paul never had shown the slightest interest in hitting the stores with her.

Leaving the skirt and blouse with the salesclerk, Mikos said, "Okay, then the only other thing we need is lingerie."

There was no "we" about it! Having him pick out panties and a bra was pushing it too far, even if he had seen her without any clothes at all. "Thanks! I'll get by with what survived the flood, at least until tomorrow," she declared, clutching the box containing her few remaining possessions as if it held the British crown jewels.

"Okay, I'll pay for this, then I'm taking you home for a *mesi-meriani anapafsi*."

"What's that?" she inquired nervously.

He laughed. "A siesta. As I told you before, they're a part of life in Greece, during the summer."

Not in her life, though, she thought, stifling another yawn. Not in the afternoon and recently, not always at night, either. Ever since her mother had wandered, at the most inappropriate moment imaginable, into the bedroom occupied by guests on their honeymoon, Gina always seemed to sleep with one eye open.

The prospect of snoozing, worry free, through the worst heat of what had been a long and tiring day, held enormous appeal. Apart from a brief nap just before dawn, she hadn't slept since Mikos had dropped her off at her hotel, yesterday, and her internal clock was in an uproar. "A siesta sounds wonderful. In fact, I could probably sleep straight through to morning."

"But you won't," he said confidently, walking her back to where he'd left the car. "After four or five hours, you'll be ready to dance the night away with me."

At the time, the possibility seemed remote, to say the least, but waking alone just after eight that evening, she realized nothing was impossible where Mikos was concerned. After they returned to the penthouse, he'd fed her sliced oranges and sweet black grapes, then taken her to bed and made slow, tender love to her. She'd fallen asleep in his arms, drugged with pleasure.

Opening her eyes now to the blades of the ceiling fan spinning lazily overhead, and the dying sun filling the room with lambent golden light, she was filled with such a sense of completion and utter contentment that she had to pinch herself to be sure she wasn't dreaming.

This wasn't real life, she remind herself sternly. Mikos had

swept her into a holiday romance which, by definition, was a transient thing, and transported her to a world very far removed from what she was used to. But it was hers only for a little while.

Wrapping the sheet around her, sari-style, she trailed through the penthouse looking for him and found him on the phone in the living room. Upon seeing her, he abruptly ended the call. "I didn't hear you come in," he said, avoiding her gaze. "You don't need to creep around, afraid to make a sound. Treat the place as your home."

If she hadn't known better, she'd have said he looked guilty as a boy caught with his fingers in the cookie jar. But then he smiled and her suspicion melted away. What, after all, had he to be guilty about, when she was the one keeping secrets?

"So here you are!"

Surprised, Mikos glanced up from the schematic he'd been studying, and found Angelo standing in the doorway. Springing up from behind the desk, he hurried to help the old man to a chair at the other end of his office. "*Yassou!* What are you doing still hanging around the office this late on a Monday afternoon? I expected you'd be halfway to Evia by now."

"Figured it was time I found out when you started keeping secrets from me, that's what."

"I haven't a clue what you're talking about."

Angelo snorted. "You've been head of security long enough to know that nothing happens around these parts that I don't get to hear about, so stop playing games with me, Mikolas. I'm told you disappeared from the party on Friday night. With a woman. No one saw hide nor hair of you over the weekend. You didn't go to Petaloutha—I know, because I checked—which leads me to assume you spent the time here. With her. And that tells me something's up, because you dislike the city in summer

and normally can't wait to leave it behind the minute the work week ends. So who is she?"

"No one you'd be interested in."

"I might be eighty, but I'm not yet blind or senile. If she's the reason for that sappy grin on your face, I'm very interested. Bring her to the house for dinner tomorrow night so I can look her over and decide if she's good enough for you."

Oh, she was good enough! Prompted by the doubts he'd entertained when he learned she hadn't been as straightforward with him as he'd first believed, he'd ordered a second investigation. The report had come in less than an hour ago from their Vancouver agent, confirming everything she'd told him.

"You might be my boss, Angelo," he replied, a spark of resentment tarnishing his euphoria, "but that doesn't entitle you to dictate how I spend my time off."

"It did when you were a snot-nosed kid scraping to get by. You were glad enough then to let me take charge."

"I'd say twenty-one years of unswerving allegiance on my part more than evens the score."

"Meaning what?" Angelo glared, his black eyes snapping. "That you can do without me? That just because you're old enough to vote, I'm supposed to stop caring about you? That's not how it works, Mikos. I thought you knew that."

"Old enough to vote?" He burst out laughing. "Come on, Angelo, that's stretching it a bit, even for you! I'm thirty-five, for God's sake."

"And smart enough, or so I've always thought, to play the field without getting in too deep with a passing fancy. Or am I wrong? Is this woman different from the ones who went before?"

Mikos scratched his head, in truth as mystified as the old man. He *was* behaving out of character. As well as being a powerhouse in his own right within the Tyros empire, he had the

reputation of being a man with a talent for avoiding romantic entanglement. Yet Gina had captivated him from the outset. He wasn't just entangled with her, he was obsessed! "Yeah, she's different."

"How?"

"Damned if I know," he admitted sheepishly. "She just is."

"Is she local?"

"No. Not even Greek."

"Then how did she get past the door at the Grande Bretagne?"

"She was covering the event for a Canadian magazine."

A shadow passed fleetingly across Angelo's face. "Canadian, huh? A long way to come for one evening's entertainment, wouldn't you say?"

"I thought so, too, at first, but she's combining it with a holiday. And face it, Angelo, you're something of a celebrity in that part of the world. Stealing a Toronto millionaire's fiancée out from under his nose twenty years ago made headline news over there at the time."

"Marrying her was the worst mistake I ever made," Angelo muttered. "The woman was a slut. I should have let him have her. *Thee mou*, she made a pass at you, a kid of fifteen who was living in my house under my protection!"

Mikos rolled his eyes at the reminder. She wasn't the first woman he'd seen naked, but she was the first to corral him in a deserted corner of the garden where he'd been trimming dead blooms from a shrub, and lift her dress to show him she wasn't wearing underpants. He'd damn near cut off his hand in shock!

"You don't need to worry that Gina's like that. She's as straightforward and aboveboard as any woman you could ask to meet."

"Which, as I understand it, won't happen any time soon, if you have *your* way. Or have I shamed you into changing your mind about bringing her to Evia tomorrow?"

He should have known Angelo wouldn't take no for an answer. It wasn't his style. And if it meant that much to him, why refuse? Mikos knew the old man was lonely, and Gina had already expressed an interest in meeting him face-to-face. "I'll ask her and get back to you in the morning."

Angelo grimaced and struggled to his feet. *"Yia to onoma to Theo,* you're in sad shape, if you have to ask! Try telling her, instead! Tomorrow night at nine. I'm counting on you, Mikolas. Don't disappoint me."

"A command performance dinner at his house tomorrow?"

"We don't have to go, if you'd rather not." Mikos shrugged philosophically. "Angelo's always been demanding, but—"

"No," Gina said, her heart leaping in her throat. "I'd like to go, really."

"You're sure?"

"Quite sure," she said, tamping down on the guilt souring what should have been her moment of triumph. *This* was why she'd come to Greece: to confront the man who'd turned his back on her grandmother. If guilt had to enter the picture, there was enough to go around for Angelo Tyros to take the giant's share.

Mikos braced his hands on either side of her shoulders, pinning her against the side of the pool, and kissed her. *"Parakalo, karthula mou.* He's a lonely old man who's trying very hard to keep up with the doings of the people he cares about because he thinks they'll forget all about him, if he doesn't."

He's a hard-hearted bastard who doesn't give a rap about anyone but himself, Gina thought, but wisely kept it to herself. Whatever her beef with Tyros, it appeared he'd shown some humanity where Mikos was concerned.

Mikos nuzzled her neck "I missed you today."

"I missed you, too," she said.

"I'm sorry I was away so long. There's always a lot to catch up on after the weekend."

"You don't have to apologize. I understand you've got a job to do, and can't be entertaining me all the time." She bit her lip, guilt of another kind sweeping over her. "You know, it really would make more sense for me to move into a hotel. I'm a distraction you don't need, and we could still see one another, if—"

But he was adamant in his refusal to consider the idea. "Stop right there, Gina! The subject is not up for discussion. As long as you're in Greece, you're staying with me, and that's final."

Was she selfish to be glad?

Unwilling to face the answer, she turned aside from the question and salved her conscience by saying, "But I'm imposing on your time and taking advantage of you."

"I came home tonight to find chilled ouzo and a tray of *mezedes* waiting on the terrace. And you, in a *mailot* that takes my breath away." He ran his finger under the strap of her bathing suit and pulled it down to bare her breast. "So tell me, *agape mou*, how are you taking advantage of me?"

"Well, of your generosity, then," she said faintly, glad that the water kept her buoyant because, with just a touch, he turned her so weak with need that she could barely remain upright.

He pressed closer, and hushed her with his mouth. "Why are you still wearing this, when I am naked as a newborn?" he murmured against her lips, stripping her suit down her limbs and tossing it onto the pool deck.

At once, the hard thrust of his arousal nudged against her belly, hot and sleek and urgent.

More than anything, she wanted to open her legs and possess him, but he teased her by climbing out of the pool for the contraceptive he'd had the foresight to leave close by.

She whispered his name on a plea, wanting him desper-

ately. Understanding, he slipped back into the water and stroked his finger between the slick folds of her flesh, seeking out the sensitized nub at her center.

She tensed, her body clenching painfully. He stroked again, more insistently. And what had started as a whisper in the back of her throat erupted into an anguished cry as she climaxed helplessly. Then, while the spasms still shook her, he slid inside her and held himself there, immobile.

"This," he said huskily, his beautiful light green eyes in stark contrast to the dense, black fringe of his lashes, "is what generosity is really all about, my Gina—you giving yourself to me so trustingly, and asking nothing in return but to let me please you."

"But I want to please you, too, Mikos," she murmured brokenly.

"You do," he assured her. "In everything you are and in everything you do, you please me very much."

Behind him, a persimmon sunset stained the sky. She closed her eyes against its brilliance, too overcome to reply. What, after all, was there to say, when no words existed to do justice to the moment—no words except, *I love you!* and she would not, dare not, utter them.

He moved. Tightened his hold and rocked against her. Slowly at first, then with increasing urgency. His breath rasped against her cheek. His heart thundered against her breast.

She wrapped her arms around his neck. Let her legs float up to lock around his waist. Felt the distant tremors of another climax and welcomed them. Reveled in the knowledge that he was coming, too; that they were united as one in every sense of the word, both hurtling through space, each clinging to the other, as if only by doing so did they have the least hope of surviving the glory of the moment.

"S'agapo!" he panted against her neck, his body shuddering mightily. *"S'agapo, psihula mou!"*

Later that evening, he sat across from her at a taverna within walking distance of his penthouse and said, "What did you do with yourself all day?"

"Discovered more of Athens. I spent several hours in the National Gallery, and did a little shopping. But," she was quick to add, "I didn't spend much—just enough to take care of a few basics."

A frown crossed his face. "I wish you'd stop doing that."

"Doing what?"

"Justifying buying things you need. It's just money."

Just money, yes—but when you didn't have any, it ruled your every waking minute. "Nevertheless, I won't take advantage of your generosity. It's enough that you're offering me hospitality."

He stroked his foot up her calf. "But look what I'm getting in return!"

"Well, you're not paying me for it! I'm not your kept woman!"

Without actually moving a muscle, his body underwent a complete transformation. His spine turned to steel, and the mouth that so easily seduced her with tenderness, flattened forbiddingly. Outrage flared in his eyes which, though still green, no longer sparkled with laughter but instead were glazed in Arctic ice. "For your information, my dear, prostitution is legal in Greece. I can take my pick from any number of willing professionals in the Red Light district, without having to invite her into my home."

"I didn't mean it like that," she said, stricken.

He glared at her, all injured male pride with a healthy dose of Greek arrogance thrown in for good measure. "No? How did you mean it, then?"

She quaked inside. He was so angry, he looked almost pale under his tan. "Oh, Mikos, I'm sorry, truly I am," she murmured, touching his hand. "I know you mean well, and I so much appreciate your kindness, but I'm just not comfortable accepting money from a man. It makes me feel cheap and...well, *cheap!* Maybe it's a cultural thing, I don't know...but please believe me when I say I never meant to insult you."

At first, she thought he'd rebuff her, that the clenched fist under her hand would remain rigid as stone. But then the tension in his shoulders relaxed and although he moved his hand out of reach and still sounded a little distant, some of the frost had left his voice when he replied, "Nor I, you. I agreed you could repay me when you're able, but in the meantime, re-concile yourself to accepting my help because what you're wearing now, charming though it is, won't cut it tomorrow night. Like it or not, you're going shopping for a cocktail dress in the morning."

"I see no point in wasting money on a dress I'll probably wear just the one time."

"Nevertheless, you will take your cue from me on this. There will be nothing casual about tomorrow night. Angelo enjoys putting on a show for visitors and as his guests, the very least we can do is cater to his idiosyncrasies."

"Dear me! I do hope I don't embarrass you with my peculiar foreign ways!"

Far too astute to miss her intended sarcasm, he directed a killing glare her way. "You're the one who'll be embarrassed, and then only if you show up inappropriately dressed. You should be thanking me on this, Gina, not fighting me."

"I might be more disposed to gratitude if you weren't quite so dictatorial."

"I am not dictatorial," he informed her with lofty male hauteur. "I am taking charge because one of us must, and you are being unreasonable. Is it perhaps your time of the month?"

"My *what?*"

He waved a negligent hand. "That time when a woman loses her sense of perspective on life. The onset of her menses."

"No, Mikos," she cooed, with deadly, saccharine sweetness. "Fortunately for you, it is not. If it were, I'd reach across this table and rip your throat out for having the nerve to ask such a question."

He shook his head in mock despair. "*Thee mou,* I have offended you yet again, and that's the last thing I intended. Can we please put our differences aside and enjoy what's left of our evening together?"

She flung him a last smoldering glare. "I suppose so."

"Good. We are friends again." He caught her hand and brought it to his mouth. His tongue swirled against her palm, a sensuous little flame that left unguarded would, in time, turn into a raging fire. "You know, Gina, if one of my friends had found himself in your unfortunate situation, I'd have reacted just the same and insisted on helping him out."

"I doubt your friends would need your help. They're probably as well-heeled as you are, and think nothing of losing an entire vacation wardrobe."

"If you believe that, then you do me an injustice. I know what it's like to be poor, probably a lot better than you ever will. And for what it's worth, I don't choose my friends on the strength of their bank accounts. I hoped you knew me better than to assume that."

Chagrined, she lowered her gaze. "I do," she mumbled. "Forgive me, please."

"You're forgiven. Now take that worried look off your face and enjoy your dinner."

They had survived their first lovers' spat, at least on the surface. But underneath, for her certainly and, she suspected, for him, too, it had left its mark. Neither of them was quite as sure of the other as they had been at the start of the evening.

She'd already experienced the generous, loving side of his nature. Now she'd seen another side, and she realized that the passion he brought to the bedroom could also serve to make him a formidable enemy. He did not take kindly to being thwarted.

CHAPTER SEVEN

YIANNIS, Angelo's manservant who'd been with him for as long as Mikos could remember, showed them to the terrace where Angelo waited to receive them. Gina seemed nervous and almost shied away when Angelo took her hand and raised it to his lips.

"Thank you," she murmured, in response to his words of welcome. *"Efharisto...Kyrie Tyros."* And promptly snatched back her hand as if he'd scalded her.

Angelo beamed. "You learn our language already," he said in English.

"I'm afraid not," she replied coolly, her face carefully devoid of expression.

She must be intimidated by the grandeur, Mikos decided. Angelo had gone all out to impress, no doubt about it. Ouzo was his preferred aperitif, but tonight, three hundred and fifty euro Pol Roger chilled in a silver ice bucket beside a tray of *mezedes* on the wrought-iron coffee table. Add to that the stunning backdrop of mountains to one side of the sprawling acre property, the panoramic view of the Aegean on the other, the Olympic-size swimming pool on the lower terrace, and the proliferation of marble statuary at every turn, and it was small wonder she was overwhelmed—and this before she'd seen

anything of the interior of the house but the wide hall leading from the front entrance to the rear terrace.

Or did her reserve have more to do with their disagreement of the night before? Theoretically they'd made peace at the taverna, but a noticeable strain had lingered, and when they returned to the penthouse, they hadn't made love. She'd pleaded fatigue and gone to bed immediately. He stayed up, nursing a glass of metaxa and staring moodily at the distant lights of Piraeus to the south. When he finally joined her, she was asleep, or pretending to be.

He'd left for work early that morning, just after six, and again she appeared to be sleeping. He'd put in a long day at the office and not returned home until after five in the afternoon. They weren't due at Angelo's until eight, so they'd shared a few moments on the roof garden, making meaningless conversation—the *How was your day? Busy. How was yours?* kind of chitchat, like that of a couple who'd just as soon not have to talk to one another at all.

Married talk, in other words, and it had reinforced his belief that a short-term mistress was preferable to a long-term wife, any day of the week. But even a brief affair could wear a man down if he'd chosen the wrong woman, and he'd found himself wondering if he'd made a mistake in getting in so deep with her.

What had they in common, after all, beyond an insatiable hunger for one another's bodies, and mothers touched by tragedy? And what the devil had possessed him that, the night before last, he'd actually forgotten himself so far as to tell her he loved her? Granted, he'd said it in the heat of passion and in Greek, and she hadn't understood. Nor, thank God, had she asked for a translation. But that he'd uttered the words at all was so far out of range of his normal way of conducting an affair that it struck him as a serious lapse not to be repeated at any price.

But all that was before. Before she left him and went to shower and change for the evening at Angelo's.

Before he walked into the bedroom just as she was trying to close the zipper running up the back of the narrow black dress she'd found, stunningly elegant in its simplicity, and designed to drive a man to distraction.

Before he said, "Let me help," and touched the vulnerable, satin-soft skin at her nape, and smelled the fresh-washed scent of her hair, and the subtle hint of whatever elegant perfume she wore.

Before he felt himself quicken uncontrollably, and instead of closing the zipper, pulled it all the way down, and stripped the dress away from her.

Before the fragile hiss of her panties tearing echoed through the room, and he freed himself from his trousers, wrestled impatiently with a condom, then pushed her down on the bed and surged into her, blinded by the desire to lose himself in the glistening, heated silk of her flesh.

"I'm sorry," he panted, "about last night."

"Me, too," she whispered, clinging to him.

After that, nothing else mattered but the feel of her beneath him, and the muffled sound she made when she came at the same time that he did. It didn't even matter that he groaned, *"S'agapo,"* again. Because, just at that moment, he did love her.

"Sit here where I can look at you, my dear," Angelo said, gesturing to a high-backed wicker patio chair on the other side of the low glass coffee table from his. "At my age, it's a rare treat to behold such fresh, unspoiled beauty."

Startled from his reverie, Mikos buried a grin. *He's flirting with her, right under my nose!* he realized. *Eyeing every delectable inch of her, from her slender, shapely legs to the hint of cleavage showing above the top of her dress!*

Mikos could hardly blame him, yet at the same time, he

knew an urge to park his own chair close beside hers, and put
his hand very firmly and possessively on her knee, just to
remind the old coot she was already spoken for.

As though anticipating just such a move, Angelo forestalled
him. "Pour the champagne, Mikolas, and leave your lady and
me to get acquainted," he instructed, before turning his atten-
tion on her again and saying, "Tell me about yourself, *kouklaki
mou*. I'm sure you lead a fascinating life."

My little doll? Mikos rolled his eyes. If that was the best
Angelo could do, it was past time for him to relinquish his self-
appointed title of ultimate ladies' man!

"Then you obviously know nothing at all about me, Mr.
Tyros," she replied bluntly. "If you did, you'd know that,
compared to the kind of women you're used to, I'm actually
very dull and ordinary."

"There's no such thing as a dull, ordinary woman," he
chuckled, mightily entertained by her spirited answer. "And I
must insist you call me Angelo because I have no intention of ad-
dressing you as Thespinis Hudson. Gina suits you much better."

She sort of smiled…or was it more of a grimace? From
where he stood attending to the drinks, Mikos couldn't be sure.
"You have a lovely home, Mr. Tyros. Do you spend all your
time here?" she asked, pointedly ignoring his request.

"I have homes all over the world, my dear, but this is my
favorite. Would you like to see more of it?"

Not about to have her disappear on a tour of the vast mansion
with a man old enough to be her grandfather and randy enough
not to care, Mikos passed around the flutes of champagne. "I'll
be happy to show you around later, if you like, Gina. Right now,
though, I'd say a toast is in order. Will you do the honors,
Angelo, or shall I?"

"I will." Angelo raised his glass. "To your lovely Gina,

Mikolas. For once I approve your choice." Then turning to Gina, he said, "Thank you, my dear, for agreeing to spend the evening with a lonely old man. I hope it'll be the first of many."

Again, Mikos couldn't be sure, but for a moment, it almost looked as if she curled her lip. Then veiling her gaze, she murmured, "I'll look forward to it."

As she might have expected from the little she'd seen of the rest of the house, the dining room was opulent to the point of ostentatious. A massive crystal chandelier shimmered from the middle of the ceiling. A quartet of enormous silver candlesticks stood sentry on a heavily carved sideboard. Intricately cut crystal, monogrammed sterling, and crested china graced a table long and wide enough to seat forty, although the three of them occupied only a small space at one end.

Too small, in Gina's opinion. She was seated opposite Mikos, but Tyros sat between them at the head of the table and, throughout the meal, went out of his way to make her the sole object of his attention.

With the oily charm of a man accustomed to having women hang on his every word, he related amusing and often malicious anecdotes about the famous people he'd met. But the black, pebble-hard gaze scouring her so relentlessly was as incapable of human warmth as Gina had known it would be. He was horrible! She didn't know how Mikos could stand to work for him.

"I talk too much and you must forgive me," he said, as the meal at last drew to an end, and actually dared to stroke his age-spotted old hand over her wrist. "You must find my ramblings very dull."

"Far from it," she said, steeling herself not to cringe at his unwelcome touch. She couldn't afford to offend him by being squeamish, when he'd just presented her with the opening she'd been hoping for ever since she'd learned she'd finally meet him

in person. "As a matter of fact, the main reason I'm in Greece at all is because of you."

"Mikolas mentioned something about that. You write for a magazine, I believe he said."

"That's right."

He bared his teeth in a smile that would have done the wolf in Red Riding Hood proud. "I'd like to hear more about it—and about you, my dear."

Oh, he'd hear plenty, and wish he'd never asked! But not now, with Mikos in attendance. Considering how generous he'd been, the least she could do was leave him with his illusions intact regarding his mentor. Furthermore, what she had to say to Angelo Tyros was meant for his ears alone, and she doubted he'd want to share it with anyone, least of all his protege who thought him such a sterling character.

"Do you know what I'd like, Mr. Tyros?" she said, smiling through her distaste.

"Tell me, and I will make it happen."

"I'd very much like to talk to you at length, if you can spare me a couple of hours one day."

His fingers tightened, leaving her hard-pressed not to slap his hand away. "Consider it done. When would you like to come back?"

"Whenever it's convenient. I'm free all day."

"But not all night, eh?" he cackled, winking lewdly at Mikos. "I confess I'm intrigued by this girl, Mikolas. A woman has to be extraordinary if she can make you forget you're supposed to be the tough man on my team!"

"I wasn't aware I *had* forgotten," Mikos replied evenly. "In fact, Angelo, as I believe I made clear just yesterday, I never allow my private life to interfere with my work...or vice versa."

Tyros's mouth twisted in a smirk. "In this particular case, I

wouldn't blame you if you did. Your lady is exquisite—and has exquisite taste. I've been admiring your jewelry, my dear," he went on, turning suddenly to Gina again. "This, for instance, is quite beautiful. How did you come by it?"

To her horror, he pawed at her old pendant, one of the few things to survive unscathed the plaster and debris that had rained down on her hotel room. Sliding his fingers under it, he lifted it for closer inspection.

"It's been in my family for generations," she managed to say, unable to suppress a flinch, and so close to choking with revulsion that she was afraid she might lose the panacotte with chocolate sauce she'd recently consumed.

His beady black eyes bored into hers. "An heirloom, then?"

"Heavens, no. It hardly qualifies as that."

"I'm something of an expert on old jewelry, and not sure I agree with you." He shuffled his chair nearer hers. "May I take a closer look?"

Recoiling before he could maul her a second time, she hurriedly unclipped the velvet band around her neck, slipped the pendant free and passed it to him. He examined it at leisure, turning it over in his hands several times. "Yes," he eventually murmured, returning it to her, "it is as I thought. A rare piece, I'd say. Unique, in fact. Shall we take coffee on the terrace?"

She'd become something of an expert herself, specifically in detecting nuances of change in a person's expression or tone of voice. Just because people appeared to be as they presented themselves didn't mean a thing. What was happening on the inside was what counted, and something was definitely brewing behind that wily old face of his.

But if she found his abrupt shift of topic rather odd, Mikos didn't seem at all surprised by it. "*Efkharisto*, Angelo, but if

it's all the same to you, I'm going to take Gina home," he said. "She's still not used to the hours we keep in Greece."

"Then I won't insist you stay. It's been a pleasure meeting you, *koukla mou*. I trust you've enjoyed the evening?"

"Very much," she lied. "Thank you, Mr. Tyros. I hope I'll see you again."

"Angelo, please!" he crooned, raising her hand to his lips. "And you will see me again. You may be sure of it, my dear. *Adio!*"

On the drive back to the city, they discussed the evening just past. "It went well, I thought," Mikos remarked, adding with a laugh, "Angelo really seemed taken with you, I was jealous. What did you think of him?"

"He's…interesting. But was it my imagination, Mikos, or did he seem suddenly anxious to be rid of us?"

In the dim glow from the car's control panel, she saw his expression turn sober. "It wasn't your imagination. He tires very easily these days. One minute, he's the life of the party, the next, he's snoozing into his soup. Over the last year, there've been times when he's actually fallen asleep in the middle of business meetings. We've all noticed, and wonder how much longer he can go on, but he's got a will of iron and won't consider retiring. He's the boss, and as long as there's breath in his body, he's not about to let anyone else take over the reins."

"By 'anyone,' do you mean you? Are you his heir apparent?"

He flung her a quick glance. "I'm the closest thing to family he has left, and as things presently stand, I'll become president of Hesperus International and chairman of the board, but I won't inherit his absolute power. Nor do I want it."

"Why not?"

"The cruise ship industry doesn't much interest me, except as it applies to my particular field of expertise."

"And exactly what is that? You mentioned you'd gone to university and served in the air force, then went straight from there to working with Angelo, but you've never actually explained what it is you do."

"I'm a security professional, trained to develop security policies and procedures, perform security risk assessments and create what's called 'a workable incident response plan.' Those men in dark suits following discreetly behind VIPs and other high profile individuals are trained by people like me."

"Secret Service personnel, you mean?"

"Some of them, yes. Others are just private bodyguards, hired by celebrities who like to think they're important—movie stars, rock groups, that sort of crowd."

"Or tycoons like Angelo Tyros?"

"That's right. He's one of the richest men in the world, and that makes him a target."

"For what?"

"Anyone with a grudge against him, imagined or otherwise. Anyone looking to make a fortune without having to work for it. Every nutcase who thinks he's the long-lost son left in a basket on the steps of the Parthenon, and determined to exact his rightful share of the Tyros fortune. It's my job to make sure none of them gets close enough to sabotage Angelo or his empire."

He tossed out the information lightly, as if it was all a bit of a lark, but she wasn't fooled. "It sounds like dangerous work to me," she said, a thread of worry unraveling in her mind.

He shrugged carelessly. "Face it, Gina, we live in a dangerous world. Someone's got to step up and keep the villains at bay."

"Someone like you, you mean?"

"If a security breach occurred, whether it was to Angelo himself, or within any of his various enterprises, the blame

would ultimately rest on my shoulders because it would mean I or someone under my supervision slipped up."

"Are you his personal bodyguard?"

"Not any longer. I oversee the whole security operation, and these days, much of that has to do with communications technology. But if Angelo or one of his top-flight executives needs personal protection, who's assigned to guard him depends on where he's going and what he's going to be doing, and the decision for that rests with me."

"Angelo was kidnapped once, wasn't he? And the man who negotiated his release was shot?"

"Yes."

"Were you that man?"

"Yes."

She went cold all over. "Is that where you got that scar on your shoulder."

"Yes."

"You could have been killed."

He gave another nonchalant shrug. "But I wasn't."

"How can you be so blasé about something like that?"

"Do you worry about getting hit by a car, every time you cross the road?"

"No. But I'm careful, and if I did get hurt, it would be an accident. You can hardly say the same about you, in your line of work. Imagine, if you were married, how hard it would be on your wife, never knowing if, at the end of the day, she'd end up a widow."

"I'm aware of that. It's one reason I'll never marry or have children."

It was also a very good reason she'd decided to keep a tighter rein on her feelings where he was concerned. He might be gorgeous and sexy; sophisticated and charming and intel-

ligent. But falling for a man like him was a recipe for disaster, and she had enough of that in her life already. She didn't need more.

So why the sudden sinking sensation in the pit of her stomach? Why the absurd feeling that she'd just been robbed of something incredibly precious?

She didn't want to know. The answer was too disturbing.

The rest of the week passed uneventfully. Each day, she phoned home to check on her mother. Once reassured that everything was under control there, she explored more of Athens, mingling with the swarm of humanity flowing along the narrow streets, and absorbing all the color and sound and sights of the city so that, when she was back home again, the impressions would remain sharp in her memory.

With the bulk of her loan still unused, she ate lunch at inexpensive sidewalk cafés, experimenting with fractured, phrasebook Greek to order her food. She browsed the little shops, and one day sprang for a beaded bracelet for her mother because it was bright and shiny and Gina knew she'd love it, even though she might not recognize who'd bought it for her.

She strolled past the Tyros office complex in Kolonaki district, wondering behind which window Mikos worked and if, when they were apart, he thought of her as often as she thought of him. Ever since they'd smoothed over their little contretemps, their pleasure in each other had intensified. Long, lazy evenings in intimate little tavernas merged into long, breathless nights filled with moonlight and passion.

But though she tried not to dwell on it, she knew that they'd soon be saying goodbye. That dull, sinking feeling in the pit of her stomach would rear its ugly little head again then, and she'd tell herself it was indigestion, and she'd get over it.

But it wasn't. And she wouldn't. Because despite her best efforts, with every day that passed, she fell a little more in love with him.

On the Friday, Mikos surprised her by coming home just after three in the afternoon. "Pack a bag and be ready to leave in an hour, Gina," he announced, shooing her into the bedroom. "We're leaving town and going to Petaloutha for a couple of weeks."

"That's impossible," she began, determined not to leave Athens until she'd accomplished what she'd come to do.

He stopped her with a decisive slashing motion of his hand. "It's entirely possible, so don't even try talking me out of it. I'm due for some time off, and despite what you might think, you're not leaving Greece without seeing the islands."

"I'd love to, really, but I can't!" she insisted. "I still haven't heard from Angelo. What if he calls while we're gone and I miss my chance to…interview him?"

"It won't happen. He was called away himself, just this morning, and doesn't expect to be back before the end of the month. But I'm to tell you he hasn't forgotten the two of you have a date, and he'll spend a day with you when he gets back. That should be enough time for you to interview him, surely?"

She rather thought an hour would do it, after which she'd find herself persona non grata with both of them, but it would be worth the price if, in the meantime, she had two glorious weeks alone with Mikos. Still, she hesitated. "But what about my mother? I have to keep in touch—"

He dismissed her concern with a teasing grin. "We're not talking about Siberia, *glikia mou!* Petaloutha is in the northern Cyclades, just a hop away from Andros. We have mains electricity, including a land line telephone. You'll be able to call home whenever you want, exactly as you do here."

"Well…" She was weakening rapidly, and probably visibly, too. She could feel her resolve melting, and sheer, unalloyed pleasure seeping into her pores. Two whole weeks alone with Mikos! *Two whole weeks!* She'd have had to be made of stone to turn down an opportunity like that. "Well…okay, if you say so."

"I do." He gave her a playful swat on her bottom. "So stop arguing, throw your clothes into that suitcase you bought, and do as you're told! We're flying out at four."

She thought he meant they'd be taking a seaplane. She thought they'd be staying at a seaside cottage, perhaps near a village with a church and little shops, and children climbing over a rocky shore, just like the photographs she'd seen.

She was wrong on all counts.

They went by helicopter, which he flew himself. Her first surprise, once she got past the shock of realizing she was quite literally putting her life in his hands, was the sudden upward movement as the helicopter took off. It left her feeling heavy and strange.

Good grief, it feels as if my boobs just landed in my lap! she thought, clutching her midriff.

"Don't look so terrified," Mikos said, vastly amused by her white-knuckled grip as the aircraft tilted over the rooftops of Athens, and headed southeast across the Aegean. "I haven't lost a passenger yet, although there's always a first time."

Dear God, had one thrown up on him yet? Because the way her stomach was rising up into her throat, there was going to be a first time for *that,* as well!

She must have looked as pale as she felt because he reached over and patted her knee reassuringly. "I'm teasing you, *calli mou!* Relax and enjoy the ride. I promise you'll arrive in one piece."

Within a couple of hours, they did, passing over an azure sea dotted with islands which, from the timid glances she cast

down, appeared to live up to everything she'd expected of them. White cubic houses with blue roofs spilled down hillsides to the lip of the shore, with the occasional gold cross of a domed church rising from dusty squares lined with palm trees. Fishing boats bobbed at anchor in quiet coves.

But the speck of land looming closer showed little sign of life. It was, she thought fearfully, too tiny to support anything but the heavily treed humps of two mountains separated by a series of deep gorges and waterfalls. How he'd bring the aircraft down safely when there seemed no place flat enough to accommodate anything larger than a tablecloth, she couldn't imagine.

"Where did you learn to fly this thing?" she asked him, glad of the headsets, which enabled them to hear each other over the noise of the engines.

"In the air force, which is also where I first became interested in security. I'd have been just as happy to become a career officer, if it hadn't been that Angelo thought it a waste of my talents and persuaded me to work for him."

More likely played the emotional blackmail card to get you to do his bidding! she thought acidly, but wisely kept her counsel. She would not allow Angelo Tyros to intrude on this heaven-sent time. "So you really do know where you're going?"

Mikos turned to laugh at her, sunlight shimmering off his aviator glasses. "This puppy's equipped with the latest GPS."

"What's that?"

"A Global Positioning System. It tells me exactly where I am, how fast I'm going and what time it is, twenty-four hours a day, anywhere in the world, regardless of weather conditions." He indicated a display screen on the control panel. "That's us, there, see, moving along this preplanned route toward this land mass here, which is Petaloutha."

"Is it smart enough to know you're losing altitude?"

He laughed again. "We're not losing altitude, we're coming in at an angle for landing. A glide-slope, it's called."

"Oh, goodie!" she said weakly. "That makes me feel so much better!"

She should have guessed he knew exactly what he was doing. Just when it seemed they were headed straight for the nearer mountain, he veered to the left, rounded the steep spine of the hill and swooped over a wide-open area on the southern shore.

A peach-colored stucco house with a red tile roof faced the sea, with two smaller cottages farther down the beach, and several outbuildings tucked behind a stand of palm trees. Well to the rear was a landing pad clearly marked and connected to the house by a wide, sandy path. For a moment, the helicopter hovered over it like a giant bumblebee, its rotors flattening the fronds of the palm trees, then Mikos brought it down and settled it on the pad as gently as a mother's kiss.

After letting it run a minute longer to cool the engines, he shut it down, removed his sunglasses and headset and turned to her with another grin. "Still breathing?"

"Barely." Her reply emerged as a feeble croak in the sudden, blessed silence.

His green eyes sparkled with laughter. "Ah, Gina, where's your trust? Don't you know by now that I'd never hurt a hair on your beautiful head?"

She managed a wan smile. Growing up on an island, she'd become used to float planes, but this had been her first experience in a helicopter and she'd found it too much like floating aloft in a bubble. "Let's just say I'm glad to be back on solid ground again."

"In that case, we'll get you to the house and revive you with a long, cold predinner cocktail."

Quickly he loaded her, their bags and three cases of white wine into a golf cart parked off to one side of the landing pad. Then they were rattling off down the sandy path, past a grove of lemon trees, and arriving in a cloud of dust at the back door of the house.

Tomatoes grew in terra cotta pots on either side of the steps, where a couple somewhere in their early sixties waited.

Introducing them, Mikos said, "Gina, I'd like you to meet Dimitri, my right hand man who keeps everything on Petaloutha running smoothly, and his wife and my housekeeper, Stavroula— 'Voula to her friends—who feeds me so well when I'm here that, to keep my trim waistline, I'm forced to run ten kilometers along the beach each day. 'Voula, Dimitri, *apoetho I fili mou,* Gina."

"Herete!" they said, all smiles, and drew her over the threshold into a bright, sunny kitchen.

Braids of garlic and dried peppers hung by the window, above a wide, shallow sink flanked by tiled countertops. Two chairs and a large pine table, its surface scrubbed almost white, stood in the middle of the slate floor. An electric stove and large freezer-refrigerator, separated by an archway that led to a walk-in pantry, took up space on the second wall, while an old carved dresser with open shelves filled the third. To the right of the back door, a staircase led to an upper floor, with double doors on the fourth wall giving access to the rest of the house.

Roomy and cheerful, it reminded Gina a little of the kitchen back home, except she couldn't leave a gleaming chef's knife on the table, or a pair of scissors by the sink. And she'd had to remove the knobs from the stove, because her mother had almost set the house on fire once when she tried to fry bacon.

"Kalos orisite! Big welcome!" Stavroula exclaimed. "First time Mikos brings lady friend to Petaloutha. Very good thing!"

"Thank you," she replied. *"Efharisto!* I'm very happy to be here."

Stavroula eyed her up and down, spoke sternly to Mikos for a minute, then shooed them both through the double doors and into the main part of the house. "I'm to take you outside and make you put your feet up," he explained, leading her along a central hall, its floor covered in the same slate as the kitchen. "She thinks you haven't been getting enough rest, and it's as well I brought you here so she can look after you."

"And do you always do as she tells you?"

"Almost always." He pushed open a pair of doors set with many small panes of glass, and waved her though.

She stepped out and paused, transfixed. Fine old wicker furniture with colorful cushions was grouped on a flagstone patio shaded by a grapevine covered pergola. Purple bougainvillea climbed the walls, and a fabulous scarlet hibiscus tree dominated a corner of the garden. A fat tabby cat snoozed on the sunwarmed stone of another low wall beyond which, no more than fifty yards away, the turquoise sea lapped at the creamy yellow sand of a crescent beach.

"Oh, Mikos!" she breathed. "How do you ever bear to leave this place?"

He came close behind her and slid his arms around her waist. "You like it?"

"It's perfect! Heaven on earth! I've never seen anything so lovely."

"I have," he murmured against her hair. "Ever since the moment I saw you. We haven't known each other very long, but when it's time for you to leave, I'm going to have a hard time letting you go, Gina. I find myself wishing there was some way I could keep you with me."

His words both warmed and chilled her. Would he still feel the same when he learned the truth? she wondered. Or would he find his loyalty lay not with her at all, but with the man she most hated and he most admired, namely his benefactor, Angelo Tyros—and her grandfather?

CHAPTER EIGHT

THE two weeks following were the stuff dreams were made of. Carefree, golden days filled with sunlight and the kind of tranquility Eden must once have known. Dark, passionate nights when only her sighs, and his whispered endearments drowned out the gentle swish of the waves outside their window.

Away from the pressures of work, Mikos's authoritarian edge softened. He lived to please her. "Just ask, and it's yours," he'd say. "Call home as often as you need to. Sleep late. Take long siestas. Let us spoil you. It's why I brought you here."

Gina loved the slow unfolding of the hours, and the solid, even tenor of her relationship with him. Away from the city, money was no longer an issue because everything that mattered to her on Petaloutha was free. Simple things, like the warmth in 'Voula's smile each morning, or Dimitri softly playing his bouzouki as the moon rose. And above all, Mikos's gaze warming her at unexpected moments during the day, with the promise of shared intimacy when they were alone in his bed.

She loved getting up to be greeted by the cat, Kiki, who purred contentedly on her lap as she sat on the patio enjoying her first leisurely cup of coffee of the day, which 'Voula made specially for her, in a wide bowl, with hot milk, like café au lait.

Then there were the meals. Breakfasts of hot buttered toast

with honey, or fruit and yogurt, and as a special treat on the first Sunday, *loukoumades*, which were a little like doughnut holes deep-fried and immediately drizzled with honey and cinnamon. Light lunches of tomatoes and olives and feta cheese, washed down with ice-cold retsina and big glasses of sweet spring water. Dinners of roast lamb, calamari, smoky-tasting grilled octopus and skewered prawns cooked over an open flame, served with rice or an eggplant casserole and accompanied by chilled white wine. Usually in the evening they'd also have salad consisting mostly of chunks of ripe tomato from the garden, with a little finely sliced onion, diced skinny green pepper, and thin slices of cucumber, all sprinkled with oregano, salt and olive oil. And always, with every meal, fresh-from-the-oven bread.

"Please tell 'Voula I'm putting on weight," Gina complained to Mikos, toward the end of the first week, when the house-keeper served yet another delicious midafternoon snack.

Whatever he said had 'Voula cackling with delight. *"Kala pou pachyenes ligho. E andras then thellon yenekes pout ina all kokkola!"*

Gina had learned a little elementary Greek, but this was far beyond her ability to understand. Mystified, she eyed Mikos. "What did she say?"

"That it's good you've gotten a bit fatter," he replied with a grin. "Men don't like women who are all bones."

"Do *you* like me?" she asked him, when they were alone again. They hadn't really talked about their feelings for one another, or of how they'd cope with saying goodbye. There was no such thing as "tomorrow," on the island; it was always "today." But the intensity in his gaze as it scoured her face gave her the courage to put the question to him now.

"Oh, yes," he said, his voice throbbing with dark emotion.

"I like what I see very much. You've bloomed since you came here, *karthula mou*. You're not the same woman I met at the Grande Bretagne, less than a month ago."

"I feel different," she admitted, and it was true. She felt light, buoyant, just the way she used to, before her mother had changed, and everything else with her. Then the laughter had died, along with the light in her mother's eyes, and a terrible desolation had reigned in their once happy home. Still in her mid-twenties, Gina had felt old; the parent of an aging, fractious child given to bursts of incandescent rage interspersed with increasingly rare moments of utter sweetness.

The sobering memories crowding her mind dimmed the bright day a little. Whether or not she and Mikos wanted to admit it, time was not on their side. Soon, she'd leave this island paradise and return to the problems which, for a little while, someone else had shouldered. But not until she'd confronted Angelo Tyros and forced him to acknowledge the responsibilities he'd ignored all these years.

Her mother would not end her days in residential care that was, at best, merely adequate, while he ended his in luxury. Before either of them died, there would be a day of reckoning, and it was fast approaching. Gina would see to that. Until then, she would hoard every precious moment with Mikos. Keep every tender word close in her heart, to fortify her through the difficult times she knew lay ahead.

Glancing up, she found Mikos still regarding her. "All at once, you look sad, my Gina. Why is that?" he asked.

She shrugged. "Just thinking about going home."

"Don't. We still have more than a week here, and even after we return to Athens, you don't have to leave Greece right away. What was it your doctor told you—*Take a break, or risk having a breakdown?* I suspect, if you were to phone and ask, he'd rec-

ommend you extend your holiday as long as possible, provided your mother is managing without you."

"Nevertheless, when I think of her being left with a stranger, I feel guilty at abandoning her."

"But, *mana mou*, from what you've told me, she doesn't even realize you're not with her, so where is the harm in our seizing the moment for ourselves?"

"I suppose there isn't any, not really. Not as long as she's being well looked-after."

"You say the words, but the look in your eyes remains troubled, so to cheer you up, I propose we do something different this afternoon. After our siesta, I'll take you to Choro on Andros. We'll explore the town and have dinner there. Would you like that, *agape mou*?"

"As long as I'm with you, I'm happy anywhere," she said.

His eyes darkened to jade, a sign she'd come to recognize as the stirring of desire that seemed never far from the surface with either of them, especially when they found themselves alone. "Finish your lunch, and let's go to bed," he said hoarsely.

Love in the afternoon took on a more leisurely aspect that had nothing to do with ardor. Perhaps the reason was the subdued sunlight filtering between the slats of the blinds and filling the room with a mellow glow that allowed for more minute observation of each other. Or perhaps their extended enjoyment of one another had more to do with the sultry heat that reduced every living thing to half-speed.

Whatever the cause, their coming together happened in slow motion. That afternoon, every tiny pause—and there were many—punctuated a moment of new pleasure that heightened their senses to slow-burning fever. His lips brushed her neck, then drifted down to her breast and feasted there. His hand on

her leg became a gradual gliding caress up her inner thigh; his finger, a tender discovery of her core.

Her exploration of his chest strayed to his narrow pelvis and his groin. She touched his penis lightly, wonderingly, amazed as always by its power and delicacy. She devoured it with her gaze, then let her glance slide up his torso to his face, and delighted in the tension etching his features as her fingers curled possessively around him. "You're all mine," she whispered, and lowered her mouth to him.

She'd never done that before. Never sampled the silken heat of him. Never felt such power as he shuddered at her bold advance. "*Christos*, Gina," he ground out, a fine sheen of sweat glistening over his skin, "if you keep doing that, you'll make me come."

She wished he would. She wanted to taste him as he had so often tasted her. No matter how briefly, she wanted to enslave him. But he was too unselfish a lover to allow it. Grasping her shoulders, he rolled her onto her back and reached into the nightstand drawer for a condom.

"Let me," she begged, and he did, quivering at her touch as she sheathed him.

Then, with a sigh, she opened herself to him so that he sank to the hilt in her welcoming folds. And they began again the dance of love they'd perfected so many times before, the slow, sensuous movements gathering speed until the universe spun in blinding ecstasy, and she thought her heart would implode.

Spent and exhausted, they slept with their limbs entwined, her hair splayed on the pillow, her arm beneath his neck, and his arm flung across her waist as he lay facedown on the rumpled sheet. When they awoke, they bathed together, then walked down the curving beach and swam in the limpid water of the little cove.

"If I'd come prepared, I'd take you again now," he muttered,

riding the gentle waves with her legs wrapped around his waist and his hands cradling her bottom. "I cannot get enough of you, *mana mou*."

"Nor I of you," she said, drowning in the clear green depths of his eyes, while the world around her shone the deep blue of summer.

Sensible or not, believable or not, she had fallen in love with him. Deeply and irrevocably. The knowledge exhilarated her as much as it devastated her.

They traveled to Andros by speedboat, a thrilling half hour trip that ended at the capital on the east coast of the island. A lovely little town, Choro was situated on a peninsula between two long sandy beaches. To Gina, though, its charm lay chiefly in the combination of Venetian, Byzantine and Ottoman architecture. Wandering the stone walkways and narrow alleys with Mikos, she felt transported to medieval times.

"If only I had a camera," she began, enchanted by the picturesque sight of hibiscus and bougainvillea splashing ancient white walls with color, and stately neo-classical mansions fronted by palm trees.

She should have known better than to voice such a wish because, before she guessed what he was about, Mikos darted into a shop and emerged a short while later with a little digital camera to replace the one she'd lost when her hotel room had flooded. "A souvenir from your greatest admirer," he said, preempting her insistence on paying for it herself. "I'm sure you'd never be so unkind as to refuse it."

So she accepted it graciously, not willing to spoil by even a little bit, the perfection of the day.

He took her to the tip of the peninsula, to a marble-paved square containing a statue dedicated to The Unknown Sailor.

There he persuaded another tourist to take several photographs of her and him, against the spectacular backdrop of a beautiful Venetian-style stone bridge that connected to a tiny island where the remains of an old castle stood.

"Now let me take a picture of you," she said, as they made their way back to the middle of town, and focused the lens for a close-up that she could have enlarged and framed when she was back in Canada, so that he would always be with her, no matter how many miles or differences might separate them.

'Voula had given them a list of things she needed, so on the way back to the middle of town, they shopped for her, ending up at another square, this one paved in stone and surrounded by cafés and restaurants all shaded by a huge plane tree.

With daylight fading, they sat at an outdoor restaurant, sipping ouzo diluted with water, nibbling on olives, dipping crusty bread into yummy tzitziki made of shredded onions, garlic and cucumber in thick yogurt, and watching the dying sun layer the sky in thin bands of watermelon and orange.

The moment somehow captured the very essence of the Greece she'd come to know and love—a country full of boisterous sights and sounds and colors. Street merchants and gypsies; barefoot children and soberly clad old widows. Music and laughter; voices united in song, or raised in heated argument. Emerald and lime-green, and violet and fuchsia.

Noticing the camera on the table, their waiter offered to take more pictures, capturing precious moments that would never fade, no matter how many years passed. Looking at each frame on the camera screen afterward, Gina saw a man and a woman who might have been honeymooners. In one, they were both laughing and leaning into one another, their body language speaking of a deeper, more intimate knowledge than that displayed for the public eye. In another, she was looking off to one

side, a smile on her face, and Mikos was gazing at her with such naked hunger, it almost made her cry.

But she did not. She would allow nothing to spoil the magic.

Finally they returned to the boat, stowed their purchases, and with a rising moon marking their path, headed back to Petaloutha. "Did you have a good time?" Mikos wanted to know, as they nosed up to the dock where Dimitri waited to secure the lines.

"I had a wonderful time," she said. "But I'm glad to be back here. I feel as if I've come home again."

He looked at her, a smile curving his beautiful mouth. "I know. I feel exactly the same. Leaving here is always a wrench, and I can never come back soon enough."

That night, he told her he loved her. His eyes clouded with passion, his lungs heaving, he thrust into her, his body shuddering with the power of his climax, and uttered the words she'd never thought would pass his lips. "*S'agapo*, Gina!" he panted. "I love you!"

She held her breath, waiting for him to renounce the claim. Seconds hung on a fine gold chain of suspense before he said again, "I love you, *mana mou*."

She dared to reply then. "I love you, too, Mikos," she breathed.

The remaining days merged one with another in a haze of bliss. Mikos showed her more of his island paradise. One time, they picnicked on a beach a few kilometers away, well out of sight of the house, where they stripped off their bathing suits and snorkeled, following tiny schools of brilliantly colored fish darting in the protected water of a small reef.

Later, they made love on a blanket, shaded by an old olive tree, then snoozed the afternoon away in each other's arms.

Another time, they went fishing, but somehow the lines

were left unattended because, with the boat rocking gently at anchor, she slipped off the bottom half of her bikini and, taking him by surprise, climbed astride his lap. He was hard and pulsing even before she could free him from his bathing trunks, slip a contraceptive on him and guide him into her moist center.

"I told 'Voula we'd bring back fish for dinner," he rasped. "How do I explain coming home empty-handed?"

"Tell her you caught me, instead," she said, and bit gently at the muscled curve of his sun-bronzed shoulder.

One day when the air hung heavy with heat, he took her inland. Shaded from the sun by a canopy of pines, they climbed the steep hillside behind the house, and when they came to a pool at the foot of a little waterfall, shed their clothes and dived into the cool depths.

After, they sat on a flat rock, and ate figs and cheese, and talked easily about the kind of movies and music they liked, the books they'd read, their favorite colors and foods and holiday times. Unimportant things that nonetheless helped weave in the little details that made up the fabric of their separate lives.

"When's your birthday, Gina?" he asked lazily at one point, lying on his stomach and using his folded arms as a pillow.

"August the fifth." She dropped a tender kiss on the pale scar left by a crazed gunman, years before. "When's yours?"

"April 23. So you'll be turning twenty-nine in another few weeks."

"Yes."

"Will you ever get married, do you think?"

Her spirits soared with sudden hope. The only time he'd ever mentioned marriage was when he'd told her it wasn't for him. Did his bringing it up now mean he'd changed his mind? "I don't know," she said carefully. "As things stand with my

mother, it would be asking a lot of any man to become part of my family."

"He'd do it, if he loved you enough," he said. "You're not meant to be alone. The right man will find you, sooner or later."

But it won't be you!

Her heart plummeted and she turned to face the waterfall, so that he wouldn't see the devastation she knew colored her face. He was the most beautiful man she'd ever met. His smile chased away the darkness that had shadowed her for so long, and filled her with light. When he touched her, she melted. His kisses, his tongue, his hands…they were instruments of sublime sensual delight beyond anything she'd ever dreamed of.

But he endeared himself to her in so many other ways, too. She admired his integrity, his intelligence. Loved his easy camaraderie with poverty-stricken children, his kindness in helping a crippled old woman safely cross a busy street. Loved his generosity, his fire and passion for the things he believed in. But she'd borrowed him for just a little while, and his reminder that he wasn't hers to keep shot an arrow of pain through her body that nearly killed her.

"Hey," he said, turning over and running his fingertip down the curve of her spine. "What happened? How is it that you're suddenly over there and I'm here? I want you next to me." His voice deepened, and she knew why even before he added, "I want you in my arms, Gina. I want to make love with you."

For your own sake, say no! her sense of self-preservation urged. But she was addicted to him and could no more refuse him than she could turn day into night.

Her throat was tight with misery. So tight, it hurt her to swallow. But she crawled into his waiting arms, and they came together sweetly, with the scent of pines filling the air, and the music of the waterfall chattering its melody in the background.

And for one mad minute, she wished to God that he didn't have a condom with him, and that he'd give her a baby—not to coerce him into marrying her, but to have something of him that she could keep with her, the rest of her life.

But he was always careful. Always prepared. And realistically, it was just as well. She had her hands full with her mother. There was no room in her life for a baby, as well. The most she could take home with her was the gift of memory. So she filed away each moment, each word, each caress; precious souvenirs to be savored in the future when her body would cry out for him, and he wouldn't be there to answer it.

On Saturday, the eve of their return to Athens, the serpent found its way into paradise, slithering in uninvited just as she and Mikos sat down for their last dinner on Petaloutha.

They'd had gone to Syros early that morning and spent a long day exploring Ermoupolis, the capital of all the Cycladic Islands, and then the wonderful medieval village of Ano Syros. They'd returned in time to shower and change for the evening meal, and because 'Voula had gone to extra trouble preparing a farewell feast, they dressed up more than usual.

Instead of shorts and a T-shirt, Mikos wore light gray linen trousers tailored to fit his trim hips to perfection, and a white dress shirt against which his darkly tanned skin gleamed. Gina put on the outfit she'd found in a street market in Ermoupolis just that morning: a creamy cotton dress sprigged with soft blue forget-me-nots, with a dropped waistline and a skirt that fell to her ankles.

Over lunch, Mikos had pulled a small box from his pocket and presented her with a gold chain styled in a traditional Greek design. "Come on, Gina!" he'd protested, when she said she couldn't accept such an expensive gift. "First of all, gold jewelry

doesn't cost as much in Greece as it does anywhere else because our craftsmen work for less money. And second, I want you to have a permanent souvenir of the Cyclades and our special time together. You can let me give you that much, surely?"

But he'd already given her so many other, less tangible gifts. He'd taught her to seize the moment and not waste a single precious second of it. Taught her about passion, and love, and how to laugh again. And although she'd resolutely schooled herself not to dwell on tomorrow, hearing him talk of souvenirs and a future that wouldn't include him left her hollow with sudden misery.

She, who prided herself on facing facts, had deceived herself into thinking that, when her Greek idyll came to an end, she could walk away without regret. But there, in that busy square, with the perpetual sunlight turning the street dust to motes of dancing gold, the truth had caught up with her, and she'd had to face the fact that what she'd told herself was a temporary escape, a passing affair, had woven itself thoroughly into her "real" life and become an essential part of it.

Somehow, she'd forced herself to take the chain. To smile and thank him. To hide the pain tearing her apart. She had years ahead in which to let her grief run wild. She *would not* let it ruin what little time she had left with him.

Standing in front of the mirror above the dresser in his bedroom, she'd threaded the chain through the eye at the top of her old pendant, then fastened it around her neck.

"Perfect," Mikos said, coming out of the bathroom to stand next to her, and smiling at their reflection. "What a handsome couple we make, *neh?*"

"*Neh,*" she replied, a catch in her voice. Then, because she couldn't help herself, she said, "Will you miss me when I'm gone, Mikos?"

His smile had died and his dark thick lashes swept down to hide the expression in his eyes. "So much, I refuse to think about it," he answered somberly. "How is it that you've become so much a part of me? How did I let this happen, when I've always known the day would come that I'd have to let you go?"

But you don't! her heart cried. *Ask me to stay. Tell me that the difficulties with my mother aren't insurmountable and that we can work it out so that everyone's happy!*

She was asking the impossible. There were no miracle endings, not for her mother and not for her.

He might have been reading her thoughts. "Perhaps we were foolish to think we could play with fire and not get burned. But this I tell you in all truth, my lovely Gina—I shall never forget you, and if I had room in my life for marriage, yours would be the hand I'd ask for."

He stopped short then, and lifted his shoulders in resignation. "But I do not, any more than you have in yours. Fate has set us on divergent paths, and we've always known that." He took her hand and drew her gently away from the mirror and its cruelly misleading image of the perfect couple destined for happy-ever-after. "So come, *mana mou.* Tonight belongs to us. Let's make the most of it."

'Voula, bless her, had covered the patio table with an embroidered cloth instead of the customary woven place mats, and set a bowl of flowers in the center, surrounded by votive candles in red glass holders. A dozen or more other candles glimmered in brass hurricane lamps set among the vines crawling over the low stone wall.

It was as they sat across from each other, with Mikos touching the rim of his wineglass to Gina's, that a seaplane shattered the serenity of the evening, and zooming in for landing,

turned the calm, sunset-hued waters of the bay to shards of multicolored glass.

"What the devil…?" Mikos rose from his seat, a scowl furrowing his brow. "Are you expecting visitors, 'Voula?" he asked the housekeeper who, obviously having heard the din of the engines, had come to the door to see what was happening.

She shook her head. *"Ohi."*

"Then who the hell thinks he can just drop in uninvited?"

He soon had his answer. The float plane nosed up to the dock and cut its engines. A moment later, with the help of a man who was undoubtedly one of the ubiquitous security guards, Angelo Tyros clambered out of the float plane and hobbled up the path to the house.

CHAPTER NINE

MIKOS was the first to speak. "What in the name of God brings you here, Angelo?" he exclaimed, pulling another chair to the table and seating him. "Has something happened? Are you all right?"

"As right as a man my age can be," he said, and spying 'Voula still hovering in the doorway, addressed his next comment to her.

Apart from the word *ouzo,* Gina didn't understand what he said, but the housekeeper's pinched expression and terse reply made it clear she didn't care for his lordly attitude. Tossing her head, she practically stamped her way back to her kitchen.

For herself, Gina could have wept. On this, their last night on Petaloutha, she wasn't interested in sharing Mikos with anyone, least of all Angelo. But the man was oblivious to her silent reception, and surveyed his surroundings as if he owned the island and everything on it. "Nice place you've got here, Mikolas," he allowed condescendingly. "Makes me regret having waited this long to come and see you."

At that point, 'Voula returned with a tray bearing a bottle of ouzo, a pitcher of iced water and a glass. She set them on the table in front of Angelo with a distinct thump, then turned to Mikos. "Will there be one extra for dinner?"

"Of course there will, woman," Angelo said irascibly, before

Mikos had a chance to respond. "Do you think I flew in here on an empty stomach, and aim to leave the same way?"

"*Efharisto,* 'Voula." Mikos shot her an apologetic smile. "Please don't go to any extra trouble. What you've already prepared will be more than enough for three, I'm sure."

"You never have learned how to treat underlings," Angelo grumbled, pouring himself a hefty serving of ouzo diluted with a very small amount of water, as 'Voula once again exited the patio. "You don't *ask* the hired help, you *tell* them—in no uncertain terms!"

"And you still haven't told me why you're here," Mikos reminded him coolly.

"*Christos!* Give me a moment to catch my breath and put something in my stomach. I'll get down to business soon enough." He downed a mouthful of his aperitif, then turned his attention on Gina. "Well, my dear," he remarked, his pitiless gaze raking over her from head to foot. "You're looking well fed, well browned and well rested. I take it you've enjoyed your time on Petaloutha?"

"Very much," she replied stiffly.

"And now it comes to an end."

For some reason, a shiver raced down her spine. Was she imaging the menace in his tone, or was it just her dislike of him that was coloring her perception?

"Not quite yet," Mikos interjected. "We still have the better part of twenty-four hours. How about you, Angelo? How was *your* trip?"

The old man flicked a sly glance his way. "Interesting," he drawled. "Very interesting indeed."

"When did you get back?"

"This morning."

"Then I'm even more surprised to see you here. You don't

usually stray far from home after you've been traveling. How was Penelope, by the way?"

"Cooperative, for once." He bared his tobacco-stained teeth in a smile which, in Gina's opinion, inclined more toward a leer. "We got along so well, I found myself wondering why I divorced her. Penelope," he went on, suddenly switching his attention to Gina again, "was my third wife, in case you're wondering. We were together for quite a few years before I tired of her."

A number of responses occurred to Gina, none of them pleasant, so she pasted an answering smile on her face in the hope that it hid her antipathy. "Do you keep in touch with all your former wives?"

He let out a cackle. "Only those still breathing. I'll be joining the others soon enough."

Not soon enough for me, she thought, curbing a shudder of distaste, and when 'Voula came in carrying a heavy platter of *mezedes,* Gina took it as a chance to escape.

Pushing her chair away from the table, she stood up and said, "Please tell Stavroula that she's been put to enough trouble already, Mikos, and I'm coming to lend her a hand in the kitchen."

"Absolutely not," he ordained. "She won't allow it, and nor will I. Sit down."

One arrogant Greek at the table was more than enough. Gina wasn't about to tolerate another. "In case you haven't noticed, Mikos," she replied, enunciating each syllable clearly, "I am not what your employer so scathingly refers to as an 'underling,' so his exhortation notwithstanding, kindly do not give me orders."

His mouth twitched in amusement. "If I say *efharisto*, and explain that I'll miss you too much if you go, will you stay, *calli mou*?"

"She'd better," Angelo declared, piling olives and smoked

octopus on his plate, "since she's the reason I'm here to begin with."

His response, more than Mikos's, prompted her to subside into her chair again. "I am?"

"Neh. The last time we were together, you said you wanted an opportunity for us to talk." He speared her with a sly glance, an inimical gleam in his black eyes. "And I find I have much I'd like to say to you, too, so I thought to myself, what better place for us to get down to business than here, on this little island, where neither of us can run off and hide from the other?"

She wasn't imagining things this time. The old goat positively oozed malice, and it was focused entirely on her. Well, if he thought his money and his fame and his army of sycophants could intimidate her, he was in for a surprise.

"I couldn't agree more," she said, trading stare for stare without batting an eyelash. "So why don't we stop beating around the bush, and get down to business?"

Mikos recognized Angelo's manner. It was the one he adopted when he was preparing to move in for the kill on an opponent who, knowingly or not, had earned his enmity.

Most of the time, Mikos accepted it as the price of doing business in the high-stakes international circles in which Angelo moved. Show even a moment's weakness, and a man faced the equivalent of a death sentence. He could awake in the morning, king of all he surveyed, and be ruined before sunset.

But for Angelo to make Gina his target? Not as long as Mikos had breath in his body! "If you've come here looking to pick a fight with someone, Angelo," he bit out, "then pick it with me. Gina is off-limits."

Angelo swiped a chunk of bread through the olive oil on

his plate. "Gina," he replied, unmoved, "is either a liar or a thief, or both."

"*Christos!* I've never hit a man half my size and more than twice my age, Angelo, but—!" Fist balled, he catapulted out of his chair, raw anger firing his blood.

"When did an *agapetikia*—a mere mistress whom you will discard as you have others before her—matter more to you than I, who have made you the man you are today?" Angelo sneered. "How is it that you have so little trust in my judgment or my affection for you, Mikolas, that you doubt for even a second that I would make such a claim and not be able to back it up with facts?"

"It's okay, Mikos," Gina said calmly. "Let him finish." She turned a blistering gaze on Angelo. "Please go on, Mr. Tyros. Explain what it is I lied about, or stole, or both. And when you've finished defaming me, I'll set *you* straight on a few *real* truths it's long past time you heard."

Mikos hesitated, and for a long, tense minute, his lover and his benefactor glared at one another, the atmosphere between them bristling with unspoken accusations. Angelo was the first to break the silence.

"That item of jewelry your mistress so blatantly wears around her neck is not, as she claims, something handed down from one family member to another, Mikolas. It belongs to me and disappeared from my home more than sixty years ago."

"You must be mistaken," he said. "It just looks like one you used to own."

Angelo reached into his pocket. "I'm afraid not, *yio mou*. I have here the matching earrings, which I gave to Penelope on our wedding day. She very kindly let me borrow them to corroborate my story, because I knew you would not willingly believe you could have been so easily duped."

He tossed the evidence on the table: large, cabochon-cut amethysts pavéd with diamonds set in gold. "Examine the back of them, and then ask your mistress to let you do the same to her pendant. You will find all three are engraved with my family's crest."

Mikos shoved aside the earrings. "Coincidence, pure and simple. I refuse to submit Gina to such an indignity."

"She means that much to you?" Angelo's thick black brows rose in disbelief.

She'd come to mean everything, Mikos acknowledged to himself in a blinding flash of insight. Gradually, with each passing hour, she'd eroded all his well-entrenched notions of love, and even of marriage. He'd thought he could say goodbye to her, pick up the threads of his life when she left, and carry on as before. Only now, seeing her vulnerable to attack, did he realize the impossibility of the task he'd set himself. "Yes, she means that much."

"And you're sure you know her well enough to rush so impetuously to her defense, are you, *yio mou*?"

"Quite sure."

"Then it saddens me that I must be the one to disillusion you."

"I doubt you'll ever be able to do that, Angelo."

"We'll see." He switched his scrutiny to Gina, who sat ramrod straight in her chair, her face a pale mask betraying no emotion. "Will you take off the pendant, young woman, or must I do it for you?"

Without a word, she reached up and unclasped the chain, pooled it and the pendant in the palm of her hand, and held them out, not to Angelo, but to him.

"This isn't necessary, *agape mou*," he said. "There's been a mistake."

"It's necessary, Mikos."

He wasn't easily daunted, but her tone of voice struck cold as iron at his heart. With ever increasing dismay, he accepted the pendant, inspected the back and acknowledged that Angelo had spoken the truth. The Tyros crest was clearly marked.

Looking up, he met her unblinking stare. "Did you know about this, Gina?"

"I knew it was engraved. I didn't know what the markings meant."

"How did you come by it?"

"Exactly as I said. It has always been in my family. I used to play with it as a child."

"You lie!" Angelo thundered. "It was stolen from me by a woman who thought, because I had taken her into my bed, she could blackmail me into marrying her!"

"That woman," Gina informed him, the blood surging into her face and leaving it flaming, "was my grandmother, Elizabeth Beecher. And if I had known the origins of this…this *thing,* I would never have sullied my skin by wearing it."

Angelo opened his mouth to retaliate, then snapped it closed again.

"I see you recognize the name," Gina continued coldly. "What a pity you didn't have the decency to recognize your child, whom she bore and raised alone, at a time when unmarried mothers were treated as outcasts of decent society." She paused just long enough to draw in a long, deep breath and let it out again. "Well, guess what? I'm here to make you pay for that omission."

"What are you saying?" Mikos asked, the sense settling blackly in the pit of his stomach that he, the man who always knew exactly what was going on at any given moment, had in fact been laboring under a load of misinformation for the last three weeks or more.

"I'd have thought it was plain enough," Angelo said. "She

came here with this ludicrous story in the hope that I'd offer to buy her silence. She just didn't anticipate that I'd expose her before she could put her plan into action. But now it's all out in the open, so how much are you willing to bet that *she'll* threaten to expose *me* to the press, if I refuse?" He turned on her again, his mouth twisted in a near-snarl. "Admit it, woman! You're after my money, aren't you?"

"Yes," she said flatly. "And plenty of it, too."

'Voula chose that moment to make another untimely entrance. And yet, Mikos decided, perhaps it was just as well. He was embarrassed enough at being hoodwinked by a woman he'd believed he could trust, without his making a spectacle of himself by giving in to the fury consuming him.

Spinning on his heel, he strode into the house and down the hall to the office he hadn't bothered to enter since the day he'd brought Gina Hudson to the island. Once there, with the door closed between him and the debacle taking place outside, he paced the floor, berating himself for having ignored his first instinct that she was not to be trusted.

He should have known better. She'd hoodwinked him from the outset, and he had no one to blame but himself.

He returned within minutes. Seeing the anger contorting his features, Gina shrank in her seat. This was not how she'd wanted things to happen. She'd thought she was holding all the cards and could take Angelo by surprise at a time of her choosing. Instead he'd surprised her, and even without the engraved proof to back him up, his claim that the pendant belonged to him had stirred a memory from her childhood that bore out the truth of his statement.

You shouldn't let Gina play with that, her mother had reproved her grandmother. *It's too valuable.*

Oh, let her have it. It was ill-gotten gains to begin with, Elizabeth had replied cryptically, *and served me no purpose beyond the temporary satisfaction of knowing I'd taken something he cared about, a lot more than he ever cared about me."*

"So, my dear," Mikos began, resuming his place at the table and helping himself with a steady hand to the lamb and giant prawn kebabs 'Voula had brought in during his brief absence, "you presented yourself to me, masquerading as a journalist of sorts, and now brazenly admit you came here for no other purpose than to exact money from Angelo."

"I wasn't masquerading," she protested. "I really was commissioned to cover the party."

"You're an opportunist, pure and simple," he retorted harshly. "If you hadn't been able to get past security with a press pass, you'd have found some other way to get in, because your sole objective from the start was to get to Angelo."

"It wasn't exactly like that," she told him, the unleashed contempt in his voice almost destroying her.

"Then what was it, *exactly?* Explain it to me, please, because I'm obviously too big a fool to figure it out for myself. And before you open your mouth, know that I will accept nothing less than the absolute truth. So let's have it." He glowered, his face all hard angles hewn from granite. "Now, Gina!"

"Lose the attitude," she shot back, stunned that after all they'd been to each other, he could so readily believe the worst of her. "Contrary to what Angelo seems to think, I am *not* your mistress and I don't owe you anything but the money I have borrowed and which I will repay as soon as possible."

He looked at her as if he was seeing her for the first time and was not impressed by the sight. "Is money all you ever think about or understand?"

"No," she whispered, slumping dejectedly. "I think about my mother, and…you. And you don't understand me, at all."

"Then I say again, explain yourself. And before you begin—"

"Let her speak, Mikolas," Angelo surprised her by saying, and fixed her in a penetrating stare. "Go ahead, girl. Start at the beginning and take your time. We've got all night."

She expelled a sigh and related as unemotionally as possible her mother's situation and the promise she herself had made never to abandon her. "But all that changed, the day I came home from grocery shopping to find her missing," she explained. "Two whole days and nights she was gone."

She stopped, the horror of that time as vivid in recollection as it had been in reality. "Eventually the police found her on Vancouver Island, stranded in Parksville, with no idea how she'd arrived there, where she'd come from, or even who she was. She was wearing her winter coat, her very best shoes, her pearls and nothing else. They'd traced her through her wristband and the ID label I'd attached to her coat."

Again, she stopped, tears blocking her throat. Neither man said a word. They just sat there and watched her impassively.

Struggling to regain control, she continued. "I knew then that the day I'd dreaded had finally arrived. For her own safety, I had to go back on my word and put my mother into a facility."

To her shame, the tears began to fall and she couldn't stop them. *"Facility!"* she sobbed. "The word shrieked institution, abandonment, despair! How could I do that to her?"

"A difficult decision, I grant you," Angelo said, his tone less abrasive than usual. "But what, my dear girl, has this to do with me? Why should I come to her aid?"

"Because she's your daughter!" Gina flung the answer in his face. "Haven't you heard a word I've said? She's the child

you turned your back on, and she needs the kind of help only you can give!"

"If that's true," Mikos interrupted curtly, "why have you waited this long to come forward?"

"Because I only just found out myself that he's her father."

"How convenient! You discovered Angelo is your mother's father when you happened to be on your way to Greece to interview him."

"That's not how it came about! I'd taken her for her regular check-up with our doctor, and while we were waiting to see him, she started looking through a business magazine." She shot Mikos a fierce glance. "And before you say a word, let me tell you she was a smart, intelligent, well-read woman before her illness. Not much happened in the world that she didn't know about."

"And your point?" Not a fleck of sympathy or understanding showed in his eyes. They were the cold, turbulent green of a winter-tossed sea, and equally indifferent to human suffering.

Unable to bear looking at him, she spoke to Angelo. "There was a photograph of you in there, and a write-up about your forthcoming birthday. And Mom…" She gulped on another sob. "She became agitated. Started crying, and hugging the magazine, and wailing that her father didn't love her."

"And that's your proof of paternity?" Mikos let out a scornful laugh. "You can do better than that, surely?"

She glared at him, almost hating this derisive, sarcastic side of his character. "I admit it sounds flimsy, and I was ready to dismiss the incident as yet another sign of her dementia, but when I described it to our doctor, he corroborated her story."

"How much did you have to bribe him to do that?"

"*Scasmos!*" Angelo spat. "For God's sake, Mikos, shut up and let her speak. Go on, girl."

"Rather than bring disgrace to her family by giving birth to

a child out of wedlock, my grandmother left her home in eastern Canada and moved to the West Coast, to the island where I grew up. Everyone thought she was a widow. The only person she confided in was her doctor, our present doctor's father who looked after her throughout her pregnancy and delivered my mother."

"A touching story, I'm sure," Mikos said witheringly, "but still not proof positive that Angelo was the father. The only certainty is that this woman had no husband, and her child was born a bastard."

The term, accurate in the literal sense though it might be, stung Gina to righteous indignation. "Kind of like your mother and you, then, weren't they?"

"Leave my mother out of this!"

"Gladly!" She so badly wanted to slap him, she had to clench her fists hard enough that her nails left little dented imprints in her palms. "Just as soon as *you* recognize that my mother's got enough to bear, without being saddled with that label."

"When's your mother's birthday?"

Caught up in anger with each other to the exclusion of everything else, they'd almost forgotten Angelo was there until he spoke, his voice so lacking in its normal strident arrogance that, on hearing it, both she and Mikos spun around in alarm. He'd risen from his chair and was leaning heavily against the table, his dark olive skin turned a ghastly sallow.

"March 28, 1948," she said. "And because I didn't expect you simply to accept what I said without question, I've given our doctor permission to release all my mother's medical records to you, including the results of the DNA test I authorized before I came here."

"Christos!" He staggered a little, and made a grab for the edge of the table. Was it too much ouzo that left him weaving,

Gina wondered, or too much shock to a heart already weakened by age? "Then you really are my granddaughter?"

Mikos gave her no time to respond. "Don't jump to any conclusions, Angelo. So far, we have only her word to go on, and we already know she's good at covering her tracks."

"And yet, Mikolas, I see a resemblance in her to me, when I was her age."

Oh God, please not! Gina thought, with an inward shudder.

Mikos let out a disdainful snort. "She's dark haired and has dark eyes, I grant you, but if that was all that's needed to confirm paternity, you could have sired three-quarters of the Greek population," he said, taking the old man by the arm and urging him down onto his chair.

Angelo shook off his cautionary hand. "She looks like me, I tell you! And has a look of Rhoda about her, as well."

"Rhoda?"

"Her grandmother. Rose, they call it, in English."

Mikos seized on the name triumphantly. "*You* said her name was Elizabeth," he charged Gina.

"It was," she said. "Elizabeth Rose. And if proof of that is also required, you'll find both names on her birth *and* death certificates. She grew up as Rose, but people on the island knew her only as Elizabeth, I suppose because she wanted to make a fresh start after she left home."

Angelo exchanged a telling glance with Mikos. "First, the pendant, and now the dates, the names and the family resemblance—even without medical records, this many coincidences you can't dismiss easily, Mikolas. The girl's story has the ring of truth to it."

At first, she thought Mikos would persist in denying it, but at the last, he nodded moodily and paced to the edge of the patio.

"There's one other little fact that you probably don't want

to hear," Gina said defiantly to his back, "but it seems I was named after my grandfather. My full name's—"

"Angelina," he finished for her. "I know. More fool me for not making the connection until now."

It was her turn to be taken aback. "What do you mean, *you know?*"

"It's on your passport."

"And how do you know that, given that my passport is locked in a hotel safe?"

"It wasn't, when I had one of my team investigate you."

"*What?*"

Swinging around, he spared her a chilling smile. "You're not the only one with secrets, Gina. While we were touring Evia, the night of Angelo's birthday party, I had your room searched. Or did you think it was your fascinating beauty that kept me glued to your side until dawn?"

"You're bluffing! The hotel management would never have allowed a stranger into my room without my permission."

He laughed mockingly. "The man I appointed didn't need permission. He simply used your key, the one you thought you'd lost. Except you didn't lose it. He took it from your evening bag while you were dancing with me."

She felt like Alice falling down the rabbit hole into an alien world where nothing made sense anymore. "For what possible purpose?"

"To make sure you were who you said you were."

"Well, what else did you think?" she cried, a bubble of semi-hysterical laughter bursting from her mouth. "That I was a secret assassin, out to do in your beloved Angelo in front of a roomful of people?"

"You wouldn't have been the first to try it. And I wasn't about to get involved with someone I couldn't trust."

Her laughter died, and a terrible emptiness took its place. "Dear God, you're serious!" she whispered.

"Absolutely serious. And, it turns out, absolutely right to be suspicious, because you've been anything but honest with me, even though you've had plenty of opportunity to come clean."

His admission cut so deep, she thought her heart would splinter. All this time…those nights he'd held her in his arms, the time he called her *agape mou*—all of it made possible because, throughout that first night when she'd fought so hard not to fall in love with him, he'd had one of his flunkies break into her hotel room. *Paw* through her possessions, looking for proof that she was worth his time, deserving of his attention!

"You lied, too!" she reminded him bleakly. "You said you loved me, Mikos!"

"Howling at the moon talk, my dear," he responded coldly. "The sort of thing a man says in the throes of passion."

"So you didn't mean it?"

He shrugged insultingly. "After a fashion…at the time."

"Stop it, both of you!" Angelo burst out, thumping his fist on the table. "I won't have my granddaughter and the man I love like a son ripping each other apart. There's been enough damage done, without adding more."

Gina rounded on him, prepared to tell him that *he* ought to know, since he'd dished out more than his share in his time, and that she didn't care how rich and powerful others might find him, because for her, the day he chose to abandon the mother of his unborn child was also the day he lost any right to claim kinship with her granddaughter.

But what she saw wasn't the monster she'd convinced herself he had to be. He was just an old, old man, with shock leaching the fire from his eyes and seeming to strip the flesh from his

features. The skin lay draped harshly over his prominent nose and hung loosely from his sagging jowls. He trembled all over.

Voice quavering, he asked, "Is your mother really ill?"

"Oh, yes, that much checked out," Mikos confirmed. "And they're in pretty dire straits." He jerked his head in Gina's direction. "She runs a bed-and-breakfast operation, but the house needs such serious maintenance that she hasn't bothered advertising for summer guests, this year."

Gina couldn't contain an outraged howl. "You had my *mother* investigated, as well?"

"Naturally. I'm nothing if not thorough. It's what makes me so good at what I do. You're one of my few mistakes, *koritsi mou,* but not one I intend to repeat."

The enormity of his betrayal flattened her. She had no more appetite for fighting him than she had for the prawns and lamb which lay cooling on their platter.

"You're right," she told Angelo sadly. "Enough damage has been done. Too much ever to be repaired."

She turned then and made her way to the bedroom she'd shared with Mikos, knowing that he wouldn't be joining her, not that night or any other. Between them, they'd killed whatever it was they'd once had. She'd felt as close to him as any human being she'd ever known, but in the blink of an eye, they'd found themselves on opposite sides of a yawning chasm, with no hope of bridging the distance separating them.

It had ended, not sweetly and with regret, as she'd hoped, but ended nonetheless, just as she'd always known it must.

CHAPTER TEN

"YOU did it for me, I know, but telling her you had her investigated, that you lumped her in with the dross of society…? You hurt her, Mikolas. You hurt her grievously."

Mikos knew it. Thinking back to how the color fled her face when he told her what he'd done, he knew a moment's regret. But then he looked at Angelo, and fearing for the old man's heart, hardened his own. "I let you down," he said, the metaxa he'd swallowed burning a hole in his gut. "You pay me to keep you safe, and instead I exposed you to a threat more insidious than an assassin's bullet. You look ill, Angelo. First thing tomorrow, we have to get you back to Athens, to a hospital."

"I don't need a doctor."

"You have a heart condition."

"*My* heart isn't the problem right now, Mikolas. Yours is."

He tried to smile, but the effort was as much trouble as she was. "I had an affair that went sour. Nothing fatal in that."

"Or perhaps," Angelo mused, "you fell in love."

"With a con artist?" He let out a hoot of self-disgust, telling himself he'd been taken in by a beautiful face, a willing body and a sob story, despite the nagging uneasiness which, from the very start, had warned him something about her story didn't quite add up.

It had persisted in plaguing him like indigestion after a too-rich meal—enough that he'd ordered further investigation, this time casting a wider net to include her mother. But because he'd wanted Gina more than he'd cared about the truth, he'd let himself be satisfied by what appeared on the surface, and chosen not to dig deeper.

Bottom line? His pride had taken a beating on all levels. Professionally he should have known better. And personally...? He ground his teeth in impotent rage. Even now, knowing the full extent of her duplicity as he did, desire prowled through his blood, a sullen, remorseless predator tormenting his body.

Watching him, and most likely accurately gauging the conflicting emotions chasing over his face, Angelo remarked, "We can't always control our fate, Mikolas. I only just discovered that. I'd like to think you'll learn the lesson soon enough not to repeat my mistakes."

This time, he managed a genuine laugh. "I didn't think you ever made mistakes, *yarro*."

"It seems I did when I refused to acknowledge that I might have fathered Rhoda's child."

"You really believe it's a possibility?"

"More than a possibility. We spent a whole summer together. Much," he concluded a trifle grimly, "as you have spent the last several weeks with the young woman who might very well turn out to be my granddaughter."

A flush of embarrassment warmed him. "Well, *she's* not pregnant, if that's what you're implying."

"I'm implying nothing, nor am I in any position to pass judgment." He rested his head against the back of his chair and closed his eyes. "What I *am* going to do is make sure that girl has money enough to take care of her mother."

"Even though you can't be sure she's family?"

"It doesn't matter whether she is, or not. I turned my back once on a woman who begged for my help, and all the evidence points to it being the greatest mistake of my life. She's dead now, so I can't make it up to her, but it's not too late to help Gina."

"You're making me nervous, Angelo," Mikos said, eyeing him warily. "This isn't like you."

Angelo's eyes opened and bored straight into his. "Look at me, Mikolas, and tell me what you see."

"A man who should be checked out by a doctor."

"No." He dismissed the suggestion with something of his usual acerbity. "I'm eighty, in failing health and alone. My only son is dead. My ex-wives tolerate me only when they want something from me. Apart from you, there isn't a soul in the world who gives a damn that I'm still alive, and dozens who'd be glad to see me dead. My money, my influence and my power are my only assets. Otherwise, I'm just a foolish old man trying to kid himself into believing women still find him attractive, and men want to be his friends. Yet all this time, I've had a family who've needed me and who might have loved me for myself, if I'd given them the chance. Do you have any idea how that makes me feel?"

"I know you're hurt and confused by everything that took place on this veranda tonight. But you've just admitted money can't buy love, Angelo."

"I'm not trying to buy anything. I'm simply trying to do the right thing, for a change." He uttered a weary sigh. "Go find the girl, Mikolas. Bring her to me. I want this settled tonight."

One of the benefits of having lost most of her possessions and replaced them with only a few, meant Gina was packed and ready to go within fifteen minutes. She didn't know how she'd get away from Petaloutha in the dark. She knew only that she

couldn't remain here, in this house, with its whitewashed walls
and dark slate floor, its many-paned glass doors opening to the
endless sea, its easy, casual elegance and its memories.

Most of all, its memories.

She knew she couldn't face 'Voula's sympathetic gaze, or
Dimitri's kindness, and not fall apart. That even hearing Kiki's
throaty purr would be enough to make her cry. And she knew
that once she let that happen, she'd never be able to make it stop.

Best just to look ahead, she told herself sternly, stuffing the
last of her clothes into her suitcase. *Find a way back to Athens,
collect your passport and tickets from the hotel and go home
empty-handed.*

Although she'd always known she might fail to persuade
Angelo to help her mother, she'd thought at least she'd gain
some satisfaction from confronting him with the truth of who
she was. But she'd been wrong. There was no reward to be had
from lying in order to expose another's sins. Nothing com-
mendable in knowing she'd left an old man of eighty stricken
with useless guilt.

And then there was Mikos. She hadn't meant to love him,
but it happened anyway. She'd opened her heart and let him in.
Now she had to find a way to let him go again.

Oh, yes, better for both their sakes that she just disappear
from the landscape without further fuss or ado. Yet in the end,
as she stood at the door with her suitcase, she couldn't bring
herself to make a clean break of it.

Instead she turned for one last look at the bed, with its linen
still rumpled from their late-afternoon lovemaking. At the sight,
a burst of pain knifed through her, crippling in its ferocity.

Doubled over, she staggered across the room and, falling
across the mattress, picked up his pillow and buried her face in
it. The faint scent of his shampoo, his skin, his shaving soap,

struck like tiny daggers, deepening her anguish until it became a visceral thing, tearing at her like a wild animal on its prey.

Sobs choked her. Left her gasping and fighting to breathe. Why did it have to end like this, with anger and bitterness erasing all the beauty they'd shared, and leaving only the ugliness of deceit? Why couldn't they have parted with mutual regret, with his arms around her and his lips on hers, and his thumb wiping away the tears she shed?

Because they were never meant to be, that's why! Not even for a little while.

Slapped hard by a truth she'd steadfastly refused to acknowledge before, she pushed herself upright and pressed the heels of her hands to her swollen eyes. She had to get away, if for no other reason than to preserve her sanity. Mikos might not want her, but her mother needed her desperately. She had to remain strong for her.

Mikos met her in the doorway, just as she bent to retrieve her luggage from where she'd dropped it on the floor. "Where do you think you're going?" he said coldly.

"Away," she answered, straightening and making a superhuman effort to hold herself together.

"At this hour?" His mouth curved in bitter humor. "You won't get far, unless you're planning to swim to Andros."

"I'll get Dimitri to take me there, first thing in the morning, and I'll sleep on the beach until then."

He rolled his beautiful, glacier-green eyes. "Spare us all the dramatics, Angelina. You'll sleep in here."

"With you?" Hope flared, brief and brilliant as a shooting star, only to die just as swiftly.

"No, thanks. You may recall I have guest cottages. They tend to come in useful at times like this."

Pride came to her rescue, enabling her to match his cynical

tone. "What, and have you accuse me of chasing you out of your own home, on top of my many other sins and omissions? I wouldn't dream of it."

"Why not?" he asked, with sudden, searing rage. "You've done a lot worse in the short time you've been here."

She flinched. "I've loved you," she said, forcing the words past her breaking heart. "Whatever else I'm guilty of, that much at least is true."

"Bullshit!" he roared. "I was merely your conduit to Angelo!"

"That might have been so in the beginning." Desperate to make him understand, she clung to his arm. "I was caught between two impossible extremes. Don't blame me for wanting to do the best I could for my mother, when you know you'd have done the same, had the situation been reversed. But to say I used you? Mikos, you know that's not true!"

Grasping her wrist between his finger and thumb, he disengaged her hand from his arm as if she were some loathsome insect he could barely stand to touch. "Forgive me if I find that difficult to believe."

"Well then, blame yourself for being such a fool!" she cried, unraveling right before his eyes. "If you were so suspicious of me that you had me investigated, why did you bother having an affair with me in the first place?"

Momentarily a hint of uncertainty clouded his eyes. "Don't ask me to explain something I don't understand myself. What we had might have been good while it lasted, but it's over now, and that's all that counts."

"Then why are you here, stopping me from leaving, when all I want to do is go?"

"Because you're not leaving, not yet. Angelo wants to see you first."

"Why?"

"That's for him to say. I'm just the messenger." He jerked his thumb at the bathroom door. "Go wash your face and get yourself under control. He doesn't need to see you looking like the wrath of God. You've caused him enough grief for one night."

He towered over her, so taut with angry pride, she wondered how his spine didn't splinter. So certain that she'd ruined their relationship by not being up-front with him, that it didn't once occur to him he'd been just as underhanded with her. Well, shame on her for being surprised!

"You just have to have everything *your* way, don't you, Mikos?" she snapped, a smidgen of pride stiffening her own spine. "Right from the start, you've manipulated events to accommodate what *you* wanted, and you're still doing it. You intercepted me when I tried to leave the Grande Bretagne without you. Virtually kidnapped me in a limo and coerced me into staying out all night with you—under false pretenses, I might add. You pressured me into moving in with you, and didn't let up until I agreed, then insisted on bringing me here, where you could control my every move."

"You've hardly suffered," he pointed out dispassionately.

"That's true. As long as I fell in with *your* plans, *your* wants, *your* desires, harmony reigned. But dare to oppose you or, heaven forbid, outwit you, and look how you react! And they say hell hath no fury like a *woman* scorned!"

"*Scasi*—be quiet!" he ground out. "Just shut up and get on with it. Angelo doesn't have all night, and nor do I."

"Well, never let it be said that either of you should be inconvenienced on my account!"

"You call accusing a man of fathering an illegitimate child an *inconvenience?*"

She shook her head, all the fight draining out of her. "No,"

she said. "I call it a tragedy—both for the man and the child, and I pray to God you never have to learn it firsthand."

When she heard what Angelo had planned, she refused to have anything to do with any of it. "Thank you very much, but no," she said with icy hauteur. "No more favors, if you don't mind."

"You can't afford to turn me down, girl," he informed her impatiently. "Not if you care about your mother as much as you say you do."

From his post at the corner of the veranda, Mikos watched with as unbiased an eye as he could muster up, searching for the family resemblance between the two that Angelo was so sure existed. And suddenly he found it, not overtly, but in small details easily missed if a man didn't know what to look for.

Gina had been patterned along vastly more delicate lines than Angelo, to be sure, but the mulish cast of her mouth, the proud angle of her head, the high slant of her cheekbones were all pure Tyros. As for the defiance in her dark eyes, it was as familiar to him as Angelo's, and he'd have laughed at the sparks flying from them, if there'd been one iota of mirth left in him.

"If you're really a Tyros, you should be smart enough to know a good thing when it's staring you in the face," Angelo thundered, emphasizing his point with a thump to the table that set his metaxa dancing in its glass.

Unimpressed, she leaned forward and yelled right back at him, "Don't raise your voice at me. I might have Tyros blood in my veins, but that doesn't mean I have to put up with your bullying."

He reared back, apparently too flabbergasted to reply, and into that small silence, with the clock just past midnight, the phone rang. A strident, ominous occurrence at that hour. The number was unlisted, and those few people privy to it knew it was to be used only in cases of extreme emergency.

"Who the devil's calling you in the middle of the night?" Angelo barked, swiveling to glare at Mikos.

"I'll find out," he said, and went down the hall to his office.

He returned to the veranda ten minutes later, and even before he spoke, they saw the gravity he knew was etched on his face and that whatever the news, it wasn't good. Angelo's gaze sharpened perceptibly, and as for Gina, she shrank in her seat as if, by making herself very small, unkind fate might pass by without touching her.

Dear God, how do I tell her? he wondered, his heart a leaden weight in his chest.

"Well?" Angelo was the first to speak.

Dragging his unwilling feet across the veranda, he approached the table. "I'm afraid there's been an accident."

That was all he said, but it was enough. Gina turned ashen. "My mother?" she breathed.

Coward that he was, he shut his eyes against the pain and fear he saw in hers. "Yes. I just spoke to her doctor."

"Is she…?" Her voice quivered to a hush.

Knowing what it was she couldn't bring herself to ask, he forced himself to look at her again. "No," he said firmly. "She is not dead…but she's badly hurt."

"She's in the hospital?"

"Yes."

"Oh God!" She buried her face in her hands and when he tried to comfort her with a touch, flinched as if he'd struck her.

"Tell us what happened," Angelo said.

Overcoming her resistance, Mikos grasped her hands in his. They were cold as ice. "She fell from an upstairs windowsill. It appears she'd climbed out and was trying to clean the window itself, and lost her balance. Someone passing by on the street saw her fall and called an ambulance. It happened just after nine

this morning, Pacific time. The person you hired to look after her thought she was sleeping still, and was in the kitchen preparing breakfast."

"Oh God!" she whimpered again, pleading for divine forgiveness. "It's my fault. *I* did this to her."

"It was an accident, Gina. No one's to blame."

"You're wrong. I never should have left her." She pulled away from him and, hugging her middle, rocked back and forth, tortured with guilt. "If I'd been there, it never would have happened."

"You don't know that, *calli mou*," he said, gathering her in his arms. "You told me that she'd become too unpredictable and that you yourself couldn't keep her safe anymore. It's why you came here to ask Angelo for his help."

But she was inconsolable, as he'd known she would be. "It's my fault for leaving her, I tell you! I'm the only one she trusted, and I abandoned her to a stranger." Wild-eyed, she struggled from his hold a second time. "I have to go home. You have to help me, Mikos. I need to get back home right away."

Seeing that she was shaking like a leaf in a storm, Angelo poured an inch of brandy into a glass. "And we'll see to it that you do. By tomorrow night, you will be at your mother's bedside, I promise you. But there's nothing we can do until daylight, and right now, you're in shock." He pushed the glass across the table. "Drink this down, child. It will help settle your nerves."

A shadow obscured the lamplight spilling from the house. Glancing over, Mikos saw 'Voula and Dimitri hovering nearby, their faces creased with distress. "We overheard," 'Voula said softly. "I'll look after her, while you make the necessary arrangements."

She cupped Gina's cheek and stroked it. "Come with me,

kori mou. Let me take care of you," she crooned, and taking her by the hand, led her gently away.

"How bad is it?" Angelo asked, the second they were out of earshot.

"About as bad as it can get. Her mother's in a coma. She's not expected to recover."

"Thee mou!" Angelo wiped his hand down his face. "Am I to find a daughter, only to lose her before I can put right the wrong I have done?"

"Stop talking that way," Mikos chided. "You're a fighter, Angelo, and so am I. And right now, we've got one hell of a job in front of us, so let's get on it. There'll be time enough for recriminations on both our parts, once we've done all we can for Gina and her mother."

They each knew the drill. They'd followed the same procedures a thousand times before, albeit not for the same reason. Sudden departures for foreign places were an everyday event at Hesperus International. Within the hour, the arrangements were in place. Shortly after, 'Voula brought a fresh bottle of metaxa and hot milk laced with honey.

"How is she?" Mikos asked.

"Sleeping," she replied. "I gave her hot milk, as well, and two of the pills my doctor prescribed for occasional insomnia. I thought she'd cope better with what's to come, if she could get some rest tonight."

"Good thinking." He blew out a long-held breath. "Get some rest yourself, 'Voula. We plan to leave here at first light, and could use some coffee before we head out."

"If you're flying us back to the mainland, you'd better catch a couple of hours sleep yourself," Angelo told him, after she'd gone. "I don't fancy having you nod off at the controls, midway between here and Athens."

"What about you? You're pretty beat, as well."

"At my age, I don't need a lot of sleep. I'll listen for the phone, in case there's further news from Canada."

"Then I'll take you up on the offer. No sense in our both sitting up."

He stole into the bedroom. 'Voula had left a lamp burning on his side of the bed. It showed Gina curled on her side, her cheeks flushed from crying, her eyelashes clumped together against her cheek.

Stealthily he shucked off his shoes, pants and shirt, then crawled under the sheet. Not that he thought for a second that he'd be able to sleep. But he knew an imperative need to lie beside her and hold her snug against his body. It was as close as he could come to taking her pain and making it his own.

Although she didn't awaken, she sensed his presence and sighed against his neck. "Mikos..." she moaned softly.

"I'm here," he whispered, kissing her hair. "I'll look after you. I'll make everything's all right, *khriso mou*, I promise."

The corporate jet stood ready on the tarmac. By ten the next morning, they were aboard and waiting for clearance to take off. So far, everything had gone according to plan. They'd left Petaloutha at six, arriving before eight in Athens. He'd landed the helicopter on the roof of the Tyros office complex. In line with his instructions from the night before, his car had been waiting in the parking lot.

They'd driven first to the hotel, to pick up Gina's passport, made a quick stop for Angelo to collect the luggage his valet had packed, and ended up at the penthouse where Mikos threw a few things into a suitcase and picked up his own travel documents. Throughout, Gina sat huddled in the back seat, so paralyzed with grief and worry that she might have been dead.

When he'd told her she personally had to authorize the release of her passport, she'd climbed out of the car like a sleepwalker and done as he asked with a docility that terrified him.

As soon as the jet reached cruising altitude, he tried to make her eat something. "A little fruit, or a roll, at least," he coaxed.

She turned her head away and stared out of the window. On the other side of the cabin, Angelo watched and said nothing.

"What can I do?" Mikos asked him in a low voice.

"Be there to catch her when she falls," he replied. "This is a crisis beyond our will to change, Mikolas. It lies in God's hands."

But her falling wasn't what worried Mikos. It was the fear that she might break and that even his strength and indomitable will wouldn't be enough to put her back together again.

CHAPTER ELEVEN

HIGH summer had arrived on the West Coast while she was gone. As the ship eased away from the dock, the red stripe running along the hull of the Port Angeles ferry sent a bloody ripple over the blue waters of Victoria's Inner Harbor. Masses of geraniums and lobelia spilled out of flower baskets hanging from the wrought-iron lampposts lining the streets. Tourists mobbed the promenade, buying souvenirs and taking photographs of the Legislative Building and the Empress Hotel's imposing facades. Red double-decker buses and horse-drawn carriages rattled along Government Street.

But there were no flowers in the hospital's Intensive Care Unit, and no noise except for the swish of soft-soled shoes and the hum of medical apparatus. In the cubicle where her mother lay, separated by a privacy curtain from the rest of the area, a deathlike silence hung.

"A very severe head injury," the doctor in charge had told them gravely. "I'm afraid I can offer you no hope. No hope at all."

Holding herself together by a thread, Gina approached the bed. "Hey, Momma, it's me," she said softly, taking her mother's hand and willing some of her own life force into those pale, unresponsive fingers. "Look who's come to meet you. It's your father. Open your eyes and say hello."

Not a flicker of awareness crossed her mother's composed features.

"Momma," Gina said again, louder this time, the thin edge of control she clung to so desperately, slipping from her voice and leaving it strung with panic. "Wake up, *please!*"

Standing slightly behind her and to her left, Mikos squeezed her arm. "Gina, *karthula mou,* she can't hear you."

"Don't you dare say that!" she snapped, flinging his hand away. "She's still breathing. Her heart's still beating."

This time, he brought both hands to bear on her shoulders as if, by doing so, he could contain her grief. "Because she's on a ventilator. Darling, you heard what the doctor told us. They kept her on life support until you got here, but—"

"I don't believe him!"

"For your own sake, you must. Let me help you accept what can't be changed, *agape mou.*"

"I don't want your help," she whispered fiercely. "Go away and leave us alone. You don't belong here."

At first, he didn't move. Then his breath sifted warmly over the back of her neck in a sigh of defeat. "Very well. I'll be in the waiting room, if you change your mind."

On the other side of the bed, Angelo made a small sound. Looking at him, Gina again saw not the international billionaire who, to bring her to her mother's side as swiftly as humanly possible, had cut through airport and customs control both here and in Athens like a hot knife through butter, but an old man who couldn't control his quivering chin or the tears welling in his eyes.

"Don't!" she begged, forcing the plea past the thick ache in her throat. "Don't let her see you cry. She'll think she's dying and we've come to say goodbye."

"She already said goodbye to you, yesterday," he said,

holding her gaze steadily. "Your mother's brain dead, child. Let her go in peace now. She's suffered long enough."

Gina felt her face crumple and a terrible black despair enfold her. "I can't," she wept. "I don't know how."

He hauled himself slowly out of his chair and came around the bed to stand beside her. "We'll help you, Mikolas and I, if you'll let us. Lean on us, Angelina. That's why we're here."

He bent then, and kissed her mother's brow. "I'm sorry I didn't treat you well," he murmured brokenly. "Forgive me, my daughter. *Adio, pethi mou.* God be with you forever."

With the tip of his thumb and first two fingers, he crossed himself three times, touching his shoulders from left to right, then from his forehead to his solar plexus, ending with his palm placed flat against his chest. Then, with the tears rolling down his face, he left Gina to come to terms with the decision that was hers alone to make.

She kept vigil for nearly two hours before she could bring herself to release her mother from the prison she'd endured for so long. What other choice had she when, for the first time in years, even she could see that the torment of Alzheimer's disease had melted from her mother's face and let her be herself again?

"I won't say goodbye, Momma," she whispered, choking on her tears, "because I know you'll always be with me."

The next morning, Gina went home to the island. The parade of days following passed in a blur, filled with the memories of a lifetime superimposed by the business of death. Mikos and Angelo came with her, even though she wished they'd go away and leave her alone. She didn't want them. She didn't want anybody.

But neither one paid attention. They continued to hover over her, as though they feared she might shatter if they looked the other way, and as word of her mother's death spread, island resi-

dents joined them, stopping by the house with cakes and casseroles and sympathy.

"She was a lovely woman," they said, and, "You made her very proud," and, "She was blessed to have such a wonderful, caring daughter." And worst of all, "She's in a better place now."

Is she? she wanted to scream at them. *How do you know that? Tell me, please, so that I'm not pursued by demons every waking minute.*

As if they could read her mind, they tried to comfort her. "It wasn't your fault, Gina. You mustn't blame yourself."

In between settling her mother's affairs and making funeral arrangements, she supposed she ate, but only when pressed by Mikos to do so, and never very much. Food didn't taste the same anymore, and she often couldn't keep it down, but it was easier to go along with him than resist. Even though he was gentle and solicitous with her, he was still Mikos, after all, and bent on having things his way.

She slept long and deeply, sometimes falling into bed as early as eight o'clock, only to awake still exhausted, more than twelve hours later.

"Depression," she heard a well-intentioned neighbor confide in hushed tones to Mikos and Angelo. "I recognize the symptoms. Keep an eye on her."

One night, she drifted awake when the moon was high and found Mikos sleeping next to her, but he was gone when she opened her eyes in the morning and she was glad. She knew his actions were prompted by guilt. She saw it in his eyes, every time they came to rest on her. She heard it in his voice when he spoke her name and tried to take her in his arms.

She couldn't bear it. She had enough guilt of her own to deal with, without having to cope with his, too.

One time, he cornered her and tried to kiss her, the way he

used to, before. But she turned her face aside so that he missed his mark.

"Stop pushing me away!" he said, his voice rough and deep with frustration. "I want to help you. I love you, Gina!"

He didn't, not really. It was just pity talking. "If you want to help," she replied, "please bring my mother home. I'd go myself, but—"

"Of course I will," he said, his gaze scouring her face. "Anything you need, *agape mou*, just ask and I'll see to it."

She was relieved he'd interrupted her. She hadn't wanted to tell him she felt so queasy and exhausted all the time that she wasn't sure she was safe behind the wheel of a car. She didn't need his ordering her to the doctor, added to the list of things he'd decided he must do before he went back to Greece. Bad enough that he'd spent hours mowing the lawns and had brought in a crew to replace the leaking roof.

The next day, he left her alone with Angelo and drove to Victoria to collect her mother's ashes. There was no crematorium on the island.

"You know he loves you, don't you?" her grandfather said, after he'd gone and they sat together, sipping lemonade in the garden.

She stared at the snow-capped mainland mountains laid out in panoramic splendor on the eastern horizon. "He feels sorry for me," she said dully.

"Of course he does! We all do, child! What's that got to do with it?"

Everything, she thought. Because that's not what love's about. Love should be tempestuous and glorious. A vivid Technicolor of emotion that didn't need to steal the pastel shades of pity to make it real.

"You're punishing yourself, and using him to do it," Angelo warned. "Keep it up, and you *will* lose him. He's too proud to

go on this way indefinitely. Sooner or later, he'll take his battered heart back to Greece, and if you don't think there'll be plenty of women more than willing to console him, you're not smart enough to call yourself my granddaughter."

"No lectures today, Angelo, please," she said wearily, the lemonade sitting sourly in her stomach. "Right now, I've got all I can do to get through tomorrow."

"Ah, yes, the memorial service." He sighed heavily. "I know how difficult it will be, child. But you'll do just fine, you'll see. Your mother inherited your grandmother's spirit, and *she* passed it on to you."

He was right—to a point. She held up throughout the service, and the condolences offered by the more than two hundred people who filled the church and came to the reception afterward. She pretended to sip her cup of tea, and remembered to thank everyone for their kindness.

And when it was all over, she fainted.

Her family doctor was among those who'd come to honor her mother. "Strain and exhaustion, most likely," he told them, after Mikos had carried her into the little anteroom behind the church hall. "All things considered, I'm amazed she's held up this well. She's had a rough time of it, these last few years, with very little relief. How long are you going to be here?"

"For as long as she needs us," Angelo said. "I'm her grandfather."

"I figured as much," he sniffed, unimpressed. "Better late than never, I suppose." He closed his medical bag, put on his jacket and addressed Mikos. "I don't think you need worry. Give her a couple of days to recover from the emotional stress of the funeral, and she should be fine."

"She hasn't been fine since she left Greece," he said. "She's got no appetite, and no energy. And she's lost weight."

"Not surprising, under the circumstances. But to be on the safe side, have her come in for a complete checkup. It never hurts to err on the side of caution."

"As if she'll do anything I tell her!" Mikos commented in a gloomy undertone to Angelo, as Gina showed signs of coming around. "More likely, just the opposite. I'm not sure I'm doing her any good at all by sticking around."

"Perhaps you're not," Angelo replied bluntly. "Perhaps the best thing we can both do is go home because, no matter how badly we wish we could, we can't grieve for her, *yio mou. That* she must do on her own, at her own pace, in her own good time. And if our being here delays it, then we're doing her no favors by staying."

He could scarcely believe what he was hearing. "You're suggesting we should abandon her?"

"No. I'm saying we should give her room to breathe, to heal, and perhaps to miss us a little." He lifted his shoulders helplessly. "Maybe that's necessary before she can admit to herself that she needs us."

He wanted to disagree, but in his heart, he knew Angelo was right. The more he tried to bridge the chasm separating her from him, the farther away she retreated. And by trying too hard to hold on to her, he was destroying any chance of bringing her back to him.

"All right, we'll go. But not until she's seen her doctor. I have to know she's okay."

"I'm okay," she told them, when the three of them sat down to dinner, the next Monday, and somehow she managed to sound convincing, even though she wasn't sure anything would ever be okay again. "Honestly, I'm in perfect health."

"If that's true," Mikos said, casting a critical eye over the tiny

portion of chicken and two spears of asparagus on her plate, "why do you have such a poor appetite? And why are you tired all the time?"

"I'm a bit run-down, that's all, but Dr. Irving prescribed vitamins. You can go home with an easy mind. I'll be back to my old self soon. "

"Soon" being some time in early March next year, because that's when her baby was due, if Sam Irving was to be believed.

Pregnant? She'd stared at him aghast when he'd concluded his examination and brought her back to his office to pass along the news. *How can that be?*

Through intercourse, as a rule, he replied dryly. *Are you saying you haven't had any?*

Well...um...um... Realizing she was gaping like a fish floundering to stay afloat, she snapped her mouth closed until she'd collected herself enough to stop stammering. *As a matter of fact, I did have a...fling while I was in Greece. You told me I should, and I always follow doctor's orders. But we took precautions, and were careful.*

Except when she'd taken Mikos by surprise in the shower!

But he'd barely had time to penetrate before it was over, and surely with all that water pouring down, the chances of her conceiving...?

Not careful enough, I'm afraid. Sam regarded her across his desk. *Have I met the father?*

She colored. *Yes. At Mom's memorial service.*

The young Greek fellow. I figured as much. Any chance you'll be getting married?

None at all.

Not even when he finds out you're having his baby?

He won't find out.

Why not?

Because it's over between us. He and my grandfather are returning to Greece very soon.

I see. He swiveled back and forth in his chair. *How do you feel about becoming a mother?*

I don't know. Surprised, mostly. Shocked. She laughed weakly. *Though come to think of it, I don't know why I should be. Illegitimate babies seem to run in the family.*

People don't think like these days, Gina. Unmarried mothers aren't ostracized the way your grandmother was. And in your case, it doesn't have to be a bad thing, you know. A baby would go a long way toward filling the huge void left in your life by your mom's death. He swiveled some more in his chair. *But if, after you've had time to mull it over, you decide you can't handle—*

I won't have an abortion, Sam, if that's what you're getting at.

Well, there's always adoption. Plenty of good people out there would jump at the chance to give your child a home. But it's early days yet and you don't have to decide anything right away. Give yourself time to adjust to being pregnant before you make any decisions.

Yes, she'd said. *Of course.*

But early days or not, she knew she'd never give away Mikos's baby.

Mikos spoke, jarring her back to the moment. "What kind of vitamins?" he asked sharply, pinning her in such an all-seeing stare that her mouth ran dry.

"The usual kind," she said, swallowing nervously. "Stop quizzing me like this, Mikos. I'm not on trial here."

"Maybe not, but I'd feel a lot easier in my mind if I spoke to your doctor myself."

Although her blood pressure spiked at the mere idea, she managed to reply calmly enough, "Go ahead. Just don't bother speaking to him about me, because I'm none of your business,

and although I don't pretend to know anything about the Greek medical profession, I can promise you there isn't a doctor practicing in this country who would dream of violating his patient's confidentiality without her specific permission. Not," she added, afraid she was verging close enough to vehement to arouse his suspicion, "that there's anything to disclose in my case."

"Let it go, Mikolas," her grandfather said. "Angelina's right. It's none of your business."

"So," she said, into the brittle silence that ensued, "now that I've been given a clean bill of health, there's nothing to keep you here, is there? So when do you think you'll be leaving?"

"So why are you in such a hurry to get rid of us?" Mikos snapped, with glowering sarcasm. "Have we been such onerous company?"

"No, of course not. I'm very, very grateful to both of you for the support you've shown over the last three weeks. But sooner or later, I have to learn to manage on my own, and I think sooner is better."

"Well, what the hell!" he said. "We can fly out tomorrow, if that's how you feel."

As it turned out, they didn't leave until the day after that, because their pilot needed time to file a flight plan and have the jet prepared. But early on the first Wednesday in August, they loaded their bags into their rented car and said their goodbyes.

"We're not over, you and I, that I promise you," Angelo vowed, kissing her on both cheeks. "I'll be in touch."

"I'm going to miss you," she said, and was surprised to find it was true. He was all the family she had left, and she'd become fond of him in the weeks since her mother died.

Trapping her between himself and the trunk of the car, Mikos kissed her, long and hard. "Don't expect me to echo Angelo's sentiments," he said blackly. "I'm not making any promises."

And while she was still reeling from the angry taste of his mouth on hers, he climbed behind the wheel, slammed the car in gear and drove away.

She didn't know if he once looked back. Too much grief obscured her vision.

The autumn gales swept in early that year, bringing rain and cool temperatures that sent the tourists home by the end of September. She was just as happy to see them go. Too often in the weeks since Mikos had left, she'd caught sight of a man in the crowd emerging from the ferry, tall, dark, broad-shouldered and moving with a long, purposeful stride, and her hopes had soared. But it was never him.

She stopped looking for a letter with a foreign stamp. Her heart stopped racing, every time the phone rang. What was the point in harking back to the past? Instead she raked leaves, pruned the perennials, stacked enough firewood to see her through the winter and planned her future.

After her mother's death, her first thought had been to sell the house, go back to Vancouver and resume her career. But when she learned she was pregnant, she changed her mind. She wanted to stay home with her baby, and running a bed-and-breakfast would allow her to do that. So she painted the three larger upstairs bedrooms in preparation for next summer's visitors, and turned the little sun porch off her own room into a nursery, projects which were now affordable, thanks to an unexpected windfall of cash from an insurance policy her mother had taken out, years earlier.

"Moderate exercise is good, but don't get too carried away with it," Sam Irving cautioned, when she went in for her monthly checkup. "The pregnancy's going well, but that's no reason to take unnecessary risks, and climbing ladders comes

under that heading. Not only that, you're far too thin, so slow down and start taking it a bit easier."

"I have to keep busy," she told him.

"There's a difference between keeping busy and driving yourself to the point of collapse." He looked her squarely in the eye. "When are you going to stop punishing yourself, Gina? You're not to blame for what happened to your mom."

"But I am," she quavered, the tears that were never far from the surface spilling over. "If I'd been here…"

"Instead of doing what every woman your age is entitled to do? Meeting a man and falling in love? Because that's what this is really all about. You fell in love, and she fell out of the window. She died from her injuries, therefore you don't deserve to be happy. Hmm." He scratched his jaw thoughtfully. "So tell me something. Is it also your fault that she was struck with Alzheimer's in the first place?"

"No," she sniffled, mopping her face with a tissue. "That was beyond my control."

"And so was her death, so stop condemning yourself for it, and focus on what's best for you and your baby." He shot her another probing glance. "And a good place to start might be to pick up the phone and call Mikos. I'm pretty sure, if he knew you were carrying his child, he'd been on the next flight over here."

No doubt he would, because he'd feel obligated. But she didn't want him on those terms. *I'm not making any promises,* he'd said, and she wouldn't use her baby to try to wring any from him. She'd sent him away, and either he came back of his own accord, or she'd manage without him. But missing him was a nagging pain forever twisting inside her.

The second Monday in October dawned clear and sunny for a change, with a light breeze coming in off the Strait and a hint of Indian summer in the air. Elsewhere on the island, people

had decorated their houses for Thanksgiving, but Gina hadn't bothered with her usual display of ornamental gourds and dried grasses arranged in the woven cornucopia, which had always graced the front porch in previous years. It wasn't as if anyone would notice.

But someone did. Halfway through the morning, Sam's wife, Heather, stopped by with a planter of gorgeous yellow chrysanthemums. "When I saw these at Fox's Nursery, I knew they'd look perfect here," she said, plunking the container down beside the freshly painted blue front door. Then brushing dirt from her hands, she straightened and spared Gina a long, hard look. "How are you, dear? I've seen nothing of you since your mother's memorial service."

Gina pointed to the brush and can of white enamel next to the porch railing. "Fixing the place up, as you can see. I'm afraid I let things slide around here the last couple of years, but now that I've got time on my hands, I'm trying to catch up by doing a little bit every day."

"Not this afternoon you aren't! You're taking a break to celebrate Thanksgiving at our house, with roast turkey and pumpkin pie. You need fattening up. You're much too skinny— despite that little bulge your paint shirt can't quite hide."

Embarrassed, Gina flattened her hands across her middle. "Sam told you?"

"He didn't have to. Not that he would anyway, as you very well know. But you're definitely showing, my dear. Before long, everyone on the island will know Gina Hudson's pregnant. And," she added bluntly, "if you think any of us gives a rat's behind that you're not married, you sadly under-estimate our affection for you. All we care about is that you're happy." She subjected Gina to another sweeping ap-praisal. "Are you?"

"About the baby, yes."

"I hear a 'but,' which we'll talk about further later today. Right now, I have to get back to that darned turkey. It's so big, Sam might have to amputate both its legs to make it fit in the oven. See you at four, Gina. Don't be late—and bring your appetite."

With a blast from her car's horn and a spurt of gravel from beneath its tires, she was gone, leaving behind a warmth that had been sadly missing in Gina's life of late.

Maybe I *will* go, she mused, her initial decision to decline the invitation fading. She hadn't given herself a manicure or dressed up in ages, because there'd been no occasion special enough to warrant doing so. But life, as the old saying went, had to go on, and she couldn't hibernate forever.

What's more, with the return of the warmer weather, she could leave all the windows open and air out the entire house while she was gone. Pregnancy, she'd discovered, left her unpleasantly sensitive to the smell of new paint.

Collecting her supplies, she stashed them in the garage, then headed for the house, something of a spring in her step. No doubt it was temporary, but just then she felt neither happy nor miserable, but something in between the two. What she felt was…content.

"Content." She paused at the front door, and tried out the word.

It rolled easily off her tongue. She liked its gentle cadence, and the sense of peace that suffused her as she accepted it into her heart.

So much more enduring than bliss, she decided. So much less demanding than ecstasy.

At her feet, the chrysanthemums nodded their heads in the breeze, seeming to agree with her.

DUSK was falling as Mikos drove the rental car down the ramp from the ferry, one of only about fifty vehicles on what had turned out to be the last sailing of the day.

"It's Thanksgiving, that's why," a fellow passenger had told him, when he commented how few people had been on board. "Everyone's home stuffing themselves with turkey and all the trimmings. You can't be from around here, if you don't know that."

"You're right. I'm visiting from overseas."

"Somebody expecting you?"

"No. It's to be a surprise."

The man had grinned good-naturedly. "Well, you chose the right day to drop in unexpectedly. There'll be plenty to eat at dinner."

He noticed the parking lot outside the inn on the main street of town was crowded. The place was busy, indicating a good number of island residents preferred to let someone else do the cooking.

Was Gina one of them?

Was she still on the island at all?

And if not, where would he find her?

Annoyed at the ripple of anxiety prickling his skin, he took the left turn at the fire hall too fast, startling a deer grazing at

the side of the road, and hit the brakes hard as the frightened creature leaped in front of the car and bounded away into the bush on the other side of the road.

Skata! He needed to get a grip on his emotions before he saw her again. But the fact was, they'd been out of control—*he'd* been out of control—ever since he'd left her: a bear around the office, unfit company with other people and just plain wretched alone.

He'd tried pumping Angelo for information, but the old guy wouldn't bite. "I'm not about to jeopardize my budding relationship with my granddaughter by playing middle man," he'd said. "You want to know how she's doing, Mikolas, ask her yourself."

A hundred times or more in those first weeks, he'd picked up the phone to do just that, until his pride kicked in and reminded him that she'd made it more than clear she didn't want him in her life. Only in the last few days had he admitted to himself that he wanted her in *his* life badly enough to risk having her reject him a second time.

He rounded the last curve in the two-lane highway paralleling the shore, and hung a right to the dead-end lane leading to her house. Only when he saw the windows open did some of the tension seep from his body. At least she was home, even if she hadn't yet bothered to turn on any but the front porch lights. Cruising to a stop, he reversed the car into the space between two other vehicles parked along the side of the road, and strode up her driveway with a confidence that was more show than substance.

Gina left the Irvings at nine o'clock, loaded with leftover turkey breast, dressing, cranberry sauce and a whole pumpkin pie. "Just in case you feel like a snack, later on," Heather had said, as she and Sam walked her to her car.

Not much chance of that, she thought, smiling as she backed down their driveway and headed west along the shore road.

She'd eaten so much, she could hardly walk. It was a good thing her dress was loose-fitting, or she'd be in real trouble. But the evening had been wonderful; lighthearted and fun.

She didn't meet much traffic on the way home, which came as no surprise. There were few houses along that particular stretch of highway, and fewer still on the lane where she lived. But as she turned onto her own property, she noticed that her neighbors three doors down were entertaining. Extra cars filled their driveway, with several more parked along the grass bordering the opposite side of the lane.

The temperature had dropped after sunset, leaving a damp chill in the air, and she shivered as she hurried up the steps to the front porch. "I shouldn't have left the windows open, after all," she muttered, fumbling in her purse for her house key.

The party down the lane was in full swing. Music and laughter drifted faintly across the intervening gardens, but it was another sound, much closer, that had her spinning around just as a dark forbidding figure unfolded from the bench half-hidden in the shadows at the far end of the porch.

"No, you certainly should not," a deep, accented voice declared. "Leaving the place open like this is an invitation for someone to break in. I was tempted to do so myself, but I figure I've made enough mistakes with you already, and it's not in my best interests to add to them."

The startled scream she'd been about to utter died in her throat, mainly, she thought hysterically, because there wasn't room there for it *and* her heart, which had certainly slipped its moorings. *"Mikos?"* she gasped.

He approached her with the lazy elegance that was his trademark and bent to pick up the key, which she'd dropped. "Were you expecting someone else, *agape mou*?" he inquired, inserting it into the lock and thrusting open the door.

"No." Overwhelmed on every front, she stood rooted to the spot, struggling to restore some sort of order to the incoherence laying waste to her mind. "What do you want?" she finally managed.

"You," he said. "I want you."

"Why?"

"Because I am nothing without you."

Her heart missed a beat and, suddenly light-headed, she clutched weakly at the door frame.

His hand shot out to cup her elbow. "Are you going to faint again?"

"Uh-uh." She swallowed as a wave of nausea threatened. "Just shocked to see you, that's all."

"And shaking with cold."

Oh, she was shaking all right! But cold? No, she was burning where he touched her. Burning and aching and hurting, as if she'd come close to freezing to death, and the blood was struggling to circulate through her body again. Teeth chattering, she said politely, "Won't you come in? I think I need to sit down."

A hand in the small of her back to steady her, he escorted her to the sitting room, and turned on the lamp next to the chair she chose. "Shall I close the windows?"

"Yes, please. And light the fire, if you don't mind."

"Of course." He put a match to the kindling already laid in the grate, and waited until the flames caught before turning to face her again. "Can I get you anything? A little brandy perhaps?"

"No, thank you."

For a moment, he paced about the room, more restless than she'd ever seen him. "Then may I help myself to some?" he finally burst out. "I've come a long way to bare my soul to you,

Gina, and I want what I have to say to come out right. But now that I'm here, I find I'm not as sure of myself as I thought I'd be."

"By all means," she said. "You know where it's kept."

He nodded. "In the right-hand cupboard of the sideboard in the dining room."

Left alone, she stopped trying so hard to hold herself together, and gave in to the agitation fermenting in her brain. For the first time ever, she'd seen a glimpse of uncertainty behind his cosmopolitan self-assurance.

We're not over, you and I, Angelo had declared, the day he returned to Greece.

But, *Don't expect me to echo his sentiments,* Mikos had told her. Yet he'd come back to her. And she saw no pity in his candid green eyes. No trace of guilt. Just the kind of vulnerability inherent to utter, complete honesty.

The anger had gone from his voice. In its place was a calm certainty that had nothing to do with being in control of everything around him, but rather that of a man who'd finally come to terms with who he was and what he needed.

Or was it merely resignation she'd heard?

I want you, he'd said, and had sounded sincere. But what, exactly, did "wanting" her mean? Had he somehow found out about the baby? Had Angelo forced him to come and do the honorable thing?

No. That wasn't possible. She'd written to her grandfather, and spoken to him once by phone, but she hadn't said a word about being pregnant, and there was no one else who'd have told him.

So was it possible that Mikos was here of his own free will? That he wanted more than to initiate a long-distance affair? A tiny bud of hope sprouted inside her.

"I've shut the dining room windows," he called out, startling her as he continued down the hall toward the front hall. "I

might as well close those upstairs, too, while I'm at it. There's quite a stiff breeze blowing in from the northwest."

Only then did she remember the sunporch was now set up as a nursery. "No, Mikos," she cried out in alarm, leaping to her feet and flying after him. "Leave them alone! I want them left open."

Already halfway up the stairs, he stopped and came back down to where she stood panting and hanging on to the newel post as if her life depended on it, his face mirroring his surprise. "Okay, Gina. Don't upset yourself. I just thought the bedrooms would be cold, that's all."

"But I like a cool bedroom."

"Fine. Whatever you say. I didn't come here to tell you how to run your home."

She dared to take his hand, and even so simple a touch was enough to reignite the electricity that had always sparked between them. "Why don't you tell me exactly why you are here then?" she suggested.

There was no putting it off any longer. Collecting his brandy snifter from the console in the hall, he followed her into the living room. The fire had chased away the chill and flung warm reflections over the polished surface of the coffee table.

She returned to her chair, arranged the folds of her pretty red dress and regarded him expectantly, little realizing that she held his entire future in her slender hands.

He leaned against the mantelpiece and took a fortifying swig of the brandy, wishing he knew where the hell to begin. He was never at a loss for words when it came to business. Never had a problem saying what had to be said when it was time to end an affair. But proposing? *That* was something he'd never anticipated doing, and he hadn't a clue how to go about it.

"I want to marry you, Gina," he said baldly, diving in before he lost his nerve. Never mind the romantic lead-in, the flowery prose. Simple truth straight from his heart was the best he could do.

Her lovely mouth fell open in shock. "Why?" she whispered.

"Because I love you, I have missed you more than I ever dreamed possible, and I can't imagine going through the rest of my life without you."

She opened her mouth again, this time to speak, but he was finally in gear and stopped her with an upraised hand. "Before you say anything, let me add this—I wouldn't blame you if you turned me down. I know I dealt you a vicious blow with my harsh condemnation, that last night on Petaloutha. But falling in love had never been part of my long-term plans, and I didn't know how to handle it."

"Especially when it seemed that I'd been using you," she put in quietly.

"My pride took a beating, I admit. But that doesn't excuse the way I've behaved. After your mother died, I tried to convince you I loved you, and when you wouldn't listen, I went away like a spoiled boy who wouldn't play by any rules but his own. But the truth isn't so easily dismissed, and I'm here now to tell you again. I love you, Gina. I love you with all my heart. Not because I feel sorry for you. Not because I feel guilty. But because I can't help myself. And if you can forgive me for the cruel things I've said, and believe that I'm here now for all the right reasons, I promise I'll never make you cry again."

"But you already are," she said, tears sparkling like diamonds on her lashes.

"Don't!" he begged, an agony of remorse consuming him. "Gina, my darling, my angel, my soul, if having me here speaking to you like this really makes you unhappy, of course

I'll leave, but not willingly. The only woman, the one I'd never thought to find, has come into my life when I was least expecting her, and I'm not about to let her go again unless I must. So if there's any chance—"

She blinked and brushed at the tear that escaped and ran down her cheek. "There's a chance," she said. "A very good chance. But before I give you my answer, there's something you need to know."

"I know that I will love you the rest of my life and beyond. That's all that matters."

She shook her head. "I love you, too, Mikos. I think I have from the minute I first saw you. But I tried hiding the truth from you once, and it ended up hurting both of us. I won't take the same chance again, not with so much at stake."

She unfolded herself from her chair. Although she looked thinner in the face, he thought she'd put on a little weight. She was more rounded under the soft folds of her dress.

"Come with me," she said. "There's something I want you to see."

He followed her upstairs, and down the hall to her bedroom overlooking the sea. She'd painted it since last he'd been there, a soft restful blue that matched the walls in the small adjoining bathroom, and hung white curtains at the window. "You've been busy," he commented.

"More than you know," she replied, and opened the door leading to the enclosed sunporch. "Take a look in here and tell me what you think."

"Very nice," he said, at first seeing only buttery-yellow walls and a white rug, and the same white curtains as those covering her bedroom windows. But then he noticed the furniture. A simple white dresser, and a lamp with a rabbit motif on the shade. A table of some sort in one corner, and shelves under-

neath filled with things that babies used. And next to it, one of those little beds on rockers with a hood at one end—a bassinet, he thought it was called.

"Yes," she said, as his stunned gaze traveled the room a second time, then came to rest on her. "It's a nursery. I'm expecting a baby."

She sounded brave. Defiant, even. And he knew why. She was testing him. He'd failed her once too often.

"No, *calli mou*, you're expecting *our* baby," he said firmly. "And even if you were expecting two, my proposal would still stand."

"Are you sure?"

"*Neh*. I'm very sure."

She smiled at him then, a luminous joy transforming her face. "Then yes, I'll marry you."

He did then what he'd ached to do from the moment she'd stepped out of her car. He took her in his arms and held her as if he'd never let her go. "Thank you," he muttered hoarsely, to her, and to God.

They'd never made love in her house. Never lain together, with a fluffy duvet protecting them from the night breeze sifting through her window. Never wished on the stars pricking the cool northern skies outside her window.

"When did you learn you were pregnant?" he asked.

"When I went for that checkup with my doctor. I had no idea until he told me. At first, I didn't believe him. We'd always used protection—"

"Except for that first night, when I was inexcusably careless. Yes, I remember." He rolled to his side and searched her face, his green eyes clouded. "But I was still here when you found out. Why didn't you confide in me? Were you afraid I'd turn

away from you, as Angelo turned away from your grandmother, and leave you to bring up our child alone?"

"No," she said. "I was afraid you'd stay with me out of duty, and hate me for tying you down in a marriage you never wanted."

"You'd have let me live in ignorance that I'd fathered a child?"

"Not forever, no. Every child has a right to a father, and every father willing to take on the responsibility has the right to know his child. But I would have put off telling you until after the birth. The last months have been among the most difficult of my life, Mikos. I needed to know I was strong enough to go on without you, if I had to. I needed to recover."

"And have you, my love? Enough to put the past behind you?"

"Oh, I still miss my mom," she said, a pang of grief nudging at her happiness. "I always will. But I've accepted her death. I know no one's to blame. The way she died was a blessing in some ways because, for a very long time now, she'd been a lost soul caught in a living hell with no way out. Our doctor spoke to me at length and helped me understand that, shocking though the accident was, her death was quick and merciful, not a lingering nightmare that could only get worse and might have lasted years longer. So to answer your question, I might not be all the way there yet, but I'm close enough to know I'll go the distance." She patted her thickening midriff. "I have to. I have a baby on the way."

He shaped her body with his hand, sketching the full curve of her breasts, and bringing his palm to rest on the rounded contour that was his child lying snug in her womb. "And you have me," he said tenderly. "You both have me, and you always will."

Her body quickening with need, she touched him where he was most vulnerable. "Show me," she whispered.

Except for when she'd conceived, they'd never known the freedom to pleasure each other without first thinking about

contraception. To feel him sliding into her, his flesh touching hers, the warm spill of his seed running free inside her and welding her to him, brought an element of intimacy to their lovemaking that had been missing before.

"I don't ever want you to use a condom again," she whispered, still locked to him in the rosy aftermath of ecstasy.

"Then you'd better be prepared to give birth to a soccer team or two, because I intend to make love to you whenever, and wherever the opportunity arises," he said, laughing, and illustrated the point by thrusting against her with recharged vigor.

Much, much later, she fell asleep wrapped in his arms, the perpetual ache of missing him eased at last, and the steady beat of his heart beneath her hand assuring her that he was not a figment of her imagination.

The next morning, she awoke to a languid contentment. Sunbeams played through the window, striping his big, powerful body with bands of gold. Careful not to disturb him, she stole to the bathroom, put on her robe and slippers and crept downstairs to make breakfast.

He was still on Greek time and would probably sleep a while yet. They'd talked late into the night, making plans. A quiet wedding here, within the month, they'd decided, and a honeymoon on Petaloutha right after. A house on Evia with a big garden and a view across the sea, close enough for Angelo to visit and get to know his great-grandchild. But they'd keep the penthouse, just in case they wanted to spend the night in the city.

And this house, where she'd grown up? "I'm ready to let it go," she'd told Mikos. "From now on, my home is with you."

"But the place means so much to you, my love. You don't have to get rid of it. I'll hire a couple to be its caretakers."

"The memories it holds are what matter, Mikos, and they'll go with me wherever I am."

He'd stroked her face, his eyes brimming with love. "Don't decide now. Think about it long and hard before you make up your mind."

Perhaps he was right, she thought, mixing batter for waffles. A light frost had touched the grass overnight and she knew if she stepped outside, her lungs would fill with the clean crisp air of the Pacific northwest. Perhaps she couldn't sever her ties so easily, after all.

He was lying there, his eyes still closed, when she went back upstairs with the loaded tray, but when she sat down on the mattress next to him, his hand shot out to manacle her wrist. "Where have you been?" he grumbled, his voice all raspy with sleep. "I reached out for you, and you weren't there."

"I've brought you breakfast in bed. Fresh-squeezed orange juice, and Canadian coffee, which you'll probably hate, and waffles with the last of the season's blueberries."

A smile inched over his face. "What a woman! Have I told you yet today that you make me very happy and that I love you?"

"No, as a matter of fact, you haven't."

He yanked her forward so that she fell on top of him. "You make me very happy and I love you, Angelina. Will you marry me?"

The poems, the love songs, they all said the same thing: that when you finally find the person who is your true other half, the one who makes you complete, your heart races madly.

It wasn't true, at least not for her, not at that moment. *Her* heart underwent a great wash of serenity. It knew the search was over. "I will," she said.

It was half past eight in the morning on Canada's West Coast, half past seven in the evening in Greece. Replete with waffles

and love, they decided they should phone Angelo with their news.

"Where the hell are you?" he growled, on hearing Mikos's voice.

"In bed with your granddaughter, old man."

"*Bastardo!* Have you no sense of decency?"

"Plenty," he said. "That's why I'm going to make an honest woman of her. I've asked her to marry me."

"Marry, hmm?" Angelo's phony snort of annoyance echoed across the miles. "Well, it's about time. I'm not going to live forever, you know."

Mikos tucked the duvet more securely around Gina's shoulders and pulled her closer. "We've taken that into account. It's why we're presenting you with a great-grand-child next spring. Think you can stick around long enough to give him your blessing?"

This time, silence skimmed over the line. Then, his voice suddenly quavering, Angelo spoke again. "Gina's pregnant?"

"Oh, yeah!" he boasted, so puffed up with pride, he was fit to burst. "Four months along, beautiful, and all mine. Clear your calendar and have the jet ready to go, Angelo. You're needed here for the wedding, unless you want your granddaughter walking herself down the aisle."

"I'll be there tomorrow, if they have to trundle me on board in a wheelchair," he affirmed. "Give that girl a hug from me, and don't ever forget what a treasure you've found for yourself. You're a lucky man, *yio mou*."

Mikos studied the woman curled up beside him, resilient as tempered steel, gentle as an infant's sigh; his Botticelli angel, her face radiant with inner joy, her body ripe with approaching motherhood.

Aware of his gaze, she smiled and pressed a soft kiss to his shoulder. "I love you," she mouthed.

Almost blinded by the tide of emotion that swept over him, he turned his attention to the phone again. "Yes, I'm lucky," he told Angelo. "The luckiest man in the world."

Discover more romance at

www.millsandboon.co.uk

- ❤ WIN great prizes in our exclusive competitions
- ❤ BUY new titles before they hit the shops
- ❤ BROWSE new books and REVIEW your favourites
- ❤ SAVE on new books with the Mills & Boon® Bookclub™
- ❤ DISCOVER new authors

PLUS, to chat about your favourite reads, get the latest news and find special offers:

- Find us on facebook.com/millsandboon
- Follow us on twitter.com/millsandboonuk
- ❤ Sign up to our newsletter at millsandboon.co.uk